BOOKS BY YUKIO MISHIMA

The Sea of Fertility, a Cycle of Novels:
Spring Snow (1972)
Runaway Horses (1973)
IN PREPARATION
The Temple of Dawn
The Decay of the Angel

Thirst for Love (1969)
Forbidden Colors (1968)
The Sailor Who Fell from Grace with the Sea (1965)
After the Banquet (1963)
The Temple of the Golden Pavilion (1959)
Five Modern Nō Plays (1957)
The Sound of Waves (1956)

These are Borzoi Books, published in New York
by Alfred A. Knopf

RUNAWAY HORSES

ALFRED · A · KNOPF

1973

NEW YORK

THE SEA OF FERTILITY

A CYCLE OF FOUR NOVELS

RUNAWAY HORSES

YUKIO MISHIMA

Translated from the Japanese by Michael Gallagher

THIS IS A BORZOI BOOK
PUBLISHED BY ALFRED A. KNOPF, INC.

Library of Congress Cataloging in Publication Data
Mishima, Yukio, pseud.   RUNAWAY HORSES.
(His The sea of fertility [2])
Translation of Homba.
I. Title.
PZ3.M6878Se vol. 2   [PL833.17]   895.6′3′5   72–11039
ISBN 0–394–46618–7

Manufactured in the United States of America

First American Edition

RUNAWAY HORSES

1

IT WAS 1932. Shigekuni Honda was thirty-eight.

While still a law student at Tokyo Imperial University, he had passed the judicial civil service examination, and after graduation he had been given a probationary assignment as a clerk in the Osaka District Court. Osaka was his home from then on. In 1929 he became a judge, and last year, having already advanced to senior associate judge of the District Court, he had moved to the Osaka Court of Appeals to become a junior associate judge.

Honda had married at twenty-eight. His wife was the daughter of one of his father's friends, a judge who had been forced to retire in the legal reform of 1913. The wedding was held in Tokyo, and he and his wife came to Osaka immediately afterwards. In the ten years that followed, his wife had borne him no children. But Rié was a modest and gentle woman, and their relationship was harmonious.

His father had died three years before. At the time, Honda had considered disposing of the family home and having his mother come to Osaka. She had been opposed to this, however, and now she lived alone in the large house in Tokyo.

Honda's wife had one maid to help her care for the rented house in which they lived. There were two rooms on the second floor and five on the first, including the foyer. The garden covered somewhat more than seven hundred square feet. For this Honda paid a monthly rent of thirty-two yen.

Aside from three days a week at the court, Honda worked at home. To go to the Court of Appeals he took a streetcar from Abeno in Tennoji Ward to Kitahama in downtown Osaka. Then he walked across the bridges spanning the Tosabori and the Dojima rivers to the Courthouse, which stood close by Hokonagashi Bridge. It was a red brick building with the huge chrysanthemum of the imperial crest glittering above its front entrance.

A *furoshiki* cloth was indispensable to a judge. There were always documents to take home, usually more than a briefcase would hold, and a cloth-wrapped bundle could be either large or small. Honda used a medium-sized muslin *furoshiki* from the Daimaru department store, and, to be on the safe side, carried a second one folded up within it. For the judges these *furoshiki* bundles were vital to their work; they would never trust them to a luggage rack. One of his colleagues would not even stop off for a drink on the way home without passing a cord under the knot of his *furoshiki* and then looping it around his neck.

There was no reason why Honda could not use the judges' chambers to compose his decisions. But on a day when court was not in session the crowded room would be ringing with vigorous legal arguments, as the probationary clerks stood about respectfully assimilating all they could learn. Little hope of his being able to write his decisions in peace. Honda preferred to work at home late into the night.

Shigekuni Honda's specialty was criminal law. He felt no concern that Osaka, because of its small criminal law division, was said to offer only limited advancement in this field.

Working at home, he would spend the night reading the police reports, the prosecutor's briefs, and the accounts of the preliminary examinations relating to the cases to be tried at the next session. After he had made extracts and taken notes he would pass the material along to the senior associate judge. Once a decision had been reached, it was up to Honda to draft it for the Chief Judge. The sky would already be growing light in the east by the time he finally plodded his way to "All of which having been considered, the judgment of this court is as has been hereinbefore stated." The Chief Judge would revise this and give it back to Honda, who now had to take up his writing brush and make the final copy. The fingers of his right hand had scrivener's calluses.

As for geisha parties, Honda attended only the traditional end-of-year celebration which was held at the Seikanro in the red-light district of Kita Ward. On that night superiors and underlings caroused freely together, and occasionally some-body or other, emboldened by saké, expressed himself to the Chief Justice with unwonted frankness.

Their usual diversion was drinking in the cafés and *oden* shops clustered around the streetcar junction of Umeda-Shimmichi. The service at some of these cafés knew no limits. If one were to ask the waitress what time it was, she would lift her skirt to consult a watch strapped to a plump thigh before answering. Some judges, of course, were altogether too dignified for this sort of thing, and even believed that cafés were merely places for drinking coffee. One of them happened to be presiding over an embezzlement trial, when the defendant testified that he had squandered all of the misappropriated thousand yen in cafés. The judge interrupted indignantly.

"How can you say that?" he demanded. "A cup of coffee is only five sen. Are you trying to tell us you drank that much?"

Even after the general reduction of civil service salaries, Honda had an ample income of nearly three hundred yen a month, the equivalent of a regimental commander. His colleagues gave their leisure to various pastimes: some read novels, others took up the chants and Nō plays of the Kanzé School, and still others gathered to write haiku and make sketches illustrating the poems. Most of these diversions, however, served as pretexts for getting together to do some drinking.

Then there were some judges, especially enthusiastic for things Western, who went to dances. Honda did not care for dancing, but he often heard his colleagues talk about it. Since a city ordinance forbade dancing in Osaka itself, devotees had to go to Kyoto, where the Katsura and the Keagé dance halls were popular, or else to Amagasaki, where the Kuisé stood isolated in the midst of rice paddies. The taxi ride to Amagasaki cost one yen. As one approached the gymnasium-like building on a rainy night, the shadows of dancing couples flickered past the lighted windows, and the strains of the foxtrot took on an uncanny quality across the flooded paddy fields gleaming in the rain.

Such was Honda's world about this time.

2

How ODDLY SITUATED a man is apt to find himself at age thirty-eight! His youth belongs to the distant past. Yet the period of memory beginning with the end of youth and extending to the present has left him not a single vivid impression. And therefore he persists in feeling that nothing more than a fragile barrier separates him from his youth. He is forever hearing with the utmost clarity the sounds of this neighboring domain, but there is no way to penetrate the barrier.

Honda felt that his youth had ended with the death of Kiyoaki Matsugae. At that moment something real within him, something that had burned with a vibrant brilliance, suddenly ceased to be.

Now, late at night, when Honda grew weary of his legal drafts, he would pick up the dream journal that Kiyoaki had left him and turn over its pages.

Much that it contained seemed like meaningless riddles, but some of the dreams recorded there gracefully foreshadowed Kiyoaki's early death. His dream of looking down in spirit upon his own coffin of plain wood while the pre-dawn blackness gave way to deep blue at the windows was fulfilled with unforeseen swiftness in less than a year and a half. The woman with the widow's peak who clung to the coffin was evidently Satoko, but there had been no sign of the actual Satoko at Kiyoaki's funeral.

Since then eighteen years had passed. The border between dream and memory had grown indistinct in Honda's mind. Because the words contained in this journal, his only souvenir of his friend, had been traced there by Kiyoaki's own hand, it had profound significance for Honda. These dreams, left like a handful of gold dust in a winnowing pan, were charged with wonder.

As time went by, the dreams and the reality took on equal worth among Honda's diverse memories. What had actually occurred was in the process of merging with what could have occurred. As reality rapidly gave way to dreams, the past seemed very much like the future.

When he was young, there had been only one reality, and the future had seemed to stretch before him, swelling with immense possibilities. But as he grew older, reality seemed to take many forms, and it was the past that seemed refracted into innumerable possibilities. Since each of these was linked with its own reality, the line distinguishing dream and reality became all the more obscure. His memories were in constant flux, and had taken on the aspect of a dream.

On the one hand, he could not definitely recall the name of a man he had met yesterday, but on the other, the image of

Kiyoaki came to him fresh and clear whenever he called it up, much as the memory of a nightmare is more vivid than the look of the familiar street corner that one passes the next morning. After reaching the age of thirty, Honda had begun to forget people's names, just as paint flakes away bit by bit. The reality that these names signified became more fleeting and more insignificant than any dream, a waste substance thrown off by each day's life.

Honda felt that the future had no shocks in store for him. Whatever new turmoil rocked the world, his function would remain the same, and he would bring to bear upon each disturbance the rational scrutiny of the law. He had become thoroughly acclimated to a sphere whose atmosphere was logic. And it was logic, therefore, that Honda took as valid— more than dreams, more than reality.

The vast number of criminal cases tried before him had, of course, brought him into constant contact with the more extreme forms of passion. Though he himself had never experienced such emotion, he had seen many human beings whom a single passion held fatally in thrall.

Was he really so secure? Whenever the thought occurred to him, Honda had the feeling that long ago a glittering danger had threatened him, a danger that had been destroyed in a final flash of brilliance. And from that moment, he felt, he had become invulnerable to any temptation, however compelling—a freedom that he owed to the armor that had encased him ever since. The danger of that distant past, and its temptation, had been Kiyoaki.

Honda had once enjoyed talking about the days that he had shared with Kiyoaki. But as a man grows older the memory of his youth begins to act as nothing less than an immunization against further experience. And he was thirty-eight. It was an age when one felt strangely unready to say that one had lived and yet reluctant to acknowledge the death of youth. An age when the savor of one's experiences turned ever so slightly sour, and when, day by day, one took less pleasure in new things. An age when the charm of every diverting foolishness quickly faded. But Honda's devotion to his work shielded him from emotion. He had fallen in love with his oddly abstract vocation.

When he came home in the evening, he had dinner with his wife before going to his study. Though he usually ate at six on the days that he worked at home, on court days the hour varied since he sometimes remained at the Courthouse as late as eight o'clock. Now, however, he was no longer called out in the middle of the night as he had been when he had presided over preliminary hearings.

No matter how late he came home, Rié always waited to eat with him. When he arrived late, she would hurry to warm up dinner. Honda read the newspaper as he waited, conscious of the purposeful bustle of his wife and the maid in the kitchen. Thus the dinner hour was for Honda the most relaxing of the entire day. The pattern of his own household was different, to be sure, but the image of his father enjoying the evening paper often came to his mind. Somehow he had come to resemble his father.

Still, there were differences. He was sure he did not have any of the rather artificial sternness of his father, so characteristic of the Meiji era. For one thing, he had no children to be stern to, and, for another, his household, of its own accord, functioned in a simple and orderly manner.

Rié was quiet. She never opposed her husband, nor was she inquisitive. She was bothered by a touch of inflammation of the kidneys, and occasionally her features would be swollen. Then her sleepy eyes would seem to smolder with passion, an effect heightened by the somewhat heavier makeup she wore at these times.

Now on this Sunday evening in the middle of May, Rié's face was swollen again. Tomorrow would be a court session. Honda had begun his work in the afternoon, thinking he would be able to complete it by dinnertime, and so he had told his wife before going into his study that he wanted to

keep at it until he was finished. He was not through until
eight. It was unusual for him to eat at so late an hour on a
day spent at home.

Although refined tastes meant very little to Honda, during
his long residence in the Kansai area he had developed an
interest in ceramics, and he allowed himself the modest luxury
of using good-quality dishes for even ordinary meals. They
ate from bowls of Ninsei porcelain and their evening saké
was served in Awata ware by Yohei III. Rié took great pains
to prepare such delicacies as a mustard-flavored fish salad
made with young trout, eels broiled unseasoned in the Kanto
manner, and sliced winter melon spread with a sauce thick-
ened with arrowroot starch. She was concerned about her
husband's health, bound as he was to his desk throughout
the day, and planned her menus accordingly.

It was the time of year when the fire in the brazier and the
steam whistling from the copper kettle began to seem disagreeable.

"It won't do any harm to take a bit more saké than usual
tonight," said Honda, as if to himself. "All my work is done
now, since I gave up my Sunday to it."

"How nice to have finished," said Rié, filling his cup. A
simple harmony coordinated the movements of their hands,
his holding out the cup, hers the bottle from which she was
pouring. An invisible cord seemed to link them, tugged back
and forth almost playfully in accordance with the spontaneous
rhythm of life. Rié was not a woman to disturb such rhythms.
Honda could be certain of that, just as he could tell from the
rich scent of the blossoms that the magnolia in his garden
was in bloom that night.

Thus everything that Honda wanted was tranquilly arranged within his view and within easy reach. This was the
domain established in less than twenty years by the young
man of promise. Then he had had almost nothing over which
his fingers might close with a sense of possession, but because
the lack had stirred no anxious irritation in him, all these

things had now come securely into his grasp.

After sipping his saké, he took up a steaming bowl of rice in which scattered green peas gleamed brightly. Just then he heard the jingle of a newspaper-boy's bell announcing an extra. He had the maid run out to buy a copy.

The paper, whose ragged cut edges and barely dry ink showed the haste in which it had been put out, conveyed the first news of the May Fifteenth Incident, the assassination of Prime Minister Inukai by Navy officers.

Honda sighed. "As if it weren't enough to have had the Blood Oath Alliance." Honda felt that he was above the usual run of indignant men who arose, their faces dark with passion, to condemn the corruption of the times. He was persuaded that his own world was one of reason and clarity. Now that he was a little intoxicated, its clarity seemed to shine with even greater brilliance.

"You'll be very busy again, won't you?" said Rié.

Honda felt a surge of affectionate condescension on hearing the daughter of a judge betray such ignorance.

"No, no. This will be a matter for a military court."

The affair by its very nature was outside civilian jurisdiction.

 3

FOR SOME DAYS, of course, the May Fifteenth Incident was the sole topic of conversation in the judges' chambers at the Courthouse. But by the beginning of June there was such a crush of cases pending that all the judges were too busy to concern themselves any longer with the affair.

They were already well aware of the facts left out of the newspaper accounts and had exchanged every scrap of information among themselves. Everyone knew that the Chief Justice of the Court of Appeals, Judge Sugawa, a kendo enthusiast, was very much in sympathy with the defendants, but no one was rash enough to allude to this.

Incidents of this sort, arising one after another, were like waves rolling in from a night sea to break upon the beach. First a small crest like a wavering line of white out upon the deep. Then as the wave came rushing in, it swelled enormously, only to crash down upon the sand and melt back into the depths. Honda remembered the sea at Kamakura on that night nineteen years before, when he and Kiyoaki and the two princes of Siam had lain upon the beach and gazed out at the waves as they rolled in and receded.

As for waves such as the May Fifteenth Incident, Honda thought, the beach was innocent. It was only obliged to force them back into the deep with inexhaustible patience, preventing them from rolling over the land. To force them back each time into the abyss of evil from which they had arisen, back into the primeval realm of remorse and death.

What did Honda himself think of evil? What did he think of sin? Such thoughts were really not his responsibility. He had but to guide himself by the established legal code. Somewhere deep within him, however, Honda did harbor a secret concept of sin, a concept as fragrant and stimulating as a pungent lotion soaking into dry, chapped skin. No doubt he owed this to Kiyoaki's lingering influence.

Still, this "unwholesome" notion was not so strong that he felt he had to combat it. Dominated as he was by reason, Honda lacked anything like a blind devotion to justice.

One day in early June, when the morning court session had ended earlier than usual, Honda returned to the judges' chambers with some time on his hands before lunch. He took off his black cap with its purple piping and his black legal robes with the arabesque design of purple embroidered across the front and put them away in the mahogany cabinet that reminded him of a Buddhist household altar. Then he stood looking absently out the window as he smoked a cigarette. A misty rain was falling.

"I'm not a beginner at this any more," Honda mused. "I've done my work without being swayed by the opinions of others, and I can say that I've met the prescribed standards. I've become thoroughly adept at my profession—like a potter whose clay seems to shape itself, taking the form that he wants it to."

Suddenly he realized that he was on the verge of forgetting the face of the defendant who had just stood trial before him. He shook his head. Try as he might, he could no longer clearly visualize the man's features.

Since the Public Procurator's Office occupied the third-floor rooms facing the river on the south side of the Courthouse, the view left to the judges' chambers, whose windows faced north, was a dismal one. The prison took up most of it. A passageway through the red brick wall separating the Courthouse and prison allowed defendants to go to court without being exposed to the public gaze.

Honda noticed that the painted wall of the room was dripping with moisture, and he opened the window. Beyond the red brick wall the roofs of the various wings of the white brick two-story prison were clustered together, with a guard tower shaped like a silo rising at their point of juncture. Only in this tower were the windows without bars.

The tile roofs of the prison wings and the little tile shields over the ventilation stacks all gleamed with the wet blackness of an inkstone. In the background a huge chimney towered up into the rainy sky. The view from Honda's window extended no farther than the stack.

The sides of the prison buildings were pierced at regular intervals by windows, each covered with white-painted iron bars and a screen of wooden slats. Below each window, on the rain-wet wall the color of soiled linen, a large Arabic number was painted: 30, 31, 32, 33, and so on. The first- and second-floor numbers were staggered so that directly below window 32 of the second floor was window 31 of the first. There was a line of oblong air vents, and on the first floor, just at ground level, were openings for toilet drainage.

All at once Honda found himself wondering which of those cells contained the defendant who had just appeared before him. Such knowledge had no bearing upon his role as a judge. The man was a poverty-stricken farmer from Kochi Prefecture in Shikoku. He had sold his daughter to an Osaka brothel, and then, having received less than half of what he had been promised, he had gone to see the madam. Enraged by her insults, he had begun to beat her and had become so carried away that he had killed the woman. Still, Honda could not clearly recall the defendant's face, a face as impassive as stone.

The smoke from his cigarette rose through his fingers and yielded to the misty rain. This cigarette would be a precious treasure in that other world separated from him by only a wall. For a moment Honda was struck by the absurd contrast of values between these two worlds whose borders the law defined. Over there the taste of tobacco was infinitely desirable; here a cigarette was nothing more than a means to while away an idle moment.

The exercise ground within the cluster of prison buildings was divided into a number of fan-shaped enclosures. From this window one often saw the blue uniforms and blue-shaven scalps of the prisoners as, two or three at a time, they were given calisthenics or allowed to walk around. Today, however, perhaps because of the rain, the exercise ground was as empty and still as the yard of a hencoop after all the birds had been slaughtered.

Just then the heavy, sultry silence was shattered by a noise from below, like rain shutters slammed together.

Then the silence closed in once more. A faint breeze caught the misty rain, and Honda felt a touch of moisture on his brow. As he was closing the window, his colleague, Judge Murakami, came into the room from his own morning court session.

"I just heard the sound of an execution," Honda said abruptly, as though apologizing.

"I heard one too a few days ago. Not a very pleasant noise, is it? I don't think it was a good idea to put the gallows close to the wall there." Murakami took off his robes. "Well, shall we go to lunch?"

"And what are you going to have today?"

"What else? An Ikematsu *bento*."

The two of them walked down the dark corridor that led to the dining room reserved for high officials, which was here on the third floor. It was the custom of Honda and Murakami to devote their lunch to discussing current cases. Just over a door marked "Senior Officials' Dining Room" was a stained-glass window whose intricate art nouveau floral pattern shone brightly from the lights inside.

The dining room contained ten long, narrow tables each furnished with kettles and teacups. Honda looked to see if the Chief Justice was among those already eating. He often came here for lunch in order to talk things over with his fellow judges. On such occasions, the woman in charge of the dining room, well aware of the Chief Justice's preferences, always hurried over to his table with a small kettle. This contained not tea but saké. Today, however, the Chief Justice was not present.

Seated across from Murakami, Honda opened his own lacquered *bento* box and took out the top section containing fish and vegetables. As usual its bottom was moist and sticky from the hot, steaming rice in the lower section, and grains of rice clung to its chipped red lacquer. Honda, disturbed at the very hint of waste, carefully picked off the rice grain by grain and put it into his mouth.

This scrupulous display amused Murakami.

"You were raised the same way I was," he said, laughing.

"Every morning you had to bow and offer a few grains of rice to a little bronze farmer sitting cross-legged with a straw raincoat between his legs. So did I. If I dropped a single grain on the floor during dinner, I had to pick it up and put it in my mouth."

"Samurai realized that they ate without working," said Honda. "The effects of being brought up that way still remain. How do your children behave?"

"They follow Papa's lead," answered Murakami, a cheerfully complacent expression on his face. Murakami was aware that he lacked the dignified countenance proper to a judge, and at one time he had tried cultivating a moustache, only to give it up when his colleagues and superiors made fun of it. He was fond of reading, and often talked about literature.

"You know, Oscar Wilde said there's no such thing as a pure crime in the present-day world. All crimes spring from some necessity. Take most of these recent assassinations. I feel as if I'd have to disqualify myself from presiding."

"Yes, I see what you mean," replied Honda prudently. "You might call them crimes resulting from social maladjustment. Most of these incidents seem to be social problems crystallized into crime, don't they? Furthermore, the men involved are hardly ever intellectuals. They don't know what it all means, but they come to personify the very problems."

"The farmers in the North, for example. There's a terrible situation."

"We can be thankful we have nothing that bad in our district."

The jurisdiction of the Osaka Court of Appeals was constituted in 1913 to include Osaka, Kyoto, Hyogo, Nara, Shiga, Wakayama, Kagawa, Tokushima, and Kochi—two urban districts and seven prefectures, a generally prosperous area.

The two went on to discuss at length the rapid growth of ideological crime, the policy of the Public Prosecutor's Office, and the like. As they talked, the clap of the execution still echoed in Honda's ears with a fresh, vibrant quality that would satisfy a carpenter. Nevertheless, he ate with a good appetite. Rather than disturbing him, the noise made him feel as if a thin wedge of crystal had pierced his awareness.

Chief Justice Sugawa entered to the respectful nods of greeting of all present. The woman in charge rushed to get the special kettle as His Honor sat down by Honda and Murakami. A huge, florid-faced kendo expert, the Chief Justice was a qualified instructor in the Hokushin Ittoryu school of kendo and served as an advisor to the Martial Arts Association. He was fond of quoting a classic kendo book in the course of his legal addresses and was consequently referred to behind his back as "the referee." But he was a very pleasant gentleman, and a warm humanity always informed his judicial decisions. Whenever there was a kendo meet or tournament within his district and he was asked to make the congratulatory address, he was happy to comply. And since many Shinto shrines sponsored the martial arts, the Chief Justice naturally developed ties with these and was always an honored guest at their festivals.

"I don't know what to do!" sighed the Chief Justice as he sat down. "I told them I'd come a long time ago, and now there's just no way of my being there."

His distress surely had something to do with kendo, Honda thought, and so it turned out. There was to be a kendo tournament at the Omiwa Shrine in the town of Sakurai in Nara Prefecture on the sixteenth of June. The shrine had worshippers all over the country, and even the universities in Tokyo were sending their best athletes to participate. Chief Justice Sugawa had agreed to give the main address, but, as it now happened, he had to go to Tokyo on that very day for a conference of district court heads. Since this was a matter that in no way involved official duty, he told Honda and Murakami, he had no right to ask one of them to go in his place, but did either of them, by chance, feel like lending him a hand? Faced with such a humble request, the two judges immediately consulted their appointment books. A court session on the sixteenth ruled out Murakami, but Honda was to work at home for a few days and the cases he would be reviewing were simple ones.

The Chief Justice's face glowed. "I don't know how to thank you," he told Honda. "This will keep me in their good graces, and there's no doubt they'll be quite happy about it at the shrine, knowing your father too. You'd better make it a two-day trip. You can stay at the Nara Hotel the night of the tournament. It's very quiet, and it will be a good place to work. The next day is the Saigusa Festival of Izagawa Shrine, the branch shrine of Omiwa right there in Nara itself, so you can see that too. I saw it once myself, and there isn't a more beautiful old festival anywhere. How does the idea suit you, Honda? If you think you'd like to see it, I'll send a letter off today. No, no two ways about it. It's something you can't afford to miss."

Pressed as he was by the Chief Justice's well-meaning enthusiasm, Honda somewhat reluctantly agreed. As for a kendo match, he had not seen one since twenty years before at Peers School. In those days both he and Kiyoaki had detested the kendo team and the fanatic yelling that accompanied their practice sessions. Neither of them could hear those cries without feeling their youthful sensitivity painfully affronted. Savage, strangled, revolting cries that seemed bent on exalting brazen madness to the level of something holy. Of course Honda and Kiyoaki had different reasons for loathing them. To Kiyoaki, the screams were a shock to his refined sensibility. To Honda, they were an assault upon reason itself. A reaction of this sort, however, was something that belonged to Honda's past. By now he had become so disciplined that he could hear or see anything at all without betraying himself by so much as a flicker of his eyebrow.

On days when there was a fairly long interval between lunch and the beginning of the afternoon session, Honda would take a walk along the bank of the Dojima River if the weather was pleasant. He liked to watch the lighters towing timber down the river, the logs churning up white water as though frothing at the mouth. But today it was raining. And the judges' chambers would be bustling with far too much activity for him to relax there. After leaving Murakami, he stood idly for a time by the front entrance, where the pale green and white light from a stained-glass window depicting an olive grove shone faintly upon the polished, mottled granite of the pillars that lined the lobby. A thought struck him, and he went to the accounts department to get a key. He had decided that he would climb the tower.

The red brick Courthouse tower was one of the landmarks of Osaka and, seen from the opposite bank, its reflection lying across the Dojima River, made for an aesthetically pleasing view. On the other hand, it was referred to as the Tower of London and was the subject of fables such as the one alleging that there was a gallows at its top upon which executions were carried out.

No one had ever been able to devise a use for this extraordinary whim of the English architect who had designed the Courthouse, and so the tower was kept locked and left to gather dust through the years. Sometimes a judge would climb it for the sake of the view. On a clear day one could see as far as Awaji Island.

Honda turned the key in the lock and went in. He was confronted with a vast white emptiness. The base of the tower was the ceiling of the front lobby of the Courthouse. From there to the very top was nothing but unobstructed space. The white walls were soiled with layers of dust and the rain that had seeped in over the years. There were windows only at the top, around which was a narrow balcony. One reached this by means of an iron stairway which crooked its way up the walls with the tenacity of ivy.

Honda knew that if he touched the stairway railing its thick coat of dust would blacken his fingertips. Though it was raining, the light let in by the windows above was enough to fill the interior of the great tower with an eerie illumination like an ill-favored dawn. Whenever he entered this tower and found himself enveloped in its blank expanse of walls and its absurdly twisting stairway, Honda had the impression of coming into a bizarre world whose dimensions had been deliberately expanded. Such a space, he felt, must house some gigantic statue hidden from his eyes, a huge figure whose invisible features were set in stern anger.

Were it not so, Honda thought, nothing would justify this extravagant spaciousness. It would be altogether devoid of meaning. Even the windows, fairly large close up, seemed no bigger than matchboxes from where Honda stood.

He climbed step by step, occasionally glancing downward through the iron grating that supported him. Each footstep stirred thunderous echoes within the tower. Though he had no reason to doubt the safety of the stairway, every step he took made its long metal frame shake from top to bottom with a giddy trembling, like a shiver passing down a man's spine. And dust drifted silently down toward the distant floor.

When he reached the top and looked out through the various windows, the scene spread out below him offered little that Honda had not already discovered. Although the rain cut his field of vision considerably, he could see the Dojima River following its leisurely southern course to its confluence with the Tosabori. On the opposite bank of the Dojima, directly to the south, stood the Public Hall, the Prefectural Library, and the Bank of Japan with its round bronze roof. Honda looked down at the office buildings that covered this broad strip of land between the two rivers, all of them dwarfed by the tower. To the west of the Courthouse, the Dojima Building rose up as a near neighbor, and in its shadow, the Gothic front of Resurrection Hospital. The wings of the Courthouse stretched out to either side below, its red brick lent charm by the rainy wetness. The small lawn of its inner courtyard seemed fitted in place as carefully as the green felt of a billiard table.

From such a height, Honda could not make out any human

figures below. He saw nothing but the lines of buildings, lights burning at midday, passive beneath the falling rain. In the pervading coolness, the consolation of nature, Honda began to reflect.

"Here I am in a high place. High enough to make one giddy. And I am here not because of power, not because of money, but simply because I represent reason for the nation. A height upheld by logic, like a tower formed of steel girders."

Whenever Honda came up here, far more than when he was seated upon the mahogany bench, he felt possessed of that all-encompassing vision that should belong to a judge. Now as he looked from this vantage point, all the phenomena below and all the phenomena of the past seemed to lie before him on a single rain-soaked map. If even reason had a childish playfulness, perhaps no diversion would be more natural for it than to gather all within a single view.

All sorts of things were going on below him. The Minister of Finance shot to death. The Prime Minister shot to death. Leftist teachers rounded up. Wild rumors flying about. The crisis of the farming communities deepening. Party government tottering along, no more than a step away from collapse. And what of Honda? He stood upon the height reserved for justice.

Honda, of course, was a man who could sketch all sorts of mental caricatures of himself in this role. Here he was, for example, upon the tower of justice, holding up in turn with a pair of tweezers each variety of human passion for evaluation. Here he was wrapping them up in the snug *furoshiki* of reason so that he could carry them home to use as the raw material of his decisions. Day after day, Honda's task was to thrust aside every element of mystery and set himself single-mindedly to the work of firming up the mortar that held the bricks of the law in place. Still, he thought, to stand upon a high place, to encompass human nature in a single view, from the clear upper reaches to the lower depths—there certainly was something to it. To possess an affinity, not with phenomena, but with the principles of law—there was something to it. Just as a groom smells of stables, so Honda, at age thirty-eight, had become permeated with the aroma of legal justice.

4

JUNE SIXTEENTH turned out to be unusually hot, even from early morning. The sun blazed down with an extravagant flourish as though announcing the midsummer heat to come. Honda left his house for Sakurai at seven a.m. in a car sent by the Chief Justice.

Omiwa Shrine ranked extremely high among national shrines. Most local people referred to it as Miwa Myojin, after Mount Miwa, which was considered to embody the divinity worshipped at the shrine. Mount Miwa itself was called simply the Holy Mountain. It rose fifteen hundred feet above sea level, with a circumference at its base of about ten miles, and it was covered by a thick forest of cedars, cypresses, red pines, and oaks. Not one of the trees growing here could be cut down. No defilement whatsoever was permitted. This primary shrine of the land of Yamato was the oldest shrine in all of Japan, and was reputed to have transmitted the Shinto faith in its purest form. And so all who reverenced the ancient rituals felt compelled, at least once in their lifetime, to make the pilgrimage to Omiwa.

The principal god enshrined at Omiwa was the major deity Nigimitama, "the mild god," who was worshipped throughout Japan as the patron of saké brewing. And the name of the shrine itself came, perhaps, from that of a vessel in which rice was fermented. Within its precincts stood the smaller Sai Shrine. This was consecrated to Aramitama, "the harsh god," toward whom military men had a warm devotion, and vast numbers of them came to pray for good fortune in battle. Five years before, the head of a veterans' association had proposed holding a kendo meet here each year as an act of worship. Because the grounds of Sai Shrine itself were too small, however, the wide court in front of the main shrine was finally chosen as the site.

All this the Chief Justice had explained to Honda. The car pulled up before the huge torii gate, and Honda got out in front of the signpost instructing pilgrims to proceed on foot.

The gravel pathway leading up to the shrine curved gently. White paper pendants hanging at prescribed intervals from cords linking the branches of the cedar trees on either side swayed in the faint breeze. The moss that covered the roots of the pines and oaks beyond the cedars, still soaked from yesterday's rain, gleamed with the wet greenness of seaweed. For some distance a brook paralleled the path just off to the left, and the sound of splashing water came up through the ferns and bamboo grass. From the clear sky overhead, the sun's torrid rays sought out the undergrowth, little hindered by the sheltering cedar branches. Just as Honda was crossing the sacred bridge he caught a glimpse of the curtain, white with a design of purple, that hung before the shrine. It was well beyond the crest of the winding stone steps that now confronted him. After climbing the steps, Honda stopped to wipe his forehead. Omiwa Shrine rose imposingly before him, at the foot of Mount Miwa.

The broad courtyard before the shrine had been swept free of gravel to form a square lightly covered with sand that was tinged red by the clay beneath. Here the kendo matches were to be held. Chairs and folding stools lined three sides, and a large canopy covered a portion of the spectators' section. His own seat as an honored guest, Honda thought, was there beneath the canopy.

A welcoming delegation of white-robed priests appeared and told him that the head of the shrine would be honored to receive him. Honda glanced quickly over his shoulder at the white disk of the morning sun blazing down upon the kendo ground as he followed the priests to the shelter of the shrine office.

Though he usually wore a grave expression, Honda was not an especially pious man. As he looked beyond the shrine at the towering cedars of Mount Miwa shining in the awesome brilliance of the morning sky, he had the feeling of being in the presence of divinity. Nevertheless, he was far from being possessed by a mood of devotion.

The feeling that the mystical enwraps the world like a pure atmosphere differs considerably from an outlook that, while acknowledging the mystical, simply does not think of it as having anything to do with ordinary affairs. Honda was of course sympathetic to the mystical. It was somewhat like affection for a mother. But from about the age of nineteen he had felt he could get along quite well without it, a feeling that had by now become second nature to him.

After Honda and the various local dignitaries had greeted one another at length and exchanged cards, the chief priest brought them all to the entrance of the corridor leading to the shrine itself where two *miko* were waiting. The guests put out their hands for the young girls to pour water over them according to the Shinto purification ceremony. Within the shrine were the fifty participating athletes, a cluster of blue-clad figures. Honda was accorded the place of honor as the guests seated themselves.

Ritual flutes sounded, and then a priest in tall cap and white robe advanced to the altar and began to recite a dedicatory prayer: "Here in the terrible presence of the great divinity of Omiwa, the Sacred Prince, Omononushi Kushimiga-

tama, forever enthroned beneath the heavens, forever favored
by the light of the sun, here upon this holy ground of
Omiwa . . ."

As he prayed, the priest waved above the heads of everyone
the sacred green sakaki branch hung with strips of white
paper. Taking his turn after a member of the sponsoring association, Honda, as representative of the guests, accepted the
sakaki branch and raised it reverently before the altar of the
gods. Next to make the offering was the representative of
the athletes, an old man of about sixty, whose kendo uniform
was a faded blue. In the course of all this solemn ritual the
heat grew ever more intense, and Honda was uncomfortably
aware of the rolling beads of sweat like a swarm of insects
under his shirt.

When the formal worship was at last completed, the whole
group went down into the forecourt. The guests took their
seats in the chairs beneath the canopy, and the athletes sat
down upon mats, which were also covered with a canopy.
The unsheltered seats were already filled with spectators.
Since these sat facing the shrine, they were in the direct rays
of the morning sun climbing behind Mount Miwa and had
to shield themselves as best they could with fans and hand
towels.

Next on the program was a long series of welcoming and
congratulatory speeches. Honda, too, got to his feet and expressed appropriate sentiments. The fifty athletes, he had
been told, were divided into the traditional two groups of red
and white. Today's meet honoring the gods of Omiwa, then,
would have five rounds, each consisting of at least five
matches between the two camps. The veterans' association
head rose to speak after Honda, and in the course of his address, which went on and on, the chief priest leaned over and
whispered into Honda's ear.

"Do you see that boy first from the left in the front row
beneath the canvas? He is only in his first year at the College
of National Studies in Tokyo, but he is the lead-off man for

the whites in the first round. I think that Your Honor would do well to mark this lad. The kendo world expects much of him. At nineteen, he has already achieved the third rank."

"What's the boy's name?"

"It is Iinuma."

The name stirred Honda's memory. "Iinuma? Is his father a kendoist?"

"No, he is Shigeyuki Iinuma, the head of a well-known patriotic group in Tokyo. He has always been most devoted to our shrine. But he himself has never engaged in kendo."

"Is he here today?"

"He wanted very much to see his son perform in the tournament, he told me, but unfortunately he has to attend a meeting in Osaka today."

It was Iinuma, then, beyond a doubt—the Iinuma that Honda had known. For a long time now, his name had been rather prominent, but Honda had identified him with Kiyoaki's former tutor only two or three years before. At that time, when the current ideological ferment was becoming a popular topic in the judges' chambers, Honda had borrowed some journals from a colleague making a study of it. Among the articles he read was one entitled "A Survey of Right-Wing Personalities" which mentioned Iinuma as follows: "An increasingly conspicuous figure is Shigeyuki Iinuma, a living embodiment of the Satsuma spirit. During the time he was a middle school student he was esteemed by his masters as the most promising boy in the entire prefecture. His family was poor, but, being highly recommended, he came to Tokyo to enter the household of Marquis Matsugae and serve as tutor to the Marquis's young heir. He devoted himself wholeheartedly to the furthering of both his own education and that of the young master. However, he fell passionately in love with one of the maids, a girl named Miné, and he abandoned the Marquis's service. Today this hot-blooded man has survived a time of hardship to attain eminence as the head of his own academy. He and his wife—Miné, of course—have one son."

Thus Honda learned what had become of Iinuma. He had never had much to do with Kiyoaki's tutor. The only impression of Iinuma that lingered in his mind was that of a stern figure in a somber dark-blue kimono with a pattern of white splashes leading him silently through the long, dark corridors of the Matsugae mansion. To Honda, Iinuma remained an inscrutable figure against a background of darkness.

The shadow of a horsefly darted over the clean-swept surface of the forecourt. Suddenly the fly buzzed loudly, approaching the long table covered with a white cloth behind which Honda and the others sat. One of the guests opened his fan and brushed it away. His gesture was so elegant that Honda at once remembered seeing from his name card that this man was a kendoist qualified to the seventh rank. The tedious address of the leader of the veterans' group went on and on.

From the square before him—but also from the overhanging gable of the shrine, the green of the holy mountain, the radiant sky—came the scorching breath of violence. Stray gusts of wind stirred the dust in the silent kendo square, soon to be filled with the shouts of antagonists and the crack of bamboo staves, as if the unseen breeze were a lithe phantom flexing its limbs to presage a brave combat.

Honda's eyes were somehow drawn to the face of Iinuma's son, who happened to be seated directly opposite him across the courtyard. The Iinuma of twenty years before must have been five years older than Kiyoaki and Honda. Even so, the realization that the earnest young tutor from the provinces had now become the father of a boy so mature forcibly reminded Honda, childless as he was, of the years that had slipped by unnoticed.

The boy had sat bolt upright throughout the long-winded speeches without making the least movement. Honda could not be sure whether he was really listening. His eyes glittered and he glared straight ahead, an image of steely imperviousness.

The boy's eyebrows were prominent. His complexion was dark. The line of his tight-shut lips was as straight as a blade's edge. Certainly he resembled Iinuma, but the features that had been blunted with heavy melancholy were now strikingly refashioned to express a keen vivacity.

"Here's a face," Honda thought, "that knows nothing of life. A face like new-fallen snow, unaware of what lies ahead."

The athletes sat with their masks and gauntlets arranged carefully in front of them, mask over gauntlet, a small towel partly covering each mask. Sunlight striking the metal bars of the masks flashed along the line of blue-clad knees, heightening the feeling of danger and tension that preceded combat.

The two referees took their positions, one to the front, one to the rear.

"White team: Isao Iinuma."

As soon as his name was called out, Iinuma's son arose, his body girded with protective gear, and strode forward over the hot sand in his bare feet. He made a deep bow of reverence before the enshrined gods.

For some reason or other, Honda found himself hoping that this boy would win. Then the initial shout broke from young Iinuma's mask, a wild cry like that of an enraged bird. Honda suddenly felt his own youth rushing back upon him.

He had once told Kiyoaki that in later years the two of them, their subtle emotional complexities lost sight of, would be lumped together with the members of the kendo team in the general estimate of the youth of their era. History would say they were dominated by callow faith. And now all had turned out as he had said. What was surprising, however, was that Honda's feeling toward this callow faith was now one of nostalgia. At some point in his life he had come to feel that the "foolish gods" were more beautiful than the exalted

deities that he had once vaguely acknowledged. And in fact
the cave of youth into which he had now stumbled was different from the one he had known before.

When that first cry tore the silence it was as though the
burning soul of youth had flared out through the rent. The
sharp pain that Honda had felt in the days when there were
wild flames in his own breast now gripped him once again,
as intensely as ever, though at his age he should have been
immune to it.

So it is that time reenacts the most curious yet earnest
spectacles within the human heart. The past makes its appearance again, with all its mingled dreams and aspirations,
the delicate tarnish of falsehood left undisturbed upon its
silver. And a man may thus come to a much deeper understanding of himself, a realization that was beyond him in his
youth. If one looks down on one's old village from a distant
mountain pass, whatever details of that era may have faded
from memory, the significance of having lived there becomes
vividly apparent. Even the rain-filled hollow in the stone
paving of the square, once so disturbing, now merely has a
simple, obvious beauty as it glitters in the sun's rays.

The instant that young Iinuma shouted out his challenge,
the thirty-eight-year-old judge perceived that there was some
pain tearing at this boy's breast, as though an arrowhead had
pierced it and remained fixed there. Never had Honda tried
to fathom in this manner what went on within the heart of
any young man who appeared before him in the prisoner's
dock.

The opponent from the red team, his neck pads bouncing
against his shoulders like a fish's distended gills, hurled back
his own challenge fiercely.

Young Iinuma now was quiet. The two squared off, staves
half-raised, and, thus confronting each other, circled once,
then once again. When the boy turned toward Honda, the
streaked shadow of his mask bars could not obscure the
black, well-defined eyebrows, the brilliant eyes, and the line

of white teeth that flashed when he shouted. And then when he turned his back, the shaven nape of his neck, below the neatly folded towel inserted beneath the blue mask straps, conveyed a sense of pure, youthful power.

Then suddenly there was a clash, like the collision of two boats buffeted by storm waves. The slender white pendant attached to young Iinuma's back flashed in the sunlight, and the same instant Honda heard the sound of a crashing blow. The boy from the red team had taken it upon the mask.

The spectators applauded. Young Iinuma had eliminated one of the opposition. Now as he faced another man from the red team, first squatting down, then swiftly drawing his stave from his hip, his virile grace persuaded one that he was already master of his new antagonist. Even to Honda, as little as he knew of kendo, young Iinuma's perfect form was evident. However violent the action, he maintained his poise throughout, his flawless bearing at each moment fixed in space like a classic pattern cut from blue cloth. He always kept his balance, unhindered by the clinging heaviness of the air. Though for others the atmosphere might be hot, sticky mud, for young Iinuma it seemed a light, congenial element.

He took a step forward out of the area shaded by the canopy, and his black cuirass shone with the luster of the clear sky above.

His opponent retreated a step. The blue of his kendo tunic and *hakama* was faded and uneven from many washings, especially where the cords that secured his cuirass had rubbed against his back to form a worn x-shaped pattern. A bright red pennant was attached here.

As young Iinuma advanced one step farther, Honda, whose eye was becoming accustomed to the action, recognized the ominous tension the set of his gauntlets conveyed. The forearm visible between the flaring cuffs of the gauntlets and the sleeves of his tunic showed a thickness unexpected in so young a man, the tendons straining beneath the light skin of the inner arms. The white leather of the gauntlet palms shaded into a bluish tint from their cloth backs, color as lyrical as the dawn sky.

The tips of the two staves moved cautiously together, like the noses of two wary dogs confronting each other.

"Ee-yaah!" his opponent shouted furiously.

"Ah-ree-yah, ah-ree-yah, ah-ree-yaah!" young Iinuma shouted back at him, his voice sonorous.

He swung his stave to the right to block the other's thrust at his waist, and there was a crack like a bursting firecracker. Then they closed with each other, grappling face to face until their sword arms locked together. The referee separated them.

At the official's signal to resume combat, young Iinuma, without pausing for breath, moved upon his opponent like a blue whirlwind, delivering a combination attack aimed at the head. Each blow struck with force and precision, each more intense. So overwhelming was their combined effect that the other boy, after parrying to right and to left to ward off the first and second blows, seemed to take of his own volition the third, which crashed down directly upon his mask. Both referees flung up their small triangular white pennants at the same moment.

The young athlete had thus eliminated his second opponent, and this time there were shouts of appreciation as well as applause from the spectators.

"The tactic of pressing with vigor and driving him back for the kill, you see," the kendo instructor next to Honda observed in an affected tone. "Red there was watching the tip of white's stave. No better way to lose. It just doesn't do to eye the other man's stave. You do it, and you get flurried."

Though he knew almost nothing of kendo, Honda grasped that there was something like a coiled spring within this young boy that gave off a dark blue glow. The vigor of his spirit manifested itself without a trace of disorder, and, whatever the resistance, created a vacuum within his opponent's resolve, if but for an instant. And the usual result was that, just as air is drawn into a vacuum, so this weak spot of his opponent drew Iinuma's stave. Thrust with perfect form, that stave, Honda thought, would no doubt pierce the guard of any opponent as easily as one enters through an unlocked door.

The third red opponent confronted young Iinuma, advancing with a weaving motion, as though reluctant. The edge of his towel, held in place across his forehead by his mask, was sloppily arranged. Instead of forming a white line straight across his brow, one of its edges dipped down, almost touching his right eye. He hunched his back slightly, like some sort of strange, erratic bird.

This, however, was a man to be reckoned with. Every dip and rise of his stave told something of a tough and shrewd competitor. Like a bird who snatches up the bait and then quickly darts to safety, this opponent would take distant aim for the forearm, strike home in most cases, and then withdraw swiftly to give a shout of victory. And to defend himself, he would not scruple to use any tactic at all, no matter how graceless.

Matched with such an opponent, young Iinuma's very grace, like that of a swan gliding confidently across the water, seemed vulnerable. This time his beauty and skill appeared likely to be his downfall.

His opponent disrupted the rhythm of movement and striking by constantly slipping away. He meant to infect him with his own awkwardness, his own unruliness.

Honda had forgotten the heat. He had even forgotten the cigarettes he liked so well. He realized that he had stopped discarding butts into the ashtray in front of him. Just as he put out his hand to smooth the badly wrinkled tablecloth, the priest beside him uttered a cry of alarm.

Looking up, Honda saw that both referees were waving crossed pennants.

"That was lucky," said the priest. "He was almost struck on the gauntlet."

Young Iinuma was trying to decide how to pursue an opponent who kept at such a distance. If Iinuma took a step forward, the other retreated. His opponent's defense was formidable. He protected himself artfully, as clinging as seaweed.

Then, when Iinuma suddenly attacked with a fierce cry, he countered his thrust derisively, and the two of them came together. Their two staves pointed almost straight upward, shaking slightly, like the masts of two boats side by side, and their cuirasses glistened like wet hulls. Antagonists though they were, their staves were now locked together as though united in reverence to a sky that offered no hope. The hard breathing, the sweat, the straining muscles, the force of their contention compressed into burning frustration . . . Such were the elements that went into their immobile symmetry.

Just as the referee was about to call out to put an end to this, young Iinuma, using the strength his opponent was mustering against him, suddenly broke free in a swift backward leap accompanied by the slapping sound of his stave landing a clean blow. He had struck the other's chest as he came away.

Both referees raised their white pennants, and the spectators applauded enthusiastically.

Honda finally lit a cigarette. It glowed feebly, its fire almost imperceptible within the pool of sunlight creeping over the table, and soon he lost interest in it.

Drops of young Iinuma's sweat sprinkled the dust at his feet like a libation of blood. When the boy arose from his squatting position, there was supple vigor in the way his pale Achilles' tendons stretched beneath the dusty hems of his blue *hakama*.

5

ISAO IINUMA, kendoist of the third rank, scored five victories in succession, bringing the first round to an end. When the fifth and final round of the match was completed, the officials declared the white team the winner. Furthermore, the silver cup for outstanding individual achievement was to go to Iinuma. As he advanced to receive his award, the sweat of combat wiped away but his cheeks still flushed, he showed the cool modesty suited to a victor. Honda could not recall ever having encountered so manly a young man.

He wanted to talk with the boy and to inquire about his father, but the priests were eager to escort him to the lunch being served in an adjacent building. During the meal the chief priest turned to Honda.

"Would Your Honor care to go up the mountain?" he asked.

Honda hesitated for a moment as he gazed out at the court-yard which lay at the mercy of the blazing sun.

"Of course ordinary visitors are not permitted to go all the way," the priest added. "Beyond a certain point the mountain is normally restricted to those who have been devoted to our shrine for many years. To enter there is truly a solemn experience. Gentlemen who have worshipped at the peak say that it gave them a sudden feeling of awesome mystery, as stunning as if they had been struck by lightning."

Honda looked once more at the summer sunlight shining on the foliage of the courtyard. Could mystery indeed be so bright? His imagination was stirred and he felt himself tempted.

Honda was only willing to sanction a mystery that could

flourish in the clear light of day. Thus, if there could be mystery shot through with brightness, he would gladly accept it. A miraculous phenomenon with no link to reality had only a shadowy, dubious existence. But any mystery that could maintain itself beneath the pitiless glare of the sun was a mystery fit to occupy a place beside clearly acknowledged principles. Honda was willing to make room for it in his world.

After a short rest following lunch, one of the younger priests led Honda along the path taken by pilgrims, and after a five- or six-minute walk up a gentle slope covered with lush greenery, they arrived at Sai Shrine, the subordinate shrine within the Omiwa precincts. Its formal title was the Sai Shrine of Omiwa Aramitama. Here pilgrims customarily underwent the rite of purification before proceeding farther up the mountain.

A grove of cedars encircled the unpretentious shrine, whose roof was thatched with cypress bark. So tranquil was its atmosphere that Honda felt that the harsh god whom it honored must have grown serene. Behind the shrine some red pines rose high above the roof, evoking for Honda the long, agile legs of an ancient warrior.

After Honda's purification, the young priest relinquished him to the care of another guide, a man of about forty wearing rubber-soled climbing shoes. His manner was extremely deferential. Just as they were to begin the formal climb of the sacred mountain, Honda noticed his first wild lily of the day.

"There's a lily they'll be picking for tomorrow's Saigusa Festival, I imagine."

"Indeed, sir, they will. But they'll never find three thousand on this mountain, so they've already gathered lilies from all the related shrines around here and put them in water in the sanctuary. The young men who fought in the match today will be pulling a cartload of lilies to Nara tomorrow as a sacred offering." And then, cautioning Honda that yesterday's rain had made the clay underfoot treacherous, the guide turned abruptly and started up the mountain path.

Almost a hundred valleys radiated from the forbidden area of Mount Miwa, including Omiya Valley, which opened out behind the main shrine to the west. After they had climbed a short distance, Honda could see the forbidden zone itself beyond a fence to his right. The trunks of the red pines growing there, in the grip of a tangle of vegetation, glowed like agate beneath the afternoon sun.

Within this area the trees, the ferns, the bamboo thickets, even the sunlight that spilled over everything seemed, to Honda at least, to create an air of purity and solemnity. The fresh color of the soil at the roots of a cedar, where the guide told him a boar had been digging, made him think of the stories from the old chronicles about the odd forms that the boar could assume.

Still, as he made his way up the sacred mountain, he had no strong feeling that it was either itself divine or the abode of divine beings. A little disconcerted by the swiftness of his middle-aged guide, Honda was hard-pressed to keep up. He felt grateful that the trees along the stream they were following warded off the afternoon sunlight, which was now even hotter.

Though sheltered by the trees, the path was becoming more and more difficult. There were many sakaki on the mountainside. Even the young trees had far broader leaves than the sakaki Honda had seen elsewhere, and in the midst of their dark green they showed a wealth of white blossoms. The current of the stream grew more rapid as they climbed until they at last reached Sanko Falls. The view of the falls, however, was half hidden by a shelter at the foot for those who came to undergo the water purification. Honda had heard how dark the woods were at this spot, but since sunlight was glinting all around, the impression was of being in a basketwork cage of light.

From here, the path led directly to the peak, and this was

by far the hardest part of the climb. Wherever the path gave
out, the two of them had to make use of jutting rocks and
pine roots to scale the sections of bare cliff that blocked their
way. And whenever Honda allowed himself to hope that a
relatively easy portion would last for a time, yet another rock
wall loomed up ahead in the brilliant glare of the afternoon
sun. Honda was soaked with sweat and panting for breath.
It was the intoxicating force of such harsh mortification, he
supposed, that prepared a man for the mystery that he was
approaching. That indeed was a divine law.

Honda looked down on a silent valley with red pines and
black pines over ten feet in diameter. He saw withered pines
choked with ivy and twisted vegetation, all their needles the
color of dull brick, and a lone cedar halfway up a cliff,
around whose trunk some pilgrim, sensing the tree's divinity,
had wound a length of sacred rope. Offerings were placed
before it, and a growth of lichen had turned one side of its
trunk a greenish bronze. The closer they drew to the peak of
the sacred mountain, the more every shrub and tree seemed
to have its own divinity, as if it had naturally become a god.

When, for example, the wind caught the tips of some tall
oaks and scattered their blossoms in a cloud of pale yellow
floating down through the lonely mountain forest, Honda felt
that the scene was charged with divinity, like a sudden
charge of electricity.

"Just a little more effort, sir," said the guide, his voice un-
affected by the strenuous climb. "There's the top ahead. You
can see the Iwakura and Konomiya Shrine."

The Iwakura—the seat of the gods—had suddenly appeared at the end of the steep slope in front of them. Its circumference marked by sacred rope, it was a huge, irregular
rock formation, now sharp-pointed, now jagged and blunted,
like a great ship whose back had been broken. Since ancient
times this mass of rock had defied comprehension, had never
submitted to the general order, its bulk an awesome image of
pure chaos.

Rock had fused to rock to form the mass that now lay broken and shattered. Below it more rock stretched out in a broad, flat surface slanting downward. Rather than a tranquil seat of the gods, the whole impression was that of the aftermath of battle or of something incredibly terrible. But then, perhaps any place visited by the gods would undergo a similar transformation.

The sun beat pitilessly down upon the moss that crept over the rock surface like an infection. But, as one might expect at this height, a refreshing breeze stirred the forest.

Konomiya Shrine, at the very top of the Iwakura, was 1,534 feet above sea level. The simplicity of this little shrine alleviated the wild, awesome mood of the Iwakura itself. The small cross-beams that formed a sharply acute angle over the peaked roof stood out from the green pines around it like a headband gallantly knotted across a warrior's forehead.

After Honda had paid his reverence, he wiped away his sweat, and, begging the guide's indulgence, lit a forbidden cigarette and drew hungrily upon it. Many years had gone by since he had last put his legs to such a test. Now that he had come through the ordeal, he took satisfaction from it and found himself very much at peace. In the midst of divinity of this sort, a divinity filled with brightness and the sound of pine needles rustling in the breeze, he felt as if he might be willing to believe in anything.

All at once Honda was reminded of another time, probably by the terrain and the altitude. He remembered climbing the mountains behind Chung-nan Villa at Kamakura on a summer day nineteen years before. They had come upon a distant view of the Great Buddha of Kamakura through the trees, and he and Kiyoaki had exchanged amused glances at the expense of the two Siamese princes, who had knelt in reverence at the first sight of the Buddha. Honda would never again feel inclined to mock such a display.

In the intervals between gusts of wind through the pines, the silence could come stealing back. His ear caught the buzz of a passing horsefly. The cedars pointed upward like so many spears thrust at the brilliant sky. The clouds were moving. The cherry trees were in full leaf, a study in light and shadow beneath the sun's rays. Honda was happy without knowing why. And this happiness had a trace of indefinable sadness, a light, poignant sting. It must have been the first time in years that he had felt this way.

The descent was not as easy as he had expected. He tried to use the tree roots to keep his footing, but the red clay around them was even slipperier. When they finally reached the tree-lined path that circled Sanko Falls, Honda found his shirt wringing wet once more.

"Would Your Honor care to make use of the water purification? It's very refreshing."

"But it wouldn't be right to bathe for that purpose, would it?"

"On the contrary, sir. When the falling water strikes a man, it clears his head. That's what makes it a religious exercise, so you needn't worry."

When they entered the shelter at the base of the falls, Honda noticed two or three kendo uniforms hanging from nails. Someone had preceded them.

"The students who were in the match today, sir. They'll be making the offering of the lilies, and they must have been told to come here to purify themselves."

Honda stripped to his undershorts and went through the door that faced the falls.

Sacred rope stretched across the falls high up at its crest, where a lush growth of vegetation shone in the afternoon sun. Up there were brightness and color, the green of trees and shrubbery ruffled by the wind, the white Shinto pendants dancing along the length of the rope, but as Honda looked downward, the scene before him was enveloped in the dark shadow cast by the rock walls to either side. A small shrine to the stalwart God of Fire occupied a grotto beside the falls, and ferns, spear flowers, and sakaki trees, all of them wet with spray, grew in the half-light at its foot. The gloom was relieved only by the slender white ribbon of falling water. Its sound echoed from the encircling rock walls with a full-throated roar.

Three young men in undershorts were standing side by side beneath the falls, water spilling in all directions over their heads and shoulders. Honda could hear the water beating on their resilient young flesh. Through the swirling spray he saw the reddened flesh of their gleaming wet shoulders.

When one of the young men noticed Honda, he nudged his companions, and they stepped back, bowing politely as they yielded the falls to him. It was then that he recognized young Iinuma among them.

Honda moved forward beneath the falls. But the water struck the upper part of his body with such clubbing force that he hastily drew back. Young Iinuma, laughing pleasantly, came up beside him, raised both hands high to demonstrate how to break the force of the falling water, and plunged himself beneath it. He stood there for a few moments, catching the violently tumbling water upon his palms and outspread fingers as if bearing a heavy flower basket aloft. Then he turned to Honda and smiled.

Honda was about to follow his example, when he happened to glance at young Iinuma's left side. There, back from the nipple, at a place ordinarily hidden by the arm, he clearly saw a cluster of three small moles.

A shiver ran through Honda. He stared at the gallant features of the boy who looked back laughingly from beneath the falls, brows contracted against the water, eyes blinking.

Honda remembered Kiyoaki's dying words: "I'll see you again. I know it. Beneath the falls."

6

ONLY THE VOICES of the frogs of Sarusawa Pond were audible in his quiet room at the Hotel Nara, as Honda, the legal documents untouched on the desk in front of him, passed a sleepless night lost in thought.

He had left Omiwa Shrine toward evening, he recalled, and had encountered a cart laden with lilies just as his car was passing flooded rice paddies ablaze with the scarlet glow of the setting sun. The wild lilies piled high upon the cart and held in place with sacred rope were a faint pink, as if they had been cut just at the flush of dawn. Two students with white headbands over their school caps were pushing the cart, and another was pulling it. A white-robed priest walked ahead, holding a purification wand hung with paper pendants. The student pulling the cart was young Iinuma, and as soon as he noticed Honda in the car, he stopped and raised his cap in greeting. His companions followed suit.

Ever since he made his incredible discovery beneath the falls, Honda had been unable to regain his equanimity. He had barely acknowledged the various courtesies that the priests of the shrine had shown him afterwards. And then when he had again come upon the three students, their offering of lilies and their white headbands brilliant in the sunset glow mirrored upon the surface of the rice paddies, he became still more abstracted. The young man left behind in the dust raised by the speeding auto, much as his features and his complexion differed, was assuredly in his essential being no one but Kiyoaki.

Once Honda was left to himself at the hotel, he was beset by the thought that from that day on, his world would be drastically changed. He went down to the dining room at once, but ate his dinner as if in a daze. He went back to his room. The sheets on the freshly made bed were folded back to form a lustrous white triangle. Like the pages of a book lying wide open, they gleamed in the faint light of a table lamp.

He turned on all the lights, trying in vain to keep mystery at a distance. The miraculous had invaded his own ordered world, and he had no idea what might happen in the future. Furthermore, though he had seen the marvel of reincarnation with his own eyes, it was a secret he could never reveal. If he were to speak of it to someone, he would immediately be thought insane, and the rumor would pass from mouth to mouth that he was no longer qualified to be a judge.

Still, mystery had a rationality of its own. Just as Kiyoaki had said eighteen years before ("I'll see you again. I know it. Beneath the falls.") Honda had indeed met beneath a water-fall a young man whose side was marked with the same pattern of three moles. He was reminded of what he had read about the four successive existences in the books on Bud-dhism that he had studied after Kiyoaki's death, following the teachings of the Abbess of Gesshu. Since young Iinuma was eighteen years old, his age as Kiyoaki reincarnated fitted precisely.

These four existences, marking the progression of every sentient being, were conception, life, death, and then an inter-mediate period of existence, a state midway between the pre-vious life and the reincarnation to come. At its shortest this lasted seven days, and it could extend for as long as seventy-seven. Honda did not, of course, know the date of Iinuma's birth, but it was altogether possible that it fell somewhere within the period of from seven to seventy-seven days after Kiyoaki's death in the early spring of 1914, the third year of the Taisho era.

In this intermediate state, according to Buddhist lore, one existed, not as a merely spiritual being, but in the form of a fully sentient young child of five or six. Now, however, all the ordinary powers were marvelously heightened. The eye and ear became incredibly keen. One heard the most distant sounds, one saw the most hidden objects, one was immediately present wherever one wished to be. The childlike figures thus gifted, though invisible both to men and to beasts, could be seen hovering in the air by the rare clairvoyant who had attained sufficient purity.

These invisible children nourished themselves on the fragrance of burning incense as they went about their rapid journeys through the air. Hence this intermediate state was also known as "seeking fragrance," after the divinities called Gandharva in Sanskrit.

In the course of his far-ranging flights, such a child would come upon the overwhelming sight of his future father and mother in the very act of copulating. A male child would be fascinated by the shameless disarray of his future mother's body, and yet, though he burned with resentment toward the man who was to be his father, no sooner had this man made his impure ejaculation than the child would be seized with a passionate joy as though the act were his own, and give up his free existence to take life up within the woman's womb. This instant was the next stage of existence.

Such was the Buddhist explanation. Honda, of course, had once looked upon it as a mere fairy tale. And now all at once it had come to his mind. The process, he thought, was certainly what mystery should be: something that arbitrarily made its appearance, independent of the wishes of any man. A dangerous gift. Like a shimmering sphere of changing colors, it came plunging into the midst of the cold but well-regulated structure of order and reason. Its colors, indeed, changed according to principle, but a principle that was entirely different from human reason. Hence the sphere had to be somehow hidden from human eyes.

Whether Honda was willing to acknowledge it or not, mystery had already irrevocably altered his outlook. He could not escape it. Perhaps the best course was to find an ally, someone to share the secret. There was young Iinuma himself for one. And then, too, there was the boy's father. But what assurance had he that either one was aware of the presence of mystery? It might well be that Shigeyuki Iinuma, who must have had occasion to see Kiyoaki naked, realized that the mark on his son's side strikingly resembled the one that his young master had borne. Even so, he might wish to conceal it. How could Honda question father and son about such a matter? Would not the very act of questioning them be ill-advised? Even if they were aware of the presence of mystery, would they be willing to share their secret? If they refused, the mystery might weigh heavily on him for the rest of his life.

Once more Honda felt racing through him the keen excitement that Kiyoaki had brought to his youth. Though Honda had never yearned to exchange lives with anyone, the brief beauty of Kiyoaki's life, like delicate blossoms on a branch, seemed joined to his own, the tree that for those few years had provided the needed support. And thus Kiyoaki's life gave meaning to Honda's, having flowered with a beauty that Honda's itself would never attain. Could this happen again? What was the meaning of Kiyoaki's reincarnation?

Beset though he was by the riddles that surrounded him, Honda nonetheless felt joy stirring deep within him like a subterranean spring. Kiyoaki was alive once more! The tree cut down in its youth had sprung up once more. Eighteen years ago both he and Kiyoaki had been young. Now Honda's youth was gone, but his friend's shone with undiminished brilliance.

Young Iinuma might lack Kiyoaki's beauty, but he compensated for that with the manly force that Kiyoaki had lacked. Though Honda could not be certain from so brief an acquaintance, it seemed to him that young Iinuma, in place of Kiyoaki's arrogance, possessed simplicity and fortitude, qualities hardly apparent in Kiyoaki. The two were as different as light and shadow, but they shared one characteristic: both of them strikingly personified youth.

When Honda thought about those years he had spent with Kiyoaki, he felt mingled grief and nostalgia, but now also an unexpected rush of hope. He would have to pay a price for the excitement that was building within him, but he was ready to do so without regret, no matter how severe the consequences for his once unswerving commitment to reason.

And then how strange a turn of fate that he made the incredible discovery of Kiyoaki's rebirth in Nara, a place so intimately involved with Honda's last memories of his friend!

"I'll wait until morning," Honda thought, "but there's something I should do before going to Izagawa Shrine. I'll have my driver rush me to Obitoké for an early morning visit to the convent. I'll apologize to Satoko for not having come to see her in the years since Kiyoaki's death, and then I'll tell her about his reincarnation, even if she won't believe it. She should be the first to know. Now she's the Abbess of Gesshu, after the death of the former Abbess, and I've heard that she is greatly revered. Probably the years have touched her only lightly, and I'll be able to see that beautiful face of hers lit up by pure joy."

For a time Honda felt a youthful impulsiveness. Finally, however, he prudently decided to suppress that hasty notion.

"No, I shouldn't do it," he told himself. "After all, she didn't even attend his funeral. She made her decision to turn her back on the world, and I have no right to disturb her. No matter how often Kiyoaki was reborn, it would not concern her—it would always be something that happened in the world of deceitful illusion which she has abandoned. No matter how unmistakable the proof, she would turn coldly away. For me it may be a miracle, but miracles no longer exist for Satoko in the world in which she now lives. It won't do to let myself be carried away by excitement over this. I'll not go to see her. If this strange reincarnation is the work of providence, I needn't rush to see her. Some occasion will arise for her to meet him. It's better that I wait and let events mature in their own way."

After pondering all this, Honda found sleep still more remote. The warmth of his pillow and spread became oppressive, and he gave up all hope of a pleasant night's rest.

The window was beginning to whiten. In the pane of glass enclosed by a frame carved in Momoyama style, the reflection of Honda's night lamp shimmered like a dawn moon. Against the faint light of the sky he could already make out the five-storied pagoda of Kofuku Temple rising up beyond a grove of trees encircling a pond. Only the three top stories and the spire thrusting itself upward into the dawn were visible. As he gazed at the pagoda, hardly more than a shadow in a corner of the gray sky, Honda felt as if he had awakened only to fall into another dream, like a man who thinks that he has escaped from one kind of irrationality only to find himself in the midst of another, even more persuasive. Thus did the pagoda affect him—the subtle curvature of those three upper roofs—as if it were the image of a many-layered dream. A smoky mist seemed to be rising from the topmost roof to swirl through the nine rings circling the spire and up past the flame-shaped device at its peak, finally to fade into the dawn sky. Even as he was watching this happen, Honda had no assurance that he was in fact awake. For all he knew, he might be in the midst of another dream, a dream so vivid that not even the keenest perception could distinguish it from reality.

The song of the birds became louder. Suddenly the thought struck him that it was not just a matter of Kiyoaki's returning to life. Had not Honda himself risen from death? From the death manifested by a chilled spirit, by a rigorous order like a file jammed with thousands of entries, by the tedious refrain, "Youth is gone"?

Perhaps it was exactly because his own life had once been so far encroached upon by Kiyoaki's life, so deeply buried with it, that life was now being restored to Honda too, just as the first rays of dawn brighten one branch of a tree and then the next.

At this point Honda felt a curious relief, and at last, as if falling into a light faint, succumbed to sleep.

7

HONDA AWOKE with a start, realizing that he had forgotten to ask to be called, and by the time he arrived at Izagawa Shrine the solemn ritual of the Saigusa Festival had already begun. Bending forward, he made his way through the hushed crowd to the seat reserved for him beneath the canopy. He sat down quietly, without even looking around, and fastened his gaze on the ceremony before him.

Izagawa Shrine was in Nara itself, not far from the railway station. To the rear of the shrine precincts stood three sanctuaries. The center sanctuary enshrined the goddess Himetataraisuzu, and, to either side, as though to protect her, were her goddess mother and her father, the latter the principal deity of Omiwa Shrine. A scarlet railing encircled the three small, beautifully fashioned structures, which were linked together by white screening partitions decorated with paintings of pines and bamboos done in rich turquoise and gold.

Each sanctuary was fronted with three stone steps which were swept clean of impurity. And then to reach the sanctuary door itself, one had to ascend ten wooden steps. The white paper pendants that hung from the sacred rope at the eaves seemed to stand out like fragments of pure ivory against the scarlet railing and the yellow and gold-flecked bracketing in the dark shadow of the roof.

Fresh mats had been spread upon the stone steps for today's ritual. The gravel of the courtyard had been raked into a neat pattern. To the front of the precincts was the scarlet-pillared outer hall of the shrine, an open gallery in which priests and shrine musicians were sitting on either side. Through this gallery the worshippers would observe the ceremonies.

A priest had already begun the purification ritual, and the three small bells attached to the base of a large sacred branch tinkled as he waved it over the bowed heads of the crowd. After the prayer ended, the chief priest of Omiwa Shrine, bearing a gold key hung with a crimson cord, advanced toward the center sanctuary and knelt upon the wooden steps, the back of his white robe half in sunlight and half in shadow. As he was kneeling, the assistant priests at his side twice chanted a long, drawn-out "Oh!" The chief priest then climbed the steps, inserted the key into the lock of the sanctuary doors, and reverently drew them open. The dark purple Sacred Mirror flashed from within. The stringed instruments were sounding a repeated tremolo of almost ludicrous intensity.

The assistant priests spread fresh mats before the sanctuary. Then, together with the chief priest himself, they bore oblations covered with oak leaves to a table of bark-covered wood hung with white paper pendants. And now began the most beautiful part of the Saigusa Festival.

The next offerings would be a cask filled with white saké and an earthen jar filled with black saké, both of them beautifully adorned. The cask was of plain wood and the jar was unglazed, but both were entirely covered with lilies, like two sheaves of flowers. Thus the body of the cask was completely wrapped around with the tough green stems of lilies, bound by fresh white hempen cord. Since their stems formed such a tight sheath, the flowers and leaves and buds were thrust all

together in a promiscuous tangle. The greenish red buds had
a rustic vigor, and there was a trace of green left even in the
fully opened flowers, whose petals were streaked with a delicate pink. Their inner surfaces were dusted with red, and the
tips of their petals, bent back in utter disarray, were trans-
lucent in the sunlight. Huddled together in such a mass, the
lilies stood with drooping heads.

The most beautiful of the three thousand wild lilies
brought by young Iinuma and his companions had been selected to adorn the cask and the jar, but the rest were also
brilliantly in evidence, arranged in vases before the sanctuaries. Lilies were everywhere. The breeze carried the scent
of lilies. The theme of lilies was persistent and inescapable,
as though lilies had come to express the very essence of life.
Now the priests advanced with the cask and the earthen jar.
White-robed, with black ceremonial headgear, they solemnly
held these offerings aloft, and the bound lilies trembled in
beauty over their heads. The bud of one especially long-
stemmed lily seemed as pale as a tense young man on the
verge of fainting.

The wail of the flutes filled the air. The drums throbbed.
Placed before a dark stone wall, the lilies seemed to flush
crimson. The priests crouched down beside the cask and the
jar, parted the stems of the lilies, and dipped out saké. Other
priests approached to receive it in their plain wood flasks, and
then raised them in oblation before each of the three shrines.
This ritual, with its musical accompaniment, seemed quite in
the spirit of a cheerful banquet of the gods. Within the doorway of the sanctuary the noon shadows evoked a vaguely
growing sense of divine intoxication.

Meanwhile a group of *miko*, four beautiful young girls,
had begun the Cedar Dance in the outer hall. Their heads
were bound with cedar leaves, and their black hair was
braided with red and white paper fastened with gold thread.
Over pale crimson *hakama*, they wore gossamer robes of pure
white with a silver pattern of rice leaves. The five robes worn

beneath the white outer one revealed themselves at the neck-
line in an alternating white and red pattern.

The young girls made their appearance in the midst of
lilies, lilies standing upright, petals wide open, amber-colored
stamens out-thrust. And each of these *miko*, too, held a bunch
of lilies in her hand. As the musicians played, the girls formed
a square facing inward and began to dance, their upraised
lilies starting to shake with fearful abandon. The dance progressed, the lilies now elegantly rising, now dipping to come
together, now separating once more. Again and again, like
the passes of a keen sword blade, a graceful edge of whiteness
cut through the air. As they were thus whipped about, the
lilies gradually wilted, cruelly handled, it seemed, for all the
quiet elegance of the music and the dance.

As Honda looked on, he felt a kind of intoxication overcom-
ing him. He had never seen such a beautiful ritual. The effects
of his sleepless night made the spectacle begin to blur, and
the lily festival he was now watching started to merge with
the kendo match he had seen the previous day. The girls'
lilies became bamboo staves and then, in another moment,
flashing sword blades. As the *miko* circled about with easy
grace in the sunlight, the shadows of their long eyelashes on
their white-powdered cheeks became for Honda the shadows
cast by the glittering bars of the kendo mask.

After the guests and other worshippers had lifted the
pendant-festooned sakaki branch in reverence before the sanctuary, the doors were shut once more. By noon the ritual was
over.

The Naorai, the sacred banquet following a ritual, was to
take place in an adjacent hall. The chief priest came over to
Honda with a middle-aged man he wanted to introduce. As
soon as Honda saw young Iinuma in his school cap walking
along behind him, he realized that the man was Shigeyuki
Iinuma. Iinuma's slender moustache had thrown him off for
a moment.

"This must be Mr. Honda," Iinuma said. "What memories this brings back! Has it really been nineteen years? My son Isao told me about yesterday, how kind you were to him. What a strange turn of fate!"

Iinuma pulled a sheaf of calling cards from his pocket, picked out one of his own, and presented it to Honda. As he read it, the fastidious Honda could not help noticing that one corner of the card was slightly soiled and bent:

THE ACADEMY OF PATRIOTISM
SHIGEYUKI IINUMA
HEADMASTER

What startled him about Kiyoaki's old tutor was his talkative and open manner, so unlike the Iinuma Honda remembered. Years before he had been quite different. As Honda looked more closely, he saw that some things about him were unchanged: the uncouth tuft of hair just visible at the neck of his kimono, his square shoulders, the dark, brooding eyes, with a tendency to waver. His outward bearing, however, was altogether different.

"Forgive me for addressing you so familiarly!" said Iinuma, looking up from Honda's card. "You certainly have attained eminence. The truth is, your fame came to my notice some time ago, but it seemed rude for someone like me to presume upon past acquaintance, so I restrained myself. Now that I look at you, you haven't changed a bit. If the young master were alive, you would be his most trusted friend. Anyway, as I learned afterwards, you proved the depth of your friendship by what you did for him. Everyone said how wonderful you were."

As Honda listened, feeling as though he were being slightly mocked, it occurred to him that Iinuma would not speak so openly of Kiyoaki if he were aware of his young master's reincarnation in his own son. Then again, possibly Iinuma's apparent frankness was a means of seizing the initiative and warning Honda not to intrude into this mystery.

Still, when Honda looked at Iinuma in his crested *hakama* and at young Isao standing behind him, he could only see everyday reality. Iinuma's face was marked by the years and by the common tribulations. The smell of day-by-day existence was so strong that the wild thoughts that had pursued Honda from the dreams of the night before seemed no more than ephemeral fantasy. He began to wonder if even the moles he had seen on Isao's side might have been no more than a trick of vision.

Nevertheless, despite the urgency of the work that awaited him that evening, Honda found himself asking Iinuma: "How long will you be in the Kansai?"

"I'm afraid I'll be taking the train back to Tokyo tonight."

"That's too bad." After a moment's thought, Honda made his decision. "What do you say to this? Before you leave tonight, won't you and your son have dinner at my home? It's a rare chance for us to have a leisurely talk."

"You do me too much honor. I couldn't think of imposing myself and my son upon your hospitality."

Honda turned directly to Isao: "It will be my pleasure. You and your father must come. You'll be returning to Tokyo on the same train, won't you?"

"Yes, sir," answered Isao, somewhat inhibited by his father's presence.

Iinuma, however, now said that he would accept Honda's kind invitation, and promised that, after attending to a few matters in Osaka, both of them would come to his home that evening.

"Your son was superb yesterday in the kendo match. It's really a pity that you couldn't be there. It was a performance to take one's breath away." As he spoke, Honda looked from one to the other.

Just then a lean but erect old man in Western clothes

approached them. He was accompanied by an extremely attractive woman of about thirty.

"General Kito and his daughter," Iinuma whispered into Honda's ear.

"General Kito, you say? The poet?"

"Yes, yes. That's right."

Iinuma had become tense, and his hushed, respectful tone made Honda think of a courtier sent to prepare the way of a lord.

Kensuké Kito was a retired major general of the Imperial Army, but his fame came from his poetry. Honda, urged by friends, had read his highly praised *Hekiraku*, a collection of poems that, according to critics, revived the bold spirit and style of the thirteenth-century poet Sanetomo. Such classical elegance and simple beauty were wholly unexpected from a contemporary military man, and Honda had found his poems so moving that he could recite two or three of them from memory.

Iinuma greeted the General with the utmost deference and then turned to introduce Honda: "This gentleman is Judge Honda of the Osaka Court of Appeals."

Honda would have preferred to be presented merely as an old friend, but now that Iinuma had seen fit to introduce him with such a flourish, Honda had no choice but to assume his role as an official and stand on his dignity.

The General, however, seemed quite equal to the occasion, his military background having accustomed him to distinctions of rank. He smiled, crinkling the corners of his eyes, and said quietly: "My name is Kito."

"I am a great admirer of your poetry, especially of *Hekiraku*."

"You'll have me blushing."

General Kito had the affability and utter lack of arrogance of a man who has spent his life as a soldier. Having survived a profession that offered ample opportunity to die young, he inspired a feeling of strength and steadfastness. His old age shone with cheerful detachment, like the winter sun shining through white paper stretched over a latticework of fine, aged wood, not in the least warped, beyond which patches of snow lay here and there on the ground.

As he and Honda were exchanging a few words, his beautiful daughter spoke to Isao: "I hear that you defeated five men in succession yesterday. Congratulations."

Honda glanced over toward her, and the General introduced them: "My daughter, Makiko." Makiko bowed her head politely.

During that moment Honda found himself eagerly waiting to look into the lovely face beneath her Western-style hairdo. Now that he saw her close at hand, Honda noticed by both the whiteness of her skin, almost devoid of makeup, and the faint, telltale signs, like the grain of thick Japanese paper, that she was no longer a young girl. Her smooth features seemed somehow to express a distant sorrow. The tautness at the corners of her mouth gave a disturbing hint of disdainful resignation but her eyes were brimming with a soft, gentle light.

As Honda and Iinuma stood talking with the General and his daughter about the beauty of the Saigusa Festival, young priests in white robes and pale yellow *hakama* came out and urged all the guests to take their places at the Naorai.

The General and his daughter met other friends, walked ahead with them toward the reception hall, and were soon lost in the crowd.

"What a lovely young woman!" said Honda, half to himself. "And she's still not married?"

"She's divorced," Iinuma replied. "I suppose she must be in her early thirties. It's hard to think a man would let a beauty like that get away from him." His voice sounded muffled, as if the lips beneath the neat moustache were reluctant.

The worshippers crowded the entrance of the hall, jostling

together as they struggled to remove their shoes and enter. Honda let himself be carried along by the flow of people, and, looking ahead through the crowd, caught his first glimpse of the tables set up for the banquet. A mass of wild lilies was spread over the white tablecloths.

Somewhere Honda had become separated even from Iinuma. As the crowd surged by, it occurred to him that Kiyoaki himself, alive again, was caught in this same press of humanity. How wild a fancy this seemed here at midday beneath the early summer sun! He was dazzled by the excessive brightness of the mystery.

Just as sea and sky blurred together at the horizon, so, too, dream and reality could certainly become confused when viewed from a distance. But here, at least around Honda, everyone was clearly subject to the law and, in turn, guarded by the law. His role was that of a guardian of the order established by the operative law of this world. This operative law was like a heavy iron lid upon the pot in which the multifarious stew of the day-to-day world simmered.

Human beings eating, digesting, excreting, reproducing, loving and hating . . . Honda reflected that these were the human beings under the court's jurisdiction. If worst came to worst they would appear before it as defendants.

They alone had reality. Human beings who sneezed, laughed, human beings who went about with absurdly dangling reproductive gear. If all human beings were like this, there was no basis whatsoever for Honda's fearful mystery. Even if a single reborn Kiyoaki might be hidden in their midst.

Honda sat at the place of honor to which the priests directed him. On the table before him were wooden boxes of various delicacies and jars of saké as well as plates and small bowls. At appropriate intervals stood vases of wild lilies. Makiko was sitting on the same side of the table, and he was occasionally able to catch a glimpse of her lovely profile and the wisps of hair that fell over her cheek.

The rays of the early summer sun, scattered by tree branches, fell upon the garden. Now it was the turn for humans to feast.

8

AFTER HONDA HAD returned home in the afternoon, he asked his wife to arrange for dinner guests and then took a short nap. He had a dream that Kiyoaki suddenly appeared and began telling him how joyful he was at their being reunited. When Honda awoke, however, he did not allow this to excite him. He accounted for it as merely an illustration of the lingering thoughts that had occupied his fatigued mind since the previous night.

Iinuma and his son arrived at six o'clock. Intending to leave directly by train afterwards, they had brought their luggage with them. When Honda and Iinuma sat down together, they felt awkward about immediately returning to their talk of the past, and instead began to discuss recent politics and social conditions. But Iinuma, apparently in deference to Honda's position, refrained from voicing any outright complaints about the evils of the times. Isao sat upright, hands on knees, as he listened.

Those eyes of his, which had flashed brightly even from behind a kendo mask yesterday, seemed extravagantly brilliant here in an ordinary room. They seemed to express intense determination. To have such eyes close to one, to be gazed at intently by such eyes was an extraordinary experience.

Honda sensed Isao's eyes on him as he talked with Iinuma, and he felt uneasy. "It's quite uncalled for to stare like that during a conversation," he thought, feeling tempted to say a word of remonstrance. Eyes of that kind should not be brought to bear upon the petty doings of everyday life. Honda felt somehow accused by their clear brilliance.

Two men may talk together enthusiastically for an hour or so about shared experiences, and yet not have a true conversation. A lonely man who wants to indulge his nostalgic mood feels the need of someone with whom to share it. When he finds such a companion, he starts to pour out his monologue as though recounting a dream. And so the talk goes on between them, their monologues alternating, but after a time they suddenly become aware that they have nothing to say to each other. They are like two men standing at either side of a chasm, the bridge across which has been destroyed.

Then at last, since they cannot bear to remain silent, their conversation turns again to the past. For some reason, Honda found himself yielding to the urge to ask Iinuma why he had published an article in a right-wing newspaper accusing Marquis Matsugae of being disloyal and unfilial.

"Ah, that!" answered Iinuma. "I hesitated before making an attack on the Marquis, who was so kind to me, but I felt I had to write that article regardless of the consequences. I did it solely out of concern for the nation."

Such a smooth, ready answer naturally did not satisfy Honda. He remarked that Kiyoaki, after reading the article and sensing its significance, told him he missed Iinuma.

A startling surge of emotion swept over Iinuma's face, which had already begun to show the effects of the saké they were drinking. The neat moustache trembled slightly.

"Is that right? The young master said that? He must have known how I felt. My motive in writing that article—how should I put it—was to make a public complaint, even though it meant sacrificing the Marquis, so that no one could blame the young master himself. I was afraid the young master's involvement might somehow become known, and the scandal would do him irreparable harm. By taking the initiative and exposing the Marquis's disloyalty, I could shield the young master. And then, too, wouldn't any good father want to bear the brunt of the scandal himself? That was what I expected. Perhaps it was inevitable that the Marquis would become enraged at me, but when I think how the young master understood my intentions, I feel an overwhelming gratitude.

"Judge Honda, please listen to what I have to say. It's the saké that gives me the courage to tell you this, but I'm not exaggerating. When I heard that the young master had passed away I wept for three whole days and nights. I thought that I would at least attend the wake, and I went to the Matsugae mansion, only to be turned away at the door. It seems that the arrangements concerning me were very thorough. Even on the day of the public funeral service I was kept out by their police. And so I could not offer incense for the departed young master.

"Of course I brought it on myself, but it's a grievance that I'll bear for the rest of my days. Even now I sometimes speak bitterly about it to my wife. What an unhappy fate for the young master! To die without achieving what he wished, and at barely twenty." Iinuma pulled a handkerchief from his pocket and wiped away his tears.

Honda's wife had come in to pour the saké, and sat there speechless. Young Isao, who had apparently never seen his father so overcome with emotion, had stopped eating and was looking down. Honda stared at Iinuma across the brightly lit, dish-laden table as if he were gauging the distance between them.

Honda did not doubt the genuineness of Iinuma's sentiment. Thus, since his grief expressed such finality, he could hardly have known of Kiyoaki's reincarnation. Otherwise his emotion would surely have been far more ambiguous and uncertain.

As he reflected, Honda found himself scrutinizing his own inner thoughts. Why did the sight of Iinuma's grief provoke no tears from him? For one thing, there was the tempering his emotions had undergone in a profession that prized reason. And for another, there was the newfound hope that Kiyoaki lived again. A mere hint of the possibility of reincarnation made even the keenest grief suddenly seem to lose its freshness and reality, and begin to scatter like dry leaves. Somehow that was related to man's unwillingness to tolerate any injury to the dignity that he achieved through sorrow. In a sense, such a loss was more fearful than death.

When Iinuma had gained control of himself, he at once turned to his son and asked him to go to send a telegram for him. He had forgotten to tell the students of the academy to come to meet them at Tokyo Station the next morning. Rié suggested sending the maid, but Honda, realizing that Iinuma wanted his son out of the way for a time, quickly sketched a map to show Isao how to find the nearest post office that was open at night.

After Isao left, Rié went back to the kitchen. At last Honda had a chance to question Iinuma closely, but, while he was wondering how to broach the subject, Iinuma himself began to speak of Kiyoaki.

"I failed wretchedly in educating the young master, so I intended to do my best to give my own son what I considered an ideal education. But again something was missing. When I look at my grown son, it's incredible how the young master's good qualities come to my mind. In spite of how I failed with him."

"But you have a wonderful son. From what I've seen of him, he's quite superior to Kiyoaki Matsugae."

"Judge Honda, you're being too polite."

"Well, consider Isao's physical fitness. Kiyoaki neglected his body completely." Honda felt the excitement rising within him as he tried to lead Iinuma to the crucial point of the mystery. "It's no wonder he died so early from pneumonia— he was handsome, but he had no strength. But you were with him ever since he was a child. You must have been thoroughly familiar with his body."

"By no means!" Iinuma hastily protested. "I never so much as washed the young master's back."

"Why not?"

Embarrassment contorted Iinuma's blunt features, and the blood rushed to his swarthy cheeks.

"When the young master was undressed, I could never bring myself to look at him directly."

After Isao's return from the post office, it was soon time to leave. Honda, whose profession had not equipped him to deal with the young, realized that he had yet to exchange a word with Isao.

"What sort of books do you like to read?" he asked, rather awkwardly.

"Let me show you, sir." Isao, who was just putting something into his suitcase, took out a thin paperbound book and showed it to him. "I bought this last month after a friend recommended it, and I've already read it three times. I've never been so moved by a book. Have you read it, Your Honor?"

Honda looked at the title and author's name printed in old-style characters on the plain cover: *The League of the Divine Wind* by Tsunanori Yamao. He turned over the small book, hardly more than a pamphlet, and noted that even the publisher was unfamiliar. He was about to give it back without a word when he found his hand checked by Isao's strong hand, callused from the kendo stave.

"If Your Honor is interested, please read it. It's a splendid book. I'll lend it to you. You may send it back later."

His father had just gone out to the lavatory, or he would have scolded him for his presumption. As Honda looked at the flashing eyes of the enthusiastic young man, he saw at once that Isao believed that lending his favorite book was the only way he could express his gratitude for Honda's kindness. Honda accepted the book, and thanked him for it.

"It's good of you to part with a book that means so much to you."

"No, no, I'm delighted to have Your Honor read it. I'm sure, sir, that you too will be moved by it."

The force of Isao's answer gave Honda a glimpse into a world where the pursuit of idealism was easy, where youthful enthusiasms were readily shared—a world as simple as the endlessly repeated pattern of white splashes on the coarse blue kimono of his student days. He felt a twinge of envy.

One of Rié's merits was that she never gave a critique of guests immediately after their departure. Though not in the least credulous, she had a kind of languid, bovine steadiness. Still, even two or three months after the visit of a particular guest, she would sometimes surprise Honda with a casual allusion to a shortcoming she had noted.

Honda was extremely fond of Rié, but she was not the sort of woman to whom he could pour out his fantasies and dreams. No doubt she would be delighted if he did. Certainly she would not ridicule them, but neither would she believe in them.

Honda made it a rule never to discuss professional matters with his wife, and he had no difficulty being just as secretive about the products of his by no means fertile imagination. As for the events that had so bewildered him since the day before, he intended to keep them as hidden as Kiyoaki's dream journal at the back of his desk drawer.

Honda entered his study to confront the work that had to be done before morning, but the stack of thick Mino paper on which the court proceedings had been recorded in hard-to-read brush strokes gave such a severe check to his sense of duty that he was unable to begin.

He reached out absently, picked up the pamphlet that Isao had left, and, without any eagerness, began to read it.

9

The League of the Divine Wind
by Tsunanori Yamao
PART THE FIRST
The Rite of Ukei

ONE DAY in the summer of 1873—the Sixth Year of the Meiji era—four stalwart men of high ideals gathered at the Imperial Shrine in Shingai Village five miles south of Kumamoto Castle to offer worship under the direction of Tomo Otaguro, adopted son and heir of the former chief priest. The Shingai Shrine was a branch of the Grand Shrine at Isé, and was known locally as Isé Shingai. Sheltered by a grove of tall trees and surrounded by paddies, this simple thatched-roof shrine was the most sacred place within the prefecture.

Their worship done at last, the four left Otaguro alone in the shrine and retired to the parlor of the priest's dwelling. Now Otaguro was to perform the secret rite of Ukei.

As for these four: Harukata Kaya was at the height of his powers, a man of stern visage. Kengo Ueno was past sixty. Kyusaburo Saito and Masamoto Aikyo were men in their fifties. Kaya wore his hair long and tied at the back of his head. Each of them bore a sword at his side.

Taut with emotion as they awaited the issue of the Ukei, the four of them sat erect in silence, neither wiping away their sweat nor looking at one another.

Again and again, the cicada's untiring cry pierced the sultry summer air like a needle at work on thick cotton cloth. A pine

bent like a reclining dragon shaded the pond in the garden upon
which the parlor opened. Though not the faintest breeze reached
the veranda, the irises at the pond's edge, some upright like
sword blades, others gracefully bent, trembled slightly. The
reflection of the water glimmered upon the white branches of the
delicate-blossomed crape myrtle.

Greenness was heaped up abundantly, even the leaves of the
bush clover giving way to green. Yellow butterflies fluttered
about. At the edge of the garden, between the trunks of a row of
half-grown firs, the blue sky shimmered.

Kaya, his emotion evident in the glitter of his eyes, turned in
the direction of the shrine. What he hoped for from this Ukei ran
counter to the wishes of the others.

The fore-hall of Isé Shingai was appointed thus: in its center,
mounted within a frame, hung the sword of Lord Tadatoshi
Hosokawa in its white sheath. To the left was a votive picture of
a dragon, and to the right was another depicting the white cock
and hen of Lord Nobunori Hosokawa. The inscription "The
Third Year of the Manji Era" was in the calligraphy of Sekki
Obaku. A raised platform stood ever in readiness for the clan
lord, whether he chose to worship in person or through a retainer.

The white-robed figure of Tomo Otaguro lay prostrate in the
Divine Presence. The priest's neck was thin and his face as pale
as an invalid's. It was his practice, whenever he was to address
a petition to the gods, to fast for a period of seven or ten days
and to do without cooked food for fifty or a hundred days.

The Ukei, through which the will of the gods was consulted,
was accorded the utmost reverence by Otaguro's late master, Oen
Hayashi, who had passed away three years before at this very
shrine. Indeed, Oen had written *A Treatise on the Ukei*. His
vision of Shinto went beyond Atsutané Hirata's principle of conti-
nuity between the Revealed World and the Hidden World. Oen
wrote, for example:

> Divinity is the source. The visible world is its issue. He
> who has charge of affairs, he who governs men, must view
> Divinity as source and the visible world as issue. For the ruler

who rightly integrates source and issue, the governing of the whole world will be of small concern.

And Oen taught that the Ukei, by means of which the divine will became manifest, was of prime importance within the arcane canon.

A Treatise on the Ukei began with these words:

> Of all the rites of Shinto, the Ukei is the most wondrous. As to its origin, the ineffably awesome goddess Amaterasu, together with Lord Susano, conducted the first Ukei in High Heaven, whence it was transmitted to our land of Yamato.

Among the offspring brought forth by Lord Susano in the course of the Ukei that he undertook in order to demonstrate his innocence was Lord Amenooshihomimi, who is none other than the Divine Parent of Lord Ninigi, first of the everlasting Imperial Line. Hence the Ukei was the central mystery of the Divine Ritual. Its practice, however, had fallen into abeyance for centuries, and thus it was that Oen had striven for its revival so that, in this confused world, men might once more attain the guidance of the gods and have the divine will manifested to them.

Thus the Ukei ritual was "worship of the awesome and exalted gods," and the Emperor's Land was a land whose good fortune sprang from the wondrous power of words. For it was evident that when the priest intoned the ritual, his words, fraught with sacred power, invariably called down the protection of all the gods of heaven and earth. Thus the Ukei was "worship by words fraught with sacred power."

At the clan school at Kumamoto, when someone drew upon a treatise of Neo-Confucian learning called *Eight Steps of Self-Discipline* to express contempt for the mystery of the Ukei, Oen replied in the following manner:

> In this world both he who rules and he who is ruled are but men. If a mere man as a mere man attempts to rule another, he is like one who, having no boat, plunges into the sea to rescue one who is drowning. But the Ukei is what can bear up both of them. It is the boat without which the drowning man cannot be saved.

In Shinto learning Oen favored the works of Mabuchi and Norinaga. As for Chinese learning, he was versed in sutras as well as Confucius and other philosophers. His knowledge of Buddhism embraced both the Greater and Lesser Vehicles. Indeed, he even engaged in Dutch studies to some extent. Cherishing as he did the ideal of glorifying the Imperial Tradition within the land and upholding the national honor in the face of foreign incursion, he was appalled by the vacillation of the Shogunate officials at the time of Perry's arrival and also by the tactics of those who turned away from the policy of "Expel the Barbarians" but tried to use it to overthrow the Shogunate. He became a recluse and gave himself over to the contemplation of occult wisdom.

Oen hoped for the restoration of the rule of the gods in this world. Not content with the exegeses of Mabuchi and Norinaga, he resolved to make known to all the ancient Shinto ritual as preserved in the classics and, by so doing, to set right the hearts of men and restore the pure land of the gods, a land blessed with the divine favor. The practice of the ancient worship, then, the achievement of restoration, had been his goal. He went so far as to bring Socrates of Greece into his writings, approving the view that, though Socrates did well to preach morals in a country lacking them, the superior state of the Emperor's Land precluded the need for moral teaching.

The Way of the Gods meant that worship and government were one. To serve the Emperor, the shining vicar of the gods in the world of men, was to serve the distant gods of the world hidden to men. To govern was to act always in accordance with the divine will, and to ascertain that will was a most sacred task, a task that could only be accomplished by the rite of Ukei.

The example of this man whose zeal for the gods was so notable inspired a host of pure-minded disciples, foremost of whom was Tomo Otaguro. The attitude of Oen's followers mourning his passing could be likened to that of Buddha's disciples seeing him entering Nirvana.

Now, three years after his master's death, it had come to pass that Tomo Otaguro, purified in body and in spirit, felt compelled to perform the rite of Ukei.

At the time of the Decree of Imperial Restoration, the indications had been altogether favorable that the august wish of His Late Majesty Komei to expel the barbarians would be fulfilled. But clouds soon cut off the light of Heaven, and month by month, year by year, the policy of opening the land to foreign influence had grown stronger. In Meiji 3, permission was granted to an imperial prince to study in Germany, and at the end of the same year, swords were forbidden to the common people. In Meiji 4 it was decreed that samurai could cut off their topknot and that they might go without swords. Treaties were concluded with various foreign countries, and just the previous year, Meiji 5, the Western calendar was adopted. At the beginning of the current year, six army garrisons were established with an eye toward curbing popular unrest, and, indeed, a disturbance did break out in Oita Prefecture. The world was moving further and further away from the late Master Oen's central doctrine of government and worship as one. Far from being progress, this was a heedless rush to destruction. Thus were the Master's hopes betrayed. Men delighted in defilement rather than purity. Base ambition gained the victory over lofty idealism.

What would be the late Master's thoughts if he were still in this world? And what would be the thoughts of His Late Imperial Majesty?

Though Otaguro and his companions were, of course, unaware of it, at the time of Prince Iwakura's mission to Europe and America in Meiji 4, there had been intense discussion on shipboard among such subordinate ministers as Koin Kido, Toshimichi Okubo, and Hirobumi Ito with regard to changing the national polity, and many voices were raised to argue that Japan should become a republic in order better to confront the power of America and the nations of Europe.

In the meantime, hopelessly contrary to the late Master's teaching about restoration and the oneness of government and worship, the Ministry of Shrines was reorganized in Meiji 5 as the Ministry of Religion, and soon after was abolished entirely, its functions delegated to the Department of Shrines and Temples. Thus were the places of worship revered and the most ancient traditions put on the same level with the temples of a religion brought from abroad.

Now Otaguro was about to offer two Ukei formulations to the divine scrutiny. The first of these was in accordance with the wishes of Harukata Kaya and read as follows: "To bring an end to misgovernment by admonishing authority even to the forfeiture of life."

Kaya was bent upon the use of argument, of subduing their enemy without shedding any blood but his own. He wished to insure that his admonition achieved its goal by emulating Yasutaké Yokoyama, the samurai of the Satsuma Clan who, in Meiji 3, set the seal upon his heroic remonstrance by slaying himself with his sword as soon as he had delivered his petition. Kaya's comrades, however, had misgivings about the efficacy of such a course.

The second formulation, to be proposed in the event of the first's not gaining the divine sanction, read as follows: "To cut down the unworthy ministers by striking in darkness with the sword."

Otaguro, too, if this resolution was favored by the divine will, would see it through to the last.

Although Oen's *Treatise on the Ukei* recommended the use of a saké flask and rice honey in the manner of the Emperor Jimmu, Otaguro preferred to follow the Ukei procedure preserved in the arcane tradition of the Grand Shrine of Isé, into which he had become initiated at the Sumiyoshi Shrine in Udo. He therefore selected a peach branch, and, after paring it to a straight stick, cut heavy Mino paper into strips and fastened these to the branch as sacred pendants, save for four, upon each of which he inscribed the first Ukei formulation, allowing space for a positive or negative response. Then he took up one of these, and after the words "To bring an end to misgovernment by admonishing authority even to the forfeiture of life," he wrote: "is propitious." He crumbled these into small wads and placed them upon a three-legged stand. Carrying this with him, he went down from the fore-hall and climbed the stairs leading to the sanctuary. Reverently he opened the sanctuary doors and made his way upon his knees into the midday darkness within.

It was high noon, and the heat of the sanctuary was intense. The drone of mosquitoes filled the darkness. The rays of the sun touched the skirt of Otaguro's white robe as he knelt, head bowed, just inside the threshold. Bathed in sunlight, the folds of his white raw silk *hakama* shone like bunched hibiscus flowers. Otaguro began by reciting the Great Prayer of Purification.

In the midst of the darkness, the Sacred Mirror glinted faintly. That the gods were present therein, that their eyes were upon him, Otaguro felt with the same certainty that he felt the very sweat that trickled down over his forehead and temples and past his ears. The beating of his heart became the divine life pulsing within him, and enclosed as he was by the four walls of the sanctuary, this seemed to grow to a rumble. Then with his whole body withering in the heat and his heart bursting with an intensity of yearning, he sensed that from somewhere in the darkness before him, an unseen force, as pure and fresh as spring water, was pouring out upon him.

When Otaguro picked up the branch, the sacred pendants rustled like the wings of doves. At first he waved it slowly from side to side above the stand in the manner of purification, and then, quieting his heart, lowered it till the pendants gently brushed the surface. Two of the four crumpled papers were caught by the pendants and swept from the stand. He spread out each of these and held it to the light. On the wrinkled paper of the first, he clearly saw the words "is not propitious." And on the second, too, was written: "is not propitious."

After reciting the prescribed prayer once more, he began the second Ukei rite, this time to put to the divine scrutiny the formulation "To cut down the unworthy ministers by striking in darkness with the sword." His procedure was as before, this time but a single paper being swept from the stand. When he had uncrumpled this, Otaguro read thereupon the words "is not propitious."

Three of the four comrades received Otaguro with bowed heads, awaiting the judgment of the gods. Harukata Kaya alone sat erect, looking full into the priest's pale countenance which was moist with sweat. If the gods favored his petition, the thirty-eight-year-old Kaya was resolved to take sole responsibility for admonishing the authorities, on behalf of his comrades, and then to slay himself with his own sword.

Otaguro sat without uttering a word. At length, Ueno, the eldest of the four, asked him the outcome. Thus it was learned that neither of the two had secured the divine sanction.

Though the gods had not looked with favor upon their endeavor, the will of the four to offer themselves up for the Imperial Land remained unaltered. They therefore decided to devote themselves all the more earnestly to prayer, while awaiting the approval of the gods, and to vow in the Divine Presence to make a joint oblation of their lives whenever the proper time might come. The four went back to the shrine, and, after burning to ashes the paper inscribed with the vow offered in the Divine Presence, they sprinkled these into a flask of holy water, from which each drank in turn, leaving not a drop.

As for the name of the League of the Divine Wind, "league" was a common term in Kumamoto to designate a party or group, such as the Tsuboi League, the Yamazaki League, and the Kyomachi League, local groups founded to foster the samurai spirit. The patriotic samurai who gathered about Oen, however, came to be called the League of the Divine Wind under different circumstances. In Meiji 7, when some of their number took the examination for the Shinto priesthood at the prefectural office, each of them, as though by prearrangement, responded as follows in the course of his examination: "If men were pure of heart, if they revered the Emperor above all else, the Divine Wind would rise at once, just as in the time of the Mongol Invasion, and the barbarians would be swept away."

Their examiners were quite taken aback, and for the first time Oen's disciples were called the League of the Divine Wind.

Among these patriotic samurai, youths such as Tsuguo Tominaga, Tomo Noguchi, Wahei Iida, Saburo Tominaga, and Mikao Kashima sought to realize the ideals of their brotherhood in every aspect of daily life, and so they shunned defilement and loathed all innovation.

Tomo Noguchi, because telegraph lines were something brought from abroad, refused to walk beneath them. (The telegraph system was established in Meiji 6.) When Noguchi made his daily pilgrimage to the shrine dedicated to Lord Kiyomasa, he took special care not to pass under any telegraph lines, even though this meant taking a roundabout way. If he found it impossible to avoid them, he passed beneath while shielding his head with a white fan.

It was the custom of these young men to carry salt in a pocket of their sleeve, and scatter it about to purify themselves if they met a Buddhist priest, a man dressed in Western style, or a funeral procession. Herein may be seen the influence of the famous work *The Jeweled Sash* of Atsutané Hirata, which even Masahiko Fukuoka, foremost of the group in his contempt for books, had read with appreciation.

Again, Saburo Tominaga once went to the Shirakawa Prefectural Office to cash his brother Morikuni's bonus bond and, unwilling to touch paper currency defiled with a foreign-style design, carried it home between chopsticks.

Master Oen was fond of the uncouth vigor of these young men. Most of them did not take to refinement. They loved the moon shining on the banks of the Shirakawa with the love of men who believed that it was the last harvest moon they would see in this life. They prized the cherry blossoms like men for whom this spring's blossoms were the last that would ever bloom. And so they would sing together the song of Ichigoro Hasuda, the patriotic samurai of Mito:

> I look upon the moon
> Beyond my upright spear,
> Wondering when its rays
> Will fall upon my corpse.

According to Master Oen's teaching, in the world hidden from men there is neither life nor death. The life and death of this world about us took its origin from the Ukei of the gods Izanagi and Izanami. Since men are the offspring of the gods, however, if they preserve themselves from all polluting transgression and, upright, just, and pure of heart, worship in the ancient manner, they can put off the death and corruption of this world and ascend to heaven to become one with the gods.

Master Oen was wont to recite this poem:

> As the white swan soars to heaven,
> Leave no traces here below.

In February of Meiji 7, the Saga Rebellion broke out, the rebellious forces having been raised by those who had cast their lot with the supporters of the Subdue Korea Policy. To aid in its suppression, government forces were dispatched from various encampments, including Kumamoto. And thus, for the moment, the troops left guarding the castle numbered a mere two hundred. Otaguro deemed it improper to let such an opportunity slip by.

In Otaguro's mind a strategy for sweeping away misrule had already taken form. To unseat corrupt advisors and enhance the grandeur of the Imperial Throne, there was no better way to begin than by raising a force of loyal men and seizing the camps at Kumamoto. With this stronghold as a focal point, a number of like-hearted men could be rallied to the cause from both east and west, and a vast force could be put together for an advance to the east. The first step was the seizure of the Kumamoto camps. It was a time when the enemy had become extraordinarily vulnerable, and it behooved Otaguro and his comrades to turn this to their advantage.

Thus it was that Otaguro once more consulted the will of the gods through the Ukei rite. Again, after fasting for a number of days he made his way reverently into the Divine Presence, and, raising the branch adorned with the sacred pendants, executed the rite of Ukei with a devout heart.

This time the darkness was not filled with the heat of midsummer. The chill of early spring held possession of the sanctuary. Then, too, it was just before dawn, and from the rear of the priest's house could be heard the crowing of roosters. Their cries seemed to shatter the darkness like streaks of crimson lightning.

They were rending cries, as if the dark throat of night had been burst asunder and was spurting blood.

The sage Atsutané Hirata talked endlessly of the pollution caused by death, but, as to blood pollution, he mentioned only the loss of a trivial amount of blood. Now there took form in Otaguro's mind, here before the gods, the image of pure, seething blood. As his thoughts dwelt upon this blood which was to purify the Imperial Court, he felt that the gods would not take offense. There flashed through Otaguro's prayerful entreaty terrible phantasms: glinting swords cutting down the wicked, blood spilling out on every side. And beyond the blood, what was pure, just, and honest took form, like the blue line of the distant sea.

The candles burning before the Divine Presence flickered in the dawn breeze. As Otaguro began to wave the branch with its sacred pendants, the candles guttered and nearly went out.

The eyes of the gods were fixed upon him. They evaluated the doings of men by a standard of their own, a standard beyond human knowledge. Alone able to foresee all consequences, only the gods could sanction or forbid.

Otaguro picked up the wad of paper that the pendants had caught. He opened it and read it by the candlelight. The words "not propitious" met his eye.

The patriotic samurai of the League of the Divine Wind were not unreasonably stiff men to whom the usual human emotions were foreign. Each of them yearned with all his heart to prove himself upon the field of combat, but otherwise they were simply vigorous young men.

Haruhiko Numazawa had unusual strength and excelled in wrestling. One day when he was pounding rice outside his door, a sudden shower began to fall. He immediately picked up both mortar and pestle, carried them indoors, and set calmly to work once more.

Hironobu Saruwatari had a two-year-old daughter named Umeko, upon whom he lavished his affection. One night, coming home somewhat drunk, he placed a large saké bottle in the arms of the sleeping girl and cried out: "Look, a melon! A melon!"

Umeko loved melons. Still half-asleep, she began to caress the bottle. But when his wife Kazuko laughingly remarked: "You keep saying 'Don't lie even to a child'—how can you do such a thing?" Saruwatari was stricken with remorse. He went out and searched until he was able to buy an out-of-season melon, which he brought home and gave to Umeko.

Kisou Onimaru, along with Gensai Kawakami and his companions, had once been committed to prison for a year for a political offense. He loved saké dearly, and throughout his sentence his friends regularly brought bean curd steeped in saké. On New Year's Day they carried a large box of it to the prison, having on this occasion emptied three bottles of saké into the bean curd. When the warders called attention to the powerful aroma, Onimaru satisfied them with the explanation that the bean curd had been simmered in saké.

Gitaro Tashiro was a devoted son. Since the doctor had told his father to eat beef, which the League shunned, Gitaro went each day to the slaughterhouse at Kamikawara to buy beef for him. However, in the summer that the patriotic force was raised, when his father arranged a match without consulting him and urged him to marry, Gitaro refused again and again with tears in his eyes. He had already resolved to die.

Tomo Noguchi was a man of inborn integrity, not fond of books but devoted to martial skills, especially archery from horseback. Each spring and fall at the festival of military arts held in the gardens of the Lord of Kumamoto, he drew his bow with unerring accuracy. Then, too, he was not one to forget a promise. Once a friend happened to complain that all year long he had been unable to find any radishes for pickles. Late that very night Noguchi and his brother came to this man's gate carrying on their shoulders a huge barrel of fragrant pickled radishes.

In the summer of Meiji 7, the governor, Nagasuké Yasuoka, appointed various members of the League of the Divine Wind to shrines of greater and lesser importance throughout the prefecture. Tomo Otaguro was of course appointed chief priest of the Imperial Shrine at Shingai, with Mitsuo Noguchi and Wahei

Iida as his assistant priests. Yasuoka designated Harukata Kaya as chief priest of Kinzan Shrine and Yasuhisa Koba, Tateki Ura, and Chuji Kodama as his assistants. In this manner the comrades of the League came to have custody of some fifteen shrines in all. Besides the beneficial effect that their fervent zeal had upon the general piety, shrines in every part of the province became main or subordinate bases of operations for the League.

All this had the result of strengthening the dedication of the men of the League. The more they revered the gods, the more anxious they were over the state of national affairs. As time passed, they grew ever more resentful at seeing those in authority draw the nation further and further from Master Oen's ideal of a land in which the gods would once more be worshipped as of old.

In Meiji 9 they suffered a crushing blow to their aspirations. On the eighteenth of March, the governor promulgated the Edict Against Wearing Swords, which was followed soon after by an edict forbidding the traditional samurai hair style. Yasuoka stringently enforced both of these.

Otaguro, in order to restrain the violent indignation of the League's young men, instructed them that the decree against wearing swords could be circumvented by going about with one's sword concealed in a bag. But this did not suffice to stem their anger. Together, the young men came to Otaguro and demanded to know when they would be permitted to sacrifice their lives.

If their swords were snatched from them, what means would be left to guard the honor of the gods they revered? Each of them was determined, whatever the odds, to fight to the death in the Divine Cause. To worship the gods, the sacrosanct Divine Ritual was the essential means. Thus if this sword were torn away from them, it was inevitable that the gods of Japan, so utterly disdained by the new government, would become powerless spirits, worshipped only by the ignorant masses.

Meanwhile, month after month, year after year, the gods Master Oen had said were so close at hand, the gods who had enflamed their hearts with such devotion, were being degraded. The young men felt certain that a conspiracy was afoot to rob the gods of their dignity, to thrust them off into the distance, to make them as insignificant as possible. Thus, out of fear that the Christian West might look upon Japan as an ignorant, heathen land, the ideal of worship and government as one would be slighted more and more. The gods would finally sink to the level of feeble spirits, ephemeral beings who clung to life in the shelter of sprouting reeds rippling in the wind beside remote streams.

And the sword was to suffer a like fate. The defense of the land would no longer be entrusted to the manly warrior bearing at his side the swift thunderbolt of the immortal gods. The national army created by Aritomo Yamagata gave no preference to the samurai class, nor did it honor the ideal of the Japanese as individuals rallying spontaneously to the defense of their native land. Rather, it was a Western-style professional army which, in ruthless disregard of all tradition, ignored class distinctions and depended upon a draft system to supply its manpower. The Japanese sword, giving way to the saber, had lost its soul. Now it was fated to become a mere decoration, an ornament.

It was at this time that Harukata Kaya resigned his priestly office at Kinzan Shrine and presented a formal petition of several thousand words concerning the wearing of swords to the prefectural governor. This was a superb composition in praise of the Japanese sword, and Kaya's heart's blood had nourished every word. To it he later added a preamble, intending to present the revised document to the highest authorities in Tokyo:

A Petition Concerning the Proclamation of the Edict Prohibiting the Wearing of Swords

I, Harukata, a lowly subject, holder of no office, though at the hazard of my own life, hereby submit with utmost humility a statement to the honorable members of the Council of Elders.

Edict Number Thirty-eight, issued from the office of the Prime Minister in March of this year, prohibits the wearing of swords by any citizen except military police and government officers in full-dress uniforms, as prescribed by regulations. With all due respect, I must point out that such a proclamation is not in accord with the unique national character of our glorious land, unchanged since the time of the Emperor Jimmu.

The intensity of my patriotic zeal forbade my keeping an awestruck silence and clinging stealthily to my office. Thus on April 21 I submitted to the governor of Kumamoto a detailed protest, in much the same terms as below, and also requested that he promptly relieve me of every main and subsidiary duty pertaining to my office. On June 7, however, this memorial was sent back to me on the grounds that a prefectural office could not concern itself with the matter therein since it was urged in opposition to the law of the land.

Alas, an untutored rustic such as I cannot cope with the formalities of an advanced civilization! I realize that my expression is crude, and that I am unable to marshal my thoughts adequately, and this has for some time given me pause. Nevertheless, the spirit of dogged devotion and humble loyalty ever surges up within me, and I can no longer hold back. Thus do I dare, in all humility, to present my arguments once more.

In this preamble we see the full measure of Harukata's long-stifled rage and anguish, and of his irrepressible "dogged devotion" and "humble loyalty."

In my view, the bearing of swords is a custom that characterized our Land of Jimmu even in the ancient era of the gods. It is intimately bound up with the origins of our nation, it enhances the dignity of the Imperial Throne, solemnizes the rites of our gods, banishes the spirits of evil, puts down disorders. The sword, therefore, not only maintains the tranquility of the nation but also guards the safety of the individual citizen. Indeed, the one thing essential to this martial nation that reveres the gods, the one thing never to be put aside even for an instant, is the sword. How, then, could those upon whom is laid the burden of fashioning and promulgating a national policy that honors the gods and strengthens our land be so forgetful of the sword?

Thus did Harukata, drawing from sundry sources, attest ample proof of the importance of the sword in the history of Japan from the time of the early chronicles, and of the significance of its role in exalting the Japanese Spirit. And he went on to explain how the wearing of a sword by people of all ranks was a custom that fulfilled the divinely inspired precepts of Japan's ancient rulers.

A recent rumor in the town would have it that this edict prohibiting the wearing of swords was recommended by the supreme commander of the Army, it being alleged that it would be a matter of grave consequence to the authority of the military if those outside its scope were permitted to bear

swords. After much thought, I have come to the conclusion
that such an outrageous statement could not have issued
from an Army commander but was rather the fabrication
of street-corner idlers.

Those who guide the Army are the fangs and claws of the
Imperial Throne and the very salvation of the Land of the
Gods. To their benevolence, their authority, their magnanimity, their severity the populace must ever give respectful heed.
Thus, with all those in military service as the winged limbs
of their commanders, even if the whole people of the Divine
Emperor should go about with swords and spears throughout the land, this would but magnify the power of the Army,
strengthen national policy, and temper the nation for the
shocks of greater and lesser trials. How could it possibly
obstruct the workings of government? For it would manifest
the glory of a land where the splendor of arms is abundantly
nourished. . . .

In the light of all this, I cannot forebear to observe that
never has the honor of the Land of Jimmu fallen so low as in
these present times. How could any citizen, in the least eager
to serve the nation, pass his days in idle pursuits, heedless
of national policy, and not bend his efforts to aid in promot-
ing good and suppressing evil? Now is the time for those
loyal subjects close to the Throne, the men who are the
Emperor's claws and fangs, to ponder deeply, to agonize, to
labor unremittingly. . . .

This edict is in opposition to the Imperial Decree on the
Abolition of Clans and the Establishment of Prefectures, and
turns its back on the understanding of duty, the search for
justice, the preservation of domestic tranquility, and the defense of the nation against foreign incursion. Thus it contra-
dicts the Imperial Will. Beyond doubt it would speedily
verify the proverb that a nation must ravage itself before
foreigners can ravage it, a man must despise himself before
others can despise him.

As stated in the preamble, Kaya's original petition had been
returned from the governor's office without acknowledgment. He
had supplemented it and put it in suitable form, having resolved
to go alone to Tokyo, present it to the Council of Elders, and
disembowel himself on the spot. Thus he was far from eager to
join his comrades in armed resistance.

Meanwhile Otaguro had been holding in check the hot-blooded
youths who came to him protesting: "The warrior bereft of his
sword is wretched. When, Master, will you give us an oppor-

tunity to lay down our lives?" But at last he assembled the seven leaders of the League at the shrine in Shingai. These were Morikuni Tominaga, Masahiko Fukuoka, Kageki Abé, Unshiro Ishihara, Kotaro Ogata, Juro Furuta, and Tsunetaro Kobayashi. The plan that they devised was as follows: since their comrades in other parts of the land seemed to lack the courage to set matters in motion, they themselves would strike the first blow in the righteous cause by cutting down every major military and civilian official in the prefecture and seizing the camps at Kumamoto. Placing as they did the deepest trust in Otaguro, the whole group then waited as, at their bidding, he left them to consult the gods for a third time through an Ukei.

It was late on a May night in the Ninth Year of Meiji, with all gathered together at the imperial shrine in Shingai.

Otaguro, having purified himself, entered the sanctuary.

The seven leaders sat in a row in the fore-hall of the shrine, waiting to hear the will of the gods.

When Otaguro clapped his hands, the sound echoed loudly from within the sanctuary.

Otaguro's hands were large, though emaciated, and the sharp report of their clapping was as if the palms, like hollowed, rough-hewn cedar planks, had entrapped pure atmosphere, and crushed it with an explosive burst of divinity.

Thus Tominaga, for one, felt that the clapping of those dedicated hands, hands purified by sacred ablution, echoed as if in a forest glen deep in the mountains.

Especially on a night like this, in the darkness of the small hours with the spring rains not far off, the reverberating echo of Otaguro's clapping seemed charged with yearning and devotion, and the seven heard it as striking upon the very doors of heaven.

Otaguro next began the prayer of purification. His loud, clear voice seemed to herald the dawn that would break through the curtain of night and whiten the eastern sky. To the eyes of those waiting in the fore-hall, there was perfection even in the straight seam running down the back of his white priestly robe. His clear voice seemed like a blade cutting through evil:

". . . When these entreaties are heard, all the land under

heaven, beginning with the court of the offspring of the gods, will be free of every defilement. As the winds of heaven scatter the towered clouds, as the breezes of morning and evening sweep away the mists of morning and evening, as a great ship moored in a wide harbor is freed at the prow and at the stern, and pushed out toward the deep, as the scythe blade forged in fire cuts away yonder tangled growth—so shall all defilements be purged and purified . . ."

The seven leaders held their breath in awe as they beheld the arcane ritual from the fore-hall. Unless they received the divine sanction this time, they would perhaps never be able to strike their blow.

Silence fell with the conclusion of Otaguro's chant. His tall cap seemed to sink into the darkness of the inner sanctuary as he prostrated himself in prayer.

The shrine was surrounded by open country. The night scent of fresh young leaves, of manured fields, of oaks in blossom floated in upon the breeze, an oppressive heaviness to the mingled odors. Since they sat in darkness, there was not even the drone of swarming insects.

Suddenly a sound from the roof above shattered the silence. It was the cry of a night heron taking flight. The seven regarded one another. They knew that each had felt the same shudder.

Soon the candles burning in the sanctuary were hidden for a moment as Otaguro rose to make his return. The seven awaiting him heard the very sound of his footsteps as a favorable omen.

Otaguro announced that the gods had blessed their undertaking. The divine approbation thus gained not only freed them to act but designated them the army of the gods.

Matters having reached such a stage, Otaguro set about forming a secret coalition with patriots in other areas, and dispatched comrades of the League to Yanagawa in Chikugo, to Fukuoka, to Takeda in southern Bungo, to Tsuruzaki, to Shimabara, as well as to Saga, to Hagi in Choshu, and elsewhere. As for the comrades in Kumamoto itself, they were to enter into a seventeen-day period of mortification, during which they would

pray for the success of their long-cherished enterprise. The day
to strike, the grouping of the comrades—nothing was determined
without consulting the will of the gods. As for the day, the divine
will ordained thus: "At the start of the Eighth Day of the Ninth
Lunar Month, when the moon hides herself behind the mountain."
In like manner, the comrades were assigned in accordance with
the sacred casting of lots.

Thus the entire group was divided into three units, the first of
which was then further divided into five bands. The first of these
five, led by Unki Takatsu, had the task of assaulting the residence of the commander of the Kumamoto post, Major General
Masaaki Taneda. The second band, with Unshiro Ishihara at its
head, was to attack the residence of the chief of staff at Kumamoto, Lieutenant Colonel of Artillery Shigenori Takeshima. The
third band, led by Kagesumi Nakagaki, had as its target the
home of the commander of the Thirteenth Infantry Regiment,
Lieutenant Colonel Tomozané Yokura. The fourth band, with
Yoshinori Yoshimura commanding, was to direct its attack
upon the residence of Nagasuké Yasuoka, the governor of Kumamoto prefecture. The fifth band, led by Tateki Ura, was to slay
the chief of the Kumamoto Prefectural Assembly, Korenobu
Otaguro. The total force thus committed was some thirty men
and was designated the First Unit. Once they had taken these
enemy heads, they were to signal by fire and rejoin the main
body.

The next group was the main force, and its commanders were
Tomo Otaguro and Harukata Kaya. The two elders, Kengo Ueno
and Kyusaburo Saito, were among the secondary commanders,
who also included Kageki Abé, Kotaro Ogata, Kisou Onimaru,
Juro Furuta, Tsunetaro Kobayashi, and Gitaro Tashiro, aided by
such stalwarts as Goichiro Tsuruda. Designated the Second Unit,
its mission was to assault the Sixth Artillery Battalion. Its strength
was some seventy men.

The last group, whose command was entrusted to Morikuni
Tominaga and Masahiko Fukuoka, was to attack the Thirteenth
Infantry Regiment, spurred on by the zeal of its elder, Masamoto
Aikyo, together with such men as Tsuneyoshi Ueno, Gengo

Shibuya, and Tomo Noguchi. Its strength was some seventy men, and it was designated the Third Unit.

There was one, however, who had not yet declared himself willing to join in this armed rising. This was Harukata Kaya. Kaya was a man of rigorous moral character. His heart was filled with courage, and his eyes flashed with the purity of his zeal. He was skilled in literature, composing both Japanese and Chinese poems and having an excellent prose style. As for martial accomplishments, he was adept in the Shiten School of kendo.

Since his decision would greatly affect the morale of all, Tominaga and the other leaders went in turn to try to persuade him to join them. Finally, a mere three days before the event, he told them that if the Divine Will were consulted and a favorable response elicited, he would commit himself to the enterprise.

Kaya himself having resigned his priestly office, he designated Tateki Ura to present to the gods the question of his participation. And thus at Kinzan Shrine on the Plateau of Kinzan, with Kimpo rising to the west and the haze-covered peak of Aso to the east, Ura fervently performed the rite of Ukei on his comrade's behalf. The gods indicated their approval. Earlier, with regard to Kaya's proceeding to Tokyo to present his petition to the Council of Elders at the sacrifice of his life, they had indicated disapproval.

Kaya realized that his reluctance to support the rising was something that had sprung from his own will. Now the will of the gods clearly took precedence. He believed firmly that they had enjoined him to commit himself to this seemingly hopeless resort to arms, and that, after its violence, they would somehow lay a banquet for him and his comrades upon a cloth of pure white, unmarred by the least wrinkle. And so, without vacillation, Kaya submitted to the divine will and joined the enterprise.

How did the men of the League prepare for combat? Most of all, night and day alike, by imploring the blessing of heaven. The shrines allied to them were thronged with comrades come to offer worship.

The troops opposing them numbered two thousand, and they themselves less than two hundred. One of the elders, Kengo

Ueno, proposed that some firearms be obtained, but the comrades as a whole were hotly opposed to arming themselves with the weapons of the barbarians. Thus they would carry into battle nothing but swords, spears, and halberds. In order to destroy the post, however, they secretly made several hundred grenades by joining two bowls packed with gravel and gunpowder and attaching a fuse. For the same purpose, Masamoto Aikyo purchased and laid away a supply of kerosene.

How would they garb themselves for combat? Some of them would don helmets and cuirasses, some even the tall caps and ceremonial robes of the ancient nobility, but most would wear short *hakama* over their everyday dress, with two swords thrust into their sashes. Each would wear a headband of white cloth and bind up his sleeves with strips of white cotton. And every man would fasten on a white cloth shoulder-strap bearing the character *victory*.

More than their arms and equipment, however, more than their banners, they put their trust in the Divine Simulacrum that Tomo Otaguro was to bear upon his shoulder. The god whom Otaguro would carry into battle, the Divine Simulacrum of the war god Hachiman of Fujisaki Shrine, would be their unseen commander, the one who would mysteriously direct their efforts. And herein would be the fulfillment of their late Master's dying wish.

For when in his youth Master Oen heard of the incursion of the American warships and set out for Edo in great wrath to avenge this profanation, he bore upon his shoulders this same Divine Simulacrum.

PART THE SECOND
The Combat of the Ukei

THE ENTIRE FORCE was to meet at the home of the elder Masamoto Aikyo, directly behind the Fujisaki Hachiman Shrine with its guardian rows of huge camphor trees. This house stood on high ground at the western edge of the second defense perimeter of the old castle, adjoining the Kumamoto garrison.

So that nearly two hundred armed men could gather here without being noticed, small groups met at dusk at various rendezvous and thence made their way to the marshaling point under cover of night.

Here, by Aikyo's house, they could see Kumamoto Castle rising into the night sky beneath the moon of the Eighth Day of the Ninth Month. The Great Tower, bathed in moonlight, thrust itself up at the castle's very center, and to its left rose the lesser tower. Still further to the left the outline of the level roofs of the main hall and the women's quarters stretched out for a short way before giving place to the Udo Turret, whose dark outline jutted skyward. To the right of the Great Tower, at the end of an irregular line of roofs, rose two final towers of more modest height, the Sangai Turret and the Tsukimi Turret, their tile roofs glistening in the moonlight. The Tsukimi Turret looked down upon the riding ground of Sakuranobaba just to the west of the castle, where slept the artillerymen upon whom would fall the assault of the Second Unit.

The moon set.

The First Unit whose object was the residences of major officials made its departure. The hour was drawing on to eleven. There were stars in the sky, and the deep grass of Fujisaki Heights was covered with dew.

Next to leave was the Second Unit, led by Otaguro and Kaya. And as it set out in the direction of the artillery battalion, the Third Unit also departed, bound for the infantry encampment.

The seventy-odd men of the Second Unit, the main force of the rising, went up the Slope of Keitaku, and divided into two sections, one of which was to assault the east gate of the artillery encampment and the other, the north. They found both gates firmly barred. At the east gate two expert young swordsmen, Wahei Iida, twenty-two, and Gitaro Tashiro, twenty-six years old, scaled the wall with gallant exuberance and, shouting "First over!" plunged into the camp and at once cut down the sentries who challenged them. They were followed over the wall by Tsunetaro Kobayashi and Tadajiro Watanabé. Then Tashiro, seizing a pestle from the nearby mess hall, rushed up and smashed the bolt of the gate, and the entire force came pouring in like an avalanche.

Just inside the gate, Kango Hayami overpowered a soldier and bound him with a rope, intending to press him into service as a guide.

Meanwhile, the north gate, too, had fallen, and the other section of the Second Unit dashed forward to join forces in cutting their way into the two barracks of the artillerymen. Roused from deep sleep by fierce battle cries, the troops were thrown into a panic by the sight of blades flashing in the darkness. Utterly routed, they sought safety by cowering in various corners of the barracks. The battalion headquarters duty officer on this night, Second Lieutenant of Artillery Keiichi Sakaya, ran downstairs from the second-floor duty room and engaged the onrushing swords with drawn saber. Quickly wounded, however, he escaped through a rear door and watched the scene from the shadows.

Leaderless, the soldiers fled like terrified women and children. As the lieutenant looked on, flames sprang up from the east barracks. Pressed by the billowing black smoke, the soldiers who had hidden in the barracks came tumbling from the windows, to be driven and scattered by the swords of the oddly garbed insurgents. Seeing this, the young officer grated his teeth.

The fire had been set with grenades and kerosene in the east barracks by Tsunetaro Kobayashi, Wahei Iida, and their comrades, and in the west barracks by Katsutaro Yonemura and his. Neither Iida nor Kobayashi were carrying matches, and they had had to shout out to their companions for "phosphorus," as they were called, to light the fuses.

Avoiding the glare of the flames, Lieutenant Sakaya made his way to the garrison dispensary and hurriedly bandaged his wounded right arm. Then, plunging once more into the fray, he confronted some fleeing soldiers, and tried to take command of them. The terrified soldiers would not heed his orders. When he finally put heart into a few of them, his efforts caught the eye of Kyusaburo Saito, renowned for his skill in fighting with the spear, who came running to the attack.

Lieutenant Sakaya raised his saber with his wounded arm, but was instantly pierced by Saito's spear, and fell, uttering a bitter cry. He was the first officer of the government forces to perish in the struggle.

Meanwhile, Yoshinori Yoshimura and his comrades of the fourth section of the First Unit had wounded Governor Yasuoka grievously in wild fighting but failed to take his head. They then withdrew from the Governor's residence and hastened across Geba Bridge, attracted by the battle cries and the leaping flames within the castle walls. Kageki Abé turned aside from the final routing of the enemy to greet them, thereupon learning of the outcome of their battle and of the loss of Motoyoshi Aikyo at the tender age of seventeen, the first of the League of the Divine Wind to fall.

The garrison artillerymen had not been issued small arms. Those who had been tardy in fleeing either perished in the flames or were slain by the flashing blades of the comrades of the League, and now their corpses lay heaped about. Kisou Onimaru, who had cut down the foe with exuberant zeal, happened to come up at that moment and, seeing Yoshimura, broke into a broad smile. Raising his bloodied sword so that it glittered in the noonday brightness cast by the flames that enveloped the two barracks, he gazed at it with cheerful mockery as he declared: "Indeed, such is the worth of garrison troops!" Even his garments, drenched in enemy blood, glowed crimson in the flames. Then Onimaru rushed off in pursuit of the remnants of the enemy.

The comrades of the League had crushed all resistance here. A single hour had brought them victory.

Otaguro and Kaya re-formed their force, but as they were withdrawing they saw a red blaze lighting the sky above the infantry camp within the castle's second perimeter. Realizing the fierceness of the battle there, Kaya called out to his men to help in the assault on the infantry garrison, to which they responded eagerly. Behind them flames ravaged the artillery barracks. The black bulk of Kumamoto Castle loomed up against a crimson sky. In Yamazaki, Motoyama, and other parts of the city were still more conflagrations. These flames, dancing skyward on all sides, gave witness to the fury with which their comrades had struck. In their mind's eye they saw the brave figures of their brothers in arms, forever faithful, moving through the swirling fire, each one smiting the foe with flashing blade. This was the hour for which they had so long checked their fierce rage and whetted their sword blades in secret. Otaguro's bosom heaved with an ineffable surge of joy. "Every man is fighting," he murmured. "Every man."

As for the Third Unit, led by Morikuni Tominaga, Masamoto Aikyo, Masahiko Fukuoka, and Hitoshi Araki, the seventy men of this group had left the precincts of Fujisaki Shrine at the same time as the main force commanded by Otaguro and Kaya. Its objective, the Thirteenth Infantry Regiment's camp, lay within the same castle perimeter as the shrine, though at the eastern edge of it, whereas Fujisaki Shrine was at the western. The foe's strength was close to two thousand men.

Finding the west gate of the infantry camp shut fast before them, twenty-year-old Haruhiko Numazawa clambered atop the palisades and, shouting "First over," leapt down on the other side, to be followed immediately by several other young men. The lone sentry fled across the drill field intending to sound the alarm with his bugle, but he had no more than put it to his lips when he was cut down where he stood.

Hitoshi Araki had come equipped with a rope ladder. He flung this up so that it caught upon the top of the palisade, then hastened to mount it, but so many others grasped it too that the ropes gave way. Kyushichi, Araki's loyal servant, thereupon offered his shoulders to his master, and several men, one after the other, scaled the wall by this means and opened the gate from the inside. With a great battle cry, the entire company rushed in to the attack.

Masahiko Fukuoka, wielding a massive sledgehammer, shattered one barrack's door after another, and his comrades hurled in grenades. Soon the regimental headquarters barrack as well

as those housing the first, second, and third companies of the
second battalion were engulfed in flames.

According to current military practice, no ammunition was
distributed to individual soldiers in time of peace. Thus the only
weapons of use were sabers for the officers and fixed bayonets for
their men. Beset as they were by battle cries, swirling flames, billowing black smoke, and sword blades flashing about them, the
troops had no means to resist. The captain who was regimental
duty officer was cut down before he could rally his forces, and
the corpses of his men soon lay in heaps, some clad only in their
shirts, still others stark naked, and the flames and the black
smoke rolled over them.

A lone survivor, Second Lieutenant Ono, still wielded his
saber and fought on with bitter tenacity. But then, just as two
sergeants had come rushing to his assistance, all three men were
cut down.

It was at this moment that the third section of the First Unit
poured into the camp through the second perimeter gate to join
forces with the Third Unit. In their assault on the residence of
Lieutenant Colonel Yokura, the regimental commander, the third
section's prey, had slipped through their grasp, but now the
morale of the combined forces soared to new heights.

With a full infantry regiment, however, the combat was of a
different order from that waged in the artillery compound. There
was a limit to the number of men that could be felled by blades
alone. Though each attack threw that part of the camp into
disorder, it took time for the waves of panic to spread. Thus
some were able to regain their wits. With clearer vision, they
could correctly assess the situation. And now the grenades that
had served so well to terrify the foe worked against the men of
the League. For as the flames soared up from the barracks and
the men of the League leapt about in the noonday brilliance, it
became all too clear how incredibly few they were.

One officer, having observed this, took command of some
troops and formed them into two rings on the drill field with
their bayonets pointing in every direction like the spines of a

thistle, in order to counterattack. To confront this threat, the elder Masamoto Aikyo grasped his spear, whose use he had so well mastered, and marshaling some ten of his comrades, who aligned their spears with his, charged into the massed infantrymen. The troops broke formation at once and fled. One man alone held his ground, Cadet Lieutenant Tarao, and he fell with spears through his body.

Earlier, two officers who had been quartered off post, First Lieutenant of Infantry Sataké and Cadet Lieutenant Numata, were hastening back to camp, aroused by the sight of the flames. At Hoké Slope they met some of the routed troops and learned how the issue stood. The waters of the moat which lay to the north of the slope shone scarlet from the fiery sky overhead. As the officers questioned the men, more straggled up in twos and threes, the inferno of the burning camp at their backs, and their shadows merged with those of the others.

The two officers hotly chastised the troops for being out of uniform and almost speechless with terror. Thus they managed to rally a platoon of sixteen soldiers, but one which lacked both rifles and ammunition.

It happened, however, that a man named Kichizo Tachiyama, a shrewd merchant who dealt with the military, made his appearance and proffered from his storehouse sufficient rifles, 180 rounds of ammunition, and one thousand percussion caps. The officers rejoiced immensely at this, and the morale of their battered troops rose at last. Thereupon, the two officers each took command of one half of their platoon and secretly made their way into the camp by different routes, Lieutenant Sataké by the rear gate and Cadet Numata by the emergency gate. Coming together once more, their number swelled by other survivors, the troops took up position in a still unburned barrack and commenced firing.

Lieutenant Colonel Tomozané Yokura, the regimental commander, was at his residence in Kyomachi Heights when the assault of the third section of the First Unit fell upon it. The Lieutenant Colonel's wife, Tsuruko, woke her husband the instant she heard the men of the League storming in through the front entrance, and he immediately grasped the situation and fled to the quarters occupied by his grooms. There he snatched a workman's jacket off a hook and hurriedly donned it just as two or three of the League burst into the room. One struck him a blow on the shoulder with his sword, but when he pleaded: "Spare me! I am a groom," he was able to extricate himself from his foes.

The commander thereupon fled to a restaurant, the Ichijitsu, which stood to the rear of Kinzan Shrine. There his wound was hastily seen to by the proprietor, and the commander then shaved off his moustache and further disguised himself by putting on a servingman's jacket. So attired, he made his way once more through the enemy force and at length reached the rear palisade of his infantry command.

After he had climbed to the top and looked down within the camp, he caught sight of the hurrying figures of an officer and two enlisted men. Recognizing Captain Takigawa, the commander hailed him. The Captain stopped and stared for an instant in shocked surprise at the sight of his disguised commander atop the palisade. But then realizing that it was indeed he, the Captain hurried over as the commander descended and gave him a report on the battle. By that time the duty officer of the Second Battalion, Lieutenant Suzuki, had marshaled one company and was seeking to stave off defeat, but had run desperately short of ammunition. Captain Takigawa himself, together with the two soldiers, was now on his way to the magazine to obtain the ammunition left over from maneuvers.

"Very well. Be quick about it," replied Lieutenant Colonel Yokura abruptly. Then he rushed into the midst of his scattered troops, issuing orders and rallying his routed command. With their leader restored to them, the will to carry on flared up among the common soldiers.

The supply of ammunition obtained by Lieutenant Sataké and by Captain Takigawa was augmented by that brought from general headquarters. Thus strengthened, the regiment was at last in a state to give an account of itself.

At general headquarters Major Gentaro Kodama, a staff officer and later a general, had already arrived on the scene. Flinging wide the doors of the magazine, he supplied the soldiers dispatched by Lieutenant Colonel Yokura with ammunition. Then he himself led a company up to a high point on the castle's innermost perimeter, where they were able to look down on the burning camp and see the figures of the men of the League clearly lit by flames in the fighting on the drill field. His troops took aim at the glittering armor, the ancient court robes, and the white headbands, and he gave the command to fire a volley.

The Third Battalion of the regiment had been quartered separately in the gardens of the castle, and had escaped the onslaught of the League. Also, the previous day it had been supplied with Snider rifles and ammunition. Now these were issued to the troops of both its companies, who at once went to the relief of their comrades, the First Company hastening up Keitaku Slope, the Second Company penetrating the camp by crossing Geba Bridge.

In the meantime, the Second Unit of the League under the command of Otaguro and Kaya, who had gone to aid in the assault upon the infantry garrison, smashed through the south gate into the camp only to find the tide of battle turned and themselves now entrapped. Under cover of buildings and stone walls they strove to come to grips with their foes, but helpless against the volleys of bullets, they could only grit their teeth and clench their fists. The arrival of the Second Unit had given the other men of the League their last hope. If a man exposed himself, he was struck at once. But if all clung to their cover, defeat was inevitable. There was no way to launch an attack upon the massed rifles.

Sixty-six-year-old Kengo Ueno spoke out as he crouched in hiding and surveyed his comrades around him: "Though I insisted that we equip ourselves with firearms, no one would heed me, and now we have come to this pass." In their hearts, all of them agreed.

Yet what the men of the League had been willing to risk by renouncing the use of firearms had clarified their intent. Divine aid was to be theirs, and their very purpose was to challenge the Western arms hateful to the gods with swords alone. Western civilization would, as time went by, search out weapons still more terrible, and would direct them at Japan. And then might not the Japanese themselves, in their anxiety to counter these, fall into bestial fighting and lose all hope of restoring the ancient worship so revered by Master Oen? To rise to the combat bearing only the sword, to be willing to risk even crushing defeat— in no way but this could the fervent aspirations of each man of the League take expression. Here was the essence of the gallant Yamato Spirit.

A fierce will inflaming the heart of each one, they broke from cover to charge across the fire-lit drill field.

Raising his sword crafted by Rai Kunimitsu, Eiki Fukami, his comrade Haruhiko Numazawa at his side, dashed headlong through a hail of bullets. Almost at once Numazawa was hit in his right arm. Taking cover, he tore a strip from his tunic with his teeth and hastily wrapped it about his wounded arm. Fukami, after advancing another fifteen yards or so, went down with a bullet in his chest. Masahiko Fukuoka hastened to him, but as soon as he lifted him in his arms he realized that his comrade was dead, and he cried out with anguished rage. Forthwith he brandished his sword in fury and charged the massed foe, only to fall before a murderous volley. Then Numazawa, apparently unhampered by his wound, leapt to the assault once more, but a bullet pierced his left temple from the side. This time, he did not rise.

Harukata Kaya was a master in the combined use of long sword and short. Now he raised his swords, nicked in countless desperate combats and covered with blood, and glared at the enemy. He saw his younger brother Shiro in his mind's eye, Shiro who had disemboweled himself on Mount Tenno after the abortive assault of the Choshu samurai upon the Imperial Palace. Now he too, at age forty-one, would die impelled by the same spirit. Kaya had been unwilling to make common cause with the

League in the venture, until the gods had indicated their approval only three days before. Yet he was without regrets. Here on this field he would join his fate forever with that of his comrades.

Kaya brandished his swords and led the men around him in a fierce charge, drawing upon himself the concentrated fire of the enemy. Mortally wounded, he gave one last cry, "Hachiman, God of Battles!" and fell headlong.

It was around this time that eighteen men of the League perished, among them the elder Kyusaburo Saito, together with Hitoshi Araki, Hironobu Saruwatari, and Tomo Noguchi. Some twenty others were wounded, including Masamoto Aikyo, Yoshinori Yoshimura, Kengo Ueno, and Yoshio Tominaga.

Otaguro, glaring furiously and ignoring those who shouted to him to withdraw, plunged toward the enemy line. A bullet pierced his chest.

Gunshiro Yoshioka, trusting in the keen blades of Onimaru and his comrades to check the assault of the bayonet-wielding government troops, bore up Otaguro on his shoulders and carried him down Hoké Slope, whence, with the aid of Otaguro's brother-in-law Hideo Ono, he brought him into a house.

Otaguro's wound was mortal. He kept losing and regaining consciousness, but even so managed to ask Yoshioka and Ono in which direction his head lay. They answered, in turn, that it lay to the west. "His Divine Majesty dwells in the east. Make haste to have me sit with head poised accordingly," Otaguro told them. They did so.

Then Otaguro ordered Ono to strike off his head. His voice faint, he asked them to bear it to Shingai Shrine together with the Divine Simulacrum of Hachiman.

The foe might well have come storming in at any moment. Hideo Ono had no will to strike his brother-in-law such a blow. But upon the exhortation of Yoshioka, he at last unsheathed his sword. Carefully wiping off the enemy blood that stained it, he purified its blade. Then he lifted it above his head and took aim at his brother-in-law's neck. Yoshioka had helped Otaguro to sit up, head sagging, but facing toward the east. At the very instant that his brother-in-law's torso, thus awkwardly positioned, was about to pitch forward, Ono's blade came sweeping down.

PART THE THIRD
One with the Gods

MOUNT KIMPO is less than four miles west of Kumamoto Castle, and, like the mountain in Yamato from which it takes its name, is revered as a sacred peak. At its crest stands a shrine dedicated to the deity Zao.

Though small, the shrine has a long history. In 1333—the Third Year of the Genko era—Lord Takeshigé Kikuchi ascended to it in order to implore the divine favor before going into battle. Victory was his, and in gratitude he had the shrine rebuilt. According to tradition, he himself carved the Worship Image, reciting a triple prayer after each stroke. This represented the god as standing on the mountain peak with one hand raised, gazing at the armed host he had blessed. It was an image of victory.

Now, however, the morning after the rising, early on the auspicious Ninth Day of the Ninth Month, the time of the Chrysanthemum Festival, there were gathered around the shrine forty-six hunted survivors of a defeated force. Some standing, some sitting, they stared blankly about them, though the penetrating autumn chill made their wounds sting. The clear light of the rising sun cast a striped pattern as it shone down through the branches of the few old cedars that surrounded the shrine. Birds were singing. The air was fresh and clear. As for signs of last night's sanguinary combat, these were visible in the soiled and bloodstained garments, the haggard visages, and the eyes that burned like live embers.

Among the forty-six were Unshiro Ishihara, Kageki Abé, Kisou Onimaru, Juro Furuta, Tsunetaro Kobayashi, the brothers Gitaro and Gigoro Tashiro, Tateki Ura, Mitsuo Noguchi, Mikao Kashima, and Kango Hayami. Every man was silent, sunk deep in thought, looking off at the sea, or at the mountains, or at the smoke still rising from Kumamoto.

Such were the men of the League at rest on the slope of

Kimpo, some with fingers yellowed from brushing the petals of
wild chrysanthemums that they had plucked while staring across
the water at Shimabara Peninsula.

Before the break of day, the way leading to the sea had lain
open to them in their flight. A man of the League, Juro Kagami,
had been offered six boats by a family powerful in clan days, but
these had become stuck fast in the mud left by the morning's ebb
tide and no amount of tugging or pushing could free them. Since
they were being hotly pursued, the men of the League had no
choice but to abandon the boats and make their way up Mount
Kimpo.

The foothills around them were interlaced with small valleys
dotted with villages, and there were terraced fields and paddies
far up the steep slopes. Some sort of white-flowered bush grew
here and there, along with the ripening crops of rice plants. The
mountain forest spread out over the undulating terrain around
the patchwork of small villages scattered like so many cushions
set out to dry, and the foliage of the trees, still a deep green in
this early autumn, entrapped the subtle morning light to form
delicate tracings of brightness and shadow. In these villages were
the homes of men whose upbringing had been different from that
of the men of the League. At some time in their lives, would they
too feel the powerful emotions of a decisive battle? They whose
lives now seemed so peaceful, so without incident?

To the west of Kochi, a cape in the form of a seahorse stretched
a green neck out into the sea. Still farther west was the fan-
shaped muddy delta of the Shirakawa. If a man shifted his gaze
down from the kites circling in the sky over the mountain villages nearby, he saw the mud flat swarming with the huge birds,
flapping their soiled-looking mottled brown wings.

As for the sea below, Shimabara Peninsula opposite thrust
itself out between Ariaké Bay and Amakusa Channel, its tip
pressing upon the strait at Kimpo's base. The water's color was
dark blue everywhere, except for a casual stroke of black at mid-
strait, the effect of a tidal current. To the men of the League this
seemed to be a divine omen, of uncertain significance.

Nature had never been more beautiful than on this morning

after defeat. All was clear and fresh and tranquil.

Across the water on Shimabara Peninsula, the skirts of Mount Unzen stretched out wide to either side. Rows of tiny houses were clearly visible amid the foothills. The peak of Unzen lay concealed behind towering clouds. Off to the southwest, in Saga, the crest of Tara was shrouded in mist that but faintly revealed its outline. The clouds massed in the sky were shot through with a brightness that seemed to bode divinity.

The sight vividly reminded the men on Mount Kimpo of the mystic teaching on the ascent to heaven that they had heard from Master Oen.

According to the Master, there were but two means of ascent to heaven, and these were similar in nature. A man had to use either the Pillars of Heaven or the Floating Bridge of Heaven. Though these still existed unchanged from ancient days, ordinary men given over to defilement could not even see them, much less ascend by them to heaven. If men purged themselves of pollution and with pure hearts returned to the ways of old, then, like the godlike beings of those times, they would be empowered to see the Pillars of Heaven and the Floating Bridge of Heaven before their eyes and avail themselves of the means thus offered to mount to the high place where the gods dwell.

Now divinity seemed so embodied in the bright-flecked clouds upon the mountain peaks that the watching men felt that they were viewing an epiphany of the Floating Bridge. Should they not turn their swords joyfully upon themselves and make an end to their lives? There were those, however, who had taken up a position on the cliff edge facing east and kept their gaze fastened upon Kumamoto Castle, around which thin smoke still rose.

Before them was the bulk of Mount Arao, rising to the left, and, beyond a forest of cedars, the close-packed forms of Mount Tengu, Mount Hommyoji, Mount Mibuchi, and others. Still farther stood Mount Ishigami, like a guardian lion-dog seen from the rear, its foothills projecting well into the city. Kumamoto was well endowed with greenery. The view from Kimpo afforded more the prospect of dense forest than of human dwellings, and the castle's Great Tower rose sharply from the midst of clustered trees. There was also a sweeping view of the region of Fujisaki Heights.

The watchers felt as if last night's battle, erupting at eleven and raging but three hours, and the wretched flight that followed, were being reenacted before them. Once more they were storming about with upraised blades within the camp. Or rather it was ghostly warriors and ghostly flames that now held sway on a field of combat flooded with morning light—of more substance, though, than they, the fugitives on Kimpo, who looked down upon the scene of last night's combat as though upon an ancient battleground.

Beyond the city, far to the east, the smoke that poured up from the crater of Mount Aso, merging with the clouds drawn by it, blotted out that whole portion of the sky. It seemed to hang there peacefully, but was changing from moment to moment. Smoke kept rising from the crater to thrust ever upward the smoke that had preceded it, and the swelling clouds drank it in unremittingly.

The sight of the rising smoke put heart into the watchers, and the will to strike another blow quickened within them.

Just then some of their comrades returned from a successful forage in the villages below with a cask of saké and rations for the day, and all fell to eating and drinking lustily. Every man felt his vigor returning, whether he had set his mind upon death or yearned to make another assault, and before long a resolution was formed that took into some account their actual circumstances. With Kisou Onimaru urging another assault upon the garrison and Tsunetaro Kobayashi counseling against this, it was finally determined with near-unanimity that a scouting party should first be dispatched to probe the enemy's strength and disposition.

After the departure of the scouting party, those remaining upon the mountain took counsel once more, this time to determine what should be done about the youngest members of the group. For seven were mere boys of around sixteen or seventeen: Kataro Shimada, Tadao Saruwatari, Saburohiko Ota, Tamonta

Yano, Kakutaro Motonaga, Susumu Morishita, and Kango Hayami.

These seven had been whispering among themselves with the irrepressible verve of youth: "What are the old fellows up to with their constant delays? Why do they not decide at once? Let us commit seppuku or let us attack again!" But when they learned of the sudden decision that they were to withdraw from the mountain under the command of forty-eight-year-old Goichiro Tsuruda, who had been lamed by a swollen leg, they were appalled by this unforeseen turn of events and protested fiercely.

Yielding at last to the fervent arguments of their elders, they glumly followed Tsuruda down the mountain. Tsuruda's son Tanao, since he was already twenty, stayed behind with the others. Soon it was night.

The report of the scouting party was to be heard in the house of a sympathizer in Shimazaki Village. The men on the mountain slipped down by twos and threes. Their comrades returned from their reconnaissance. According to the news they brought, troops and police were keeping a strict watch in Kumamoto and its environs, the government had issued orders forbidding all vessels to leave harbor, and the foe's patrols had penetrated even to the edge of Shimazaki.

They all made their way secretly to the beach of Chikozu, where they sought the aid of a fisherman, a former servant of Juro Furuta, in order to cross the bay. The fisherman, however, could do no more than offer them his only boat. This was wholly inadequate to the more than thirty comrades who remained.

Accordingly they decided to disband their force, letting each go his own way to seek whatever succor he could. Furuta himself, Kagami, the Tashiro brothers, Teruyoshi Morishita, and Shigetaka Sakamoto availed themselves of the precious boat and set out for Konoura. And with this the uprising came to an end.

The number of those who had retreated to Mount Kimpo was less than a third of those under arms at the time of the muster. All the rest either had been slain outright in battle or, wounded and hard-pressed in their places of refuge by government troops, had perished heroically by turning their own swords against themselves. One of the elders, Masamoto Aikyo, fled as far as the mountain pass of Mikuni, but, with three police officers closing in upon him, he abruptly sat down by the side of the road, cut open his stomach, and died. He was fifty-four years of age.

Saburo Matsumoto, twenty-four, and Suehiko Kasuga, twenty-three, returned to their homes and killed themselves. Tatenao Arao, twenty-three, returned to his home and, revealing to his mother his intent to kill himself, apologized for the grief he would cause her. However, she had only praise for him. Arao, weeping tears of joy, thereupon went to do reverence at his father's grave, and, at the graveside, valiantly committed seppuku.

As for Goichiro Tsuruda, who had been entrusted with leading the seven boys down from Mount Kimpo, he saw the youngsters to their various homes and then returned to his own home and prepared to take his life.

After his wife Hideko had set out food and drink, he exchanged a last cup of saké with her, wrote a death poem, and told her that she should not lose heart, since their only son, Tanao, was still alive. It was now the night of the second day after the uprising. Tsuruda also had two daughters, aged ten and fourteen. His wife wished to wake them so that they might say farewell to their father, but Tsuruda insisted on letting them sleep. And having unfastened his garments, he cut open his stomach and then thrust his blade into his throat. With his own hand he drew it out again, and he toppled over just as his older daughter, awakened by chance, came into the room and burst into bitter sobs.

Around dawn, word was brought that Tanao, the only son, had also committed seppuku. Thus on the morning after her husband had died telling her to place all her trust in her son, the news of that son's death came to Hideko's ears.

After the disbandment at Chikozu, Tanao had made his way to Shingai Shrine accompanied by Buichiro Sugé and Masura Ito.

Parting from his friends, he journeyed on alone to the village of Kengun. His plan was to escape to Choshu.

He had an uncle named Tateyama in Kengun, and when he came to him for assistance, Tanao learned that his father had visited his uncle earlier that very afternoon, and had explained his own intentions, and had asked him to look after his family. No doubt his father had already killed himself. When he heard this, Tanao lost all desire to escape.

Granted the use of the garden in front of his uncle's house, Tanao spread a mat of fresh straw beneath a tall tree there. Facing the east, he bowed in worship three times to the distant palace of the Emperor, after which he turned in the direction of his parents' house, not far away, and bowed again. Then he took up his short sword, cut open his stomach with it, and plunged it into his throat. This word was carried to the Tsuruda home at once.

After Masura Ito and Buichiro Sugé had parted from Tanao Tsuruda, they headed toward Udo, a region just to the south of Kumamoto. The village of Mikka in Udo was the home of Ito's elder brother, Masakatsu. When he saw his younger brother, however, he berated him harshly for his rashness, and would not let him enter his house. The two young men had no choice but to go away. That night they sat down facing each other on the bank of a clear stream behind the village and carried out their ritual suicides with extraordinary grace. People who lived nearby heard the echo of repeated clapping coming from the direction of the stream late in the night. Tears filled their eyes as they realized that it was someone clapping in reverence to the gods and the Emperor before committing seppuku.

Ito was twenty-one. Sugé was eighteen.

Then as to the seven youths whom Goichiro Tsuruda had conducted to their homes, three among them, Ota, Saruwatari, and Shimada, slew themselves heroically with their own swords.

Just before the uprising, the sixteen-year-old Tadao Saruwatari had composed the following poem, writing it upon the white headband that he would wear the night of the battle:

Our land divided, sold to barbarians,
The Sacred Throne in peril.
May the gods of heaven and earth
Behold our loyal devotion.

When he reached home he learned of the suicides of many of
his comrades. Disregarding all attempts to dissuade him, he exchanged a farewell cup of saké with his father and mother and
relatives and then retired alone to another room. There he cut
open his stomach, and thrust his sword into his throat. The blade
hit the bone and was slightly nicked. Saruwatari called for one
of his family to bring him another sword, and this time, cleanly
pierced by the blade, he fell forward.

Saburohiko Ota was seventeen. As soon as he returned home
he threw himself upon his bed and began to snore. When he
awakened the next morning his face was glowing with health.
He announced his intent to his sister and asked her to invite two
young friends of his, Shibata and Maeda, to the house. When
these two came, he told them that he was saying farewell forever
and requested that they attend to whatever matters he would
leave unresolved.

After the young men had left, Ota rose and went into another
room alone. An uncle, Fusanori Shibata, waited in an adjoining
room with only a sliding paper door between them. He became
aware that Ota had cut himself open. Then he heard his nephew
cry out in a heartrending voice: "Uncle, Uncle! Please help me a
little." When Shibata flung open the sliding door, Ota's dagger
was already thrust into his throat. With Shibata's hand guiding
his own, the youth brought his life to a brave conclusion.

Kataro Shimada was eighteen. As soon as he arrived home, his
family wanted him to escape by disguising himself as a Buddhist
monk, but he would have none of it. He had determined to kill
himself, and after the farewell saké, he entreated Juzo Uchishiba,
a man renowned for his skill in judo, to come to his house and
instruct him in the ritual of seppuku.

After Shimada had cut open his stomach, he pressed his blade
to his throat.

"Master, is this the correct place?" he asked. When Uchishiba

answered that it was, the youth plunged the blade in with graceful dispatch.

After the defeat of the uprising, three men, Kazuo Jugé,
Namihei Imura, and Hisaharu Oda, were sheltered in the village
of Kakihara by a prominent family named Oyano. Having gone
to Abumida one day, they met two of their comrades, who were
among those just come down from Mount Kimpo, Tateo Narazaki and Taketsuné Mukunashi. These two they asked to join
them, and all five were kept hidden by the Oyano family. Their
place of shelter was the grotto of Rakugen Temple, and the
Oyano family attended to all their needs.

Seven days had passed since the uprising. In the interval the
five men in the cave began to get word from various sources of
the suicides of their comrades, and they came to the decision that
to hide themselves further was unthinkable. Accordingly they
left the grotto and went to the Oyano home to make their last
farewells. The family, struck with grief at such a parting, set
out food and drink for them.

Jugé ate very little, thinking how unseemly to have the food
pour out when the sword cut into his stomach. Such considerations, however, hindered the lusty Narazaki not at all as he ate
and drank his fill. Afterwards these two begged some cosmetics
of a woman of the family, and brushed their cheeks lightly with
rouge. They wished the glow of health to remain there even
after death.

The five waited until nightfall to leave the house, and then
went to a place close by called Nariiwa. It was the Fifteenth Day
of the Ninth Month, a night on which the moon was full. Its
bright beams seemed to scatter jewels through the dewy grass.
The five men sat upright upon the grass, and after each had recited a farewell poem, Oda, the youngest at twenty, cut open
his stomach, after which each of the others in turn fell forward
over his own sword. Imura was thirty-five, Narazaki and Mukunashi twenty-six. Jugé was twenty-five.

Tsunetaro Kobayashi, who had parted from Kageki Abé and
Unshiro Ishihara at Abumida, returned to his home late the

evening of the Eleventh Day of the Ninth Month, accompanied by Kisou Onimaru and Mitsuo Noguchi.

Though he was but a youth, Tsunetaro Kobayashi combined courage and intelligence to a remarkable degree. He had generally taken a position opposed to the rash counsels of the extravagantly bold Onimaru, but these two comrades of opposite temperament chose to meet death at the same time and place. Now that the three of them had learned of the immense obstacles in the way of a second rising and of the utter dissolution of the League, they all committed seppuku side by side the evening of the following day.

Before doing away with himself, Kobayashi expressed his regrets to his mother for preceding her in death, and then withdrew to a separate room with his wife Mashiko, a girl of nineteen, whom he had just married the previous spring. Out of pity at causing her to pass the rest of her life as a widow, he offered to divorce her. But Mashiko burst into tears and refused.

The three men went into a room at the back of the house while the family waited in the kitchen. Kobayashi called out: "Let no one enter here. Draw some water and put it on the veranda." Then the three took up a tatami mat in the center of the room and laid it over another. Onimaru sat down facing the east upon the double mat and unfastened his kimono.

Those in the kitchen heard Kobayashi call out again: "Noguchi has performed the service of severing Onimaru's head." At length no further sound came from the room.

When the members of the family entered, they found the three facing the east, Onimaru in the middle, the act of ritual disembowelment carried out to perfection.

Onimaru was forty years of age. Kobayashi was twenty-seven. Noguchi was twenty-three.

Ikiko Abé was the wife of Kageki Abé. The eldest daughter of Kishinta Torii, she was born in Kumamoto in 1851, the Fourth Year of the Kaei era. Her elder brother Naoki studied the Japanese classics under the tutelage of Master Oen, learned military tactics from Teizo Miyabé, and so became an ardent patriot with the slogan "Honor the Emperor and expel the barbarians" ever on his lips.

Ikiko grew up hearing the opinions of her brother and his comrades, which made a deep impression upon her. The family was poor, and she worked hard to aid her mother.

When she was sixteen, a certain wealthy man desired her as his bride, but since Ikiko had resolved to marry only a militant patriot, she was not at all inclined to assent. Her brother and her mother were of like mind. However, the village headman was the matchmaker, and moreover the family was in the rich man's debt. Thus there was no avoiding the marriage.

Ikiko asked her mother, "Well, then, if I marry this man, will that fulfill all obligations?" Her mother replied that it would. The wedding took place. That night Ikiko sat upright and did not allow her husband to approach her, and when dawn came, she fled to her mother's house. Bowing low before her mother she said: "I have gone through with the marriage. Is anything else required of me?" That very day her husband divorced her.

She reached the age of eighteen. In 1868, the First Year of the Meiji era, her brother, Naoki, was appointed to serve at the Imperial Court.

It happened at this time that Kageki Abé, together with his comrade, Morikuni Tominaga, went to do worship at Hommyo Temple, sacred to the memory of Lord Kiyomasa. As they were approaching the black gate, they encountered a nubile young beauty. Perceiving that she was the sister of their comrade Naoki Torii, they bowed courteously. After they had walked on for a bit, Tominaga abruptly asked: "What would you say to marrying that girl?" Abé replied that he would have no objections. With Tominaga as go-between, the marriage soon took place. Abé at that time was twenty-nine. Ikiko's hopes had been fulfilled. She had become the wife of a patriot. But no child was born of the marriage.

Ikiko became twenty. A comrade in Kurumé named Kii Kagamiyama escaped from prison and was given shelter by Abé. Then after Kagamiyama had left, Abé himself was taken into custody, examined severely, and thrown into prison.

As long as her husband was imprisoned, Ikiko would eat no food in the morning, she prayed constantly to the gods that this unjust punishment be lifted from her husband, and at night she did without a mosquito net, though it was the height of summer, and slept upon bare boards so that her husband's sufferings would be ever in her mind.

After he had been freed, Abé was taking a stroll through the town when in one shop he came across a fine belly band. But the price was so high, as he told his wife, that he gave up all thought of buying it. Ikiko secretly sold a kimono and sash and presented her husband with the amount of money he needed. He thanked her and bought the belly band. And this is what girded his body the night of the rising.

As the rising drew nearer and nearer, the Abé house became a kind of headquarters. Ikiko and her mother-in-law spared no efforts in treating their guests with the utmost hospitality. And when some ten men gathered to prepare to take to the field, the women assisted them in every way, making ready food and drink. Noticing with a shrewd eye that one of the group was somewhat flurried, Ikiko admonished him quietly: "One must go into battle with a tranquil heart."

On the night itself, when Ikiko and her mother-in-law, Kiyoko, saw from a distance the angry flames flaring up from Kumamoto over the castle, the fires burning at five places in the Kyomachi, Yamazaki, and Motoyama districts, she leapt with joy, crying: "It's done! It's done." She lit vigil lamps before the household shrine and implored the gods for the success of the rising and her husband's good fortune in battle.

But with the morning, reports of setbacks came in thick and fast, and there were endless rumors of men falling in battle or perishing upon their own swords. With her husband's whereabouts unknown, Ikiko prayed to the gods yet more fervently for his welfare.

Three days were to intervene before his return. It was just before daybreak on the Twelfth Day of the Ninth Month.

After the disbandment of their force at the beach of Chikozu, Kageki Abé, accompanied by Unshiro Ishihara, left there to spend the following day, the tenth, in hiding in the mountain vastness of Shioya. As soon as it was dark they set out for the shrine of Kitsuki in Abumida and arrived in the middle of the night at the home of Oki Sakamoto, the shrine priest. There they were reunited with Tsunetaro Kobayashi, Onimaru, and Noguchi, and, staying the night of the eleventh, they debated their future course of action. When a response of the gods to a question put by Oki Sakamoto held out hope for a second rising, all took heart, and Abé and Ishihara left Kobayashi and his party and made their way each to his own home.

Ikiko awoke to the sound of a voice calling softly through a chink in the wooden shutters. It was her husband. Her heart leapt as she slid open the shutters. He came in without a word, and then, facing Ikiko and his mother, who had risen and joined them, gave a brief account of the defeat. Ikiko stripped off her husband's bloodstained kimono and buried it in a bamboo grove behind the house. In the days that followed, Abé spent the daylight hours hiding beneath the floor of his study, a dagger grasped in his hand. When the sun had set he came up into the study. He sent Ikiko secretly to the Ishihara house so that she could consult with Ishihara's wife, Yasuko.

Ikiko and Yasuko made a frantic search for a boat for the passage to Shimabara Peninsula, but the ban on leaving harbor was stringently enforced, and all hope of an escape by sea vanished.

On the dawn of the fourteenth, Unshiro Ishihara, determined to break through the police cordon that blocked the roads or to die at his own hand, said farewell to his wife and children and left his house.

Abé had invited his uncle, a man named Baba, to his house, and in the dawn hours, the three men, Ishihara, Abé, and Baba, discussed a plan of action. Baba explained that the strict measures taken by the police seemed to make flight impossible. And with that he departed.

Yasuko Ishihara went to the home of her husband's elder brother, Kimura, to beg for help. She had heard the thump of the boots of a search patrol coming along the road toward her house, and Kimura advised her to hurry to the Abé house to tell them that the time was past for flight.

Yasuko hired a rickshaw but got off just before reaching the Abé house, where she knocked softly at the rear door and asked that Ikiko come out. She explained to Ikiko briefly that a patrol was approaching their house in Ishihara's absence.

Ikiko made a gesture of striking at her own throat, and Yasuko nodded. Ikiko urged Yasuko to see her husband once more, but Yasuko said she had no wish to become an obstacle on her husband's path to the other world. Then she left as though fleeing.

Ikiko immediately reported all this to her husband and Ishihara. For their part, from the time they had heard Baba's intelligence, both leaders had cast away all hope for a second rising and had set their minds upon death.

Reverently the two bowed and offered worship before a scroll depicting the Grand Shrine of Isé. Ikiko placed three earthen cups upon a three-legged stool of plain wood. Urging the men to partake of the final draught of saké, she herself took up one of the cups.

Abé and Ishihara opened their kimonos and took their short swords in hand. As for Ikiko, she quietly drew a small dagger from within her sash.

Her action provoked consternation in Ishihara as well as her husband, and they tried to stop her, but Ikiko would not turn aside from her resolve. She had no children, she told her husband, so why should he prevent her from accompanying him? Since she gave no sign of retreating, Abé did not venture to deny her her will.

At the same moment that the two men cut open their stomachs with a precise thrust of their swords, Ikiko struck her throat with her dagger.

It was the Fourteenth Day of the Ninth Month. The time was shortly past noon. Abé was thirty-seven years of age. Ikiko was twenty-six. Ishihara was thirty-five.

Hardly a moment after their suicides the door of the Abé house shook with a violent knocking. The patrol had come. Abé's old mother called out in a loud voice: "They have just committed seppuku." An officer flanked by his troops forced his way into the house and was confronted with the three fresh corpses.

When the force had disbanded at Chikozu, the group of those who embarked in the lone fishing boat and made their way to Konoura in Udo, just south of Kumamoto, numbered six men.

There was the twenty-eight-year-old Juro Furuta, who together with Tsunetaro Kobayashi was one of the most youthful of the leaders. In the struggle within the garrison walls, he broke two swords, took up a third, and kept on fighting. It was he who cut down Lieutenant Colonel Kunihiko Oshima as well as many others, though he himself also sustained a wound.

There was Juro Kagami, forty years of age and a master of the ancient court music.

There was Gitaro Tashiro, twenty-six years of age and a master swordsman. He was the first man upon the palisade of the artillerymen's camp.

Tashiro's younger brother Gigoro was twenty-three and had fought valiantly in the combat with the infantrymen.

Teruyoshi Morishita was twenty-four. He struck down Major General Taneda, and then joined the struggle at the infantry garrison and slew another officer, greatly distinguishing himself.

Shigetaka Sakamoto was twenty-one.

The six had placed their hopes in the aid of the priest of Konoura Shrine, their comrade and fellow-disciple of Master Oen, Takeo Kai. He most certainly would have joined in the rising, but word of it had not reached him in this distant place. Kai gave them a cordial welcome.

They passed the night at Kai's house, taking counsel with one another as to a second rising. Kagami offered a suggestion for procuring funds for traveling and military supplies. He had learned that his former lord, Eijiro Mibuchi, happened to be staying at the Matsui residence in Ueyanagi, and so he entrusted a letter to Kai, asking Mibuchi to provide funds for their journey. Kai set out with the letter at once.

Everyone waited anxiously for Kai to come back. The following day, the Twelfth Day of the Ninth Month, passed without his return.

When Kai arrived at the Matsui residence, not only was Mibuchi no longer there, but Kai himself was recognized by the police on guard as one of those in sympathy with the League, and he was taken into custody.

The six who waited realized that every moment that Kai's return was delayed heightened their peril. And once a certain limit was reached, they knew they would have to prepare to meet their fate.

Three of them, Gigoro Tashiro, Morishita, and Sakamoto, racked by impatience, climbed to the top of the nearby peak of Omigataké just as the sun was setting. They gazed at distant Kumamoto Castle. Seen thus from afar, the castle tower's appearance gave no hint of any extraordinary activity within. But when the comrades casually questioned the mountain folk, they were told that by night the castle was ablaze with lights and by day search patrols were dispatched without letup in every direction. When the three came down from the mountain, they urged their three comrades to resign themselves to the inevitable.

They set their minds upon death. As for the place, they chose Omigataké. As for the time, they chose dawn of the following day.

Not long after the first cockcrow, the six climbed to the crest of Omigataké. The previous evening, the Tashiro brothers had selected there a level portion of unspoiled ground and marked it off into a square bordered with sacred rope which they hung with Shinto pendants. Now at dawn these white pendants fluttered in the breeze. Gazing up at the trailing clouds as daylight broke over the mountains, Juro Kagami composed his farewell poem:

> I have lived long in this world
> By the grace of the gods of Yamato,
> And today I at last set foot
> On the Floating Bridge of Heaven.

As need hardly be said, his poem was based upon the mystic teaching of Master Oen on the ascent to heaven. Kagami told his comrades that he would very much like to have played for them in this final hour the ancient music in which he had been schooled, and that the lack of an instrument grieved him.

The six stepped within the sacred rope, they partook together of the farewell cup of saké, and Gitaro Tashiro, singled out by the others, agreed to administer the finishing stroke to each of them. Whereupon Kagami, thinking it a pity that Tashiro should undergo the last agony alone, said that he would wait and die with him.

Juro Furuta was the first to expose his flesh to the autumn breeze of morning and to cut his stomach straight across. Tashiro then severed head from body.

After that, Morishita, Gigoro Tashiro, and Shigetaka Sakamoto committed seppuku in turn. Finally Gitaro Tashiro and Kagami, performing the ritual together, cut open their stomachs and thrust their blades into their own throats.

Inspector Yoshitaka Niimi, alerted by an informer, began leading several policemen up the mountain. While still on the middle slopes, he met a hunter rushing down excitedly, who told him that six members of the League of the Divine Wind were committing seppuku on the mountaintop. Halting his impatient group with the words, "We will rest here before going on," Niimi sat down at the base of a tree and lit a cigarette. He did not wish to disturb the last moments of these men.

When the police reached the crest of the mountain, the last traces of the night's darkness were gone. Within the square cordoned with sacred rope, the corpses of the six patriots lay slumped forward in perfect fulfillment of the ritual. The white paper pendants that hung from the rope, many of them flecked with fresh blood, shone in the rays of the morning sun.

After the rising had been suppressed, one of its leaders, Kotaro Ogata, consulted the gods and was told that he should surrender. Ogata did so, and, while in prison serving a life sentence, wrote a short book entitled *The Romance of the Divine Fire*. In it he addressed himself to the problems of why the Divine Wind had not blown and why the Ukei had proved fallible.

With dedication of such unparalleled intensity, with wills so purged of impurity, how was it that divine assistance was not forthcoming? Such was the riddle with which Ogata struggled vainly in his prison cell for the rest of his life. Ogata's thoughts, as he recorded them in the following passage, merely represent his own interpretation, his personal conjecture. The will of the gods is hidden, and, indeed, it does not lie in man's province to know it:

> How wretched and pitiable that men so splendidly faithful should, counter to all expectation, perish in a single night, like blossoms scattered by a storm, like the fleeting frost and dew, and in an enterprise conceived and executed under the guidance of the divine will! Thus in my foolish heart did I wonder why it was that events had so come to pass, and I even began to feel doubt and bitterness. But I came to believe that the end was foreordained, that it was what the divine will had intended.
>
> Had the gods once more frowned upon the enterprise for which these hardy men, so fierce and bold, had sought their approval, what they had planned would no doubt become known to the world, and a most perilous situation would have come about. Even if that danger could have been surmounted, surely some of them would have taken their own lives, out of sheer frustration and despair.
>
> And so the great gods, moved to pity, fashioned a marvelous providence whereby these men would vindicate their honor at one stroke and thereafter render their service in the world to come.
>
> Though stricken with awe, so do I reason within myself.

A keen regret lies hidden in these words that Ogata wrote to console both himself and the souls of his comrades. And in the simple exclamation that follows, one that truly expresses the mind of this group of men who let no obstacle deter them, Ogata may be said to have given voice to the spirit of the samurai: "Were we to have acted like frail women?"

10

THE RAINY SEASON had already begun. Isao Iinuma paused before leaving home for his morning classes to glance inside the large envelope that had just arrived bearing Honda's name. After seeing that it contained a letter as well as his *League of the Divine Wind*, he put the envelope into his bookbag, intending to read it at his leisure once he had reached school.

He passed through the gate of his school, the College of National Studies. Just inside the entranceway of his classroom building stood a huge drum which well embodied the spirit of the school. It was a venerable-looking drum with the inscription "Yahachi Onozaki, drum-maker, Temma," and had a large iron ring hanging from its cylinder. The broad circle of taut-stretched leather was like an expanse of early spring sky hazy with yellow dust. And the spots of wear inflicted by numerous blows were like clusters of white clouds floating in such a sky. But on a muggy rainy-season day like this, Isao thought, the drum, its vigor gone, would probably give off a sluggish, muffled sound.

As soon as he entered his second-floor classroom, he heard the drum being beaten to announce the beginning of the school day. His first class was ethics. Since neither that subject nor its decrepit teacher roused Isao's enthusiasm, he stealthily took out Honda's letter and began to read it.

My dear Mr. Iinuma:
    I am returning to you your copy of *The League of the Divine Wind*. I read it with keen appreciation indeed. Thank you.
    I well understand why this book stirred such admiration

in you. And rest assured that I, too, who had regarded this uprising as nothing more than an affair of discontented samurai fanatically dedicated to the gods, have had my horizons broadened by learning of the purity of motive and feeling of those involved. My appreciation, however, probably differs from yours, and it is about this difference that I would like to write in more detail.

That is to say, when I reflect upon whether, were I your age, the emotions aroused in me would be the same, I cannot help but doubt this. Rather I think that, whatever regrets, whatever envy I might have concealed within my heart, I would have smiled derisively at these men who staked everything upon a single blow. When I was your age I thought of myself as on the way to becoming a useful and proper member of society. At that age, my emotional balance was carefully preserved, and my intellect had come to function in a more or less clear if prosaic manner. I was convinced that the usual passions were altogether "unsuitable" for me. Just as one cannot take on a body other than one's own, so I believed that one could not speak any lines other than those allotted one in human life. When I saw passion in others, it was my practice to search out the incongruity there as quickly as I could, the necessary contradiction, however small, between the man himself and his passion, and then to smile a little derisively—to protect myself. When one has this bent, it is easy to discover "unsuitability" anywhere. This kind of derision was not necessarily malicious. I might even venture to say that my very derision contained a kind of cordiality and tolerance. Why? Because at that age, the realization had begun to take form in me that passion by its very nature is something born of man's failure to perceive this kind of incongruity in himself.

It happened, however, that a close friend of mine, Kiyoaki Matsugae, whom your father, too, has spoken to you about, put a great strain upon this so carefully ordered awareness of mine. He fell passionately in love with a girl, and I, with the eyes of a friend, perceived this from the first as the most extraordinary of incongruities. For I had thought of him up to that time as having no more warmth than a glittering crystal. He was maddeningly capricious, he was given to sentiment, but I, as an observer, had concluded that his all too exquisite sensitivity would preserve him from heedless and simpleminded passion.

Things did not proceed as I had thought, however. Even as I watched, I saw this naïve, heedless passion changing my friend. Love was feverishly at work, transforming him into a person suited for love. His passion, altogether foolish, altogether blind, made him into one altogether suitable. Just at the moment of his death, I saw his face become the very face of one who had been born to die for love. All incongruity was wiped away at that moment.

I, whose eyes had witnessed so miraculous a transformation, could myself hardly remain unchanged. My callow faith in my own indomitable nature became a prey to misgivings, and I had to work to maintain it. What had been an act of faith now became an act of will. What had been something natural now became something to be sought after. This was an alteration that brought with it a certain profit valuable to me in my role as a judge. When I deal with a criminal I am able to believe, unswayed by theories of retribution or re-education, or by optimism or pessimism toward human nature, that any man, regardless of his situation, is capable of being transformed.

At any rate let me return to the emotions I felt after reading *The League of the Divine Wind*. Strangely enough, I, who now am thirty-eight, discovered myself capable of being stirred by this narration of an historical event shot through with irrationality. What came to my mind most vividly was Kiyoaki Matsugae. His passion was no more than a passion dedicated to one woman, but its irrationality was the same, its violence, its rebelliousness was the same, and its resistance to all remedies but that of death was the same. Still, even in the midst of my excited appreciation, I felt secure in knowing that at my present age I can be aroused by such accounts without incurring any risk. Perhaps precisely because of the immutable truth of my never having done such things myself, I am now able to contemplate with safety everything that I might have done in the past. Thus, with no danger at all, I can fix my imagination upon such events, and I can let myself bathe in the poisonous rays of my own reveries reflected from them.

At your age, however, every excitement is dangerous. Every excitement that can send one pitching headlong is dangerous. And some are especially dangerous. For example, judging from that light that flashes from your eyes to disconcert those around you, I would think that your very nature makes a tale of this sort "unsuitable" for you.

Having reached my present age, I find myself no longer adverting to the incongruity between men and their passions. When I was young, concern for my own welfare certainly made such fault-finding a necessity, but now not only is this necessity gone but the disharmony in others resulting from their passion, which in the past I would have considered a weakness worthy of scornful laughter, has become but an allowable imperfection. And with that perhaps I have lost the last vestige of my youth, whose vulnerability made it fearful of the wounds incurred by reacting emotionally to the erratic conduct of others. Now, indeed, it is the beauty of danger rather than the danger of beauty that affects me with the utmost vividness, and there is nothing comical to me about youth. Probably this is because youth no longer has any claim on my self-awareness. When I consider all this for a moment, there is something frightening about it. My own enthusiasm, innocuous as it is for me, may well have the result of further stimulating your dangerous enthusiasm.

Because I realize this, I want very much to admonish you in this regard, to urge restraint upon you—though my efforts may well be useless.

The League of the Divine Wind is a drama of tragic perfection. This was a political event so remarkable throughout that it almost seems to be a work of art. It was a crucible in which purity of resolve was put to the test in a manner rarely encountered in history. But one should by no means confuse this tale of dreamlike beauty of another time with the circumstances of present-day reality.

The danger of this account lies in its leaving out the contradictions. The author, Tsunanori Yamao, seems to have written in accordance with historical fact. But for the sake of the artistic unity of this slim volume, he has, without doubt, excluded a number of contradictions. Furthermore, he focuses so insistently upon the purity of resolve that pertained to the essence of this affair that he sacrifices all perspective. Thus one loses sight not only of the general context of world history but also of the particular historical necessities that conditioned the Meiji government which the League chose as its enemy. What the book lacks is contrast. To give an example, you yourself are aware, are you not, of the existence at the same time in the same Kumamoto Province of a group called the Kumamoto Band?

In the 1870s, a retired American captain of artillery named L. L. Janes, who had distinguished himself in the Civil War, came to take an assignment as a teacher at the school of Western learning founded in Kumamoto. He began to give Bible classes, and to slip into the role of a Protestant missionary. In the same year of the rising of the League of the Divine Wind, 1876, thirty-five of his students, led by Danjo Ebina, gathered on Mount Hanaoka on January thirtieth. And under the title of the Kumamoto Band they took a vow "to Christianize Japan, to build a new nation based upon this teaching." Persecution arose, of course. The school was finally closed, but the thirty-five comrades were able to flee to Kyoto, where they helped Jo Niijima build up Doshisha University. Though their ideals were diametrically opposed to those of the League, here, too, do we not see another example of the same purity of resolve? In the Japan of that day, even the most eccentric and unrealistic ideas were not without some faint possibility of realization, and diametrically opposed concepts of political reform manifested themselves with the same naïveté and lack of sophistication. One should realize how much different that era was from the present when the structure of government has taken on a definite form.

I am no advocate of the novelties of Christianity, nor am I one to scorn the zeal for the past and the stubborn narrow-mindedness of the men of the League. However, if one is to learn from history, one should not concentrate solely upon a single portion of an era but rather make a thorough investigation of the many complex and mutually contradictory factors that made the era what it was. One must take the single portion and fit it into its proper place. One must evaluate the various elements that went into giving it its special character. Thus one must look at history from a perspective that offers a broad and balanced view.

This, I believe, is what is meant by learning from history. For any man's view of his own era is limited, and he has great difficulty in trying to obtain a comprehensive picture of his time. Precisely because of this, then, the comprehensive picture offered by history both provides information and constitutes a pattern for one's guidance. A man who lives bound by the limits of the minute-to-minute present is able, by means of the broad vision offered by time-transcending history, to avail himself of a comprehensive picture of his world and so correct his own narrow view of things. Such is the enjoyable privilege that history offers men.

Learning from history should never mean fastening upon a particular aspect of a particular era and using it as a model to reform a particular aspect of the present. To take out of the jigsaw puzzle of the past a piece with a set form and attempt to fit it into the present is not an enterprise that could have a happy outcome. To do so is to toy with history, a pastime fit for children. One must realize that yesterday's sincerity and today's sincerity, however much they may resemble each other, have different historical conditions. If one seeks a kindred purity of resolve, one should seek it in a "diametrically opposed ideology" of the present day, existing under the same historical conditions. A modest attitude of this sort is appropriate for the characteristically limited "present-day me." For thus one is at last able to abstract this purity of resolve as a historical problem, and to make this "human motive" which transcends history the object of one's study. Then the historical conditions common to the era become no more than the constant factors in the equation.

What a young man like you should be especially warned against is the blurring together of purity of resolve and history. The immense esteem, then, that you have for this book on the League of the Divine Wind makes me fearful. I think it would be well if you would try to think of history in terms of a vast stage of events, and of purity of resolve as something that transcends history.

All this has probably been a show of excessive solicitude, but such is my advice and admonition. I suppose that, without realizing it, I have arrived at the age of pouring out advice to anyone younger than myself. But, beyond that, I value your intelligence. Why should I admonish at such length a young man whom I expected to amount to nothing?

As for the almost sublime strength that you displayed in the kendo match, as for your own purity of resolve and passionate feelings, I cannot withhold my admiration. But placing still more reliance upon your intelligence and your zeal for truth, I would like to express the deeply felt hope that you will be ever aware of your primary duty as a student, ever assiduous in your studies, and so turn out a man valuable to your country.

Again, whenever you come to Osaka, please take the opportunity to visit me. You will always be welcome.

Finally, though there should be no need for such concern with a man as excellent as your father always at hand, nevertheless, should any especially grave problem arise to trouble you and you feel the need of consulting with someone else, I would be willing at any time to talk things over with you. Please do not have the least hesitation in this regard.

Sincerely yours,
Shigekuni Honda

The young man sighed when he came to the end of the long letter. What was written there did not please him. He was opposed from first to last to what it said. Then there was something else. Even though this man was an old friend of his father's, Isao could not fathom his motive in sending a letter of such length, one furthermore which was so cordial, so carefully fashioned, so obviously sincere, to a boy whom he, a judge of the Osaka Court of Appeals, had met only once.

To be so singled out was a unique privilege, but what impressed Isao was not the letter itself but the frankness and warmth of its style. Never before had an eminent man demonstrated so sincere a regard for him.

Isao could draw but one conclusion: "There's no doubt that he was moved by the book. His age and his profession have turned him into a coward, but Judge Honda, too, must be a man of 'purity.'"

Though the letter was filled with phrases that offended his feelings, at least his boyish eyes could find no corruption lurking there.

But even so, had not Honda's skillful freezing of history, stripping it of time, had the effect of reducing everything to a map? Was that how a judge's mind worked? The history of an era in terms of his "comprehensive picture" would become no more than a map, a scroll, a thing with no life.

This man understands nothing at all of the blood that flows in Japanese veins, of our moral heritage, of our will, the boy thought.

Isao looked up to find the lecture still drowsily in progress. The fall of rain outside the window had intensified. The damp and sultry atmosphere of the classroom was filled with the heavy acid odor given off by the young flesh of growing boys.

The lecture ended at last. There was the same feeling of relief with which one sees a frightfully squawking chicken suddenly breathe its last and become tranquil.

Isao went out into the corridor, which was damp from the rain. Izutsu and Sagara were waiting for him.

"What's on your minds?" asked Isao.

"Lieutenant Hori said he wasn't on duty today and he'd be back at his quarters by three o'clock," Izutsu told him. "The place will be quiet at that time, and we'll be able to talk. He said we're to have dinner with him too."

Isao answered without hesitation: "Well, I'll skip kendo practice today."

"Won't the captain have something to say about that?"

"He can say what he likes. He doesn't dare put me off the team."

"How wonderful to have such power!" replied Sagara, who was small and wore glasses.

The three of them walked together to the next class, since all three had chosen German for their foreign language.

Izutsu and Sagara both deferred to Isao's leadership. It was Isao who had roused their enthusiasm by letting them read *The League of the Divine Wind*. Having by chance received his book that morning from Osaka, Isao decided to lend it next to Lieutenant Hori, whom he would meet that afternoon. It was hardly likely that the Lieutenant's reaction would be anything like the temporizing response of Judge Honda.

"A perspective that offers a broad and balanced view," Isao thought, the phrase from the letter he had just read coming to his mind. He smiled slightly: "That man would never touch hot fire tongs. He'd touch only the hibachi. But how different fire tongs and the hibachi. One is made of metal, the other of clay. He's a man who is pure, but he belongs to the clay category."

The concept of purity was something that came from Isao and entered deeply into the minds and hearts of the other two. He had composed a motto, "Learn from the purity of the League of the Divine Wind," which had become the motto of their group.

Purity, a concept that recalled flowers, the piquant mint taste of a mouthwash, a child clinging to its mother's gentle breast, was something that joined all these directly to the concept of blood, the concept of swords cutting down iniquitous men, the concept of blades slashing down through the shoulder to spray the air with blood. And to the concept of seppuku. The moment that a samurai "fell like the cherry blossoms," his blood-smeared corpse became at once like fragrant cherry blossoms. The concept of purity, then, could alter to the contrary with arbitrary swiftness. And so purity was the stuff of poetry.

For Isao, to die purely seemed easy. But what about laughing purely? How to be pure in all respects was a problem that disturbed him. No matter how tight a rein he kept upon his emotions, there were times when some trivial thing would arise to make him laugh. Once, for example, he had laughed at a puppy frolicking at the side of the road, with a woman's high-heeled shoe, of all things, in its mouth. It was the kind of laugh that he preferred others not to see.

"Do you know how to get to the Lieutenant's place?"

"Trust me. I'll get you both there."

"I wonder what the Lieutenant is really like."

Isao spoke up: "I think he is someone who will give us a chance to die."

THE THREE BOYS, carrying their umbrellas and wearing their school caps with the white piping, got off the streetcar at Roppongi and walked down the street that began its descent at No. 3 Kasumi-cho and led around toward the main gate of the Azabu Third Regiment.

"That's it," said Izutsu, pointing his finger at a house at the foot of the slope. All three stopped to look.

It was a two-story house so worn with age that one wondered how it could have survived the disastrous earthquake. Its garden seemed rather large, but there was no gate, the board fence that surrounded it opening immediately upon the door. At the front a narrow porch ran along the second story backed by a line of six glass doors, which seemed to brim over with the twisted reflection of the dark, wet sky. As soon as he had observed the rain-soaked bulk of this house from the slope above, Isao had had an eerie impression. This could not be the first time he was looking upon it, he thought. There the house stood wrapped in falling rain like a ludicrously oversized cabinet too old to be of any use and so abandoned to the elements. The trees and shrubs of its garden, unpruned and unclipped, flourished immoderately, and made the fence seem like a trash box stuffed with weeds. Isao felt that this place of so melancholy an aspect was connected with a past event of ineffable sweetness, a memory of which stirred deep within him like the bubbling of dark honey. How odd it seemed that he should have such an uncanny but distinct impression of having been here before. Perhaps this was founded upon the actual experience of having been brought to this neighborhood by his parents when he was a child. Then, too, he might have once seen a photograph of this house. Whatever the case, he felt that the form of this house had remained perfectly preserved within his heart like a tiny but fully detailed garden wreathed in mist.

In another moment, Isao shook off these reflections which the dark shadow of his umbrella might have provoked. Ahead of the other two, almost running, he hurried down the steep slope awash with muddy water.

They stood before the entranceway. There was a nameplate fastened at the top of the closely worked lattice of the door, but the wind and the rain had taken such a toll of its wood that only the part inked over with the name "Kitazaki" seemed to have any substance left. The rain had penetrated even the moldering threshold.

An officer cousin of Izutsu had introduced him to Lieutenant Hori, the infantry officer whom they had come to see today. Izutsu could well expect the Lieutenant to be especially receptive to his bringing with him the son of the headmaster of the Academy of Patriotism.

Isao's mood was that of a vigorous young man newly enrolled in the League of the Divine Wind on his way to meet Harukata Kaya, and his heart thumped furiously. Now, however, the era was one in which the League was a thing of the distant past, and Isao well understood that the situation today

was not that of sword-wielding samurai of the League clash-
ing with the soldiers of the Meiji government, with friend
and foe clearly marked like opposing pieces set up on a chessboard. He knew that today the samurai spirit was alive deep
within the Army, and that those who had it viewed with
sorrow and indignation the "Meiji mentality" of the militarists
and the important ministers who were their allies. That one
of these possessed of the samurai spirit should live within
such a wretched house seemed to Isao as though a scrub
citrus tree hidden in the shadowy dampness of a forest should
bear a single, bright-colored orange.

Isao completely lost the cool reserve that he was able to
maintain even before a kendo match. The man he was about
to meet was someone capable perhaps of lifting him to the
heavens—though every dream and hope that he had up to
now placed in someone else had been betrayed.

The old man who answered the door sent a chill through
the three youths. He was tall but bent forward so that, with
his white hair and his deep-set eyes, he materialized in the
gloom of the entranceway as though swooping down upon
them. He was the sort of birdlike creature one might expect
to meet in a mountain fastness, an ancient with broken wings
folded.

"The Lieutenant eagerly awaits your visit. Please come
this way," said the old man, pressing his palms to his knees.
Then he went off through the darkness of the damp corridor
as though using his hands to direct the motion of his legs.
Though the materials that had gone into the house seemed no
different from those of any other lodging house, the very
walls were permeated with the smell of leather, and the distant sound of the morning and evening bugle calls of the
Third Regiment seemed to have been compounded with the
fiber of its sliding panels. Apparently no other lodger but the
Lieutenant had yet returned, so deep was the silence throughout the house. The old man's breath grew labored as he began
to climb the creaking stairway. Then he stopped halfway up,

and, as if to gain a moment's rest, called to the second floor: "Lieutenant Hori, your guests have come." There was a youthful, almost insolent vigor to the voice that shouted in response.

The room that Lieutenant Hori lived in was a single one of eight mats, and, aside from a desk and a bookcase, it had no furnishings at all, Spartan surroundings altogether suited to a bachelor officer.

He had already changed into a splashed-pattern summer kimono with a carelessly fastened sash, and, so dressed, he seemed an ordinary young man of dark complexion. His uniform was neatly arranged upon a hanger which hung from a beam. The red tab at the collar and the brass numeral "3" gave the room the only bit of color that caught the eye.

"Well, come right in. I was duty officer this week, and I was relieved at noon. That's why I'm home early." The Lieutenant's voice rang with self-confidence.

His head was close-cropped, and his scalp was like a text proclaiming the rough vigor of his spirit. And though his eyes were clear and his glance penetrating, yet, dressed as he was, there was nothing to set him apart from any other young man of twenty-six or seven from the provinces. Save, perhaps, for the thick forearms which told of his mastery of kendo.

"Now make yourselves comfortable. Don't bother about the tea, old fellow. We'll take care of it."

When the old man's footsteps on the creaking stairs had grown faint, the Lieutenant began to talk cheerfully as he leaned forward to take up a thermos bottle containing the hot water for the tea. His words were obviously meant to put the tense boys at ease.

"This place looks like a haunted house, but both it and that old man there have a momentous history behind them. He was a hero of the war with China, and then, during the Russo-Japanese War, he opened this lodging house. Many great military men started to make their own way in life right here. So it's a house with good associations. Then it's cheap and it's also handy because it's close to the barracks, and so there's never an empty room in it."

As the Lieutenant laughed, Isao watched his face. A visit about the time the cherry blossoms had begun to fall would have been preferable, he thought. How much better if the Lieutenant had come home after drilling on a windswept parade ground beneath a dusty yellow sky, had pulled off soiled boots to which clung cherry blossom petals, and had greeted the boys dressed in a khaki uniform that gave off the scent of spring and of manure, a gleeful flash of red and gold at the shoulders and collar.

The Lieutenant was evidently a man who cared little about the impression he made upon others. His tone was free and easy as he began to talk about kendo.

Izutsu and Sagara held their breath, intent on saying something. What they both wanted to say was that Isao, already a third-level kendoist, was a young man from whom the world of kendo expected much. At length, Sagara, small and bespectacled, stammered out this information. Isao's face reddened, and the Lieutenant's expression suddenly took on a kind warmth as he looked at Isao.

This is what Izutsu and Sagara had been hoping for. In Isao they saw the perfect embodiment of their hopes, and so, with the aggressiveness which is the privilege of youth, they wanted him to be on an equal footing in any confrontation with an outsider. Of course Isao would never resort to verbal trickery, but only bring to bear upon his opponent the piercing force of the purity to which they all were dedicated.

Suddenly the Lieutenant changed his tone and, eyes sparkling, put a direct question. Izutsu and Sagara felt their hearts throb; it was the moment they had been awaiting.

"All right, let me ask Isao here. What ideal do you hold?"

Isao, still sitting erect though he had been told to make himself comfortable, threw out his chest and answered succinctly: "To form a Showa League of the Divine Wind."

"The rising of the League failed. Doesn't that trouble you at all?"

"That was not a failure."

"No? All right, what are you going to put your trust in?"

"Our swords," answered Isao, not mincing a word.

The Lieutenant said nothing for a moment. He seemed to be rehearsing the next question in his mind: "Well and good. But let me ask you this: what do you wish for more than anything else?"

This time Isao was silent. He had been keeping his eyes fixed upon the Lieutenant's, but now he turned them slightly away. His glance went from the damp wall to the tight-fast window of ground glass. That was as far as he could see. He knew that beyond the close-worked lattice of the window was a thick curtain of rain. Even if the window had been opened, there would have been nothing but rain in view. Still Isao seemed about to speak of something that was not close at hand but far off.

When he spoke, though his voice stammered slightly, his words were bold: "Before the sun . . . at the top of a cliff at sunrise, while paying reverence to the sun . . . while looking down upon the sparkling sea, beneath a tall, noble pine . . . to kill myself."

"Hmm," said the Lieutenant.

Izutsu and Sagara looked at Isao in shock. Though he had never before made such a momentous confession, certainly not to his two friends, he had expressed himself in these terms to a man whom he was meeting for the first time.

Fortunately for Isao the Lieutenant did not respond with harsh skepticism but gave every indication of weighing with the utmost seriousness this declaration which seemed little short of madness. Finally, he spoke: "So that's how it stands. But it's not easy to die beautifully, you know. Because it's not up to you to choose the moment. Even for a military man, there's no guarantee that he'll be able to die exactly the way he wants."

Isao gave no heed to the Lieutenant's words. Subtle discourse, exegesis, the "on the one hand this, on the other that" approach—all these were foreign to his way of thinking. His ideal was drawn upon pure white paper in fresh black ink. Its text was mysterious, and it excluded not only translation but also every critique and commentary.

Isao's manner now became very tense, and, fully prepared to receive perhaps a slap across the face, he looked directly into the Lieutenant's eyes and spoke, his shoulders square.

"Would it be permissible to ask a question?"

"Go ahead."

"Is there any truth to the rumor that before the May Fifteenth Incident Lieutenant Nakumura of the Imperial Navy made a visit to Lieutenant Hori?"

For the first time, a cold, hard expression flickered across the Lieutenant's face.

"Where did you hear a rumor like that?"

"Someone said it at my father's school."

"Was it your father himself?"

"No, it was not my father."

"It doesn't matter. Everything will come out at the trial. You shouldn't let yourself be taken in by stupid rumors."

"Is it a stupid rumor?"

"A stupid rumor, yes."

The Lieutenant lapsed into silence, and the anger which he had checked seemed to tremble in the interval like a compass needle.

"Trust us. Please tell us the truth. Did you meet with him?"

"No, I didn't. I never meet with any of them from the Navy."

"Did you meet with Army men?"

The Lieutenant attempted a carefree laugh.

"I meet with them every day. I'm a soldier after all."

"That does not answer my question."

Izutsu and Sagara looked fearfully at each other. How far would Isao dare to go?

"Do you mean with comrades?" asked the Lieutenant after a pause.

"Yes."

"That's something that doesn't concern you."

"Please, we really must know."

"Why must you?"

"Because if . . . if we should ever come to ask something of you, we have to know ahead of time whether or not Lieutenant Hori is a man who will try to restrain us."

Even before hearing the other's answer, Isao, taught by what had happened so often before, felt the unpleasant time had come when a chill would isolate him from the man sitting opposite him. The personality of his companion, which a moment before had seemed so radiant, would lose all its luster. This was a change that was perhaps painful enough for the one who underwent it but decidedly more painful for the one who witnessed it. As though the tension of a drawn bow were suddenly relaxed, the arrow unreleased, the bowstring slack again before one's eyes. As though the heaped-up duration of day-to-day living, like a pile of rubbish, were manifested at one stroke. Was there not one man among their elders who would throw aside discretion and the caution brought on by his years and respond at once to the keen thrust of their purity with a sharp-pointed purity of his own? If there were definitely none, the purity that Isao envisaged had to be something that the bonds of age strangled. (This despite the example of the men of the League of the Divine Wind.) If it was in the nature of purity to fall victim to age, then purity was something destined to waste away before his eyes. No thought could make Isao more fearful. If this was true, he had no time to lose.

The way for elders to cure the impetuosity of youth is to give it their unqualified approval, but this is a bit of wisdom that they never seem to learn. And so the young put all their trust in the fierce purity which they feel will of its very nature vanish on the morrow, and they go to extremes in their pursuit of it. And the fault lies with no one but their elders.

Isao and his two friends stayed in Lieutenant Hori's room until nine that evening, the Lieutenant treating them to a dinner brought in by a caterer. Once he had abandoned his subtle questions, Lieutenant Hori's conversation became both interesting and profitable, quite capable of arousing their zeal. The shameful state of foreign affairs, the government's economic program which was doing nothing to relieve rural poverty, the corruption of politicians, the rise of communism, and then the political parties' halving the number of Army divisions and, by championing the cause of arms cutbacks, bringing constant pressure to bear upon the military. In the course of this conversation, the Shinkawa *zaibatsu*'s exertions in purchasing American dollars came up, something of which Isao had already heard from his father. According to the Lieutenant, Shinkawa's group had been making a great show of restraint ever since the May Fifteenth Incident. However, the Lieutenant went on to say, there were no grounds at all for placing any trust in the self-control of people of that sort.

Japan was sorely beset. Storm clouds were piling up in an ever-growing mass, and the situation was enough to make a man despair. Even the august person of His Sacred Majesty was affronted. The boys' knowledge of current evils to be deplored was greatly expanded. In any event, the Lieutenant was a good man.

As they were leaving, Isao said: "Our ideals in their entirety are contained in this." He then handed *The League of the Divine Wind* to the Lieutenant. Since he had not made it clear whether he was giving the book or just lending it, if he ever wanted to visit the Lieutenant again, he thought, it would suffice to say that he was coming to get the book.

12

EARLY ON SUNDAY MORNING, Isao conducted a kendo practice for young boys in the drill hall of the neighborhood police station. The officer in charge was an admirer of his father, and from time to time visited the Academy of Patriotism. With his father as go-between, Isao could hardly refuse the officer's request. As for the boys' regular instructor, since he was thus able to sleep late on Sunday at least, he welcomed the opportunity to turn his charges over to Isao, whom the boys were not only fond of but looked upon as a hero.

The grade-school youngsters formed a line, their thin arms thrust out from the sleeves of their drill uniforms with the hemp-leaf pattern stitched in black on the white cloth, and one by one they charged at Isao with reckless abandon. As each pair of earnest young eyes behind their mask came rushing at him, Isao felt that he was being assaulted by a hail of brightly polished stones. Bending his body in accordance with the height of each antagonist and deliberately remiss in maintaining his guard, he dodged back and forth, taking blow after blow from the bamboo swords of the boys, much as though he were being whipped by young branches springing at him as he made his way through a thick grove. Isao felt his own youthful body glow pleasantly as the torpid mood of the rainy-season morning was shattered by the ever more fierce cries of the boys.

While Isao was wiping off his sweat after practice, a detective named Tsuboi, a man in his early fifties, who had been an interested spectator, came over to talk to him.

"You know, when I was watching you," said Tsuboi, "I realized what they mean about no kind of kendo practice demanding as much of you as when you're working with young boys. What a splendid sight! And then at the very end, the final reverence to the gods, when the oldest boy shouted out the order, 'Divine Presence!' with such force even though he's so young, I saw right there the effect of good education. I tell you, it was a splendid sight!"

Tsuboi was a second-level kendoist, but his technique had no flexibility and power, all of his strength being in his shoulders. Sometimes when Isao would practice with the policemen at the station, Tsuboi would very affably put himself under his tutelage, a youth some thirty-five or six years younger. With his sunken eyes, which were devoid of expression, his long nose with its florid, unsightly tint, the garrulous and sentimental Tsuboi scarcely looked like a detective assigned to thought control.

Just as the boys were leaving by twos and threes through the gate in front of the drill hall, a patrol wagon turned into the yard. When it had stopped, a group of long-haired young men, bound and fastened to one another, got down from it. One was dressed like a workman, the two behind him wore drab business suits, and the fourth was dressed in a fashionable kimono.

"Well, well! Looks like we have some visitors this Sunday morning," said Tsuboi, getting sluggishly to his feet. He gripped a kendo sword with his bare hands and executed a few strokes as he was about to leave. Isao could not help noticing that his hands were distastefully soft and weak, their veins standing out as though under nervous tension.

"Who are they?" he asked Tsuboi, impelled by no more than normal curiosity.

"Reds. You couldn't tell just by looking at them? Your Reds today don't dress like they used to. They make it a point either to dress so you don't notice them or to look like foppish playboys, one or the other. The one in work clothes

is probably an organizer. The rest of them are most likely
college students. Well, we'll have to make them feel right at
home." So saying, he twisted his weak hands suggestively
about the handle of the sword, then put it aside and went out.

Isao felt a touch of envy toward these young men being
thrown into prison. Sanai Hashimoto had been imprisoned
at twenty-five and executed at twenty-six.

Was it possible that Isao himself might one day become a
prisoner like Sanai? For a number of reasons, he found himself discontented that prison seemed so remote from him. Yet
would he not choose to kill himself rather than submit to imprisonment? Very few of the League of the Divine Wind
had been imprisoned. Surely, once he had plunged into a
heroic enterprise, he would not await capture and all its in-
dignities, but would put an end to himself with his own hand.

He wished that some morning, were it possible, the death
that he was intent upon—to die atop a cliff swept by a breeze
fresh with the scent of pine overlooking a sea bright in the
morning sun—would somehow partake of the atmosphere
reeking of urine that the rough and clammy concrete walls of
a prison enclosed. But how could the two be mingled?

He was always thinking of death, and this had so refined
him that the physical seemed to fall away, freeing him from
the pull of earth and enabling him to walk about some distance above its surface. Indeed he felt that even his distaste
and hatred for the affairs of the world no longer stirred him
deeply. That was what Isao feared. Perhaps then the dampness of prison walls, the bloodstains upon them, the stink of
urine, might serve to quicken his hatred. Perhaps prison was
something he needed.

Since his father and the students had already finished
breakfast when he returned home, Isao ate alone, served by
his mother.

His mother had grown rather fat, so much so that her
movements had become cumbersome. The blithe young girl
with a roving eye and imperturbably sunny outlook now lay

concealed beneath a melancholy burden of excess flesh which seemed to give expression to a temperament as cheerless as a heavily overcast sky. There was a sharpness to her gaze that suggested constant anger, but, even so, the erotic movement of her eyes had not changed from what it had been years before.

Since Miné's function at the Academy of Patriotism was to attend to the needs of some ten or more students, she surely had much to do. As demanding as her duties were, however, she had reached an age where playing the role of mother to so many young men should have given her a certain amount of pleasure, but Miné had built a wall around herself, as though for some reason she had rejected all intimacy. Whatever leisure she had she fervently devoted to the sewing of bags, and every corner of the house was filled with examples of her handicraft. The spectacle of brocade and Yuzen work scattered throughout an institution as purposefully austere as the Academy was like bright-colored seaweed twined around the unpainted hull of a fishing boat.

Here in the kitchen, the base of a large saké bottle was jacketed with red brocade. The rice tub from which Miné now was serving her son was wrapped in a quilted cover of gaudy purple Yuzen muslin. It was obvious that her husband disliked this affectation more suited to a lady in waiting, but he had never gone so far as to reprimand her for it.

"I can't rest even on Sunday, you see. Master Kaido's lecture will be at one o'clock. Since the boys are sure to overlook something, I'll have to be there too to see to all the arrangements."

"How many will be coming?"

"Maybe about thirty. But there seem to be more every time."

The Academy of Patriotism served as a kind of church on Sundays. Besides the students, all those in the neighborhood who were interested came to attend the lectures of Kaido Masugi on the history of imperial decrees, which were prefaced by a welcoming address by the headmaster himself. These sessions ended with all present chanting in unison the prayer for prosperity, and provided an occasion for inviting donations to the school. This afternoon Master Kaido was to take up a decree of the Emperor Keiko, "The Empowering of Yamoto Takeru to Subdue the Eastern Barbarians." Isao had memorized a text from this: "Then, again, evil spirits infest the mountains, devils ravage the countryside, road-ways are blocked, pathways cut off, and multitudes are made to suffer." He thought of it as a passage that could be well applied to his own era. The evil spirits in the mountains and the ravaging devils were flourishing.

From across the table Miné gazed fixedly at the face of her eighteen-year-old only son as he silently disposed of one serving of rice and then another. She was quite taken with the masculinity evident in the line of his jaw beneath the cheeks so vigorously occupied with the rice. Miné turned to look out into the garden at the cry of a passing peddler hawk-ing morning glory and eggplant seedlings. A hedge bounded the gloomy luxuriance of the shrubbery beneath an overcast sky, but it was too thick to afford a glimpse of the man. There was a heat-induced weariness to the peddler's voice, and in Miné's mind his morning glories were drooping. The man's lethargic tone conveyed the feel of the garden, teeming with tiny snails at this hour of the morning.

All at once Miné found herself thinking of her abortion, the time she lost the first child that she conceived. This was a decision that Iinuma had forced upon her because no amount of calculation of the time involved had been able to satisfy him that the child was his own and not Marquis Matsugae's.

"This boy, Isao," she thought, "he doesn't smile. Why not, I wonder. He almost never jokes. And lately he'll go for a long time without saying a word to me."

She was reminded of the young Iinuma in the Matsugae household, but there was a significant difference. The Iinuma of that period could hardly hide his tortured soul from even a casual observer, but Isao, whatever the circumstances, had an awesome poise. And this in the period of pimply adolescence when most boys were like puppies panting beneath the summer sun.

An abortion in first pregnancy makes the birth of the second child difficult, but Isao was delivered with remarkable ease, and it was not until afterwards that Miné suffered ill effects. Whether or not Iinuma had meant to show pity by finding fault with her feelings rather than with her physical disability, sometimes, as they lay beside each other at night, he berated her more severely and more sarcastically than ever about her former liaison with Marquis Matsugae. All of this was a severe mental and physical strain for Miné, but, instead of growing thin, she put on her gloomy burden of flesh.

The Academy of Patriotism had flourished. When Isao was twelve years old, Miné became altogether too friendly with one of the students. When Iinuma learned of this, he gave her a frightful beating. She was in the hospital for nearly five days.

From that time on, as far as anyone could tell, relations between husband and wife were tranquil. Miné lost all her vivacity, the price that had to be paid for the severe restraint she laid once and for all upon her wayward heart. Iinuma himself, as though freed from a spell, did not mention the Marquis again. The past had become something never to be touched upon.

Nevertheless, Miné's stay in the hospital could not have helped but make some sort of lasting impression upon Isao. He had never said a word about it to his mother, of course, but his failure to refer to it even in passing showed all too clearly that he had something stored up within him.

Miné was sure that someone must have told Isao of her old misdemeanor. Oddly enough, she found herself provoked by the desire to hear an accusation from Isao's own mouth. That her son entertained doubts about her qualifications as a mother was not without some satisfaction for her. The prospect had a certain sweetness. Troubled by a headache that made her imagine that she had a shallow pool of stagnant water somewhere at the back of her head, she kept gazing at her son from beneath her heavy eyelids, which crinkled when she was tired. His cheeks were still filled with rice.

Iinuma had enjoined her by no means to let Isao know how much the financial situation of the household had brightened immediately following the May Fifteenth Incident. Nor did Iinuma himself inform Isao of the school's circumstances, insisting that, when his son became an adult, there would be time enough to tell him whatever ought to be told. Miné, however, with the advent of this new prosperity, could not keep herself from increasing the allowance that she secretly gave him.

When Isao had finished eating, Miné took a folded five-yen note from her obi and, saying, "Don't tell your father, now," stealthily passed it under the table to him.

Isao smiled slightly for the first time and said thank you as he quickly slipped the money into his kimono. He seemed to begrudge the smile.

The Academy of Patriotism stood in the Nishikata section of Hongo. Iinuma had obtained possession of the building ten years before. It had belonged to a well-known Western-style painter, and a separate wing that had served as a studio of massive proportions had been redesigned as a meeting hall and shrine. The main house, which had evidently been occupied by a number of the artist's apprentices, was now given over partly to the students of the Academy. The pond in the garden to the rear had been filled in and left that way, with the thought that it would eventually become the site of a drill hall. Until such time the students made do with the meeting hall for the practice of their martial arts. The floor, however, lacked the proper resilience, and Isao disliked practicing there.

To avoid setting his son apart from the other pupils, Iinuma had him join in mopping the floor each morning before he went off to school. Exercising a careful control, Iinuma did not permit Isao to be treated either as the master's son or as one altogether on the same footing with his fellow students. He tried to keep him from becoming too friendly with any of them. And though he trained the students to confide in himself, the headmaster, in all matters whatsoever, he discouraged them from opening their hearts to his wife and son.

Despite this, however, Isao spontaneously established a cordial rapport with the oldest of the students, a man named Sawa. Since he was forty, and had left his wife and children in his native place to come to Tokyo, Sawa's case was extraordinary enough to provoke astonishment. He was stout and droll, and, whenever he had even a few moments free, his head was buried in a swashbuckling adventure magazine, *Kodan Club*. Once a week he would go to the courtyard before the Imperial Palace, where he would sit down in a formal position on its gravel surface and bow until his forehead touched the ground. Believing that a man must be ready to offer his life for the fulfillment of the Imperial Will at any moment, he washed out his clothes energetically every day, to keep himself scrupulously clean. On the other hand, he gambled with the young students, and, in the course of one bet, sprinkled flea powder on his rice before eating it, with no ill effects. Whenever the headmaster sent him with a message, Sawa would relay it in such an absurd way that the person it was meant for would be utterly confounded, for which offense Sawa was always being scolded by the headmaster. Still, he had no equal for his reliability in confidential matters.

Isao, leaving his mother to her work of cleaning up after him, walked down the connecting corridor to the meeting hall. The shrine, with its doors of plain wood, stood upon a raised platform in the middle of the far end of the hall. Above it hung the curtain that concealed the portraits of Their Imperial Majesties the Emperor and Empress. From where he stood at the door of the hall, Isao faced in that direction and bowed reverently.

Though Iinuma was some distance away, giving directions to a group of students within the hall, his son's act of reverence caught his eye. It seemed to him that Isao always spent too much time at it. Also, in the course of the monthly pilgrimage to Meiji Shrine and Yasukuni Shrine, Iinuma had had occasion to notice how much longer than the others Isao took in offering his worship. And he had never confided any reason for it to his father. When he looked back on his own youth, Iinuma tried to recall those things that he had prayed for with such angry anathemas during his morning devotions before Omiyasama on the Matsugae estate. Compared to himself at the same age, Isao was a boy whose status was secure and so had no cause to resent the world and call down curses upon those around him.

Isao looked on as the students were busy rearranging chairs in the dim light filtering down through the broad skylight. Since the sky was heavily overcast, the patch of light above gave the hall the subdued glow of an aquarium.

The boys had by now put the chairs and benches in good order, but Sawa, alone among them, was still at work in his own inefficient way, pushing the same chair this way and that, eying its position, then moving it once more, a good portion of his plump torso visible as usual at the neck of his loose kimono.

Sawa escaped the headmaster's wrath only because Iinuma was busy overseeing the arrangement of the platform, taking pieces of chalk from the blackboard tray and lining them up neatly. The students, wearing Kokura *hakama*, carried in the desk that was to serve as a lectern, covered it with a cloth, and then placed a pine bonsai upon it. As they did so, light from the skylight caught the tree and caused its green porcelain vase to flash and its needles to brighten as though life had suddenly quickened within it.

"What are you doing there?" Iinuma called out as he turned around on the platform to face in his son's direction. "Are you going to be quick and give us a hand or not?"

Isao's friends Izutsu and Sagara came to hear the lecture on imperial decrees, and he brought them to his room afterwards.

"Show it to us," said little Sagara, pushing back his overlarge glasses with his forefinger, his nose pointed and quivering with curiosity like that of an eager ferret.

"Just a minute. First let me tell you I happen to have plenty of money on hand, so I'll stand you to a treat later," said Isao, tantalizing his friends ingenuously. The eyes of the two boys sparkled. Isao's manner made them feel that something was about to be accomplished then and there.

His mother came with some fruit and tea, and as soon as the sound of her footsteps had faded in the corridor, Isao unlocked and opened a drawer. He took out a folded map, and spread it out on the floor. It was a map of Tokyo, parts of which were heavily shaded with a purple pencil.

"Here's how it is," said Isao, with a sigh.

"That bad?" asked Izutsu.

"Yes, that bad. The corruption has already gone this far." Isao took a shaddock from the bowl and began to rub its bright yellow lava-like skin with his hand. "If the inside of this fruit was as rotten, it wouldn't be fit to eat, and you'd have to throw it out."

Isao had used the purple pencil to indicate the presence of corruption, marking every critical spot. From the vicinity of the Imperial Palace to Nagata and throughout the entire Marunouchi area near Tokyo Station the color was a deep purple, and even the palace area itself was not without a purple tinge. The Diet Building wore a heavy coat of it, and this saturation area was linked by a dotted line to the purple mass that covered Marunouchi, the home ground of the *zaibatsu*.

"What's that?" asked Sagara, pointing to a spot of purple a little distance removed in the neighborhood of Toranomon.

"The Peers Club," Isao answered coolly. "They like to call themselves the Emperor's 'Shield of Flesh,' but they're just parasites on the Imperial Household."

In the Kasumigaseki area, as was hardly surprising, the avenue lined with government bureaus, whatever the variations of shade, was purple from one end to the other. The Foreign Ministry, the chief architect of the weak and vacillating foreign policy, had taken such severe punishment from Isao's pencil that it gave off a purple glow.

"So, this is how far the corruption has spread! And the Army Ministry, and the General Staff too!" Izutsu exclaimed, his eyes flashing and his voice surprisingly harsh and loud for his age. Izutsu's voice, however, expressed true belief, its tone one of quick and ready affirmation surging up through a channel free of all impurity.

"Of course. I put my pencil to work only where I had certain knowledge."

"I wonder what we could do to purify this all with one sweep?"

"The men of the League of the Divine Wind would disapprove perhaps, but if you want to do it all at once there is no other way but this," Isao answered. He lifted the shaddock in his hand above his head and let it fall upon the map. The shaddock struck with a dull plop and bounced heavily a single time before rolling to one side and coming to rest upon Hibiya Park. When it stopped rolling, its reflection sluggishly took form as a broad circle of pale yellow over the cocoon-shaped pond of Hibiya Park and the winding paths that surrounded it.

"I see," exclaimed Sagara, so excited that he nearly let his glasses slip from his nose. "We drop bombs from an airplane."

"That's it," answered Isao, smiling easily.

"Of course, what else?" said Izutsu. "In that case, though

Lieutenant Hori is a wonderful man, we must make contact
with somebody in the Air Corps. If we tell the plan to the
Lieutenant, he'll introduce us to the right man. I'm sure
Lieutenant Hori will soon be one of our most valuable comrades."

Izutsu's credulity was almost a thing of beauty, and Isao
allowed himself a moment to savor it. Izutsu would be obedi-
ent to the end, to any decision Isao made. His character was
such, however, that he became completely taken up with
whatever good qualities he discovered in those whom he met.
This credulity turned the world of his ideals into something
as bright and level as a meadow. Izutsu had no fear of en-
countering contradictions, and, in his world which was without complexities, evil, as he conceived it, took the flattest
imaginable form. He thought of himself, no doubt, as crushing evils like so many wafers, and here lay the source of his
rash boldness.

"All very well," said Isao, after letting Izutsu's credulity
sink in, "but as for bombs, let me remind you that Kengo
Ueno of the League of the Divine Wind wanted to use firearms, but his plan was rejected. Our ultimate reliance too
must be upon the sword. Never forget that. We can only
rely on our swords, and on bombs made of our flesh."

13

LIEUTENANT GENERAL KITO's home in Haku-
sanmae was within easy walking distance of the Academy of
Patriotism. Isao knew by heart the number of the thirty-six
stone steps that one climbed to reach the house after crossing

the stone bridge that lay at the foot of the rise upon which it stood. In the surroundings of his home, the General's manner was especially gracious. He was a widower, and he was content to entrust the running of his household entirely to his daughter Makiko, who had returned home after an unsuccessful marriage. His relations with the Academy were cordial, and since he had always shown special fondness toward Isao, Iinuma did nothing to prevent his son spending a great deal of time at the General's home, beyond warning him not to make too much of a nuisance of himself.

Whenever Isao went there with his friends, the task of entertaining the young men always fell to Makiko. Her kindness was extraordinary. The General and his daughter both assured them that, though they were to come whenever they liked, they were especially welcome just before dinner since nothing could give the two of them greater pleasure than to feed young men whose appetites so well showed their appreciation.

Makiko's manner was one of unvarying impartiality. Cheerful, gently graceful, coolly reserved, she never had a single hair out of place or the slightest disarray in dress.

Since it was a Sunday night and Isao, Sagara, and Izutsu had no particular place to go in mind, they decided to spend the evening at General Kito's. Izutsu and Sagara had persuaded Isao to forget about his promise to treat them, and to put aside the money, however little, so that it could be of some use when the time came to carry out their plan. And so the three had to go somewhere that did not require money.

Makiko met them at the entranceway, wearing a kimono of light purple serge. Isao felt a sudden chill at the sight of it, hoping that it did not recall to Izutsu and Sagara the map splotched with corruption which he had just shown them.

"Good evening. Please come right in," Makiko greeted them, her arm curved gracefully about a hall post like a handle on a delicate vase. "Father is away on a trip, but that doesn't matter. Do come in. You haven't eaten yet, I hope?"

Her manner was as cordial as ever. Then, as rain suddenly began to fall, she peered outside into the dusk and said: "What lucky young men you are!" her soft tone blending with the light rustle of rain. When she spoke like this, she sometimes seemed to be talking to herself. Isao, feeling that it would be impolite to attempt any sort of clever response, said nothing as he stepped up into the dark house.

Makiko turned on a hanging ceiling lamp in the guest parlor. But just as she was reaching up for the switch above the shade, the lamp swayed and her hand slipped. The light went on and off for an instant, and then on again. During the brief time that she stood there on tiptoe, the seductive whiteness of her *tabi*-shod feet attracted Isao's eye. He somehow felt as though he had penetrated one of this woman's secrets.

The ability of the Kito household to have ever on hand an ample selection of dishes no matter how unexpected their guests was always a source of surprise to the boys. This, however, was a long-standing custom of the household dating from the time when they had had to be prepared for the appearance at any moment of young officers with hearty appetites. Dinner was served immediately. Makiko ate with them, having the maid do the serving. Isao had never seen anyone who could eat with Makiko's grace. She bent her head supplely and moved her chopsticks with a fluid grace, holding but the smallest portion of rice or fish between them. And, furthermore, even while laughing at the boys' jokes, she nimbly finished her dinner as though skillfully attending to some small task suited to a woman.

"Shall we listen to some records?" asked Makiko when dinner was over.

The atmosphere was hot and humid, and so, despite the light shower, Makiko had the maid open the glass doors facing the porch, and they sat down by them. A mahogany-colored cabinet phonograph stood in one corner of the room. Although electric phonographs had become popular everywhere, the Kito household clung stubbornly to its imported wind-up model. Izutsu undertook the work of winding it up. Isao might well have done so himself, but Makiko was at that moment standing near the phonograph as she looked over the records, and the thought of going beside her made him hesitate.

Makiko selected a twelve-inch record with a red label, a Chopin "Nocturne" played by Cortot, and put it on the turntable. Though this was something outside of the boys' cultural background and they made no pretense of being familiar with it, they meekly gave themselves over to the selection offered to them. They began to feel as if they had slipped into agreeably chilly water and were swimming about in it. When Isao compared the quiet passivity of spirit he experienced now with his customary state at his father's Academy, he felt that the latter was like a constant masquerade.

As though to confirm this insight, the music set his mood drifting one way and then another. Vivid memories of things seen and heard during his visits to the Kito home flowed through his mind one by one, carried along by the current of piano music, each one, as though marked with a crest, bearing a small image of Makiko.

Once, on a spring afternoon while the General, Makiko, and Isao were talking, a pheasant flew down into the garden. "Oh, look! It must be from the Botanical Gardens," Makiko had exclaimed. Her cheerful voice still echoed clearly in Isao's ears. As the memory flashed before him, the womanly voice seemed to come from the crimson-winged pheasant itself. "It must be from the Botanical Gardens"—her tone seemed to suggest a luxuriantly wooded spot such as he had never seen, a domain of women.

Then the piano music caught Isao's memory again and swept it along this way and that.

On an evening in May the same voice had spoken: "I was just on my way to flower-arranging class the other morning. It had been raining for days, so I opened my umbrella and was going down the stone steps when a swallow darted by and almost flew into the umbrella. It was a close call, believe me." But when the General replied that it was indeed fortunate that she had not taken a bad tumble down the steps, Makiko protested that that was not what she meant. She had been concerned, rather, lest the swallow injure itself upon the umbrella's pointed ribs. And Isao, listening to her, instantly re-created in his mind this critical moment and its captivating circumstances. The face of a woman flashed before him, somewhat pale in the faint green light that shone through the oiled paper of her sheltering umbrella, her cheeks moist from the misty rain, her expression taut with concern. Here was the quintessential woman, a woman standing upon the precipice of womanhood. And then the swallow, secure in the woman's concern, revels in her pity, risking the ultimate as it flirts with death. Intent on wounding though it will itself be wounded, the swallow obeys a rebellious impulse, like a blade cutting through the purple irises of May, its eye upon the supreme moment. But the moment does not come. The anxiety resolves into a gentle poetic mood: a beautiful woman on her way to practice flower arranging, a darting swallow— they brush past each other and go their separate ways.

"Are you taking good care of the lilies that you received at Izagawa Shrine?" Makiko asked Isao, and her question was so direct and unexpected that Isao could only say "I beg your pardon?" in response. The record had finished.

"The lilies I was given there, the lilies you brought from Omiwa Shrine."

"No, no. I gave them all away."

"You kept not even one for yourself?"

"No."

"What a shame! No matter how withered they get, one should keep them until the next year. People say they are a safeguard against epidemics. At our house we lay them reverently on the family altar."

"Did you press them?" asked Sagara without thinking.

"No, I didn't think it would be proper to crush the flowers of the gods under a heavy object, so I put them on the altar just as they were and I've been giving them fresh water ever since."

"But they're already a month old!" Isao retorted.

"It is a marvelous thing, but they never wither to an unsightly color. I will show you. There can be no doubt that they are the flowers of the gods."

So saying, Makiko went out of the room to return in a few moments, her step slow and reverent, bearing in upraised hands a vase of white porcelain filled with a profusion of lilies. She placed them on the table for the boys to look at. The lilies certainly had withered, as cut flowers would, but they had not turned the usual ugly color as though scorched by fire. Their white had become a somber ivory. As though anemia afflicted them, the green shading of their veins had become sharply etched. Each blossom seemed to have shrunk in the same proportion. They were as though transfigured into flowers of some yet undiscovered species.

"I will give one to each of you, and you must take them home and carefully preserve them. They will guard you from sickness." With a small pair of scissors Makiko began to clip off a lily for each of them, cutting the stems close to the blossoms.

Izutsu laughed. "Even if you didn't do us this favor, we wouldn't have to worry about getting sick."

"You shouldn't talk like that, after Isao showed such devotion in bringing these lilies from Omiwa Shrine. And besides, it's not only for sickness," replied Makiko cryptically, still snipping with her scissors.

Embarrassed at the prospect of having to go over to accept a flower from a woman, Isao remained obstinately by the porch. He sensed something he could not define about the now-silent Makiko, and, without realizing what he was doing, he looked at her. As she leaned upon the rosewood table that held the vase, her profile was turned toward him. At that moment, Isao knew she was fully aware that his eyes were upon her profile.

Seeing his two friends standing close to her, ready to take their lilies, he spoke out as though threatening them, his outlandish tone altogether unsuited to the setting: "Listen to me, you two. If in Japan today you could kill only one man, who do you think it would be best to kill? The sort, that is, whose murder would be at least a step toward the purification of Japan."

"Jugoro Itsui?" replied Sagara, turning the lily Makiko had given him in his fingertips.

"Don't be stupid. He has money, but he's unimportant."

"What about Baron Shinkawa?" asked Izutsu as he came over to Isao to hand him the lily that he had taken for him. His eyes were flashing.

"If you could kill ten, I rather think he'd be one of them. But he's only an opportunist. He's learned something from the May Fifteenth Incident, and he trims his sails to suit whatever wind is blowing. Naturally, he deserves punishment as a traitor."

"Premier Saito?"

"He'd surely be one if you killed five. But Saito stands in front of a black curtain that hides the world of big money. And who's behind that curtain?"

"Oh! Busuké Kurahara?"

"He's the one," answered Isao decisively, as he quickly slipped the lily Izutsu had given him into his kimono. "Kill him and Japan is much the better for it."

Even as he spoke, Isao's eyes held fast to the sight, as though at a far distance, of a woman's slender white hand curved upon a rosewood table and a pair of scissors giving off a sparkle like flashing water beneath the lamp. Makiko's practice was never to obtrude upon the boys' conversation among themselves, but she could hardly fail to note from Isao's manner that he wanted her to be aware of what he was saying. The look she turned toward him was warm with a maternal affection, but her eyes had a distant focus to them, as though she was perhaps looking beyond him into the garden outside, seeking out the last of the blood-red glow of the setting sun all but concealed by the wet foliage of the garden shrubbery.

"Evil blood," said Makiko, "is blood that cries to be shed. And those who shed it may indeed heal our country's sickness. Those cowards who now stand at the bedside of our stricken nation do nothing but wring their hands piteously. Japan will die if the issue is left to them."

Makiko's tone was as light as if she were reciting a poem. Isao felt his grim tautness ease.

Hearing the sound of heavy panting behind him and of something coming through the grass, Isao glanced back over his shoulder. He felt embarrassed at the quickening of his heartbeat. A stray dog had probably slipped into the rainy garden. The unpleasant snuffling noise it made as it pushed its muzzle through the vegetation confirmed this impression.

14

LITTLE RAIN MARKED the latter half of the rainy season. Day after day the skies, heavy with brownish gray clouds, persisted in trapping the sunshine, but finally they cleared. The colleges began their summer vacation.

Isao received a postcard from Lieutenant Hori with a message scrawled with a thick, coarse lead pencil. He had found *The League of the Divine Wind* quite stimulating, he wrote, and since he wanted to share it with his friends, he was keeping the book at the regimental headquarters. He would be happy to see Isao any time that he wished to come to retrieve it.

Isao went one afternoon to visit the Lieutenant at the garrison of the Azabu Third Regiment. The barracks and parade ground lay transfixed by the glare of the summer sun.

Off to the right of the main gate as one entered stood the conspicuously modern barracks that the regiment so prized. But, rather than this, the dust that swirled up beyond the trees by the drill field and the smell that came drifting from a stable somewhere were the qualities that most conveyed the sense of *army* that permeated all that Isao saw spread out before him, qualities that merged with the consecrated fame of the regiment to rise up into the dust-laden sky.

As Isao passed through the gate, a platoon drilling in a distant corner of the parade ground caught his eye at once, the figures of the men like so many upright khaki crayons beneath the blazing afternoon sun.

A private first class on guard showed him the way. "Lieutenant Hori is drilling some trainees over there. They should finish in about twenty minutes," he said. "You can watch if you like."

Isao followed the private across the parade ground, feeling the sun's heat pressing down upon him. Everything lay sharply etched beneath its rays. When the two at length came up to the platoon, the brass of the soldiers' buttons and regimental "3's" flashing in the sun and the massed red collar patches of the infantry stood out in vivid contrast from the khaki mass.

The men were now marching straight ahead and the thumping echo of their booted feet was like the champing of massive teeth. Lieutenant Hori held his drawn saber at his right shoulder, and as he bellowed the commands of close-order drill, his voice soared over the ranks of silent men like a fierce bird of prey.

"Platoon right . . ." came the warning command, fol-

lowed a moment later by the command to execute: "March!"
At that instant, the pivot man on the inside file immediately
turned his sweaty face to the right, and for the next few paces
marched in place as he waited for the outside file to perform
its wide turn. The other files in the meantime seemed to open
up like wide-spaced picket fences only to come together again
with the ease of a folding fan closing.

"Squads on line left . . . march!"

At the Lieutenant's shouted command, the formation dissolved without an instant's delay, and the troops rushed forward with mathematical precision to form a single rank
pivoting upon the guidon bearer. And when the maneuver
was completed with the file on the outside flank moving up
into position, the platoon resumed its forward march.

"By the right flank . . . march!"

The Lieutenant's virile shouts, accompanied by the flashing
of his saber, were like shots discharged into the summer sky.
The long rank changed its line of march again. Now as the
men drew away from him, Isao could see their backs, the
shirts stained and darkened with sweat. From the strain so
evident in the set of their shoulders, Isao realized what frantic
effort they were putting into checking the harsh breathing
provoked by the maneuver just accomplished.

"Fall out!" shouted the Lieutenant. And with that he turned
and ran back to Isao's direction before pulling up abruptly to
shout: "Fall in!" While the Lieutenant was running, Isao
saw beneath his black visor, which was glinting in the sunlight, beads of sweat flying from the sunburnt bridge of his
nose and from his tight-set lips.

The soldiers, too, in accordance with their officer's new
position, came rushing toward Isao as though racing one
another, and, after the maneuvers that had taken them so
far off, formed up in two ranks right before Isao, jostling one
another in their eager haste.

After inspecting their order with severe thoroughness, the
Lieutenant once more barked out the commands "Fall out!"

and "Fall in!" Clutching their rifles, the men dashed over the sun-baked earth. The commands were repeated over and over. Sometimes the area just beside Isao and the private was ravaged by a whirlwind of dust and sweat and the smell of leather and the laboring breaths of some twenty men. Afterward the dry ground lay darkened with drops of sweat. Dark splotches also covered the Lieutenant's back where he now stood some distance away from Isao.

Beneath a summer sky encircled by a low bank of distant, dreamlike clouds, oblivious to the thick and lovely shade cast by the trees bordering the drill field, the little band of soldiers performed like a finely tuned engine as they fell in, fell out, changed direction, and altered formation. They seemed to be moved by a giant, unseen hand reaching down from above. That hand could only belong to the sun itself, Isao thought. The Lieutenant was no more than a lone representative of that hand which manipulated the soldiers as it willed, and when one thought in such terms, even his powerful voice took on a hollow ring. The unseen hand which shifted pawns about on a chessboard—in the very sun above was the force that guided it, the blazing sun which dealt out death, too, whenever it wished. Here was the power of the Emperor himself.

Only on this drill ground was the hand of the sun working with a mathematical clarity and precision. Only here! The will of the Emperor penetrated the sweat, the blood, the very flesh of these young men, piercing their bodies like X-rays. From high above the entranceway of regimental headquarters, the golden chrysanthemum of the imperial crest, brilliant in the sunshine, looked down upon this beautiful, sweaty, intricate choreography of death.

And elsewhere? Elsewhere throughout Japan the rays of the sun were blocked.

When the drill was finished, Lieutenant Hori, his creaking leather puttees white with dust, came over to Isao. "Glad to see you here," he said and then dismissed the private: "Very good. I'll take over now."

They began to walk toward a huge yellowish oval-shaped building.

"What do you think of it?" asked the Lieutenant proudly. "The most modern barracks in Japan. It even has an elevator."

As they were going up the stone steps that led to the entrance facing the stables, Lieutenant Hori remarked: "I gave them quite a workout today. But I imagine you could tell they were recruits."

"No, I didn't notice anything at all go wrong."

"Oh? Well, we let them take a siesta in the summer. And afterwards when you give them a workout like that, you really wake them up."

As a company officer, Lieutenant Hori worked in the third-floor room assigned to the officers of the First Battalion. The room was austere, with five or six sets of the protective gear used in bayonet practice hanging upon one of its walls. His desk was by a window, and the straw stuffing had begun to project from the upholstery of his chair. While the Lieutenant stripped off his jacket and went out to wipe away his sweat, Isao looked down from the window at the oval inner courtyard of the building. An orderly brought in tea and left it on the desk.

A detachment of soldiers was at bayonet practice in the courtyard, and the sound of their exertion seemed to thrust itself up past the window. Six exits fronted by stone steps opened into the courtyard. On this side the building had four floors with one level half underground, but on the opposite side there were only three, including the one half underground. Large white numerals were painted over each of the doors. Three gingko trees stretched out their full-leafed branches, something almost menacing in their manner. White buds hung from the tips of the branches of the many Himalayan cedars with not a breeze to stir them.

The Lieutenant made his appearance again, dressed in a short-sleeved white shirt, and after he had thirstily gulped down his tea, he called the orderly and told him to bring more.

"All right then," he said to Isao, "let me give you back your book." He casually reached into the drawer of his desk, took out *The League of the Divine Wind*, and laid it down in front of Isao.

"And what did you think of it?"

"It really moved me. And now I understand more how you feel. You've got that same spirit, haven't you? But I'd like to put one question to you," said the Lieutenant with a faintly ironic smile. "When it comes time for you to fight somebody, are you going to be like the League and pick the Imperial Army?"

"Of course not."

"All right, who then?"

"I thought that, if nobody else, Lieutenant Hori at least understood us. The real foe of the League was not the Army. There was something that lurked behind the troops of the garrison—and that was the budding military clique. It was the militarists whom the men of the League saw as their enemy and took the field against. For they firmly believed that the army of the militarists was not the army of the gods. They believed that their own League of the Divine Wind was the Emperor's army."

Before replying, the Lieutenant glanced around the room. He and Isao were alone.

"All right, all right, but one doesn't shout out things like that for everyone to hear." The loyalty and affection evident in the Lieutenant's words made Isao's spirits soar.

"But there's no one else here. Now that I'm with you, sir, I can't help pouring out all the things that have been building up within me. The men of the League fought only with the Japanese sword, and we, too, I feel, when the supreme test comes, must depend upon the sword alone. Still, if our plan is going to be on a large scale, there's room for other approaches . . . Would there be any chance of your introducing us to an officer in the Air Corps?"

"Why?"

"So that we can have support from the sky, to have the key points bombed."

The Lieutenant only snarled in response, but he did not seem especially angry.

"Somebody must take action. If not, Japan is lost. There is nothing else to be done if the heart of the Emperor is to be put at rest."

"Don't jabber about grave matters," said the Lieutenant, his voice suddenly harsh.

Isao realized, however, that the Lieutenant had no animosity toward him, and meekly apologized: "I was wrong. I'm sorry."

Had the Lieutenant, Isao wondered, perceived something that lay within him? Yes, the Lieutenant's fierce gaze must have penetrated the very soul of a boy not long out of high school. And Lieutenant Hori, from what Isao had heard of him, was no man to be swayed by considerations of age or rank.

Isao well knew that his words were immature, but his determination made up for their deficiency. He had been supremely confident that his own inner fire would provoke flames in the man opposite him. And then, too, it was summer. The two of them sat facing each other in heat as smothering and oppressive as a heavy wool garment. It was as though even a spark would set off a conflagration or, for want of a spark, the heat would simply melt everything down to a pitiful remnant like metal in a furnace. Isao had to seize this opportunity.

"Since you were kind enough to visit me," said the Lieutenant, breaking the silence, "suppose we do something to forget the heat. How about going over to the drill hall and running through the kendo forms without masks? Sometimes I practice that way with one of the sergeants. There's nothing better for strengthening your will."

"Yes, sir, I like that kind of practice," Isao readily agreed.

Among the military, winning or losing took on critical significance, and so Lieutenant Hori no doubt rarely competed seriously, because of his comrades' eyes upon him. At any rate, the thought that the Lieutenant wished to communicate with him through the sword was pleasant to Isao.

Surrounded by the aged wooden walls of the drill hall, Isao felt a congenial shiver. Three pairs of men were practicing kendo, but he could tell at once that they were novices. Their handling of the staves was flurried, and their footwork erratic.

"Take a break, all of you," the Lieutenant shouted unceremoniously. "I'm going to do the forms with this visitor. Watch us and you'll learn something."

Isao stepped out on the floor wearing a borrowed kendo suit and holding a borrowed stave of hard wood. The six reduced to spectators took off their masks and sat down on the floor attentively in a neat line. After he had made his obeisance to the gods, he stepped forward to face the Lieutenant. Lieutenant Hori was to take the offensive role and Isao the defensive.

The rays of the sun poured down from the high windows on the western side of the hall and the polished floor beneath shone as though spread with a glistening oil, as the insistent chant of cicadas outside wound round the building. The boards, hot beneath the soles of the feet, had a good spring to them, their smooth resilience like that of pounded rice cake.

The two squatted down facing each other for the opening ritual of touching the tips of their kendo staves together. Then they rose and held their staves at middle position. Though blending with the song of the cicada, every sound seemed to strike the ear with an intense clarity, even the faint rustle of the pleats of their *hakama*.

Isao quickly sized up the Lieutenant's stance. The impression he received was one of hearty magnanimity. Somehow, too, there was a touch of bold negligence to his bearing which saved it from being rigidly orthodox. And the glimpse of his chest visible at the loosely fastened neck of his faded blue jacket increased the sense of vitality that the Lieutenant gave off, as fresh as the early morning air of a summer's day. His ease and lack of strain marked him as an outstanding swordsman.

Each of them moved his stave to his right, retreated five short paces, and lowered it to complete the salutation. Then began the first round. Once again they faced off, and, after the initial confrontation at middle position, the Lieutenant raised his sword to high left and Isao, his to high right, and they advanced steadily toward each other.

"Yaah!" Lieutenant Hori shouted as he moved forward on his right foot and swung straight for the head with his stave.

This first vigorous blow came down toward Isao's head with the suddenness of a burst of hailstones. The wooden stave concentrated all its power on a single spot, and it was there that the heavy, thick, woolly garment of heat was ripped asunder. An instant before Isao would have taken the Lieutenant's blow he moved his left foot to retreat a step, drew his own stave back further in the upper right position, and then brought it down toward his opponent's head as he shouted: "Toh!"

The Lieutenant's eyes glared fiercely. Isao's stave came whistling down, aimed directly at the top of the Lieutenant's close-cropped head. At the same moment, their eyes met, and Isao sensed a communication pass between them too swift for any words. The Lieutenant's jaw and the bridge of his nose had been burnt relentlessly by the sun day after day, but the skin of his forehead, protected by the visor of his cap, was light, which made his eyebrows more prominent. And it was this white forehead that Isao's stave threatened with a stroke of shattering force. Just before the blow would have landed, at the instant the stave stopped in midair, an intuitive force swifter than light passed between the two of them.

After checking the blow aimed at the Lieutenant's head and making a thrust at his throat, Isao coolly raised his sword to the upper left position, showing himself prepared to receive another attack.

So ended the first round. The two faced off once more at middle position, and the second round began.

After they had poured water over themselves to wash away their sweat and were on their way back to the barracks, the Lieutenant, still young himself and at the moment feeling especially cheerful and vigorous, spoke to Isao as though they were equals. His newly gained experience of Isao's kendo ability no doubt further prompted this familiarity.

"Have you ever heard much about Prince Harunori Toin?"

"No, sir."

"He's now a regimental commander in Yamaguchi. He's a splendid man. He was trained in the Imperial Horse Guards, and so I was in a different branch, but just after I was commissioned, a classmate at the Academy took me along to an audience with the Prince, and he showed me real cordiality. It was 'Hori this' and 'Hori that.' He's a man of determination, and he especially likes to hear about young men's aspirations. He takes good care of those who serve under him, and there's nothing arrogant about him—a prince of the Imperial Family and a brave and splendid soldier. What do you say—should I ask for an audience for you? If we could let him see that there were young men like you around, I'm sure His Highness would be delighted."

"Yes, sir. Please do."

Isao was not especially exhilarated at the prospect of meeting such an august personage. But because he realized that

this was a mark of the Lieutenant's special favor, he acquiesced.

"His Highness will be in Tokyo for four or five days
during the summer, and he's told me to come see him then.
When I do, I'll take you along," said Lieutenant Hori.

15

MARQUIS MATSUGAE, who had some time before
disposed of Chung-nan Villa in Kamakura and now spent his
summers at Karuizawa, received an invitation to a banquet
at the huge Karuizawa villa of Baron Shinkawa. Its arrival
provoked but a single thought in the Marquis, one that he
was extremely reluctant to face. Though all of the other invited guests were "targets," Marquis Matsugae alone among
them was no one's target.

No anonymous threatening letters or even letters of a
milder sort had come to Marquis Matsugae from radicals on
either the right or left. Past sixty and a member of the House
of Peers, the Marquis had always been quick to lend a hand
in shelving whatever proposed bills had the least radical
flavor about them, but no one seemed to have noted this.
When the Marquis looked back upon the past, he realized
that, strangely enough, the only attack that he had sustained
had been the peculiar essay that Iinuma had published and
signed nineteen years before in a right-wing paper. As he
reflected upon the unnatural period of calm that had continued uninterrupted since then, the Marquis was drawn to
speculate that someone was working behind the scenes to pro-

tect him, someone who was none other than his former attacker, Iinuma.

It was a line of reasoning injurious to the Marquis's pride. Then, too, the more he thought about his situation, the more absurd it seemed to him. Because of the influence his rank commanded, it would be a simple matter for him to discover the true circumstances. But if his speculation was correct, he would find himself greatly in Iinuma's debt, and his position would become still more untenable. And if the speculation was unfounded, he would be shamed by the realization that he had, after all, been capable of provoking rancor in no one.

Baron Shinkawa's banquets were always showy affairs. The bodyguards assigned to guests were served their own meal during the banquet in a room immediately adjoining, and they made almost as large a group as those invited. Thus in the Shinkawa villa two meals progressed at the same time, so different in the number and quality of courses as to make ordinary comparisons impossible. Of these two banquets, when one took into consideration such points as the indescribably seedy look of the suits worn by the detectives, their sharp, restless eyes and coarse features, their manner of eating in silence and turning their heads like surly hunting dogs in the direction of the slightest noise, the uninhibited way in which they rushed to take up toothpicks after the meal and poke earnestly about their mouths, one would have to judge the detectives' banquet a superior spectacle. But, sadly enough, a bodyguard for Marquis Matsugae was not there among them.

The Marquis had no hopes of remedying this shameful situation by resorting to artifice. For the police had declared in unequivocal terms that there was no threat to the Marquis's personal welfare, and so if he demanded a guard on his own initiative, he would only make himself look ridiculous.

The matter had implications that the Marquis found extremely distasteful. For the era was such that a man's power was measured in terms of the danger that stalked him.

And so, though the Shinkawa villa was within easy walking distance, the Marquis took pains, at least, to be driven there in his Lincoln. Marquise Matsugae carried folded upon her lap a small wool blanket on account of the arthritis that affected her husband's right knee. For the Shinkawas liked to entertain their guests by serving the before-dinner drinks outside until the sun had set and the air grown chilly. And all this time, scattered among the white birches that filled the Shinkawas' broad garden laid out to exploit the view of Mount Asama, the bodyguards would stand until their figures faded to crudely cut silhouettes. They had been instructed to remain inconspicuous, but this only made them seem like lurking assassins intent upon the guests who were sipping apéritifs in the garden.

Baron Shinkawa had already passed his fiftieth year. In the surroundings of his Edwardian villa, the Baron was accustomed to reading the editorials in the *Times* each morning before turning to the Japanese newspapers. And like an English colonial official he would wear one or another of his half-dozen white linen suits every day. As for the Baroness, her intrinsic bent for chattering about herself had remained unchanged through the years. The lady was blessed with the ability to discover in herself ever fresh sources of wonder, though she was at the same time able to forego discovering that she was in fact little by little growing fat.

The Baroness had had quite enough of "New Thought." The Heavenly Fire Group too, which had championed the Blue Stocking movement, had long since disbanded. The occasion for her perceiving the danger of "New Thought" was the suicide of her niece, who came out of a women's college to join the Communist Party and, the very evening she returned home after being released from prison on bail, slashed her jugular vein.

However, since Baroness Shinkawa was as overflowing with energy as ever, she simply could not think of herself as being a member of a class "on its way to destruction."

When her husband, a chillingly cynical man who saw nothing as worth fighting for, was put on the right-wing blacklist, and she found that both far right and far left looked upon the two of them as their sworn foes, she felt as if she and her husband were fair-skinned people of a higher civilization compelled to live in some barbarian land. On the one hand she found the situation stimulating, on the other, she longed "to go home" to London.

"This Japan, it's an altogether distasteful place, don't you think?" the Baroness had taken to observing from time to time. Once a friend of hers who had been to India told her that an Indian acquaintance had lost her son when the boy plunged his hand into a toy box and was bitten by a poisonous snake hiding in the bottom of it. "That's just how things are here in Japan," the Baroness had commented. "All one has to do is plunge one's hand in, intent only on a bit of amusement, and there's a poisonous snake in there waiting. Ready to bite and kill a person who has done nothing to it, an innocent, harmless person."

The evening was clear, and as the cry of cicadas echoed quietly across the lawn a distant rumble of thunder came from one corner of the sky. The guests, five married couples, were gathered in the garden. Marquis Matsugae sat in a rattan chair, and the brilliant red of the plaid blanket that his wife was arranging over his knees gave a touch of color to the dusk sweeping over the garden.

"I think it's hardly likely that one or two more months will pass without the government's recognizing Manchukuo," said one man, who was the Minister of State. "For the Prime Minister really intends to do just that." After which, turning to Marquis Matsugae, he remarked pleasantly: "That matter of Count Momoshima's son which we spoke of, is it proceeding well?"

The Marquis uttered a noncommittal grunt. "This fellow,"

he thought, "he talks to the others about Manchukuo, and then asks me about my adopting a son. What effrontery!"

After Kiyoaki's death Marquis and Marquise Matsugae would not hear of adopting an heir, but lately they no longer felt the will to resist the arguments of the Bureau of Estates. Preliminary negotiations were now under way.

Mount Asama rose in the failing light, visible through a break in the trees where a path led down to a stream. It was hard to determine from which direction the distant thunder came. The guests, however, enjoyed watching the shadow of evening steal over their hands and faces while the thunder afforded the further pleasure of thrilling to a peril far removed from them.

"Well, since all the other ladies and gentlemen have arrived, I imagine that it must be just about time for Mr. Kurahara to make his appearance," Baron Shinkawa remarked to his wife, loudly enough for everyone to hear and join in the laughter.

It had become Busuké Kurahara's invariable practice to arrive last, a never-excessive tardiness that bespoke the immensity of his power.

He seemed totally indifferent to his personal appearance, without a hint that this might be a pose, and his inability to speak otherwise than with a stiff formality was rather appealing. He certainly in no way resembled the monopolistic capitalist who appeared in left-wing cartoons. When he sat down, he had the habit of choosing the chair upon which he had just laid his hat. The second button of his suit coat had a great affinity for the third buttonhole. He left off arranging his tie well before it was tucked beneath his collar. At the banquet table, he inevitably reached out to his right to seize the roll on his neighbor's bread dish.

Busuké Kurahara spent his summer weekends in Karuizawa and all the others at Izusan, where he owned a tangerine orchard of five or six acres. He took pride in the luster of his tangerines and their sweet taste, and derived much pleasure from making gifts of them not only to his friends but to orphanages and welfare hospitals. It was hard to realize that he was indeed the object of widespread resentment.

No doubt it seemed astonishing that a man so cheerful in his private life could hold such dourly pessimistic views on public affairs. The guests gathered in Baron Shinkawa's garden, however, were always thrilled and titillated to hear from the mouth of Japan's supreme capitalist accounts of tragedy, of dire foreboding, and of evils to come.

More than the death of Prime Minister Inukai, Kurahara mourned the retirement of Finance Minister Takahashi. Prime Minister Saito, of course, had no sooner formed his cabinet than he was paying a call on Kurahara and protesting, perhaps a bit too much, that he could do nothing without Kurahara's cooperation. Nevertheless, Kurahara sniffed something unsavory in the new prime minister's manner.

Takahashi had indeed been an insider of the Inukai Cabinet which had imposed another embargo on the export of gold as one of its first acts, but, secretly influenced by classical hard-currency advocates, he acted to sabotage this newfangled government policy so that he could then contend that since this policy had not lived up to expectations and provided quick relief, since conditions were no better and prices still in the doldrums, failure to such a degree proved that the old ways were after all the best.

Baron Shinkawa, on the other hand, who avidly kept up with all that went on in London, had closely studied in the *Times* the details of England's going off the gold standard in September of the previous year and had made up his mind at once. The Wakatsuki Cabinet had kept proclaiming that it would never enact an embargo on the export of gold, but with every government proclamation, dollar speculation had increased, despite the anger of the right wing, who branded all dollar buyers as plunderers of the nation. The Baron himself had been a dollar speculator, but after he had stored away all the money that would not bear scrutiny into Swiss banks, he was unwilling to wait for an overnight shift in government policy, and came to the side of those supporting the gold export embargo and the policy of "reflation." Thus he had had enough of the halfway economic measures of the previous cabinet, and his hopes were bound up with the new cabinet. Beyond the issue of internal recovery through reflation lay the glittering prospect of the industrialization of Manchuria. Though the Baron's air was as abstracted as ever, here in the midst of Karuizawa, whose volcanic soil was so barren of resources, the image of the underground wealth of Manchukuo rose up in his mind like a seductive phantom, those resources that were as rich and varied as a menu of the Café Royale. Surely, the Baron thought, he could even kindle an affection for stupid soldiers.

Years before, Baroness Shinkawa had found it hard to countenance men carrying on a discussion all to themselves, but, as she grew older, her feelings altered. Now she was quite willing to let the men carry on with their talk, provided that the women were able to function as overseers.

"Well, they're already well into it," she said, turning to Mrs. Kurahara, Marquise Matsugae, and the other ladies, after noticing the men gathered around Kurahara. Marquise Matsugae's eyebrows, whose tilt gave her face its sorrowful look, grew almost over to her hair, now noticeably gray and brushed down over her ears.

"Just this spring," Baroness Shinkawa chatted on, "I wore a kimono to an affair at the British Embassy, and the Ambassador, who had only seen me in Western clothes, simply could not get over it. He outdid himself with his compliments, protesting how becoming a kimono was to me and all that. Really, how frustrating! Even a man of his refinement—he never notices Japanese women except as Japanese women. Of course, the kimono I wore that night, at the suggestion of my designer, was like a Momoyama Nō costume, red with a snow-covered willow and butterfly circle pattern, the whole thing worked in gold and silver lacquer thread, obviously quite showy. Because it flashed so brightly, I felt no more Japanese than if I were wearing Western clothes." Intent on being hospitable, the Baroness began by offering herself as a topic of conversation.

"Junko, perhaps the Ambassador meant stunning clothing was becoming to you," said the wife of the Minister of State. "When you wear Western clothes you're not so daring, indeed you tend to be rather restrained."

"How true!" replied Junko Shinkawa, quick to agree. "The colors of Western clothes are really so sober. And if one does wear some sort of gaudy flower pattern, it only makes one look older, like some grandmother from Wales."

"But that dress is such a lovely color, Junko," said Marquise Matsugae, offering the flattery that circumstances made imperative. The truth was that all that concerned the Marquise at the moment was the pain in her husband's knee. This was a pain that seemed to her somehow associated with the pain that affected the entire Matsugae household, a malady that seemed on the verge of discommoding the joints of everyone involved. The Marquise gave a quick glance in the direction of her husband sitting with the blanket over his knees. The man who in the past had seemed so frank and unconstrained, so fond of monopolizing the conversation, now listened quietly to what people had to say.

Since it was Baron Shinkawa's practice scrupulously to avoid controversy, he prodded Viscount Matsudaira to take on Kurahara. The Viscount was a young man who agreed with him and who, furthermore, was not in a position of real responsibility. And so this naughty boy, a member of the House of Peers and on friendly terms with the military, turned to Kurahara, his manner one of calm challenge.

"I don't especially care for all this talk about whatever we do, we're in danger, that this is a time of crisis, and so on," said Viscount Matsudaira. "Everything has started to take a turn for the better. The May Fifteenth Incident was a tragic event, of course, but it has given the government the strength to act decisively so that Japan can be pulled out of this economic slump. And in the last analysis, I think that it will have the effect of putting Japan upon the right course. It will be this affair that changes our fortune from bad to good. Isn't it in such a manner, after all, that history moves forward?"

"We will indeed be happy if it turns out as you say," answered Kurahara plaintively, a quiet gruffness to his voice. "I, for one, have no such expectations. What is this reflation, after all? It can be termed a controlled inflation, the idea being that although the fierce beast of inflation is let out of his cage we can still breathe easily because he has a chain fastened to his neck. But that chain is not going to hold long. The vital thing is not to let the beast out of the cage. I can well imagine how things might go—save the farmer, rescue the unemployed, introduce reflation—all of which seem splendid at first, and no one wants to sing a contrary tune. But soon reflation will turn into an inflation based on the demand for military supplies. The fierce beast will snap his chain and run wild. And once he starts, no one will be able to stop him. When the military itself finally awakes to the peril, it will be too late to catch him again. The wise course, therefore, is to keep him shut in the shiny cage of gold reserves. For nothing could be more secure than such a golden cage. It has a tough flexibility. If the beast grows larger, the space between the bars grows larger. If he grows smaller, it narrows. If we keep our specie reserves adequate, we prevent a falling off of our exchange rate, and we gain the confidence of other nations. That is the only way for Japan to get along in the world. If you let the fierce beast out of his cage as a means of bringing about a recovery, you achieve only the most transitory of results and you dash Japan's long-range hopes. However, even though what should be done, given this enactment of a second gold embargo, is to adopt a vigorous policy of strengthening the currency by supporting it with specie, with the aim of promptly returning to the gold standard, still, the government has been scared out of its wits by the May Fifteenth Incident and is rushing in the opposite direction. That is why I worry."

"This is merely my opinion," said the Viscount, unwilling to be shaken off, "but if the hardship of the farmers and the discontent of the workers continue as they are, it won't be a matter of anything as mild as the May Fifteenth Incident. A revolution may well break out, and then it will be too late for all remedies. Did you see the farmers who pushed their way into the special session of the Diet in June? Are you aware of the strength embodied in the groups that presented the petition demanding an immediate moratorium on farmers' debts? Furthermore, when they didn't get what they wanted from the Diet, they went to the Army, and the result was that a joint petition of farmers and military men was drawn up and a report of it carried to the Throne itself by a regimental commander.

"And then you said, sir, that attempting recovery through reflation would offer only a temporary advantage, but if the economy does become inflated, effective domestic demand will increase. Then with the drop in the interest rate, small businessmen and manufacturers will get a new lease on life. By opening up Manchuria, our development will proceed on the continent. With the increase in military expense, the construction of heavy industry and chemical plants will be stimulated. The price of rice will go up, and the rural communities will be saved and the jobless farmers put back to work—all in all, a multitude of good effects, don't you think? Wouldn't it be well for us, while taking pains to avoid the danger of war, to advance our industrialization step by step? If I were to propose the plan I thought ideal, this would be it."

"The young are optimistic," said Kurahara. "But older men, because of the knowledge that the years have brought them, find it hard to entertain such bright expectations. I hear 'the farmers, the farmers,' from you, but that's mere sentimentality and has no bearing on the nation's plight. At a time when every citizen must grit his teeth and endure hardship, these complaints that disrupt the national unity—'Oh, the villainy of the upper classes! Oh, the villainy of the financiers!'—all come from the mouths of self-seeking men.

"Just think for a moment. The rice riots of 1918 made us aware that the Country of Abundant Rice could be imperiled by want, but now, with the increased yield from the crops of Taiwan and Korea, there's more than a generous supply of rice throughout the country, is there not? And since all our citizens, aside from the farmers, have benefited from the sharp drop in farm prices and so have no worries about buying what food they need, there's been no upsurge of the revolutionary spirit preached by the left wing, despite the high unemployment rate that this severe depression has brought about. As for the farmers themselves, they're not at all the sort to listen to the blandishments of the left wing, no matter how much threatened they are by starvation."

"But aren't incidents always begun by military men?" the Viscount retorted. "And isn't the Army an Army sprung from the farming villages?"

Though the young man's assertive manner might well have struck the onlookers as somewhat lacking in deference, Kurahara was not one to be provoked into an emotional response. His words, ever controlled, ever preserving the same inflection, flowed from his lips like the white pennants issuing from the mouths of the saints and sinners in medieval religious prints. Since Kurahara was drinking a Manhattan, the moisture that wet his lips served to smooth and sweeten his hoarse voice. A smile seemed to be on the verge of flickering over his stern features, and when he put the red cherry on its toothpick between his lips, he seemed to be swallowing with it the batch of concerns that were then troubling society.

"But on the other hand," said Kurahara, in gentle rebuttal, "isn't the Army feeding the able-bodied sons of poor farmers? Comparing last year's disastrous crop with the record harvest of two years ago, I cannot help but suspect a touch of sabotage on the part of those farmers vehemently opposed to the use of foreign-grown rice."

"If they did anything of the sort, wouldn't they risk starving themselves to death?" the smooth-cheeked Viscount asked.

"Well, at any rate," said Kurahara, not answering the question put to him, "however one may analyze the present situation, I have been talking with an eye to the future. The citizens of Japan—what sort of a people are they? I imagine that, depending upon whom you ask, you would receive all sorts of definitions. But as for me, I would reply that the citizens of Japan constitute a race blind to the dire perils of inflation. A race that, when inflation strikes, lacks even the wisdom to turn its money into property to protect itself. It behooves us never to forget for a single moment that this people with whom we have to deal constitute a naïve and ignorant, a passionate and emotional citizenry. There is a certain beauty in a nation's lacking even the wisdom to preserve itself. Indeed, an undeniable beauty. And because I love the people of Japan, I cannot help but hate those who would exploit this beautiful ignorance in order to gain popular favor.

"Stringent economic measures are never popular, and any government policy that embraces inflation is sure to gain the favor of the people. For our part, however—we who know what is the ultimate happiness of this ignorant race of ours— we must strive with this ever in mind even if a certain number of people unavoidably are victimized."

"The ultimate happiness of the people, you say. What is that?" asked the Viscount aggressively.

"Don't you know?" asked Kurahara tantalizingly, tilting his head slightly to one side as a smile lit his features. His intent listeners, under his spell despite themselves, tilted their own heads. The trunks of the white birches outside seemed restless in the long twilight, like the pale shins of a row of young boys. The evening darkness was a huge throw-net cast over the lawn. At that moment all present confronted the glittering phantom of ultimate happiness like men about to receive a revelation. When Kurahara spoke, it was as though, before their very eyes, a giant fish leapt up vigorously from the tightening net of evening, its golden scales flashing.

"You don't know, eh? Well . . . it happens to be a stable currency."

So struck was his audience that they stood speechless as shudders of uncertain dread ran down the backs of their necks. Kurahara took no notice of the reaction that he had provoked. Like a thin varnish, a light coat of sadness seemed to spread gradually over his compassionate expression.

"It's peculiar about secrets. For the very reason that certain things are so simple, so well known, they become secrets. Be that as it may, those of us who know this secret have, indeed, a heavy responsibility laid upon us.

"And though we lead this ignorant people, persisting in their ignorance, step by step along the path that leads to the ultimate happiness, they become disheartened by its steepness. They give ready ear to the devil that whispers: 'Look here, see how much easier this path is.' And when they look and see how delightful a path the other is with a profusion of flowers blooming along it, they make a headlong rush for it and end by plunging down into the abyss of ruin.

"Since economics is not a benevolent enterprise, one must foresee that some ten percent will become victims while the remaining ninety percent will be saved. But if we take no hand at all, the full hundred percent will go happily to their destruction."

"I presume, then," replied Viscount Matsudaira, "that the ten percent who are the farmers must reconcile themselves to death by starvation?"

The Viscount had been rash enough to speak of starving to death, and such a choice of words before such a gathering was not likely to have the effect he wished. Certain words seem empty but forbiddingly moral. Even without an adjective, they contain an intrinsic element of exaggeration. From the standpoint of taste, they leave much to be desired, being far too strident and having by their very nature the ring of radicalism. As well he might, the Viscount felt embarrassed for having been so imprudent.

While Kurahara had been eloquently holding forth, the French maître d'hôtel had come to whisper in the Baroness's ear that dinner was ready to be served, but the Baroness had no choice but to wait until Kurahara's zest for his own conversation began to pall. When she was at last able to break in, Kurahara rose from his chair. And there on the seat, visible despite the thickening darkness, was a silver cigarette case which lay open to reveal its contents arrayed like a row of white teeth, thoroughly crushed, however, by Kurahara's bulk.

"Oh no! Not again!" cried his wife when she saw this, and everyone laughed heartily, as they always did at Kurahara's idiosyncrasies.

"Really," said Mrs. Kurahara, picking up the crushed cigarettes, "how could you!"

"I've had trouble before with its coming open so easily."

"But, my goodness! Couldn't you feel it underneath you?"

"That's the sort of thing only Mr. Kurahara could carry off, I believe," said Baroness Shinkawa teasingly as she made her way through the patches of brightness that spilled out onto the lawn from the windows.

"I still don't understand. Surely it must have hurt you, open like that," said Mrs. Kurahara.

"I thought it was just the rattan chair."

"Yes, yes, that's true. Our rattan chairs do cause some pain," exclaimed the Baroness, provoking more laughter from the guests.

"Still and all," offered Baron Shinkawa, his manner abstracted as ever, "they're far better than the ones in that mo-

tion picture house." There was an old movie theater in Karuizawa in a converted stable.

Marquis Matsugae had no place in such conversation. And
when he had taken his seat at the dinner table the wife of the
Minister of State, who sat beside him, found herself short of
suitable topics.

"Have you spoken recently," she ventured, "with Marquis
Yoshichika Tokugawa?"

The Marquis thought for a moment. It seemed that he had
not talked to Tokugawa for a very long time. Then, again, it
seemed that he had spoken with him just two or three days
before. And in any case, Marquis Tokugawa had never at
any time discussed anything significant with Marquis Matsugae. Whenever they had met, either in the lobby of the House
of Peers or at the Peers Club, they had never done more than
exchange a few words about wrestling.

"Well," replied Marquis Matsugae, "I haven't seen too
much of him recently."

"He's been rather active lately among the veterans, getting
together groups like the Moral Light Society," said the lady.
"He's quite fond of that sort of thing, Marquis Tokugawa."

"Yes," agreed a gentleman across the table, "he seems to
take great delight in letting right-wing malcontents use him
as a figurehead. Bit by bit his playing with fire is turning into
something earnest."

"If a man must play with fire, women are preferable, I
suppose," declared Baroness Shinkawa in a voice that seemed
loud enough to split the petals of the flowers that decorated
the table. When she spoke of playing with fire, without a
trace of feeling of innuendo, it was immediately obvious that
she was a woman incapable of misconduct.

Once the soup course had been served, the conversation
turned to the kind of topic that the upper classes were more
accustomed to talk about. A discussion arose as to what
sort of costumes would be suited for incognito participation
in the villagers' Bon Festival that year. In Karuizawa the

Bon Festival was celebrated in August in accordance with the old calendar. Marquis Matsugae was reminded of the Bon Festivals at his mansion in Tokyo when the eaves outside the parlor were hung with Gifu lanterns. And then he remembered how his mother had been vexed by something up until the moment of her death. It had been she who had bought the hundred and twelve acre Matsugae estate in Shibuya for three thousand yen which she had obtained from the sale of stock. Midway through the Taisho period, about 1920, she sold seventy-five acres of it for five million yen, but the buyer, the Hakoné Realty Company, was extremely tardy in making good the money due, a cause of grief that stayed with his mother until she drew her last breath.

"Have they paid yet? Do we have the money?" she asked again and again during her final illness. Those who were with her, wanting to put an end to such a scandalous show of concern, told her that the payment had indeed been made, but the woman on her deathbed would not be deceived.

"It does no good to lie," she said. "If all that money came walking into this house, the floor would creak and groan under its feet. I haven't heard anything like that, have I? I want to hear its footsteps so that I can die in peace."

After his mother's death, with the passage of time and after many vicissitudes, the account was at last paid in full. In 1927, however, at the beginning of the Showa period, the Marquis lost more than half of this in the failure of the Fifteenth National Bank. The lame steward, Yamada, oppressed by his sense of responsibility, hanged himself.

Because his mother had said not a word about Kiyoaki but had spoken of nothing but money, her death, as far as the Marquis was concerned, was robbed of all that was lyric and exalted. In his heart, he could not avoid the presage that there would be little noble afterglow left to light his own decline and death.

Since the Shinkawa household was governed according to the English manner, the male guests remained in the dining room after dinner to be presented with cigars, while the ladies retired to the parlor. Furthermore, according to Victorian custom the gentlemen did not rejoin the ladies until they had enjoyed their postprandial drinking to the full. This was a source of acute distress to Baroness Shinkawa, but, since it was an English custom, she accepted it as something that could in no way be amended.

Rain had begun to fall halfway through dinner. And since the evening had grown more chilly than normal, the servants quickly kindled a fire of white birch logs in the fireplace. The Marquis then had no need of his blanket. The lights in the room were extinguished, and the men relaxed around the fireplace.

The Minister of State began to speak, addressing Kurahara and returning to a topic that excluded Marquis Matsugae.

"With regard to what you were saying before, I'd like very much to see you give so exhaustive an explanation to the Prime Minister. Though he would like to remain above such matters, he cannot help but find himself under pressure from the flow of events."

"Exhaustive explanations are my forte," replied Kurahara. "And I haven't spared the Prime Minister. What a bother I must be to him."

"Ah, but it's not by being a bother to prime ministers that you run risk," replied the Minister of State. "There was something I had to refrain from saying before out of consideration for the nerves of the ladies, but really, Kurahara, I'd like to see you have a proper regard for your safety. Since you are a pillar of our economy, it would indeed be catastrophic if you were to go the way of Inoué and Dan. However much you take precautions, there's no possibility of your being over-careful."

"Since you're kind enough to tell me this, I presume that you're well acquainted with the actual circumstances," replied Kurahara in his hoarse voice, his features without expression. Even if a wave of distress had swept over his face, the restless flames that made the shadows dart across his fleshy cheeks would have concealed it. "All sorts of declarations from would-be assassins come to my home, and the police show much concern. However, having lived as long as I have, I am not the least worried about my personal safety. What fears I have pertain not to myself but to the future of our nation. I take the greatest delight, just like a child, in slipping away from my guards and doing whatever I like. There are those who are so fearful they urge bothersome measures upon me, and there are also those who tell me to use money to protect myself, offering to act as go-betweens. But I have no inclination to do anything of the sort. At this late date, I'm not going to start buying life."

So confident was Kurahara's declaration that his companions became ill at ease, but he was not a man to take ready notice of such reactions.

Viscount Matsudaira was warming his smooth white hands over the fire. They had turned a delicate pink, all the way back from the well-trimmed nails. Gazing intently at the ash of the cigar he held at his fingertips, he began a story whose evident intent was to dismay.

"This is something I once heard from a fellow who was a company commander in Manchuria. It impressed itself on my memory because I had never heard such a tragic story. One day this officer received a letter from the father of a private in his company who came from a poor farming district. The family, the father wrote, was crushed by poverty and tormented by hunger. Though there was no way that the father could make amends to his dutiful son for so wishing, he nevertheless hoped for his death in battle as soon as possible. For, without the bereavement payment they would then receive, the family had no means of surviving. As might well be expected, the company commander didn't dare to show this letter to the son but hid it away. And just a short time later, he told me, it happened that the son died a heroic death in battle."

"This really happened?" asked Kurahara.

"I have the story from the company commander himself."

"Really!"

The sap from the logs sputtered in the flames of the fireplace in the silence that followed Kurahara's response. After a few moments, Kurahara took out his handkerchief, and the sound of his blowing his nose attracted the attention of the others. They saw several tears, bright in the firelight, rolling down over the heavy flesh of Kurahara's creased cheeks.

These enigmatic tears had a strong emotional effect on all present. The man most startled to see them was Viscount Matsudaira, but he was content to congratulate himself on his story-telling ability. From Marquis Matsugae, however, Kurahara's tears drew still more tears. That so unsentimental a man would weep in sympathy with another could perhaps be explained only by concluding that his thoroughly egoistic cast of character had been unable to maintain itself before the advance of age. But as for Kurahara's tears, which would remain something of a mystery in the face of all explanation, perhaps Baron Shinkawa alone was able to view them accurately. Since the Baron's heart was cold, he ran no risk in any situation. Tears, however, were dangerous. Supposing they did not necessarily proceed from the approach of senility.

The Baron, then, was somewhat moved, somewhat taken aback, and as a consequence, though he made it a practice to discard his cigars half-smoked, neglected to toss the one he was holding into the fire.

16

Isao made up his mind that, when he had his audience with Prince Toin, rather than express himself in personal terms, he would bring with him *The League of the Divine Wind*. Since there could be no question of merely lending this to the Prince, he would buy a new copy to present to him. For the first time, he found his mother's talents to be of some use. He asked her to make a brocade cover for the presentation copy, choosing a pattern as conservative as possible. She went to work with her needle at a pitch of enthusiasm.

The matter, however, came to the ears of his father. Iinuma summoned his son and told him that he was not to see the Prince.

"But why not?" asked the startled Isao.

"Because I said so. There's no need for an explanation."

His son had no way of knowing how tangled was the skein of Iinuma's emotions and to what deep and obscure region it led. Still less could he know the part that Prince Toin had played in the events leading to the death of Kiyoaki.

Since he realized that his anger was impossible to explain, Iinuma himself grew more and more uncomfortable with it. Though he was well aware that the Prince's role in the affair was obviously that of an injured party, nevertheless, whenever Iinuma traced events back to the remote causes of Kiyoaki's death, he invariably found himself vexed with the image of a man he had never met, Prince Toin. If there had been no Prince, if the Prince had not been present at that particular time and place . . . Iinuma's complaint always moved toward this same conclusion. The truth was that if there had been no Prince Toin, Kiyoaki's irresoluteness would have been still more likely to prevent him from winning Satoko even for a time, but, knowing little of the particulars, Iinuma tended to fasten his resentment doggedly upon the person of the Prince.

Iinuma was still tormented by the long-standing discrepancy between his political tenets and the turbulent emotions that were their source. For the burning, emotional loyalty that had taken form in Iinuma in his boyhood—a loyalty that at times had been shot through with anger and contempt, at times had poured down like a waterfall, at times had erupted like a volcano—this loyalty that was so much a part of him was a loyalty wholly to Kiyoaki. To define it still more precisely, one might well say that it was a loyalty dedicated to Kiyoaki's beauty. It was a loyalty swerving almost to betrayal, a loyalty ever choked with a dark anger. And for that very reason it was an emotion to which one could give no other name.

He called it loyalty. Well and good. Yet it was something quite other than being dedicated to an ideal. He struggled against the ineffably beautiful temptation that would lure him far from his idealism. He was intensely eager to reconcile idealism and beauty, both of which had such a hold upon his heart, and moreover his emotion flowed from a kind of powerful need to reconcile the two. His was a loyalty that from its inception had the character of a lonely, single-minded fidelity. It was an emotion fated for him from boyhood, a dagger that had been thrust into his grasp.

In teaching his classes, Iinuma was fond of using the expression "love for the Emperor." Whenever these words passed his lips he felt a surging power go out of him which made his students tremble with emotion and their eyes sparkle. Clearly the source of this inspiration was some experience of his own boyhood. Otherwise, where could it have come from?

Since Iinuma had little self-awareness, he was quite capable of forgetting all that pertained to the distant source of his emotions. Freely transcending time, he directed the fire within him wherever he wished, setting blazes where it pleased him, letting himself rest in the flames, letting himself taste the burning ecstasy and suffering no significant pain in the process. Yet if Iinuma had been more honest with himself, he would undoubtedly have noticed that he used an excessive number of metaphors having to do with emotion. He would undoubtedly have recognized himself as one who had indeed once lived out the original poem but who now made do with mere echoes of it, constantly applying the images of the moon, snow, and blossoms of long ago to scenes' that were altering with every passing year. What he did not realize, in short, was that his eloquence had grown hollow.

Thus with regard to reverence for the Imperial Family, though he, Iinuma, should have been ready to cut down on the spot anyone who cast doubt upon this virtue, a chill shadow, like the wavering but constant image of rain flowing down a glass roof, fell upon his own sense of reverence—the name of Prince Toin.

"Who is it that was going to take you to see Prince Toin?" asked Iinuma in a somewhat quieter and roundabout manner. The boy said nothing.

"Who? Why don't you answer?"

"I can't answer that question."

"Why can't you answer?"

The boy fell silent once more. Iinuma grew furious. To say "Don't see Prince Toin" was for him an order from father to son. There was no need for explanation. But, to Iinuma, for Isao not to tell him the name of his intermediary was equivalent to rebellion against his father. The truth of the matter was that Iinuma, as Isao's father, should have been able to explain the basis of his repugnance for the Prince so that his son could have readily understood it. He should have been able to say that Isao was not to see the Prince because he had been involved in the circumstances that had driven to his death the young master whom Iinuma had served. Shame, however, like a rock glowing red with heat, blocked Iinuma's throat and prevented all explanation.

And for Isao to go against his father like this was most extraordinary. In his father's presence, Isao had always been reticent and deferential. For the first time Iinuma realized that there was an inviolable core within his son, and now he, who had failed in attempting to form Kiyoaki, in another time and in quite different circumstances, felt the same enervating frustration with Isao and could not stem a sudden rush of anguish.

As father and son thus sat confronting each other, the light of the setting sun, brilliant after an early evening shower, shone from the puddles scattered through the garden outside the room, and the green foliage sparkled as though the trees and shrubbery were growing in the Pure Land. The breeze was cool and refreshing as it blew across their faces. Isao's anger was sharply defined, like something lying at the bottom of a clear brook. He sensed its presence like a stone that he could place on a Go board wherever he wished. But the emotions that raged within his father were, as always, opaque to Isao, beyond his understanding. The cicadas kept up their solemn chant.

The copy of *The League of the Divine Wind* in its sober rust-and-green brocade cover lay on the table. Isao abruptly picked it up and got to his feet, intending to leave the room without another word. His father was too fast for him. He snatched the book away from his son, and he, too, got to his feet.

For one instant their eyes met. Isao saw that his father's eyes were utterly cowardly, that no courage shone in them. But in those eyes, like distant pounding hoofs drawing closer, anger was rushing up from the depths of his heart.

"Have you a tongue in your head or not?"

Iinuma threw the book into the garden. The gleaming orange surface of one of the puddles was rent as the book meant for a prince splashed into it and came to rest. The instant that he saw the muddy water close over the object that he had invested with so sacred a character, Isao felt a shock of anger, as if a wall had suddenly burst before his eyes. He clenched his fists without realizing it. His father trembled. He slapped Isao across his face.

At the sound, Isao's mother came into the room. To Miné the figures of the two men standing there seemed gigantic. The next instant she noticed that her husband's kimono was in disarray, while that of her son, whom he had just slapped, was not. She looked beyond into the garden sparkling in the glow of the setting sun. Miné remembered her husband's violent passion at the time that he had beaten her half to death.

Slithering across the tatami floor, Miné interposed herself between the two of them and cried out: "Isao! What are you doing? Apologize to your father. How dare you show such a face to him! Bow down before him and apologize this instant."

"Look at that," said Isao, paying no attention to the blow he had taken on his cheek. He knelt on one knee, and, tugging at his mother's sleeve, directed her gaze toward the garden. Above her head, Miné heard her husband panting like a dog. Contrasted with the bright garden, the interior of the house was very dark. Miné had the feeling that something was floating in that darkness, filling it—something so uncanny that she could not bear to keep open her upturned eyes. Half in a dream, Miné was thinking of that long-ago time in the library of Marquis Matsugae. And still, as though in a delirium, she kept saying: "Apologize. Apologize at once."

Slowly she opened her eyes. The object that took clear form before them was of glittering green-and-rust brocade half-sunk in a puddle of water. Miné was aghast. The brocade that sparkled in the evening sun from the midst of the muddy water affected her so that she felt it was she herself who was being punished. As for what kind of book it might be, not the faintest inkling crossed Miné's mind.

The Prince had informed Lieutenant Hori that he would receive them on Sunday evening, and the Lieutenant took Isao with him to pay their respects at the Toinnomiya residence in Shiba. The Prince's family had been visited by a series of misfortunes. After his elder brother, who had never enjoyed good health, passed away, so also, within a short time, did his father and mother. Thus the sole heir of the Toinnomiya family was the vigorous Prince Harunori. When he was away on duty, his wife and children had the mansion to themselves. And since his wife was a lady of extremely quiet disposition who came from a family of the court nobility, a lonely stillness, as might be expected, hung over the residence most of the time.

Isao had had great difficulty in obtaining a third copy of *The League of the Divine Wind*, but at last had found one in a secondhand bookstore, and he carried it under his arm as he walked along in his Kokura summer uniform beside Lieutenant Hori. He had taken care to wrap it in good paper at least and to draw in ink the characters designating it as a gift. In leaving the house this evening, he had used deception against his father for the first time.

The huge gate of the Toinnomiya mansion was closed, and only a dim light burned before it. There was no indication that the master of the house was in residence. A small door beside the gate was open, and a guard light shone down on the gravel. When the Lieutenant stepped through this door, the scabbard of his sword rattled as it brushed lightly against the frame.

Though the guard had been informed ahead of time of their coming, he took care to inform the house by an inside phone, and in the interval Isao, noticing how clearly he could hear the wings of the moths, the small beetles, and the other insects fluttering about the light that hung from the eaves of

the old guard post, became aware of the profound silence
that brooded over the trees surrounding the mansion and the
sloping gravel road that shone a brilliant white beneath the
moon.

A few moments later, they were climbing the gravel road.
The heavy, sucking noise of the Lieutenant's boots echoed
as though he were on a night march. Isao felt a faint warmth
still in the gravel, a reminder of the torrid heat of midday.

In contrast to the altogether Western-style Yokohama villa
of the Toinnomiyas, this mansion was in Japanese style.
Above the broad expanse of gravel, white in the moonlight,
where vehicles pulled up, there rose the heavy roof of a
Chinese gable over the entrance.

The mansion's administrative office was apparently to the
side of the entranceway, but no lights were burning there this
late. The old steward came out to meet them and, after taking
charge of the Lieutenant's sword, escorted them into the
house. There was no sign of life anywhere within. The corridor was spread with a maroon rug, and one of its walls was
wainscoted in Western style. After opening a door to a darkened room, the steward flicked a switch. Light struck Isao's
eyes, the radiated brilliance of a massive chandelier hanging
in the center of the room. Its countless fragments of glass
floated in the air like a glittering mist.

Isao and the Lieutenant sat stiffly in linen slipcovered arm-
chairs as the breeze from a sluggish fan brushed their cheeks.
They heard the rustling sound of the insects that fluttered
against the window. Since the Lieutenant kept silent, Isao,
too, kept silent. After a short wait, a servant brought them
some chilled barley tea.

A huge Gobelin tapestry depicting a battle scene hung
upon the wall. A mounted knight was thrusting his lance
through the breast of a foot soldier bent back by the force of
the blow. The tapestry had faded with age, and the gushing
blood that blossomed at the man's breast was tinged with the
russet color of an old *furoshiki*. Blood and flowers were alike,

Isao thought, in that both were quick to dry up, quick to change their substance. And precisely because of this, then, blood and flowers could go on living by taking on the substance of glory. Glory in all its forms was inevitably something metallic.

The door opened and Prince Harunori, wearing a white linen suit, came into the room. Though there was nothing pretentious about his entrance, and though its very lack of ceremony brought a measure of warmth and ease into the somewhat tense atmosphere of the room, the Lieutenant at once leaped from his chair to a position of rigid attention, and Isao followed his example. For the space of a moment, Isao studied the Prince, the first member of the Imperial Family whom he had ever been so close to. His Highness was not especially tall, but his physique gave a decided impression of sturdiness. His suit bulged at the midsection, putting a strain upon his jacket buttons. His shoulders and chest were so well fleshed that his white-suited figure with its knotted tie of reddish yellow might at first glance seem to be that of a politician. But the beautifully tanned complexion, the close-cropped head, the splendid, rather aquiline nose, the majesty that shone from the long, slender eyes, and the carefully trimmed jet-black moustache all revealed that, beyond a doubt, here was a man who combined a commanding martial presence with the graceful bearing of the nobility. The Prince's eyes were bright and lively, but he gave the impression of seldom shifting his penetrating gaze.

The Lieutenant introduced Isao at once, and he bowed deeply.

"Is this the young man you spoke to me about? Well! Sit down then, make yourself comfortable," said the Prince affably. "As far as young men today go, I haven't met a single one outside the military. And so I thought, if this lad's a civilian and truly a young man worthy of the name, then I want very much to meet him. Isao Iinuma, is it? I've heard of your father."

Since the Lieutenant had told Isao to say whatever came into his mind, he asked abruptly: "Your Highness, has my father ever had an audience with you?"

When the Prince replied that he had not, the riddle of his father deepened and became more complex. Why should he harbor such feelings toward a man whom he had never met?

The Prince and the Lieutenant began to tell old stories with a freedom that came of their both being military men. Isao watched for an opportunity to present his book. He had little hope that the Lieutenant would make the effort to offer him such an occasion. Lieutenant Hori seemed to have forgotten all about the book.

Consequently, Isao remained silent, having no choice but to sit stiffly correct while he observed the Prince across the table engaging in pleasant conversation. The whiteness of the Prince's untanned forehead gave off a serene brightness beneath the chandelier. The light shining upon his close-cropped head showed the newly cut hair bristling in perfect order.

Perhaps becoming aware of Isao's piercing look, the Prince suddenly turned his gaze, which had been fixed on the Lieutenant, toward Isao. For a moment their eyes met. It was as if the clapper of an old, rust-covered iron bell, long silent, had been loosened by some errant tremor and struck an unexpected note. What the Prince's eyes said at that moment Isao could not comprehend, nor in all likelihood could the Prince himself. But that fleeting moment of communication was charged with an emotion that transcended ordinary love and hate, an emotion that sprang from some uncanny tie. For an instant some far-off sorrow seemed to pour from the Prince's unmoving eyes, as though he meant to quench Isao's burning gaze with the water of his sadness.

"The Lieutenant, too, looked at me in just this way during kendo drill," Isao thought. "But that time, down deep, there was something definite that he conveyed to me without words. And in the Prince's gaze, there's nothing of the sort. Perhaps

His Highness's impression of me is unfavorable."

By then the Prince, who had turned back to his conversation with the Lieutenant, was nodding in vigorous assent to something the latter had said that had escaped Isao.

"You're right," the Prince said. "The nobility, too, is guilty. It sounds splendid to call the nobility the 'living ramparts' of the Imperial Family, but there are those among them who, sure of their power, tend even to make light of His Sacred Majesty. This is nothing new. There have been examples of it since ancient times, you know. And as for the necessity of chastising the overweening pride of those who should be the mirror of conduct for the common people, here, especially, I am entirely of the same opinion as you."

17

ISAO WAS SURPRISED at the intensity of the hatred that the Prince reserved for the nobility, with whom he had such close affinity. But when one took into consideration the Prince's position, he thought, there were no doubt numerous occasions when the corruption of the nobility offended His Highness's nostrils. As for that of the politicians and the entrepreneurs, no matter how far off it was, it struck the nose as squarely as the stink of a dead animal's carcass drifting across the fields in summer. But the nobility were capable of disguising their unsavory odor with the fragrance of incense. Isao wanted to hear from the Prince the names of those he considered the worst among the nobility, but His Highness prudently refrained from mentioning them.

Since he now felt somewhat at ease, Isao took up the book in its paper wrapping and addressed the Prince: "Desiring to present this to Your Highness, I have brought it with me. Though it is an old and soiled book, all our spirit is contained within it, and my hope is to be one who carries on this spirit." The words now came easily to his lips.

"Oh? *The League of the Divine Wind*, is it?" said the Prince, unwrapping the book and looking at its cover.

"I believe the book gives an excellent presentation of the spirit of the League," said the Lieutenant, coming to Isao's assistance. "These students seem to have vowed to establish a like brotherhood for the Showa era."

"Indeed? Well, then, instead of the garrison at Kumamoto, have they been slashing into the Third Regiment at Azabu, I wonder?" said the Prince. Though he joked, he showed no trace of disdain as he courteously turned over the pages. Then, suddenly lifting his eyes from the book, he looked at the boy sharply as he spoke to him: "I'll ask you something. Suppose . . . suppose His Imperial Majesty had occasion to be displeased with either your spirit or your behavior. What would you do then?"

A question like this could only have come from a member of the Imperial Family. And then, too, even among the Imperial Family, certainly no one but Prince Harunori could have been expected to ask it. The Lieutenant and Isao once more became rigid with tension. They intuitively grasped something from the quality of the moment: the Prince's question, though seemingly directed to Isao alone, really included the Lieutenant. The Lieutenant's as yet unspoken aspirations, his intention in deliberately bringing this unknown boy with him to the Toinnomiya residence—these were some of the things the Prince must have had in mind in asking his question. Isao perceived that the Prince, though not a direct superior, found it awkward as a regimental commander to question a lieutenant pointblank, and he suddenly awoke to his own situation. Both the Prince and the Lieutenant were using him as an interpreter, or a puppet that conveys another's intent, or a piece on a chessboard. Although the dialogue in progress was disinterested and offered no advantage to those involved, Isao, for once in his young life, felt himself in the midst of something like the whirlpool of partisan politics. Even if this left a somewhat unpleasant taste in his mouth, Isao would not have been true to his character if he had not responded as frankly as was in his power. The Lieutenant's scabbard rattled lightly as it struck against the arm of his chair.

"Like the men of the League, I would cut open my stomach."

"Indeed?" The martial prince's expression indicated that he had grown used to hearing such answers. "Well, then, if he was pleased, what would you do?"

Isao replied without the least hesitation: "In that case, too, I would cut open my stomach at once."

"Oh?" For the first time a gleam of interest flashed from the Prince's eye. "And what would be the meaning of that? Explain yourself."

"Yes, Your Highness. It refers to loyalty. Suppose I make steaming rice balls with rice so hot it burns my hands. My sole purpose is to present them to His Majesty, to offer them in his sacred presence. Now as to the outcome. If his Majesty is not hungry, he will curtly refuse my offering or perhaps he may even be pleased to say: 'Am I to eat food so tasteless?' and hurl it into my face. In which case I will have to withdraw, the grains of rice still clinging to my face, and gratefully cut open my stomach at once. Then, again, if His Majesty is hungry and is pleased to eat the rice balls with satisfaction, there will still be no course of action open to me but to withdraw at once and gratefully cut open my stomach. Why? To make rice balls to serve as food for His Sacred Majesty with hands so common is a sin worthy to be punished with a thousand deaths. But, then, suppose I were to make rice balls as an offering but keep them in my hands and not present them, what would happen then? After a while the rice would certainly rot. This, too, would be an act of loyalty,

I suppose, but I would call it a loyalty without courage. Courageous loyalty belongs to the man who, with no fear of death, dares to present the rice balls that he has thus made with single-minded devotion."

"While knowing he's sinning? Is that what he's to do?"

"Yes, Your Highness. The gentlemen of the military, Your Highness foremost among them, are indeed fortunate. For the soldier's loyalty rests in casting away his life in obedience to the Emperor's commands. But in the case of an ordinary civilian, he must be prepared to sin by reason of his unsanctioned loyalty."

" 'Obey the law'—isn't that a command of His Majesty? And the law courts—they are, after all, His Majesty's courts."

"The sins I refer to have nothing to do with the law. And the greatest sin is that of a man who, finding himself in a world where the sacred light of His Majesty is obscured, nevertheless determines to go on living without doing anything about it. The only way to purge this grave sin is to make a fiery offering with one's own hands, even if that itself is a sin, to express one's loyalty in action, and then to commit seppuku immediately. With death, all is purified. But as long as a man goes on living, he can't move either right or left, or take any action whatever, without sinning."

"Ah, this has become a very complex matter indeed," said the Prince, smiling as though somewhat taken aback by Isao's sincerity.

Gauging the situation, the Lieutenant restrained Isao: "That's enough. You've made your point."

But the excitement aroused in Isao by this examination of his ideals persisted. The exchange was with a prince of the Imperial Family. To face such a personage and to respond with utter frankness to his questions had made Isao feel that he was facing a brilliance not of this world shining from behind the Prince, and was giving full expression to his innermost self. He had been able to give an immediate answer to whatever question the Prince asked, proof that for some time his thoughts had been refined and tempered within him.

When he pictured himself standing, arms folded, doing nothing at all, Isao shuddered as though he had imagined himself a leper. The easy course was to accept such a posture as man's ordinary, sinful condition, as inescapable as the earth upon which one walked or the air one breathed. But if he himself would become pure in the midst of this, his sin had to take another form and he had, in any event, to draw his nourishment from the very source of sin. Only by doing so would he join together sin and death, seppuku and glory, atop the precipice swept by the pine breeze before the rising sun. His reason for not wanting to enter either the army or the naval academies was that there ready-made glory would be provided, there the sin of inaction would be purged. But perhaps, in order to attain the glory that he alone had in mind, he had begun to love sin for its own sake.

Isao did not think of himself as being pure and immaculate in accordance with the doctrine of Oen Hayashi, the beloved Master of the League of the Divine Wind, who taught that all men were sons of the gods. But he burned with a constant impatience to draw near enough to purity to touch it with his hand. So that his fingertips could reach it, he was making use of stepping stones that offered but treacherous footing, aware all the time that the next instant these might give way beneath him. He knew that Master Oen's rite of Ukei had no relevance to the present age. Still, this rite by which one asked the will of the gods seemed to contain an element of danger not unlike a footing that could give way at any moment. And what was this element of danger but sin? Surely nothing could so resemble sin as did the inevitability of danger.

"Well, well, so a young man like this has turned up," said the Prince as he turned back to the Lieutenant, his voice filled with emotion. The thought struck Isao that he was like a model on display before the two of them, and a painful shock ran through him as the desire seized him to fashion himself to fit the pattern that he saw reflected in the Prince's eyes. To do so he would have to die.

"When I realize that Japan has produced students like this, I have somewhat more hope for the future. One never hears such an outburst from those in the military. You've done me a favor in bringing so fine a lad here." Since the Prince deliberately ignored Isao and expressed gratitude to the Lieutenant, the Lieutenant gained honor, and Isao himself felt the warmth of the Prince's benevolence far more than if he had been praised directly.

The Prince summoned his steward and had him bring in some fine Scotch and some caviar. Pouring with his own hand, he urged the Lieutenant to drink, and Isao too: "I don't suppose you're of age, Iinuma, but you've just given such a display of perceptiveness that I consider you a grown man. So drink up. And don't worry. If you overdo it, I'll send you home in my car." Though the Prince spoke most graciously, Isao shuddered. For at that moment there arose in his mind the image of his father's face as he received his son coming home dead drunk in a car from the Toinnomiya residence. It was enough to jolt the hand that held his glass as he stood up to receive the Scotch from the Prince. The whiskey spilled out of the tipped glass and fell onto the delicate lace cloth that covered the table.

"Oh!" Isao cried. He pulled out his handkerchief and desperately wiped the spot.

"Please forgive me," he said, his head hanging low as tears of shame welled up in his eyes.

Isao remained standing there with bowed head, and the Prince, seeing his tears, spoke to him humorously: "That will do now. Look up. Don't carry on as though you're going to cut your stomach open right here and now."

"Permit me to apologize for him, Your Highness," said the Lieutenant at Isao's side. "I believe that it was the excitement of the occasion that made his hand shake."

Isao sat down at last, but, altogether taken up with

thoughts of his blunder, he was unable to say a single word. At the same time, however, despite his mortification, the Prince's words were like a warm current coursing through his body, affecting him far more than did the whiskey. The Prince and the Lieutenant then began to discuss the political situation in detail, but Isao, occupied as he was with his shame, could not attend to what they were saying. While the Prince was thus enthusiastically engaged in discussion and apparently paying no attention at all to Isao, he suddenly turned to him and spoke in a loud, cheerful voice which to some degree showed the effect of the Scotch he had drunk: "Come now! Pull yourself together. You're quite a disputant yourself, aren't you?"

Having no other choice, Isao took a modest role in the discussion. He now felt that he realized why, just as the Lieutenant had told him, the Prince enjoyed such immense popularity among the military.

It was getting very late. After the Lieutenant, surprised at the hour, had expressed their gratitude, the Prince presented him with a bottle of excellent whiskey and some cigarettes in a box with the imperial crest. To Isao he gave a package of cakes, also bearing the imperial crest.

"It looks as if His Highness was quite taken with you," said the Lieutenant on the way home. "I think he'll be willing to help you, when the time comes. Considering his position, though, it would be quite improper to give the appearance of wanting anything from him. At any rate, you're a lucky fellow. And don't worry about that little faux pas."

When he left the Lieutenant, instead of going straight home, Isao stopped at Izutsu's house. After a servant had roused Izutsu, who was already in bed, Isao handed him the package of cakes.

"Take good care of this. Don't let anyone in your house see it."

"All right."

Izutsu stuck his head out through the entranceway door in

the dead of night, the nape of his neck stiff with tension, and took the package. A look of uncertainty crossed his face as he felt its lightness. He was sure that any package received from his comrade at such an hour would have to contain explosives.

18

THAT SUMMER the number of Isao's recruits grew to twenty. Only the most trustworthy students with the highest principles were allowed to enter his circle, after having been screened by Izutsu and Sagara and then interviewed and approved by Isao. Of foremost use in the process was *The League of the Divine Wind*. After reading this, each candidate had to write an essay describing how it affected him, which served as the basis for his first evaluation. There were those among them who, though their style and their comprehension were superior, left too much to be desired with regard to their strength of character.

Isao came to lose his fervor for kendo. When he announced that he was not going to participate in the summer training camp, he narrowly missed the unpleasant experience of being dealt with summarily by those upperclassmen who had been counting upon him to win the coming tournament for the school. One upperclassman was particularly aggressive in demanding to know the reason for Isao's change of heart.

"Are you plotting something? Is there something that fascinates you more than kendo?" he asked. "I hear you've been getting students to read some kind of pamphlet. You're involved in some ideological movement, aren't you?"

Isao forestalled him by answering: "I imagine that was *The League of the Divine Wind*. What I'm doing is talking with people about organizing a group to study Meiji history."

In fact, Isao's kendo career was of great help in secretly gathering new comrades. When a student was confronted with his laconic presence and his brilliant, piercing glance, respect for his reputation was immediately transformed into devotion to him.

Having advanced thus far, Isao decided to gather all his comrades together at the same time so that he could test their maturity and enthusiasm. During the summer vacation, accordingly, when most of them were away from Tokyo, he sent them telegrams ordering them to return, deliberately choosing a time a full two weeks before the new semester began. During vacation the school grounds would serve as an ideal place to preserve their secrecy. The students were to meet before the shrine on campus at six in the evening, a time when the heat of the day would still be lingering.

All the students at the College of National Studies referred to this as simply "the shrine," and a gathering of students in front of this small place of worship dedicated to the myriad gods was not at all unusual. Students from the Shinto department, destined to succeed their fathers as priests of the family shrine, always came here to practice their chants, and members of the athletic teams would come either to pray for victory or to ponder defeat.

One hour before the time set for the meeting, Isao was waiting for Sagara and Izutsu in the woods just to the rear of the shrine. He wore *hakama* over a white splashed-pattern summer kimono, and a school cap with white piping. When Isao sat down on the grass, the bright rays of the evening sun, coming from beyond the precincts of Hikawa Shrine as it sank toward the heights of Sakuragaoka in Shibuya, struck the chest of his white kimono and the black trunks of the oaks. Despite this, Isao did not seek the shade, but rather, pulling the peak of his cap down over his eyes, sat facing the

sun. The heat given off by his sweat-covered flesh built up
beneath his kimono and crept up toward his brow, melding
with that which radiated from the sun-soaked grass. The
whirring song of the cicadas filled the woods.

The bicycles that moved along Hakadori Street, just below him, gleamed in the sun. The bright rays seemed to
stitch together the low roofs that lined the street. At one point
among the eaves, there glittered as bright as the sun itself
something that resembled a tilted mass of glass. When Isao
looked more closely, he saw that an iceman's truck was
parked there. He could sense the peril of the ice catching the
full force of the evening sun. He felt as if he could hear distant, shrill cries of pain as it was being ruthlessly dissolved
by the final heat of summer.

When Isao looked over his shoulder, the drawn-out shadow
of one oak seemed to him the very image of his ambition here
beneath this end-of-summer sun, a thing he had been dragging behind him to no purpose. The slipping away of summer affected him keenly. This parting with the sun. He
dreaded seeing that massive, scarlet-glowing symbol of ideal
devotion begin to fade with the change of seasons. This year
too he had let slip the chance to die one morning before the
blazing summer sun.

Again he raised his eyes, and he saw great swirling clusters of red dragonflies, as if the glow of the gradually reddening sky overhead, filtering down through the closely bunched
branches of the oak, had given wings to every crevice. This
was yet another presage of autumn. These signs of a cool
reason, slowly, leisurely taking form from out of the midst of
hot passion, would make some men happy, but to Isao they
brought sadness.

"Why wait in such a hot place?" said Izutsu in surprise,
as he and Sagara came up, wearing white shirts with their
school caps.

"Look there!" said Isao, sitting up straight in the grass.
"There in the evening sun is the face of His Majesty the Em-

peror." His words had a magical effect upon Izutsu and Sagara. As always, they were quick to fall in with his mood even while feeling intimidated. "And His Majesty's face is troubled."

Izutsu and Sagara sat down in awed silence beside Isao, and for the moment, as they twisted blades of grass between their fingers, they steeped themselves in the feeling that was theirs whenever they were close to him—that of having drawn near to a naked sword. At times Isao seemed frightening to the two boys.

"I wonder if they'll all come?" said Sagara, pushing up his glasses as he broke the silence, hoping to account for a misgiving he did not understand.

"They'll come. What other choice have they?" answered Isao with casual assurance.

"You finally escaped the kendo training camp, eh? Good for you!" said Izutsu, expressing his admiration to a somewhat embarrassing degree. Isao was about to explain his reason, but changed his mind. Their activities had not yet become so busy that he had to deny himself the least diversion. Rather his reason for not participating was simply that he had had enough of the bamboo sword. He had grown weary because victories came too easily with it, weary because the bamboo sword was no more than a symbol; weary, finally, because it carried with it *no real danger*.

The three of them began to talk earnestly among themselves about how remarkable it was that they could enlist as many as twenty comrades. At that very time, at the Olympic Games in Los Angeles, the Japanese swimming team was gaining glory for the homeland, and so it was quite easy at any school to get swimming candidates to turn out. But what Isao and his friends were doing was a different story from the recruitment of the sports clubs. The appeal of their group had nothing to do with faddish popularity. For each student whom they had selected had to be asked to entrust his life to them. Furthermore, until he unqualifiedly trusted his life to them, they could give him no clear concept of their purpose.

Finding young men willing to give their lives and getting them to declare their intention was not so difficult. Each and every one of them, however, was eager to embrace a cause that he could brag about to others and hoping for the most exquisite of funeral wreaths to mark his passing. Some of the students had secretly read Ikki Kita's *An Outline Plan for the Reorganization of Japan*, but Isao had sniffed out the odor of a devilish pride there. This book, far, far removed from the "dogged devotion and humble loyalty" of Harukata Kaya, certainly stirred up the hot blood of many of the students, but such young men were not the kind that Isao wanted.

Beyond a doubt, Isao's comrades would be chosen not for what they had to say but because of something deep and inscrutable, manifested only when their eyes met his. This was something not in the realm of thought but of a more distant origin. Further, it gave rise to a clear, outward expression that would yet pass unrecognized by anyone who did not hold a like aspiration. It was this element alone that would cause Isao to choose his comrades.

The candidates had come not just from the College of National Studies but from various schools, some of them from Nihon University and some even from high school. One Keio University student had been introduced to Isao as a candidate, but, though this boy had a ready facility with words, his dilettantish manner made him unsuitable. There was even one student who, after professing the greatest enthusiasm for *The League of the Divine Wind*, gave himself away in more casual conversation as a fraud, odds and ends of vocabulary revealing him as a left-wing activist intent on spying.

A quiet and unsophisticated manner and a cheerful smile went in most cases with a character that could be relied upon, a brave disposition, and, as a consequence, a spirit that had little regard for death. Talkativeness, high-sounding words, an ironic smile, and the like all too often went with cowardice. A pale face and a sickly body were in some cases the

source of extraordinary zeal. Fat youths in general were not
only cowardly but indiscreet, while lean and logical-minded
ones lacked intuition. Isao thus became aware of how much
the face and outward bearing could communicate.

There was, however, nothing about the city-bred students
to indicate kinship with the more than two hundred thousand
children then suffering privation in farming and fishing villages. The very term "undernourished child" had become an
expression popularly used to ridicule gluttons and had lost
almost all of its old deep-seated anger. Yet it had been reported that even in Tokyo, at an elementary school in Fuka-
gawa, school inspectors were disconcerted to find that pupils
who received the rice balls supplied to undernourished children took them home at once for their younger sisters and
brothers. In Isao's college, however, no one was from this
part of Tokyo. Many were the children of provincial middle
school teachers and Shinto priests, and while few came from
wealthy families, still fewer came from families hard put to
lay food upon the table. As members of the families of moral
leaders they were well acquainted with the severity of the
conditions in the desolate and impoverished villages. Their
fathers, for the most part, were grieved at what they saw and
angry at what they did not see. All they could do was become
angry. For as schoolteachers and priests they had no responsibility for the dreadful poverty or for the fact that it was
ignored.

The government was skilled in relegating rich and poor to
separate boxes, from which they could hardly see each other.
Party politics, keeping to an accustomed rut that excluded
any changes either for better or worse, had lost the power to
deal the kind of killing blow to the spirit that had been embodied in the ordinance of the Ninth Year of the Meiji era that
forbade the wearing of swords. Its methods left its victims
still half-alive.

Isao had not drawn up any statement of principles. Since
the world was such that all that was evil in it applauded in-

ertia and weakness, the determination to act, whatever the act, would be their only principle. Consequently, when Isao interviewed his candidates, he said not a word to them about his intentions nor did he make any promises. When he had reached the point with one of these young men where he felt that he might admit him, he relaxed his hitherto unremitting sternness, and, looking him full in the eye with a kindly expression, asked simply: "What do you say? Are you with us?"

Izutsu and Sagara, following Isao's directions, had made up a dossier with a picture for each of the twenty students who had been admitted in this way. Although the information, of course, came from the candidate himself, it included full details on his family, the occupations of his father and brothers, his own character, his physique, his particular skills, his favorite books, and even the state of his relationship with girls. Isao was quite pleased that eight of the twenty were the sons of Shinto priests. The affair of the League of the Divine Wind was by no means something terminated long ago by death. The average age of the twenty was eighteen.

As Izutsu presented him with one dossier after another, Isao read each of them once again, storing the data in his head and making it a point to join each name in his memory with the proper picture. Even in regard to a comrade's personal affairs, he had to be prepared to speak sympathetically at the proper moment, in words that would reach his heart.

The firm conviction that the political situation was in sorry shape was, in fact, very well suited to the youthful tendency to think that reality itself was in sorry shape. Isao never worried about confusing the two. As far as he was concerned, whenever the slovenly beauties that covered the garish kiosks on the street corners troubled his thoughts on the way to school, this for him was an indication of the corrupt state of politics. He and his comrades had formed a political union that was necessarily based upon their boyhood sense of shame. Isao was ashamed of the present state of things.

"Only a month ago you couldn't even tell a fuse from a detonator," said Sagara in the midst of a minor dispute with Izutsu.

Isao smiled and said nothing. He had told his two friends to investigate thoroughly the manner of dealing with explosives. Sagara had asked a cousin who was an engineer to instruct him, and Izutsu had made the same request of a cousin in the Army.

"And you," Izutsu retorted, "I'll bet even you didn't know whether you cut a fuse straight across or diagonally."

The two then plucked blades of the pampas grass at their feet to represent fuses, and broke off a section of a thin and hollow dry branch for a percussion cap. They were ready to practice setting off a charge.

"Here's a well-made percussion cap for you," said Sagara boastfully as he packed dirt into the short branch with his fingertips. "You leave half of it hollow, and you stuff as much powder as you can into the other half." The wooden branch lacked, of course, the ominous fascination of a red brass percussion cap, like a metallic caterpillar, which concealed with capricious unreliability enough explosive power to blow off one's hand. It was no more than a thin branch reduced to its dry and withered shell. However, the lingering beams of the warm summer sun sinking into the woods of Hikawa Shrine shone through the busy, soiled fingers of the two boys, and from the direction toward which time was slipping came the distant, burnt odor of the inevitable killing to come. The odor, which might well have been nothing but the smoke from the kitchen fires of the nearby houses, combined with the sunlight to effect the sudden transformation of dirt into gunpowder and dry branch into percussion cap. Izutsu carefully inserted a thin blade of grass into the percussion cap and drew it out to gauge the length of the section not filled with gunpowder. He marked it with his fingernail and then laid it against the stalk of pampas grass that was to be the fuse and measured off an equal length. Finally, he slowly inserted this fuse into the percussion cap to the proper depth. Were he carelessly to thrust it too far, the percussion cap would explode.

"We don't have a crimper."

"Use your fingers. And no nonsense while you're doing it," said Sagara.

The color that suffused Izutsu's sweat-covered face showed his earnestness. Just as he had been taught, he grasped the percussion cap with his left hand, his forefinger at its tip, middle finger against the powder-filled portion, and his third finger and thumb close to the opening at the hollow end. Then as he placed the thumb and forefinger of his right hand, doing duty as a crimper, at this opening, he brought both hands down firmly to his left side and turned his face sharply to the right. Twisting his right hand, he skillfully performed the function of securing the fuse to the percussion cap. He kept his face turned away during this process, not looking at what he was doing, in order to protect his face on the off chance of the cap's exploding.

"You're overdoing it, looking away like that," said Sagara teasingly. "You've got your body so twisted that your hands won't be able to do the important job they're supposed to. And why so much bother to protect a face like yours?"

All that was left was to insert the cap securely into an explosive charge and light the fuse. Sagara, looking serious, helped with this, a clod of dirt serving as the explosives. Now to put a match to it. The flame of the match held against the still-green stalk of pampas grass quite obviously lacked the power to set it afire. The flame, all but invisible in the sunset light, burned halfway down the stem of the match before going out. A thirty-inch fuse allowed some forty or forty-five seconds. The stalk of pampas grass had been broken off at a length of thirty-five inches and so the two boys gazed at the second hand of their watches as it measured off fifty seconds.

"Hurry, run!"

"It's all right. I'm already a hundred meters away."

Still seated as before, the two made as if they had fled far from the spot, acting as though they were short of breath and laughing as they looked at each other.

Thirty seconds passed. Then ten seconds more. Thanks to their imagination, and to the time elapsed, the explosive charge with the cap thrust into it was now far from them. But the fuse had been lit, and all the conditions necessary for the explosion had been fulfilled. The flame crawled along the fuse like a ladybug with set purpose.

Finally the imagined charge, at its imagined distance, detonated. Something ugly and corrupt suddenly heaved as though giving a violent hiccough, and the evening sky was rent for a moment. The oaks shook in the surrounding grove. Everything became transparent. The very report itself was transparent as it beat against the red sky and spread its force. At last all was still.

"Better the Japanese sword," said Isao abruptly, looking up from the dossiers he had been scrutinizing. "We need twenty swords without fail. Some of our friends can surely slip them out of their homes for us."

"Wouldn't it be good to learn how to draw and strike at close range, and how to test a sword on a dead criminal?"

"We don't have that much time," said Isao. His voice was quiet but his words had a poetic fervor for the two boys. "Instead, before the end of vacation if possible, or else after the fall term begins, we should all attend Kaido Masugi's training camp on the rites of purification. We can talk about anything there, and he won't object to whatever kind of training we do. And if that's where we're going, we'll have a good reason for leaving our houses."

"It's not much fun to listen to Master Kaido from morning to night on the evils of Buddhism."

"That's something you'll have to bear with. He's a man who understands us thoroughly," Isao replied. He looked at his watch and got to his feet at once.

. . .

Isao and his two companions, deliberately waiting until somewhat past the designated hour of six o'clock, peered toward the shrine through the low door beside the already-shut main gate. The light of the evening sun fell upon a group of students. They faced uncertainly in various directions, their uneasiness quite apparent.

"Count them," said Isao in a low voice.

"Every one of them is there," said Izutsu, unable to restrain his happiness. Isao, however, knew how imprudent it would be to let himself steep in the satisfaction of being the object of such trust. Every man being present was certainly preferable to having absentees. But they were gathered there because of a telegram. Because they expected action. Because, in other words, of the reckless courage of youth. In order to temper their resolution, he would have to take this opportunity to plunge it into cold water.

With the setting sun behind it, the shrine's copper-tiled roof was dark, but the sun's rays caught the splendid ornamental crossbeams of its gable among the glossy branches of the surrounding ilexes and zelkovas. The slanting sunlight fell upon the black granite gravel spread within the shrine fence, catching a little of each pebble and giving it its own shadow, black as grapes at the end of autumn. Two sakaki trees were half in the shadow of the shrine while their upper branches shone brilliant.

The twenty young men were grouped around Isao, who stood facing them with the shrine to his rear. As they watched him silently, he felt the brightness of their eyes, due as much to their inner fire as to the sun striking their faces, he felt their longing for some incandescent power that would lift them up to the heavens, he felt their almost frantic dependence upon him.

"You have performed well in assembling here today," he said, breaking the silence. "Nothing could have made me happier than your coming here like this, from as far away as

Kyushu, with not a man missing. But my summons was not, as you thought, because I had some purpose. There was no purpose whatever. From all over Japan you've come, holding fast to the vision within your hearts, and you've gathered here utterly in vain."

Suddenly there was agitation among the group, and a murmur arose.

Isao raised his voice: "Do you understand? This meeting today is absolutely meaningless. There's no purpose to it. I have no work at all for you to do."

He said no more, and the murmuring subsided. Silence settled upon the gathered boys even as the night was overtaking them.

Then a single angry voice shouted out. It was a boy named Serikawa, the son of a Shinto priest in the far northeast: "What are you doing to us? If I thought I was being mocked, I couldn't stand it. I drank the farewell cup of water with my father before leaving home. My father has never ceased being indignant over the plight of the farming villages, and he told me that the time had come for the young to take action. So when the telegram arrived, he said nothing but raised the farewell cup with me and sent me off. If he learns I've been made a fool of, do you think my father will have nothing to say?"

"That's right," another boy chimed in promptly. "Serikawa is right."

"What kind of nonsense is this? I don't recall making any promises. You took my telegram telling you only to meet here, and you let your imaginations run wild. Isn't that what you did? Was there anything else in that telegram—anything other than the time and the place? Tell me," Isao demanded, keeping his voice calm as he ridiculed them.

"There's such a thing as common sense. If you decide to take some important action, are you going to tell people about it in a telegram? We should have decided on a code and a clear commitment from you. If we had, this wouldn't have happened," said Seyama, a student at the First High School, who was the same age as Isao. Since he lived in Shibuya, however, coming here could hardly have been much trouble for him.

"Just what wouldn't have happened? Isn't that simply going back to a situation where nothing will occur?" said Isao, quietly refuting him. "Isn't that simply realizing that what you all imagined was mistaken?"

The twilight was deepening so that it was becoming harder and harder to make out one another's features. There was a long silence. Only the chirping of insects filled the darkness.

"What are we to do then?"

When someone asked this in a pathetic whisper, Isao's response was immediate: "Whoever wants to go home, go home."

One white-shirted figure at once detached itself from the group and hurried toward the college gate. Then two more drew away and walked off. Serikawa did not leave. He squatted down by the shrine hedge and held his head in his hands. In a few moments, the others heard Serikawa's sobs. The sound seemed to penetrate the gloom in their hearts like a chill, white stream, a tiny Milky Way.

"I can't go back! I can't!" Serikawa muttered as he wept.

"Why don't all of you go home?" Isao shouted. "Despite what I've told you, you still don't understand?"

Not a single voice answered him. Furthermore this silence differed markedly from the one that had preceded it. It was a silence that gave the feeling that some huge, warm-blooded beast had risen up in the darkness. For the first time, Isao sensed firm response. It was hot, it had an animal smell, it was filled with blood, its pulse throbbed.

"All right then. You that are left, with no hopes, no expectations whatsoever, are you willing to throw away your lives on an act that probably will amount to nothing at all?"

"Yes," one voice spoke out with a forceful dignity.

Serikawa rose to his feet and began to walk toward Isao. His eyes, wet with tears, approached through the darkness so thick that a face could barely be seen until it was very close. His voice was choked from weeping, and when he spoke out boldly, its tone was frightfully low: "I'm still here too. I'll follow anywhere at all, and I'll keep quiet."

"Good enough. All right, let us make our vows together before the gods. Let's offer worship. Then I'll recite the vows. Say each one of them after me, all together." The sound of Isao, Izutsu, Sagara, and the remaining seventeen clapping their hands in worship echoed sharply through the darkness, as regularly as the night sea slapping a wooden gunwale.

Isao intoned: "Be it thus that we, emulating the purity of the League of the Divine Wind, hazard ourselves for the task of purging away all evil deities and perverse spirits."

The youthful voices of the others responded as one: "Be it thus that we, emulating the purity of the League of the Divine Wind, hazard ourselves for the task of purging away all evil deities and perverse spirits."

Isao's voice reverberated from the dimly visible plain wood doors of the inner shrine. Strong and deep, it rose up from his chest with all the poignance of the misty fantasies of youth. The stars were already out. The noise of streetcars jangled from far off. Isao chanted again: "Be it thus that we, forging deep friendship among ourselves, aid one another as comrades in responding to the perils that confront the nation."

"Be it thus that we, never seeking power and giving no thought to personal advancement, go forth to certain death to become the foundation stones for the Restoration."

As soon as they finished reciting the vows, one boy grasped Isao's hand and held it with both of his own. Then all of them were clasping each other's hands, and jostling in their haste to clasp Isao's. Beneath the starry sky, as their eyes grew more accustomed to the darkness, they thrust out their hands

again and again on all sides, seeking other hands still un-
grasped. No one spoke. Any words would have been inadequate.

Grasping hands were everywhere as though a growth of
tenacious ivy had sprung up from the darkness. Each tendril,
whether sweaty or dry or hard or soft to the touch, was filled
with strength as it held fast for a brief moment marked by a
mutual sharing of the warmth of their bodies and their blood.
Isao dreamed that he would some night stand like this with
his comrades upon the field of battle, taking wordless farewell before their deaths. Bathing in the marvelous satisfaction of having seen the task through to the finish and in the
blood that flowed from his own body, yielding his consciousness to that peak of sensitivity where the scarlet and the
white threads of ultimate pain and ultimate joy are woven
together. . . .

Since there were twenty of them in all, they could not
safely meet at the Academy of Patriotism. His father's eye
would be likely to search out Isao's plans. On the other hand,
Izutsu's home was too small and Sagara's, too, was unsuitable. This had been a concern of the three of them from the
beginning, but no workable plan had suggested itself. Even
if the three were to put their pocket money together, they
could not cope with the cost of all twenty meeting at a restaurant. And then a coffee shop would hardly be the place to
speak of grave matters.

Now, after the handclasps beneath the stars that sealed
their alliance, it was Isao who felt a reluctance to put an end
to things that night without something further. Then, too, he
was hungry. No doubt all the boys were hungry. He turned
perplexed eyes toward the main gate, where a dim light was
burning.

Below the gate light, a little to one side, was something
like a moonflower that seemed to be floating in the air. It was
the face of a woman who was standing there, her head
slightly bowed, not wanting to be seen. Once his eyes had

discovered her, he found he could not turn away.

Somewhere in his heart he had recognized who she was. His dominant wish, however, was to go on a little longer without recognizing her. The woman's face floating in its dark seclusion, no name yet attached to it, had the character of a mysterious, lovely apparition. It was like the scent of the fragrant olive which, as one walks along a path at night, tells of the blossoms before one sees them. Isao wanted to keep things just as they were, if only for an instant more. At this moment a woman was a woman, not someone with a name attached to her.

And that was not all. Because of her hidden name, because of the agreement not to speak that name, she was transmuted into a marvelous essence, like a moonflower, its supporting vine invisible, floating high up in the darkness. This essence which preceded existence, this phantasm which preceded reality, this portent which preceded the event conveyed with unmistakable force the presence of a substance yet more powerful. This presence which showed itself as gliding through air—this was woman.

Isao had yet to embrace a woman. Still, never so strongly as at this moment, when he keenly sensed this "womanliness that preceded woman," had he felt that he too knew what ecstasy meant. For this was a presence that he could even now embrace. In time, that is, it had drawn near with an exquisite subtlety, and in space it was only a little distant. The affectionate emotion that filled his breast was like a vapor that could envelop her. And yet once she was gone, Isao, like a child, could forget her entirely.

However, after Isao had for some time let his thoughts dwell upon this presence, he found himself, despite his earlier wish to preserve the moment, unable to bear the uncertainty any longer.

"Wait for me," he ordered Izutsu in a voice loud enough for all to hear, and sprinted toward the gate. There was a dry, faint stutter of scampering clogs as his white splashed-pattern kimono disappeared into the darkness.

Isao went through the low door beside the gate. Just as he had imagined, the woman standing there was Makiko.

Makiko's hair was arranged in a different manner, something that even the inexperienced Isao noticed at once. It was a stylish hairdo that covered her ears, leaving only a wavy border about her temples and cheeks, pressing in upon her features and giving her face a heightened air of mystery. Although she was not one to use much makeup, the nape of her neck seemed to stand out like a carving in relief above the crepe of her Akashi kimono, which seemed a solid navy blue in the darkness. A whiff of some fragrant scent from her body struck Isao with unnerving force.

"Miss Makiko! What are you doing here?"

"What am I doing? All of you came here at six, didn't you, to recite your vows?"

"How did you know that?"

"Don't be stupid!" Makiko's teeth gleamed as she laughed. "Didn't you yourself say so?"

Thus challenged, Isao had to conclude that a few days ago, concerned as he was with the ever-present worry of not having a place to meet, he had probably happened to let slip the time and place of the vows in her presence. He had always been willing to confide anything to Makiko, but he felt ashamed at the thought of revealing something important and then forgetting about it, with her of all people. Perhaps he lacked some quality essential in one who was to lead men and bring about events. In his carelessness in so grave a matter, Isao could not fail to detect a certain unmanly dependence upon her. Though quite different before his comrades, in Makiko's presence he felt a subtle desire to seem a heedless young man.

"Well . . . it's just that you took me by surprise. But why have you come?"

"I thought that, after gathering a large group of students together, you might be hard put for a place to bring them.

First of all I imagine you are quite hungry, aren't you?"

Isao scratched his head with a fresh, boyish candor.

"We'd be happy to offer all of you dinner at our house, but since it's a long way from here, Father suggested that I treat you to a sukiyaki dinner in Shibuya, and he gave me the money for it. He was invited to a poetry composition party tonight, and so I'm here in his place to offer you gentlemen our hospitality. Don't worry, I can take care of the bill."

Then Makiko, as though drawing up a fresh-caught fish, held up a large Panama handbag with a quick motion of her white hand. Despite the fragile grace of the slender wrist that appeared from the sleeve, however, it was a hand that seemed to convey something of the fatigue of late summer.

19

ABOUT THIS SAME TIME, Honda was attending a performance of *Matsukazé* at the Osaka Nō Theater in Tennoji-Dogashiba at the invitation of a colleague fond of performing Nō chants himself. It was a production featuring Kanesuké Noguchi from Tokyo as *shité* with Yazo Tamura assisting him as *waki*. The theater stood upon the eastern slope of Uemachi Hill between Tennoji and Osaka Castle. This had been a section of fine villas at the beginning of the Taisho period and was still a secluded area containing high-walled mansions. One of these functioned as a Nō theater under the auspices of the Sumitomo family.

Most of the guests were merchant princes, and Honda recognized many of them. As for the famous actor, the harsh-voiced Noguchi, Honda's colleague had warned him beforehand that, although his intonation might sound like a goose being strangled, Honda was not by any means to laugh. And he predicted that, ignorant of Nō though Honda was, once the play was underway he would suddenly find himself emotionally aroused.

Honda had reached the age at which advice of this sort did not provoke any childish antipathy. Although the reason that had been his foundation had begun to crumble when he met Isao Iinuma at the beginning of the summer, his usual habits of thought had not changed. Once again he found himself believing that, just as he had never contracted venereal disease, neither had he ever experienced emotional arousal.

As soon as the exchange was finished between the *waki* as a priest and the clown, the *shité* and his companion made their entrance along the passageway at the left rear. Honda's colleague explained to him that the serene and tranquil accompaniment now being played was ordinarily limited to that entrance scene in god plays. *Matsukaze* contained the sole exception to this rule. Such was the high regard, it seemed, in which this music was held as expressing the full force of the occult.

Matsukazé and Murasamé, both clad in white robes revealing scarlet underskirts spilling out beneath, faced each other on the entrance bridgeway, and then began to chant in unison as quietly as the rain falling and sinking into a sandy beach: "Drawing our brine cart along, how briefly we live in this sad world, how fleetingly!"

Though Honda was distracted by the reflection of the pointed pines falling on the highly polished cypress floor of the stage, gleaming too brilliantly beneath the rather harsh lighting of this Nō theater, the final "how fleetingly!" rang clear in his ear, as the lighter and brighter tones of the companion entangled the deeper and more melancholy voice, ever on the verge of breaking, of Kanesuké Noguchi.

Since there was, of course, nothing to interfere with listening, the words were easily recalled.

"Drawing our brine cart along, how briefly we live in this sad world, how fleetingly!"

No matter how lean, how slender of body, the graceful figure of the verse took on significant form in Honda's mind. At that moment he shuddered without knowing why.

Then the companion began to chant the second verse: "The waves beat close to us, here at the Bay of Suma. Even the moon moves us to tears that wet our sleeves."

After the two had joined together to chant the concluding words, the *shité*, as Matsukazé, began a vigorous soliloquy: "The autumn wind saddens the heart. A little away from the sea . . ."

Although Kanesuké Noguchi wore the mask of a beautiful young woman, his voice had nothing that would recall a woman's charm. It was a voice that made one think of the rasping together of rusty, discolored metal. Furthermore, his recitation was broken by interruptions, and his style of chanting seemed to be tearing the beauty of the words to shreds. But despite all this, the mood inspired was like the outpouring of a dark and ineffably elegant mist, like the sight of a moonbeam shining into a corner of a ruined palace to fall upon a mother-of-pearl furnishing. Because the light passed through a worn and ravaged bamboo blind, the elegance of the shattered fragments shone all the more.

Gradually, then, his harsh voice became far from irritating. Rather, one had the feeling that only through this harsh voice could one for the first time become aware of the briny sadness of Matsukazé and the melancholy love that afflicts those in the realm of the dead.

Honda at some point began to find it hard to tell whether the images that shifted to and fro before him were reality or illusion. On the gleaming cypress surface of the stage, like the mirroring sea at the shoreline, was reflected the glittering embroidery of the white robes and scarlet underskirts of two beautiful women.

Mingling with the words of the soliloquy, the first line still held stubborn sway in Honda's heart: "Drawing our brine cart along, how briefly we live in this sad world, how fleetingly!"

What came to his mind was not the meaning of this line but the significance of the unaccountable shudder that he had felt when the *shite* and his companion had stood together on the bridgeway and recited it, the moment of recitation imbued with perfect stillness, the chant falling like quiet rain.

And what was that significance? Just then beauty itself had begun to walk before him. Like the beach plover, strong in flight but unsteady on the ground, the white *tabi*-shod feet moved on tiptoe as though come for a few brief moments to make their way through the world known to man.

This beauty, however, would occur but once. A man could do nothing but commit it to memory immediately and reflect upon it thereafter. Then too it was a beauty that preserved a noble futility, a purposelessness.

Keeping pace with Honda's thoughts, the Nō drama of *Matsukaze* flowed on, a small stream of never-failing emotion.

"Dwelling in this world we find thus so wretched, even while envying the carefree moon clear above us, come let us ladle out the tidewater she summons."

That which chanted and moved about on the stage bathed in moonlight was now no longer the ghosts of two beautiful women but something beyond description. One might call it the essence of time, the pith of emotion, the dream that stubbornly obtrudes upon reality. It had no purpose, no meaning. From moment to moment it fashioned a beauty not of this world. For here what hope is there that one moment of beauty will follow at once upon another?

Thus did Honda gradually become drawn into a mood of somber detachment. His thoughts had now become clearly focused. Kiyoaki's existence, his life, its consequences— Honda realized that it was a long time indeed since he had concentrated so intently on all this. It was easy to think of

Kiyoaki's life as a breath of fragrance that had wafted faintly over a single era before vanishing. Even so, Kiyoaki's sin, Kiyoaki's heartbreak remained. And Honda himself would never be able to make reparation.

Honda recalled a morning of melting snow on the campus of the Peers School before classes began. He and Kiyoaki, sitting in an arbor encircled by flowerbeds and listening to the fresh sound of trickling water, were deeply involved in a long conversation, something rare with them.

That was early spring in the second year of Taisho, 1913. Kiyoaki and Honda were both nineteen. Since then nineteen years had passed. Honda remembered insisting that like it or not, a hundred years later he and Kiyoaki would be included in the thought of the era, lumped together with those they had the least regard for, classified with them on the basis of a few meager similarities. He remembered also that he had talked of the irony of the human will's relationship to history, vehemently maintaining that every strong-willed person was in the last analysis frustrated and that there was only one way to participate in history: "To function as a shining, forever unchanging, beautiful nonwilling particle."

His terms had been entirely abstract; yet as he had been speaking on that morning of melting snow, his eyes had been resting upon the shining, beautiful features of Kiyoaki. Obviously, with Kiyoaki before him, a youth so lacking in will, so single-mindedly devoted to the vagaries of emotion, Honda's words had of their own accord fashioned a portrait of Kiyoaki himself: "To function as a shining, forever unchanging, beautiful nonwilling particle"—a clear definition of Kiyoaki's manner of living.

When a hundred years had passed since that morning, the perspective would, no doubt, once more be altered. Nineteen years before was too recent a time for generalizations and too distant for minute assessment. Kiyoaki's image was not yet confused with the rough, wholly insensitive image of boys of the kendo team pursuing their cult of toughness. Nevertheless, Kiyoaki's particular kind of "heroic figure," as a fore-runner of that brief and fleeting period at the beginning of the Taisho era when a wholehearted surrender to the emotions enjoyed favor, had already, viewed from across the years, lost much of its vividness. The earnest passion of that time, except for its fond persistence in a man's memory, had now become something to provoke laughter.

Each passing year, never failing to exact its toll, keeps altering what was sublime into the stuff of comedy. Is something eaten away? If the exterior is eaten away, is it true, then, that the sublime pertains by nature only to an exterior that conceals a core of nonsense? Or does the sublime indeed pertain to the whole, but a ludicrous dust settles upon it?

When Honda reflected upon his own character, he had no choice but to conclude that he was a man possessed of a will. At the same time, however, he could not avoid misgivings as to the ability of that will to change anything or to accomplish anything even in contemporary society, let alone in the course of future history. Often his courtroom decisions had determined whether a man lived or died. Such a verdict might have seemed of extreme significance at the time, but as the years passed—since all men were fated to die—it turned out that he had merely hastened a man's fate; and that the deaths had been neatly consigned to one corner of history, where they soon disappeared. And as for the disturbing conditions of the present world, though his will had had nothing to do with bringing these about, he as a judge was ever at their beck and call. How much the choices made by his will proceeded from pure reason and how much, without his realizing it, they were coerced by the prevailing thought of the period was a question he was unable to decide.

Then again, when Honda looked at the world around him, no matter how searchingly, nowhere did he see any effect traceable to a youth called Kiyoaki—to his violent emotion, to his death, to his life of beauty. Nowhere was there evidence that anything had come about as a result of his death, that anything had changed because of it. It seemed to have been smoothly expunged from history.

In the course of such reflections, Honda came to realize that his exposition of nineteen years before had contained an odd presage. For, after explaining the frustration in store for a will that insisted upon having an effect on history, Honda had at last discovered that his own usefulness lay exactly in the frustration of that will. And now, nineteen years later, he found himself envying Kiyoaki's lack of anything remotely like it, envying Kiyoaki's having left not a single trace in the world. He could not help but recognize in Kiyoaki, whose image had become lost to history, an inner substance superior to Honda's for participating in history.

Kiyoaki had been beautiful. His life had been useless, devoid of any purpose whatsoever. He had passed swiftly through the world, his beauty severely limited to but a single lifespan, to an instant like that depicted in the chanted line: "Drawing our brine cart along, how briefly we live in this sad world, how fleetingly!"

The truculent face of another young man rose sharply into view amidst the swirling froth of vanishing beauty. It was Kiyoaki's beauty alone that would truly occur but once. Its very excess made a renewed life essential. There had to be a reincarnation. Something had remained unfulfilled in Kiyoaki, had found expression in him only as a negative factor.

The face of that other young man . . . He had ripped off his kendo mask, its bars glittering in bright summer sunlight. Sweat poured down over his features. His nostrils flared as he breathed violently. His lips formed a line as straight as a sword.

The figures that Honda gazed upon on a stage misted with light were no longer the gorgeous figures of the *shité* and his companion as two women dipping up sea water. The two who were there carrying out a task imbued with futility, now standing, now sitting with a singular elegance in the moon's rays, were two young men of diverse eras. Two young men the same age. From a distance, they looked alike, but, seen closer, their diametrically opposed characters became evident. The sturdy hands of one of them callused from the sword handle, the white hands of the other soft from indolence— these hands were devoted in turn to dipping up water of the sea of time. At intervals the sound of a flute, like a moon-beam darting through a break in the clouds, pierced the mortal forms of the two young men. By turns, they were drawing the brine cart, its two fourteen-inch wheels hung with scarlet damask, through the mirroring water at the sea's edge. This time, however, what sounded in Honda's ear was not the elegant, somewhat wearied verse "Drawing our brine cart along, how briefly we live in this sad world, how fleetingly!" The lines suddenly altered to a sutra verse: "Six paths for reborn sentient beings to tread, like the turning wheel, without respite." And on stage the wheels of the brine cart began turning round and round.

Honda thought of the various doctrines of transmigration and reincarnation that he had encountered when he had on occasion given himself over to this study. The word for both transmigration and rebirth was "samsara" in Sanskrit. According to the doctrine of transmigration, mankind's lot was to traverse the six states of the Sphere of Illusion without surcease—the Earth Hell, the Hell of Starvation, the Hell of Beasts, the Hell of Pandemonium, human existence, and ethereal existence. The term "rebirth," however, was sometimes used to designate the transition from the Sphere of Illusion to the Sphere of Enlightenment. In that event, transmigration would be at an end. Transmigration necessarily involved rebirth, but rebirth did not necessarily involve transmigration.

At any rate, Buddhism recognized that there was a subject who underwent this transmigration, but it did not recognize this subject as constituting a constant and unchanging core. Since Buddhism denied the existence of the self, there was no place in it for the existence of the soul either. There was nothing but an extremely subtle nucleus at the center of mental activity, something that pertained to the innermost functioning of the phenomena surrounding the continual birth and death that accompanied transmigration. This, then, was the subject—something that the doctrine of *Yuishiki*, "awareness only," designated "Alaya Awareness."

Since none of the things of this world, even sentient beings, had souls as their core subject, and since insentient beings, emerging through causality, lacked even a core subject, there was nothing within the universe truly possessed of its own substance.

If the subject of transmigration was the Alaya Awareness, then the mode of activity of transmigration constituted its Karma. The theories thence grew quite numerous, the "one hundred thousand diverse exegeses" that characterized Buddhism. One theory held that the Alaya Awareness was already defiled by sin and was therefore itself Karma. Another held that the Alaya Awareness was half-defiled, half-undefiled, and hence could serve as the bridge to salvation.

Honda remembered having, in the course of his study, gone through these intricate theories of Karma and of the origin of things as well as through the difficult metaphysics of the Five Aggregates, which were the source of continuation, but the truth of the matter was that his grasp of them had grown uncertain.

In the meantime, *Matsukazé* had advanced to the climax of its first half.

SHITÉ: Into this pail, too, has the moon's image entered.
CHORUS: Fortunate event! Into it, too, has the moon's image entered.
SHITÉ: The moon is but one.
CHORUS: Two are its images. We bear the moon itself, shining in the floodtide, on our cart tonight. Now this toil no longer seems wretched, as we draw our burden home.

For Honda it was once more the beautiful Matsukazé and Murasamé who held the stage. The *waki*, in the role of a priest, arose from his position by the *waki* pillar. Honda could now clearly distinguish the face of each spectator and hear each beat of the drum.

That sleepless night at the Hotel Nara after he thought he had been confronted with proof of Kiyoaki's reincarnation now seemed to Honda like a vaguely remembered event of the distant past. A crack had certainly appeared in the foundation of reason. But earth had filled the crack at once, and the lush grass of summer sprouted from it, completely hiding the memory of that night. As in the Nō drama before him, a phantom had confronted his reason, and his reason had for a brief time suspended its function. Isao was not necessarily the only young man to have a cluster of moles in the same spot as Kiyoaki. The meeting beneath the waterfall was not necessarily beneath the falls that Kiyoaki had spoken of in his delirium. Two chance occurrences of this sort provided but a flimsy basis for concluding that Kiyoaki had been reincarnated.

Now it appeared extremely rash to Honda, versed as he was in the procedural methods of criminal law, to have come to that conclusion on no stronger evidence. The desire to believe in Kiyoaki's reincarnation shone within him like a small puddle of water at the bottom of a dry well, but Honda's reason had already told him in unequivocal terms that the well was dry. Whether or not there was something dubious about the very foundation of his reason was a matter that was certainly better left unexamined. The wisest course was to let matters stand as they were.

"How foolish!" he exclaimed, feeling as if he had suddenly come to his senses. "How very foolish! Hardly a thing to be expected from a thirty-eight-year-old judge."

However subtle the systems that Buddhism constructed, they pertained to problems outside of Honda's jurisdiction. He felt refreshed, as though he had that instant skillfully solved the vexing riddle that he had been mulling over these many months. He had regained his clarity of soul. He was now not at all unlike those accomplished men around him, who had come to this Nō theater to escape for a time the urgent demands of their work.

The Nō stage, so close at hand, shone like the world beyond. Spirits walked there, and Honda was stirred. That was sufficient. When he thought of how, that night in Nara, the pain of a bereavement incurred nineteen years before had quickened again within him and caused him to succumb to a delusion of such proportions, he saw that what had been reborn in all likelihood was not Kiyoaki himself but merely his own sense of loss.

When he returned home, Honda, for the first time in long months, felt the urge to read the dream journal that Kiyoaki had left to him.

20

OCTOBER BEGAN with a stretch of fine weather. Isao was returning from school and had almost reached home when, drawn by the sound of the wooden clappers used to attract children to a storyteller's "paper theater," he turned into a side lane, making a slight detour. A crowd of children had gathered at a street corner.

The warm rays of the autumn sun struck the curtain of the tiny stage mounted on the rear of a bicycle, where a succession of pictures would illustrate the tale. It was clear at a glance that the storyteller was a man out of work. He needed a shave. He wore a wrinkled jacket over his dirty shirt.

The unemployed of Tokyo—as though acting in concert, it seemed—affected an appearance that made obvious their being out of work, giving not the least indication that they wanted to hide their condition. Some kind of invisible pock-mark covered their faces. Those who had caught the disease of unemployment, like men struck by a secret plague, seemed anxious to be recognized as set apart from others. The story-teller, striking his sticks together, glanced hastily in Isao's direction. Isao knew that the man saw him as a naïve, shel-tered schoolboy.

The children, eager for the storyteller to open the curtain, were imitating the laugh of the Golden Bat. Isao did not stop, but as he passed, the image that appeared through the part-ing curtain caught his eye: the glaring yellow skull mask, of the Golden Bat, who, in green tunic and white tights, trailed his crimson cloak as he flew through the sky. It was a crude and distorted image. Isao had once heard that pictures of this sort were drawn by poor boys, who were paid the consider-able wage of one yen, fifty sen a day.

The storyteller cleared his throat and began his prelim-inary narration: "Well now, the Golden Bat, the champion of justice . . ." The sound of his gravelly voice followed Isao as he walked on, leaving the paper theater and the crowd of children behind him.

As he turned into a quiet street in Nishikata with a wall running along one side of it, that gold-skulled phantom who soared through the sky pursued him. How grotesque an image of justice was that bizarre golden figure!

He found no one at home when he got there, and he walked around to the back yard. Sawa was doing his laundry at the side of the well, humming the while. He was quite pleased that the weather was so suited to drying.

"Welcome home. Nobody's here. They all went to help with Mr. Koyama's seventy-seventh birthday celebration. Your mother too."

The old gentleman was a luminary of the world of the right, and Iinuma was one of those who had long enjoyed his patronage. Sawa, for fear of committing some breach of etiquette, had probably been ordered to remain behind to look after the house.

Since Isao had nothing better to do, he sat down on a ragged clump of grass. Now, at noontime, the faint chirping of insects gave way to the noise of Sawa's splashing. The sky, piercingly clear, was mirrored, then shattered again and again in the tub water belabored by Sawa. Everything was right with the world. The elements seemed to be doing their best to reduce Isao's design to a flight of fancy. The trees, the bright sky joined in cooling his burning will, calming the torrent of his violent passion. They were trying to make him seem to himself like one altogether out of touch with reality, possessed by the illusion of a reform that was unwanted. His youthfulness, however, was like a steel blade, and the autumn sky, dazzling blue to no purpose, was at least in harmony with that.

Sawa seemed to have no difficulty in sensing what was behind Isao's silence.

"Have you been going to kendo practice lately?" he asked as he bunched up a white wad in the tub and kneaded it with his thick hands as though making rice balls.

"No."

"That so?" Sawa did not ask why.

Isao stole a glance into the tub. The amount of Sawa's laundry seemed hardly in keeping with his extravagant efforts. For Sawa would wash no one's clothes but his own.

"As hard as I work to keep myself clean," he said, somewhat out of breath, "I wonder if the day will ever come when I'll be of service."

"Maybe tomorrow will be the day," said Isao, baiting him gently. "And where will Mr. Sawa be but bent over his washtub?"

Sawa never explained what he meant by "be of service" beyond an unswerving insistence that when the hour struck it would be unfitting for any man to be clad in other than dazzling white underwear.

He wrung out his clothes at last. The water struck the dry ground in glittering black drops. Without looking at Isao, he began to speak in a droll tone of voice. "Well, it seems to me that, rather than wait for the master, it might be best to look to young Mr. Iinuma for an early opportunity."

When he heard this, Isao's first concern was whether his expression had changed. There could be no doubt that Sawa had sniffed out something. Had Isao himself been guilty of some lapse?

Not giving the least sign that he had caught Isao's reaction, Sawa draped his laundry over one arm and hastily wiped off the drying pole with a rag.

"When will you be going to Master Kaido's training camp?" he asked.

"Well, I'm assigned to the week beginning the twentieth of October. It's all filled up until then. I hear that nowadays a lot of businessmen are attending."

"Who's going with you?"

"I asked the ones in my study group at school."

"You know what? I'd like to go too. Let me see if it's all right with the master. After all, what good am I but to watch the place when everybody's gone? So I think he might let me go with you. It would toughen me up and do me a lot of good to get in with you young fellows. When you get to be my age, no matter how eager your spirit is, your body's got a will of its own. Come on now, what do you say?"

Isao found himself without an answer. Indeed, if Sawa did ask his father, the reply certainly would be yes. And if he were to go with them, it would spoil the chance for the crucial talk with his comrades that Isao had gone to such trouble to arrange. Sawa might even be aware of what was up and be trying to draw him out. Furthermore, if Sawa meant to convey his dedication, his request might well be nothing but a roundabout way of communicating his desire to be numbered among Isao's comrades.

Turning to Isao, Sawa ran the pole through his undershirt

and drawers and then fastened his Etchu loincloth to it by its string. Since he had not wrung them out as well as he might, water from his clothes ran down the slanted pole and dripped from its end, but this did not trouble him at all. While he was thus occupied, the back that bulged beneath the khaki shirt, the whole heavy, insensitive mass of flesh before Isao's eyes, seemed to be pressing him for an answer. Still, Isao did not know what to say.

Just as he had set the drying pole at a convenient level, a gust of wind caught a corner of the wet cloth and slapped it against Sawa's cheek. Startled as though a huge white dog were licking his face, he pushed it away and stepped hurriedly back. Then, turning to Isao in a carefree manner, he asked: "Is there any reason why you really wouldn't want me to come along?"

Had Isao been a youth of some sophistication, he might have turned Sawa aside with a light answer. But since he was indeed thinking that Sawa's coming would cause difficulty, joking was out of the question.

Sawa did not pursue the matter. Instead, he asked Isao to come to his room to share some delicious cakes he had. The room was a full three mats and Sawa had it to himself in deference to his age. There were no books to be seen, only a few tattered copies of *Kodan Club*. When chided on this point, Sawa would reply that those who read books to imbibe the Japanese Spirit were "pseudopatriots."

He poured Isao a cup of tea and offered him the rice cakes, a kind called higomochi, which his wife in Kumamoto had sent.

"Anyway," said Sawa with a sigh, apropos of nothing, "there's no doubt that the master loves you."

Then after rummaging through the debris that littered the floor he came up with a fan decorated with a picture of a pretty woman, but when he tried to present Isao with this holiday gift from a neighborhood saké dealer, whose name and phone number were prominently displayed on it, he was rebuffed. The slender lady with a faraway look somewhat resembled Makiko around the eyes, and this was what lent an undue severity to Isao's abrupt refusal. Sawa, however, had not meant to imply anything, apparently, and his proffering the fan was but another example of his idiosyncratic behavior.

"Would you really like to go to the training camp?" Isao asked, regretting the harshness of his rebuff and wanting to end at once the lingering tension between them.

"No, not really," answered Sawa, putting him off casually as though he had lost interest in the matter. "I'd probably be busy and couldn't go anyway. I was just asking." Then, as though to himself, he repeated his irrelevant remark. "Yes, there's no doubt that the master loves you." He wrapped both of his hands, their plump flesh dimpled at the joint of each finger, around the sturdy mug that held his tea and began a story that was wholly unsolicited.

"This is something I think young Master Isao is old enough to know. It's only recently that the Academy has been so well off. When I started here, we had all we could do to make ends meet. You were never told, and I know that this was in keeping with the master's theory of education. But if I might say so, it's getting to be time for you to learn some unpleasant things. Because if your education leaves out anything that you should know, then later on you'll be scandalized.

"It was three years ago, I think, that the *New Japan* came out with a piece attacking Mr. Koyama, the very one whose birthday it happens to be today. The master said it wouldn't do to let this go by and say nothing. He went to see Mr. Koyama, but I never found out exactly what decision they came to. Anyway, the master told me to go to the newspaper office and demand that they print a thoroughgoing apology. The instructions he gave me were certainly strange. 'If they offer money, don't take it. Throw it back at them angrily and leave,' he said. 'But if they don't offer any money, it's a sign that you've handled things badly.'

"It's rather fun to pretend to be angry when you really aren't. And I don't mind seeing a frightened look on people's faces. Especially in this case, it helped matters that the one they picked to deal with me was a rather cheeky young editor.

"The master's strategy was wonderfully worked out. He sends somebody like me to begin the negotiations. If I do say so myself, I seem to be a likable sort of person, and nobody takes it too seriously even if I'm boiling with rage, so this fellow thinks he can settle the matter with a little money. Then when to his surprise I break off the meeting, the other side starts to get a bit uneasy.

"The master arranges matters so there's never a direct meeting with Mr. Koyama, and in the course of the negotiations he puts five actors on the stage, five hurdles, each steeper than the one before. Each one of these gentlemen is more formidable and prestigious than the last. The other side gets in deeper and deeper without having any idea how far we're going to go before we settle. Furthermore there can be no question of extortion, since we keep insisting that 'This isn't a matter of money,' and so they have no grounds for going to the police. The second actor to take the stage is Mr. Muto, who was involved in the June Incident. And it's at this point that the *New Japan* becomes aware, to its great surprise, that this is no simple matter.

"Furthermore, in going from the second actor to the third, the interval is made as indefinite as possible, and while offering the hope that a settlement can be had by a meeting with the third actor, the master arranges it so that this meeting seems as though it's never going to take place. And then when it finally does come off after all the anxiety, authority has been switched to a fourth party, unknown to them. At this stage, the number of 'young men who can't contain their wrath' soars to far more than a mere one or two hundred, though none of them makes an appearance.

"As might be expected, the newspaper loses no time in hiring a former detective, and this fellow comes rubbing his hands obsequiously, carrying his letter of sanction from the publisher. The master was also very careful in picking out just the right meeting places, and when our fourth actor, Mr. Yoshimori, goes on stage, the setting is perfect. He has connections with a construction company, and so the master makes it the shanty office on a building site.

"After four months of harassment, a smooth big shot who looks easygoing finally appears on the scene as our fifth actor. I can't tell you his name, but thanks to his hard bargaining, an agreement was reached. The place was in Yanagibashi. The publisher of the *New Japan* himself was there, and kowtowed to us, but with all that, they handed over something like fifty thousand yen. It seems the master got ten thousand as his share. That took care of the Academy very well for a year."

Isao had been trying to suppress his irritation as he listened. Vanity compelled him to show that petty evils of this sort could by no means upset him. What was hard to bear, however, was the realization that he himself had up to now been enjoying the fruits of such petty evils.

Nevertheless, to suppose that Isao was having his eyes opened for the first time to the true state of affairs would be an exaggeration. Isao himself would not deny that his unwillingness to look into certain fundamental aspects of his life had somehow been the basis for his sense of purity, as well as the source of the strange anger and disquiet that troubled him. To plant one's feet upon evil and yet render justice was an overblown concept flattering to the vanity of youth. The problem was that Isao's imagined evil had been of somewhat greater dimensions. But, whatever the case, this did not offer adequate cause for Isao to have misgivings about his purity.

Calming himself with an effort, he asked: "Does my father still make a practice of doing this?"

"Now things are different. Now he's an important man. That kind of struggle isn't necessary any more. What I wanted you to know is what the master had to go through before he got where he is."

Then Sawa, after a slight pause, made still another incongruous statement, and though he tossed it off carelessly, it stunned Isao: "You can go after whoever you want. But don't go after Busuké Kurahara. If anything should happen to him, the one who'll suffer most will be the master. Go ahead out of a sense of loyalty, and you'll find yourself utterly betraying your father."

21

Isao left Sawa's room abruptly and, determined to probe the significance of his words, shut himself in his own room.

Just as hot pepper becomes less pungent as it numbs the inside of the mouth, so the shock of the words "Don't go after Busuké Kurahara" was not that intense after a time. They did not necessarily imply that Sawa had penetrated Isao's secret. For Busuké Kurahara was in the eyes of many men the very personification of capitalistic evil.

If Sawa had perceived that Isao had some plan or other in mind he might well imagine that Kurahara's name would, as a matter of course, come up as one objective. And his advice not to single out Kurahara would not really depend upon his knowing that Isao had already done so.

There remained a single problem: Sawa's implication in linking his father's name to Kurahara. Was Kurahara actually an important financial backer of his father? A secret patron of the Academy of Patriotism? The thought seemed unbearable. But since this was a problem that Isao was unable to solve in his present circumstances, the truth or falsity of the allegation was a matter that would have to be set aside for a time. The irritation that burned greedily within him came more from this uncertainty than from anger.

Actually, Isao knew nothing of Kurahara other than what he had gained from studying photographs of him in newspapers and magazines and carefully reading about what he said and did. Kurahara was the unmistakable incarnation of a capitalism devoid of national allegiance. If one wished to portray the frightening image of a man who loved nothing, there was no better model than Kurahara. At any rate, in an era when everyone was choking, the fact that this man alone could evidently breathe with ease was in itself grounds enough for suspecting that he was a criminal.

One of his best-known comments, quoted by a newspaper, displayed a heedlessness that seemed carefully contrived: "Naturally, having a large number of unemployed is unpleasant. However to equate this immediately with an unsound economy is fallacious. Common sense tells us that the contrary is true. The welfare of Japan is not bound up with there being good cheer in everybody's kitchen." Such words stirred anger and resentment and were never forgotten.

The evil of Kurahara was that of an intellect that had no ties with blood nor with native soil. In any case, though Isao knew nothing of Kurahara the man, Kurahara's evil was vividly clear to him.

There were the bureaucrats of the Foreign Ministry, anxious to please England and America, oozing charm, only able to play the coquette. The financiers, giving off the stink of profit and greed, sniffing along the ground for their dinner like giant anteaters. The politicians self-transformed into lumps of corruption. The military cliques, so armored with the cult of careerism that they were like immobilized beetles. The scholars, bespectacled, sodden white grubs. The speculators eager to exploit Manchuria, their beloved bastard child.

And the sky itself reflected a panorama of poverty, like sunrise colors spread wide over the land. Kurahara was a cold, black silk top hat placed in the midst of this piteous landscape. Without saying so, Kurahara looked forward to many deaths, he welcomed them.

The sorrowful sun, the sun glittering with a chill whiteness, could give no touch of warmth, yet rose up sadly every morning to begin its course. This was indeed the figure of His Majesty. Who would not long to look up again to behold the joyful countenance of the sun?

If this Kurahara . . .

Isao opened the window. He spat. If the food he had eaten at breakfast, if his lunch, too, had come through Kurahara's bounty, then, in his ignorance, he had already corrupted his innards and his flesh with poison.

Suppose he confronted his father and questioned him severely. But would his father tell him the truth? Rather than hear skillful evasions, he preferred to keep silent and pretend to know nothing.

If only he did know nothing, if only he could have gone on without learning of this, thought Isao, stamping his feet and cursing himself for having heard it. He also felt resentment toward Sawa for having sprinkled the poison into his ears. And however much Isao feigned ignorance, Sawa might sometime tell the father what he had revealed to the son. Then, too, he would become a son who knowingly betrays his own father. He would be a traitor who kills the benefactor of his family. The purity of his conduct would be subject to question. An act conceived as bold and pure seemed in danger of becoming most impure.

How was Isao to guard his purity? Do nothing at all? Remove Kurahara's name from the list of those to be assassinated? No. If he did that, would not the cost of his being an unhappy but dutiful son be to overlook something that threatened the entire nation? Would it not be the betrayal of His Sacred Majesty as well as the betrayal of his own sincerity?

When Isao reflected, he saw that his not knowing Kurahara well was a circumstance that augmented the justice of his action. The evil of Kurahara should be kept as distant and abstract as possible. Only when the murderer could put aside not only all thought of favors granted or personal enmity but even the most elementary human considerations of liking or disliking did his act have a foundation in justice. Thus Isao's distant awareness of the evil of Kurahara was quite enough.

Killing a hateful man was an easy matter. Cutting down a despicable person was a pleasure. But Isao had no desire to seize upon an enemy's lack of humanity in order to steel himself to the act of killing. The massive evil of Kurahara as fixed in Isao's mind had nothing to do with such petty and inconsequential evils as buying off the Academy of Patriotism as a safeguard against assassination. The young men of the League of the Divine Wind had not killed the Kumamoto garrison commander for any incidental human failings.

Isao groaned with pain. How easily such a beautiful act could be destroyed! The possibility of his carrying out this beautiful act had arbitrarily been torn from him. All because of a few words!

The sole possibility left to him, if he were to act, was to become evil himself. But Isao was committed to justice.

A wooden kendo stave was leaning against the wall in one corner of the room. He seized it and rushed out to the back yard. Sawa was nowhere to be seen. Advancing step by step over the bare, flat ground next to the well, Isao made one stroke after another with furious abandon. The scolding whine of the wooden sword cutting through the air chafed his ears. He tried to make his mind a blank. He raised the sword high above his head, then brought it down. Like a man who hastily gulps saké to make himself drunk, he wanted this burning, oppressive exertion to race through his body. Though his breath was a searing flame, now trapped, now released from his heaving chest, the sweat that should have

covered him would not come. All was in vain. He thought of
an old poem that a senior kendoist had taught him:

> To try to avoid thought
> Is of itself to think.
> Thus even "Think not!"
> Is not to be thought.

And then another:

> Since rising and setting
> Are one to the unthinking moon,
> No mountain ridge
> Can vex its heart with shadow.

But these brought no relief. The lovely sky of early evening shone through the worm-eaten leaves of a chestnut tree.
Sawa's laundry seemed to be growing lighter by degrees, as
though whiteness were seeping through it.

Still carrying the stave, Isao went to Sawa's room a second
time and knocked on the door.

"What is it?" asked Sawa, opening his door. "Are you
hungry? Tonight we could send out for something to eat.
What do you say?"

Isao thrust his face abruptly against Sawa's.

"Was what you said before true?" he demanded. "Is Kurahara somehow connected with the Academy?"

"Don't threaten me, bringing a bamboo sword like that
with you! Anyway, come in."

In the course of his energetic sword drill, Isao had come to
the conclusion that no matter how passionate he might grow
in cross-examining Sawa, he need have no fear that he would
give away his true state of mind. For it was only natural that
an innocent young man would become thoroughly indignant
upon learning that Kurahara had aided the Academy.

Sawa was silent.

"Tell me the truth," said Isao. He had placed the sword at
his left side and sat down in a stiffly formal position.

"And if I tell the truth, what do you intend to do?"

"I don't intend to do anything."

"Nothing, eh? Then this business needn't bother you."

"It bothers me. You suppose it makes me happy to hear someone say that my own father is in league with the scum of the earth?"

"But if he isn't, are you going to give it to that fellow?"

"It's not a matter of giving it or not giving it to anybody," answered Isao, attempting a touch of sophistry. "What I want to do is to preserve the images I have of my father and of Kurahara. Of Kurahara as the perfect villain."

"Will that make you perfect too?"

"Perfection is no concern of mine."

"If it isn't, why do you let things bother you so?"

Isao was finding himself outmatched.

"Mr. Sawa, only cowards beat around the bush. I want to get at the truth. I want to confront it as it is."

"Why? Could the truth shake that strong faith of yours? Have you been following some kind of mirage all this time? If your dedication is so weak, then you're well rid of it. I just thought I'd put a little doubt into your world of faith. If that makes the whole thing start to shake, there's something missing in your dedication. Where is that indomitable conviction that a man should have? Do you really have it? If you do, speak up right here and now."

Isao once more found himself at a loss for words.

Sawa no longer seemed to be the man who read nothing but *Kodan Club*. He was attacking Isao; he was twisting his arm to make him spew up the burning lump lodged in his throat. Isao felt the blood rush to his cheeks, but, with an effort, he suppressed his emotion as he replied: "I'm going to stay here until Mr. Sawa tells me the truth."

"I see." Sawa remained silent for a time, as the small room was darkening in the twilight. A stout, forty-year-old man, he sat cross-legged in a baggy-kneed pair of the headmaster's old flannel pants. His head drooped forward so that the flesh of his shoulders swelled beneath his khaki shirt as though he

were wearing a quiver across his back. The keen aggressiveness seemed suddenly blunted. Isao could not tell whether he
was pondering or drowsing.

Sawa stood up abruptly. He opened a drawer and searched
through it. Then he returned to sit upright across from Isao
once more, and placed on the floor before him a dagger in a
plain wooden sheath. He drew it out. A pale, sharp-edged
crevice split the darkness of the room.

"I said what I said because I wanted to talk you out of it.
You're the heir of the Academy of Patriotism, and so your
life's too important. The master loves you very much.

"But as for myself, it doesn't make any difference. I have a
wife and children, but I'd have no regrets on that account.
And on their side too, they've already given me up. So I feel
apologetic for going on living, when I could have died at any
time. In my case I wouldn't have to involve the master, I could
just hand in my withdrawal notice and be free to stab Kurahara. I could stab him, all on my own. Anyway, I know one
thing: that fellow's the very source of the evil. Even if worst
comes to worst, as long as he gets it, all those politicians and
industrialists that are doing his dirty work will be choked off.
No matter what, he's one man that has to die. This is the
conclusion I came to a while ago. So, please, since someone is
going to get the job of cutting him down, let it be me. Let it
be this short sword that does it. Please turn this Kurahara
over to me. And then, once he's dead at my hand, if Japan
still doesn't improve, that's the time for you young men to
gather together and do whatever you have to.

"But if you think you've got to kill Kurahara yourselves,
then let me be one of your comrades. I know I can help you.
I'm the only one who can do the killing without any harm to
the Academy. Please take me. Look, I bow down and beg
you. Please tell me your mind."

Sawa's sobbing plea rang in Isao's ears as he watched him
wipe his eyes with the sleeve of his khaki shirt. Isao had now
lost all chance of further pressing Sawa about Kurahara and

his father. Sawa's words and his whole manner seemed to imply the existence of a relationship between the two men, and yet, depending upon how one interpreted them, Kurahara may well have been no more than a means used by Sawa to set the stage for his fervent plea. In any case, the one who was now hard-pressed was Isao.

He had no idea what to do, but at least there was no longer any danger of his losing control of himself. Now Isao was the one who stood in judgment. While he gazed down at the rather thin hair on the top of the weeping Sawa's bowed head, he had time to make a carefully formulated decision.

In those few moments, profit and loss, benefit and harm, like the sharp-pointed pales of a bamboo palisade jabbing the sky, stood lashed together. Isao could make Sawa one of his comrades or he could refuse. He could open his mind to Sawa or he could shut him out and persist in the course he had set for himself. He could hold fast to beauty and purity or he could let them go.

Were he to make Sawa one of his comrades, he would open his mind to him. And in return he could ask him the truth about Kurahara. From that moment Isao's intended Restoration could hardly remain the unblemished ideal it had been, but Sawa's rash thrust toward action could be thereby checked, the consequent danger avoided, and Sawa's energies channeled into the blow that Isao intended to strike.

If he did not make Sawa one of his comrades, there would be no need to open his mind to him, and, as a consequence, no need for Sawa to divulge what could be an ugly truth. But if Sawa rushed headlong to assassinate Kurahara, other enemies would be put on their guard, and the Restoration itself might suffer a setback.

Isao came to a cruel decision. In order to guard the beauty, the purity, the justice of his own conduct, it was best to let Sawa cut down Kurahara, but without a word of approval. Never would he give the least indication that he was delegating this task to Sawa. For if he were to do this, Isao would

be one who used impure means to guard his purity. Everything had to come about naturally. Perhaps, by the time he
had reached this decision, Isao had unconsciously begun to
hate Sawa.

He let the smile of an adult form upon his lips. He was
now the leader.

"Mr. Sawa, we've talked enough," Isao said. "I got excited
a while ago over something trifling, and perhaps I gave you
the wrong impression. You talk about my 'comrades'! My
friends and I have no plot in mind. We meet to study the
history of the Meiji period, and there are some great talkers
among us, that's all. Since we're young men, it's only natural,
isn't it? You've misinterpreted all this, Mr. Sawa. But now
you'll really have to excuse me. A friend has invited me over
to dinner tonight, and I have to be going. So please don't
trouble yourself about getting anything to eat for me." He
dreaded the strain of having dinner alone with Sawa. Isao got
to his feet, leaving the naked dagger gleaming upon the floor
like a rivulet in the darkness. Sawa made no move to stop him.

Isao had decided to go to Izutsu's house. Suddenly he
found himself concerned about whether or not Izutsu had
been taking proper care of the lily that Makiko had given him.
But what of his own lily?

So that it would not be thrown out in his absence, Isao had
placed his lily in a slim vase which he then put into a bookcase with a glass door. At first he had changed the water
every day, but recently, he was ashamed to recall, he had become careless and forgotten to do so. He opened the glass
door of the bookcase, removed the books he had put in front
of the vase, and peered in. The lily drooped in the darkness.

When he took it out to hold it under the light, he saw that
the lily had been reduced to the mummy of a lily. Were he to
touch his finger to the brownish petals even a little ungently,
they would surely crumple to dust at once and drop from the
stem, which still kept a slight tinge of green. It could no
longer be called a lily, but the memory, the shadow of a lily.

It was like an abandoned cocoon after the immortal, lustrous lily itself had gone its way. Nevertheless, there was a hint of fragrance which told that it had once been a living flower. The rays of the summer sun had once poured over it, and now, like a dying ember, it still held a faint warmth.

Isao gently touched his lips to the petals. If he were to feel their texture clearly, he would have gone too far. The lily would crumble. His touch had to be like that of the dawn upon a mountain ridge.

Isao's young lips had yet touched no other lips, and he brushed them delicately against the petals of this withered lily with all the exquisite sensitivity that they possessed.

"Here is the source of my purity, the warrant for my purity," he told himself. "I am certain that it is here. When the time comes for me to turn my sword against myself, lilies will surely rise from the morning dew and open their petals to the rising sun. Their scent will purify the stench of my blood. So be it! How can I have any more doubts?"

 **22**

THE CURRENT AFFAIRS CLUB met once a month at the Courthouse, and it was here that Honda learned something about the revolution in Siam of the previous June which brought a constitution to that country. Since the club had been formed at the suggestion of the Chief Justice, a sense of obligation insured a large turnout at the beginning, but gradually more and more of its members, busy with their work, failed to make an appearance. At this meeting in the small auditorium an outside lecturer had been brought in, and his talk was followed by informal discussion.

Even though Honda had never communicated with the Princes Pattanadid and Kridsada after their return to their homeland, the memory of former friendship made him extremely interested in the lecture, for once, and he listened attentively to the speaker, the head of the foreign branch of a large corporation who had happened to find himself in Siam at the time of the revolt.

The revolution began and ended quietly on the bright morning of June twenty-fourth without the citizens of Bangkok being aware of it. Launches and sampans thronged the Mae Nam River as usual and the shouts of hagglers filled the marketplace. In the government buildings, affairs crept on at the usual torpid pace.

Only those citizens who went by the palace and noted how its appearance had altered during the night were aware that something was amiss. Tanks and machine guns commanded every approach, and soldiers with fixed bayonets halted any car that drew near. The lofty windows of the upper stories of the palace bristled with machine-gun barrels glittering in the sunlight.

The King, Rama VII, was at the seaside resort of Pa-In together with the Queen. The country was an absolute monarchy, but the actual ruler was the regent, the King's uncle. The regent's residence had been attacked at dawn by a single armored car, and the pajama-clad Prince meekly allowed himself to be brought to the palace in it. One policeman was wounded in this incident, the only blood shed in the revolution.

Besides the Prince himself, the members of the royal family and the officials who constituted the main support of the monarchy were brought to the palace one after another, where they were gathered together to hear Colonel Pahon Ponpayuhasena, the leader of the coup d'état, explain the ideology of the new government. The National Party had seized power, and a temporary government had been set up.

This information was conveyed to the King himself, and after he had sent a wireless dispatch the following morning indicating that he favored a constitutional monarchy, he returned to the capital by special train to be greeted by the cheers of the crowd.

On June twenty-sixth Rama VII issued a proclamation approving the new government, immediately after receiving in audience the two young leaders of the National Party, Luang Pradit, a civilian, and Pya Pahon Ponpayuhasena, a colonel who was the representative of the young officers. The King showed himself altogether disposed in favor of the constitutional draft they presented to him, and at six o'clock that evening he bestowed the royal seal upon it. Siam had become a constitutional monarchy in both name and reality.

Honda had been anxious to hear something of Prince Pattanadid and Prince Kridsada. But since the only blood shed was that of the wounded policeman, he felt sure that no harm had come to either of them.

Though they gave no outward sign of it, those who listened to this account, aware as they were of the deplorable state of Japan, could not help but make comparisons and wonder why attempts at political reform in their own country had to be abortive affairs such as the May Fifteenth Incident, marked by senseless bloodletting and never proceeding temperately to a successful conclusion.

Soon after this lecture, Honda was ordered to attend a judicial conference in Tokyo. It was not an especially demanding assignment, and indeed one of the Chief Justice's intentions in sending him was to bestow some reward for his long service. He was to leave on the evening of October twentieth, the night before the conference. The day after it, the twenty-second, was a Saturday, and there was no need for him to return to Osaka until Monday. His mother would no doubt be happy to have her long-absent son spend a weekend in Tokyo.

It was early in the morning when Honda stepped down upon the platform in Tokyo Station. Since there was not enough time for him to go to his mother's house to freshen up after his trip, he decided to take a hot bath at the Shoji Inn within the station as soon as he had paid his respects to the delegation that came to meet him. Perhaps it was the early hour, but the Tokyo atmosphere, which he had not breathed for so long, now seemed to have something unfamiliar about it.

The crush of people moving between the platforms of the station and the lobby was just as before. Women in oddly long skirts caught Honda's eye from time to time, but this was already being seen in Osaka. He could not put his finger upon the exact difference. But something like an unseen gas seemed to have enveloped everything without anyone having noticed. People's eyes were moist. They walked as though in a dream. It seemed as if everyone was waiting anxiously for some impending event. The underpaid white-collar workers with their briefcases, the men in formal Japanese dress, the women in Western clothes, the girls at the cigar stands, the shoe-shine boys, the station personnel in their uniform caps— the mood of all alike made them seem bound together in a secret communication. And what was this mood?

When society was waiting fearfully for some event to occur, when the time had become fully ripe and the circumstances such that nothing could possibly prevent its occurrence, did not an expression of this sort appear on every man's face?

It was something not yet to be seen in Osaka. Honda felt as though he were listening to the spasmodic laughter of a frightened, goose-fleshed Tokyo, a city confronted with a huge, bizarre phantom which as yet revealed but half its bulk. Honda could not suppress a shudder.

His work done, Honda spent most of Saturday relaxing at his mother's house, and that evening it suddenly occurred to him to telephone the Academy of Patriotism. It was Iinuma who answered. His voice rang with exaggerated nostalgia.

"What a surprise to find you here in Tokyo! I am honored that you should take the trouble to call. And you've already shown me such hospitality at your home, even including that boy of mine—I was quite overwhelmed."

"How is Isao?"

"He left Tokyo the day before yesterday. He's at a place called Yanagawa. Kaido Masugi is conducting a training camp there on the rites of purification. In fact, I myself must pay a visit to Yanagawa tomorrow, Sunday, to thank Master Kaido for taking care of my son. If Your Honor has sufficient leisure, what would you say to accompanying me? I'm sure that the trees in the mountains will be in full color."

Honda hesitated. His past tie with Iinuma was reason enough for a visit to his home, but he was afraid that if he, as a judge, were deliberately to attend a right-wing training camp, even if he refrained from taking part in the purification rites themselves, it might give rise to untoward rumors.

And then too, either the next night or early the morning after, he would have to catch a train for Osaka. Honda refused, but Iinuma grew insistent. Perhaps it seemed his only way to show hospitality. Finally Honda agreed to go along on condition that he remain incognito. Since Honda wanted to sleep late, at least during his stay in Tokyo, they arranged to meet at Shinjuku Station at eleven o'clock the next morning. Iinuma told him that it would take two hours by the Chuo Line to get to Shiozu and from there they would have to proceed on foot along the Katsura River for about two and a half miles.

Yanagawa was in the district of Minamitsuru in what was once Kai Province. In a section of it called Motozawa, the Katsura River formed a right angle and turned into rapids, and here it was that Kaido Masugi owned some six acres of rice land which projected out into the river like the

apron of a stage. Facing the rice land was a drill hall which
also served as a dormitory for a considerable number of students. And there was a shrine. To the west of the drill hall
stood a hut at a point where a suspension bridge crossed the
river, and from here steps led down to the place of purification. The students of his academy cultivated the rice fields.

Kaido Masugi's aversion to Buddhism was celebrated.
Since he was an admirer of Atsutané, this was only to be
expected, and it was his practice to make Atsutané's diatribes
against Buddha and Buddhism his own and to deliver them
unchanged to his students. He condemned Buddhism for
denying life and, as a consequence, denying that one could
die for the Emperor, for knowing nothing of the "abundant
life of the spirit" and, as a consequence, shutting itself off
from the essential, life-giving source that was the object of
true devotion. And as for Karma, that was a philosophy of
evil that reduced everything to nihilism.

"Siddhartha was the name of the founder of Buddhism, a
very foolish man who buried himself in the mountains and
gave himself over to all manner of austerities, without suc-
ceeding in discovering a way to escape the Three Calamities,
age, sickness, and death. . . . But he had the perverse inspiration to stay on in the mountains for many years longer,
during which time he became adept at sorcery. And with this
occult lore to bolster him, he became the so-called Buddha
. . . and he concocted the theory that Buddha is a being to
whom all reverence is due. So this founder of Buddhism, by
virtue of his blasphemous fallacy, opened to men a path to
destruction and turned himself into a devil racked with the
Three Torments. . . . Even before the coming of Buddhism, the advent of the so-called Confucianism had already
made men's hearts cunning and corrupt. And then with the
extravagant fable of retribution that Buddhism brought with
it, all traces of manliness were wiped away, and it was not
long before high and low alike became enslaved to false
doctrine. Moreover, as this belief grew more flourishing, men

naturally drew away from that vital source that was theirs from olden times, the oracles of our ancestral gods, and they began to neglect the ancient rites. And even these rites became corrupted by Buddhist influences. . . ."

Such were the Atsutané sermons that Master Kaido poured into the ears of his students with a never-flagging zeal, and so Iinuma instructed Honda during the journey not to let slip any casual remark that was at all favorable to Buddhism.

Kaido Masugi turned out to be a different sort of person from the imposing elder with the long white beard that Honda had pictured from the bits of information that had come his way. He was an amiable little old man with several teeth missing, but his eyes were the eyes of a lion, and the impression he made upon Honda was a strong one.

After Iinuma had introduced Honda as a government official who had shown him great kindness years before, Kaido's lion's eyes looked fixedly into Honda's eyes as he responded: "You seem to be a man who has had dealings with all sorts of people. And yet your eyes are not clouded with the least impurity. That is a rare thing. I do not wonder at the respect that Iinuma here has for you. Yet you still seem young." And then, the compliments out of the way, he immediately began to lash out at Buddha: "I realize that we have only just met, but, really, that fellow Buddha was a fraud. I suspect he's the rascal that robbed the Japanese of their Yamato Spirit, and their manly courage. Doesn't Buddhism deny all spirit?"

Since Iinuma had hastily gone off to perform the ritual of purification, Honda found himself sitting alone with Kaido in the drill hall, left for the time being to bear the brunt of his sermon.

When he saw Iinuma reappear in white robe and white *hakama*, accompanied by Kaido's chief disciple, Honda felt a surge of relief.

"Your water is indeed fresh and pure," Iinuma said. "I have been cleansed in mind and body. I thank you. And now I wonder where I can find my son."

Kaido ordered his chief disciple to call Isao. Honda's interest was aroused by the prospect of seeing Isao appear clad in the same type of white robe and *hakama* that his father wore.

But there was no sign of Isao. The disciple reappeared and knelt at the threshold.

"According to the students, Isao was very angry over your taking him to task a little while ago, and he borrowed a hunting gun at the gatekeeper's house and said he was going to shoot a dog or a cat to get it off his mind. It seems he headed out toward the mountains, probably to Tanzawa."

"What? Shedding the blood of animals after being purified? Such infamy!" Kaido stood up, his lion's eyes blazing. "Assemble every man in that study group of Isao's. Tell them that each is to take an oblation branch in his hand and go out to confront Isao. He'll be as bad as Lord Susano himself, defiling our sacred precincts."

Strength seemed to drain out of Iinuma as his consternation deepened, a plight that the bystander Honda had to view with some amusement.

"But what could my boy have done? Why was it that you had to scold him?"

"For nothing serious. Don't worry. But in that son of yours the harsh god is too strong. I reprimanded him because unless he works hard to be more receptive to the mild god, he'll stray from the right path. In your son it's the heedless and intractable spirit that's dominant. Since he's a boy, that's fine, but he goes much too far. When I admonished him, he hung his head dutifully and listened, but then, afterwards, it must have been the harsh god suddenly breaking loose."

"I must take an oblation branch myself and go along to purify him."

"That would be well. Go quickly then, before he defiles himself."

Hearing all this, Honda at first felt somewhat cowed by the uncanny atmosphere, but suddenly his intelligence was affronted by the utter absurdity of it. These people around him took no thought of the flesh but were altogether absorbed in the spirit. Here was a quite ordinary incident of an independent young man becoming furious when reprimanded, but they viewed it as a manifestation of the dread power of the realm of spirits.

Now Honda regretted that his strange sense of rapport with Isao had made him come to such a place. But some unknown peril to Isao seemed to be taking form before him, and he felt that he should do whatever lay in his power to hold it back.

When they went outside, some twenty young men, each holding a sakaki branch hung with white paper pendants, stood gathered there with tense expressions. Iinuma raised his branch and started to walk. The entire group fell in behind him. Honda, who alone was wearing a suit, took his place immediately in back of Iinuma.

At that moment Honda had a peculiar feeling. What he was doing seemed somehow linked to a distant memory despite its being not at all likely that he had ever found himself in the midst of a white-clad group such as this. Yet he seemed to hear a metallic sound, as though a hoe were at work unearthing a memory of inestimable value and striking against the first rock that lay in its way. The sound echoed strongly within his head, but then it was gone like a phantom. The impression had held him but for an instant. What had caused it?

It was as though a length of beautiful, thick golden thread had arched its graceful way past the needle of Honda's perception, barely grazing it. It had touched the needle, but, just as it seemed about to pass through the eye, it had turned aside and was gone. As though fearful of being woven vigorously into the embroidery material, blank but for the faint pattern sketched upon it, the thread had slipped to one side of the needle's eye and passed beside it. The fingers that guided it were huge yet slender and extremely supple.

23

IT WAS ABOUT three o'clock on a late October afternoon, an hour when the sun had already begun to conceal itself behind the surrounding mountains. The light from the cloud-streaked sky enveloped the wooded ridges like mist.

The procession led by Iinuma crossed the old suspension bridge in silence, three or four men at a time. As Honda looked down, he saw that to the north of the bridge the water was still and deep, but on the south side, where the place of purification was located, the river ran swift and shallow between graveled shores. It was this rotting bridge that marked the division between the depths and the shallows.

After he had crossed, Honda turned and looked back at the young men solemnly marching behind him on the bridge, their oncoming footsteps sending shudders along its planks.

The young men, each holding up his sakaki branch, moved forward against a background formed of the oaks on the opposite side, the mulberry fields, the ravaged red leaves of the nurudé trees, the hut atop the bank, and one black-trunked persimmon from which a single red fruit hung with sensuous grace. Their figures shone in the few rays of the setting sun that just then broke through the clouds hovering over the mountain ridges. The sunlight threw into sharp relief the pleats of their *hakama*, and gave such brilliance to their white robes that each marcher seemed to be his own source of brightness. The leaves of the sakaki branch he carried gave off a dark green luster, and the white pendants hung upon it were flecked with delicate shadows.

There was some delay before the entire group of almost

twenty men had crossed. Honda gazed around him once more at the autumn mountain scenery that he had already had leisure to study on the two-and-a-half-mile walk from Shiozu to Yanagawa.

Since this was in the heart of the mountains, the varied dark and light colors of near and distant slopes were superimposed one upon the other and seemed to press in on the viewer. Every mountain had a generous share of cedars that stood out darkly with severe aloofness from the mild red warmth that surrounded them. Autumn was not yet advanced, and the seasonal coloring, though apparent, was like a mantle of shaggy yellowish wool mottled with rust red. A listless mood seemed to weigh upon the reds, yellows, greens, and browns, muting their brilliance. The smell of wood smoke and the mistlike sunlight enwrapped everything. The more distant slopes were sharply etched in pale blue beneath their shroud of light mist. None of these mountains, however, offered a forbiddingly steep aspect.

When everyone had crossed the bridge, Iinuma set out in the lead again, Honda still behind him. The ground beneath their feet had been covered with fallen oak leaves on the other side of the bridge, but now, along this high, rocky road, it was the leaves of cherry trees that predominated. From the bridge on, these lay like fallen red flowers. Some wet leaves, already decaying, had faded to a pink that was the color of the dawn. Why should decay take the color of the dawn? Honda wondered, the pointless question nagging at him. A fire tower stood at the top of the cliff, its small bell silhouetted against a pale blue sky. Now it was the leaves of persimmon trees that covered the path. On either side there were cabbage fields and farmhouses. Reddish purple wild chrysanthemums were everywhere, and each yard had its persimmon trees, bare except for a remnant of fruit which hung from their branches like New Year's ornaments. The path wound this way and that, between the hedges of the farmhouses.

Just as they had passed one of these houses, a much wider view abruptly opened before them. The path too, at a point where a Buddhist requiem stone from the Kaei era stood overgrown with weeds, suddenly turned into a broad road amid the farmland.

To the southwest there was but one small mountain. Directly in front of the marchers, tall Mount Gozen, together with the other mountains that filled the northern horizon, rose up beyond the river and the road. So far in their journey, except for this village in the foothills of Gozen, there had been no sign of a human dwelling.

Clusters of red-flowered knotgrass bloomed along the straw-littered side of the road. The chirping of crickets could be heard faintly. Rice-drying racks lined many of the fields, and in others the new-cut sheaves were spread out upon the dark, cracked ground. A young boy, proud of his new bike, turned to gawk at the strange procession as he slowly pedaled by.

Autumn tints, like smudged powder, covered the small mountain to the southwest. Before them, the way lay open to the north as far as the bank of the Katsura. A lone cedar, torn by lightning, stood in a nearby field, its rent trunk bent back and its withered needles the color of dried blood. Its roots were partially pulled up out of the ground, and bearded grass sprung out in all directions from them.

It was then that a figure dressed in white appeared ahead on the road, and one of the young men called out: "There he is."

Honda felt an unaccountable shiver run down his spine.

A half hour earlier, Isao, his eyes bloodshot, had ranged over this same area with a Murata rifle in his hand. He was not angry at Master Kaido's scolding. But in the course of it an intolerable idea had come to him. He found he could not help thinking that the crystal vessel of beauty and purity he sought had already fallen to the ground and lay in fragments, and that he was stubbornly refusing to acknowledge it. Was it not true, he wondered, that if he wanted to take action he now had no choice but somehow to make secret use of the thrust of evil and let its strength drive him forward? Just as his father had done? No, certainly not. This had nothing in common with his father's behavior. For him there would be no diluting righteousness with evil and evil with righteousness. The evil that he wanted to store within himself had to be pure evil, no less pure than the righteousness within him. In any event, once he had attained his purpose he would turn his sword against himself. At that moment, he felt, the pure evil within him would also die in the clash with the pure righteousness of his act.

Isao had never felt like killing anyone out of personal hatred. How was the desire to kill stirred up, he wondered. And what connection did it have with the sober events of everyday life? It was a problem that had long troubled him. He would first have to perform a small act of pure evil, commit a minor sacrilege.

Master Kaido, as a devoted follower of Atsutané, had lectured on the defilement brought about by the flesh and blood of beasts. And so Isao had borrowed a rifle and set out, hoping to hunt down a deer or a boar in the autumn mountains or, if that proved too difficult, to shoot a dog or a cat and bring the bloodied carcass back to Yanagawa. If that meant that he and his followers would be expelled from the camp, he was prepared to accept it. Indeed it would no doubt instill in them a new kind of courage and resolution.

He walked toward the southwest, his eye fixed upon the small mountain wrapped in scarlet leaves. He could see that a mulberry field encroached upon the gentle western slope of the mountain, and that a narrow path led uphill between the field and a bamboo thicket. The cedars were dense above the mulberry field, but someone had told him that the path climbed on up through them.

The Murata rifle, about two and a quarter feet in length,

was like an iron bar in his hand, and the autumn air chilled its metal so that it squealed beneath the touch of his fingers. It was hard to believe that the bullet already in the chamber had the power to give heat to the metal. And the three bullets he carried in his robe, their chill, metallic touch pressing against his chest as he walked, seemed not so much murderous pellets as three cold eyes focused upon him.

Since there was no dog or cat to be seen, Isao decided to follow the path between the bamboo thicket and the mulberry field up the mountain. The interior of the thicket was a tangle of red-berried creeper vines and ivy. A moss-grown heap of mulberry roots, dug up and piled beside the field, stood in his way. From somewhere close at hand, he heard the song of a green finch. Isao imagined the figure of an unwary stag lazily taking form before the muzzle of his rifle. He was sure that he would fire without hesitation. He would have the will to kill. The victim would be unaware of it. There was no need for hatred. And in dying the stag would for the first time expose the full force of evil. It would shine in the dark gleam of the blood pouring out from the heart of the beast.

Isao pricked up his ears. There was no sound of movement over the fallen leaves. He stared at the path ahead. There was nothing that looked like a deer's track. If something was holding its breath, it was, Isao felt, not in fear, not out of hostility, but in derision of his intent to kill. The teeming silence of the scarlet-leafed forest, of the bamboo thicket, of the rows of cedars—he felt it ridiculing him.

He climbed to where the cedars began. The very spaces between the trees were packed with a dark silence. There was no sign of life. He began to walk across the slope and found himself in a sparse, sunlit grove. Suddenly a pheasant burst into flight from under his feet. It was an explosive target that preempted his field of vision. This had to be the moment to "let go," as the gatekeeper had instructed him. He raised the gun at once and fired.

The mingled yellows and reds of the leaves above his head were suffused with the glow of the setting sun. A heavy, flashing crown of green seemed to hang poised for an instant against a patch of melancholy evening sky. This hurled crown dissolved in a flapping of wings, its glory shattered. The violent beating seemed to churn the air into a thick, sticky liquid which immediately clung to the wings like birdlime and took its toll. The bird, all unaware, was suddenly no longer a bird. The struggle to keep its wings going caused it to veer off its intended course, and it plunged abruptly downward, disappearing among the trees. The spot was not far distant. Isao estimated that the bird had fallen into the thicket which he had passed earlier.

Intent upon that spot, he ignored the path as he rushed down out of the grove, holding the rifle under his arm, black smoke still seeping from its barrel. Thorns caught at the sleeves of his robe and tore them.

An underwater glow filled the bamboo thicket. He used the gun to thrust aside the vines that clutched at him. He stared intently at the ground, anxious lest the pheasant be lost amid the colors of the fallen bamboo leaves. At last he found it. Isao knelt down, and as he picked up the lifeless body of the bird, blood spurted from its breast and fell upon his white *hakama*.

The bird's eyes were tight shut. The plumage that surrounded the closed eyes had the scarlet speckles of a toadstool. It was a somberly plump bird with a metallic sheen that seemed to turn soft feathers into armor, its color a rainbow against a black sky. As its head hung down over his arm, he noticed that the plumage of its bent body was less thick and the luster of a different sort.

The feathers about the head were a purple almost as deep as black grapes and they clustered as close as scales. From the breast to the belly, dark green feathers meshed as though to form a protective tunic that glinted in the fading light.

It was down these dark green feathers that the blood was flowing from an unseen wound.

Judging the location of the wound, Isao inserted his finger. It encountered no resistance as he plunged it deep into the breast torn by the bullet, and when he drew it out, it was covered with a red wetness. How does it feel to slaughter? he asked himself, burning for an answer. The action, that instant of aiming the gun and pressing the trigger, had been a rapid flow of movement, with only the barest feeling of wanting to kill. That had amounted to even less than the wisp of black smoke that later trailed from the muzzle.

A bullet certainly substituted for an intent. He had not begun to climb the mountain with the thought of killing this pheasant, but the gun itself would not let such a dazzling opportunity pass. And so a small shedding of blood and a small death had instantly taken place, and there was this stilled pheasant lying across his arm, a matter in no way out of the ordinary.

As for righteousness and purity, these he coolly rejected like bones left upon a plate. His appetite was not for bones but for meat. He wanted this thing that was quick to decay, this thing that shone, this thing that was so soft. It was no more than a savor barely caught by the tongue. He had experienced this taste, and from it had come the almost numbing rapture that he now felt, and the repose of fulfillment. This was what engaged his senses.

Had the pheasant been transformed into the embodiment of evil? By no means. As Isao looked closer, he saw that tiny winged insects were moving in its feathers. And if it were left lying there, ants and maggots would certainly soon be swarming over it.

He was irritated at the bird's tight-shut eyes. Like an arbitrary refusal, they seemed to shut him out coldly from something that he was desperately eager to know. But this thing that he wanted to know—Isao found himself unable to tell whether it was, after all, the sensation of killing or that of his own death.

He picked the bird up roughly by the neck, and, using his gun to slash at the undergrowth, made his way with difficulty out of the thicket. He cut away one hanging vine laden with red berries which fell around his neck and draped itself, its fruit trembling, about his chest and shoulders. Since neither hand was free to dislodge it, Isao left it as it was.

He came down to the mulberry field and began to cross it on a path along one of its ridges. Lost in thought, he paid no attention to the profusion of red flowers that he was trampling underfoot.

Ahead stood a shattered cedar, its needles already half brown. At a right angle to this path, he had noted before, was the road he had come by, a broad road through open fields. He turned onto it.

Some distance ahead a white-clad group was approaching. Though he could not yet make out their faces, the pendant-hung branches that each carried gave him an odd feeling. White robes in such a place had to indicate Master Kaido's students, but Isao would not have expected his own comrades to come marching out solemnly in this manner led by another. The leader seemed older, and behind him walked one man dressed in a suit. Isao was startled when he saw at last that the man in the lead had the neat moustache of his father.

At that moment the sky above, still lit by the sunset glow, was suddenly filled with the cries of a vast flock of small birds that had appeared from the shelter of the mountain. The white-clad marchers seemed distracted by this, and halted briefly until the birds had passed over.

As the distance separating Isao and the group lessened, Honda somehow began to feel excluded from the tableau taking form in the fading light of the open fields. Gradually he veered off the road until he was separated from the column and threading his way through rice-drying racks. Some moment of extreme significance was drawing near. What it was he did not know. Isao's figure was now clearly discernible. Honda saw upon his chest something that looked like a necklace of red crescent beads, apparently a kind of berry.

Honda's heart throbbed violently. An irresistible power was approaching, a power that would deal a smashing blow to his rational outlook. He could already feel the rush of its wings and its breath as it came bearing down. He did not believe in premonitions, but if there were something that could come to warn a man of his own death or the death of one close to him, would it not, he wondered, be a sensation like this?

"So you only bagged a pheasant, eh? Well, that's not too bad."

Iinuma's voice rang in his ears. Honda, standing there in the field, could not help looking toward them.

"That's not too bad," said Iinuma again. And then, as though in jest, he raised his sakaki branch and waved it over Isao's head. Its paper pendants flashed a pure white in the dusk. Their rustling sound had a poignant freshness.

"What a way to behave! Even taking a gun with you! Master Kaido had you sized up all right: You are heedless and intractable. You have proved it beyond all question."

The instant Honda heard these words the memory that lay within him was at last revealed with pitiless clarity. Beyond any doubt, what had been fulfilled before his very eyes was the dream that Kiyoaki Matsugae had dreamed one summer night in the second year of the Taisho era. Kiyoaki had recorded this extraordinary dream in great detail, and Honda, just the previous month, had reread that section of the dream journal. It had been vividly realized in every particular before his very eyes, becoming part of reality after the passage of nineteen years.

That Isao was Kiyoaki reborn, even if Isao himself was

unaware of it, was now, as far as Honda was concerned, something impervious to all the power that reason could bring to bear against it. It was a fact.

24

THE NEXT EVENING, after classes, Isao led his comrades to the place where they had their secret meetings every day. There no one would see them, or even if someone did, the circumstances would resemble nothing more than a group of boys getting together for some carefree exchange. At a spot where the farmland that belonged to Kaido's Academy faced the cliff of Motozawa stood a huge rock covered with vegetation, like the artificial mountain of a landscaped garden. Once behind it, one was hidden from the eyes of anyone looking from the direction of the lecture hall. Right below were the rapids, and on the opposite side rose the towering cliff wall. The small grassy spot behind the rock was ideally suited for sitting in a circle and holding a discussion. In summer it would have been quite pleasant, but in Kai in late October the evening wind was extremely chilly. But so enthusiastic were the boys who gathered here that the cold did not trouble them.

As Isao led them along the path that crossed the fields, he noticed the charred traces of a fire which had not been there the previous day. The fine ash of burnt straw had traced a gray pattern upon the path, but where it had gathered in a rut it was a dense black. This black mingled with the red of the loam in a way that captivated Isao. Oddly, it was not the mixture of gray ash and a few remnants of fresh straw that stirred thoughts of the bright fire at its peak, but the black rut crushed into the earth by a wheel. The strong, barbaric red of the flames, the vulgarly strong black of the rut—here was the perfect expression, the perfect contrast. To flame up, then to be trampled out—both had the same vivid power. The near association that all this provoked in Isao's mind, obviously enough, was the specter of revolt.

The group followed Isao in silence to the huge rock with its sheltering trees at the south end of the fields and sat down in a circle. They could hear the rushing water of the rapids below them, where the Katsura River made its sharp bend. The gray rock surface of the cliff that soared up on the opposite bank seemed to embody a stern and enduring fortitude. The red leaves that hung from the trees clinging to the face of the cliff, the first trees to be lost to the sun, had a gloomy tinge, while far up, through the trees that lined the top of the cliff, the evening sky could be seen in a turmoil of bright-flecked clouds.

"Today the time has come to decide when we will strike. We're all resolved, aren't we? But first we'll confirm the general plan and each man's responsibility, and Sagara will report on our funds. As for the exact time we strike, it would certainly be fitting if we could decide it by an Ukei, like the comrades of the League. Anyway, let's take it up later." Isao's tone was businesslike as he opened the meeting. However, the trifling affair of the day before still affected him. His father and Honda had had a light supper and returned to Tokyo immediately. But even though it was supposed to be a courtesy to Master Kaido, what had prompted his father to make such a long trip to see how things were here? Could it be that he had had a talk with Sawa? And then what of the odd behavior of Honda? There had been no sign yesterday of the detached and well-modulated kindness so evident in the first conversation and in the long letter, but, rather, Honda had said hardly a word to Isao, and his complexion had been very pale. Then later, in the course of supper, Isao had noticed that

Honda kept staring at him from where he sat in the place of honor.

Isao wrenched away this dark lever that had forced his thoughts back to the past, and he spread the written plan out on the grass before him:

1. The month, date, and hour:
2. A summary of the plan:

Our objective is to throw the capital into disorder, bring about a state of martial law, and thereby promote the establishment of a Restoration government. We are fully resolved to sacrifice ourselves for such a Restoration, hoping to achieve the maximum result with the minimum number of men. We believe that others who share our ideals will rise in response throughout the country. We will have copies of our declaration scattered from an airplane, contending that an imperial command has been issued to Prince Toin, and we will see to it that in short order this will in fact be the case. With the proclamation of martial law, our mission will be accomplished, and no later than the following dawn, whether we have succeeded or failed, we will commit seppuku honorably together.

The purpose of the Meiji Restoration was to return the governing power and the control of the military functions to His Imperial Majesty. The purpose of our Showa Restoration is to place finance and industry under the direct control of His Imperial Majesty, to uproot capitalism and communism, those doctrines of Western materialism, and thus deliver our people from their misery, and here beneath the bright light of the sun to seek the direct rule of the Emperor that will glorify the Imperial Way.

As for throwing the capital into disorder, we will first blow up every transformer substation throughout the city, and in the dead of night we will assassinate the ringleaders of industrial capitalism: Busuké Kurahara, Toru Shinkawa, and Juemon Nagasaki. At the same time, we will occupy the Bank of Japan, the kingpin of the Japanese economy, and set it afire. We will then gather by sunrise at the latest before the Imperial Palace and put an end to ourselves by committing seppuku as one. Should we be unable to meet, there is nothing to prevent our turning our swords against ourselves in whatever place each man happens to find himself.

3. Table of Organization:

A. First Unit (The attacks upon the Tokyo Electric transformer substations)

Kamedo Substation:	Hasegawa
	Sagara
Kinuden Substation:	Seyama
	Tsujimura
Hatogaya Substation:	Yoneda
	Sakakibara
Tabata Substation:	Horié
	Mori
Mejiro Substation:	Ohashi
	Serikawa
Yodobashi Substation:	Takahashi
	Ui

B. Second Unit (The assassinations)

Toru Shinkawa:	Iinuma
	Miyaké
Juemon Nagasaki:	Miyahara
	Kimura
Busuké Kurahara:	Izutsu
	Fujita

C. Third Unit (The occupation and burning of the Bank of Japan)

The action will be carried out by fourteen men under the command of First Lieutenant of Infantry Hori, with two men, Takasé and Inoué, joining the twelve men who will assemble rapidly by bicycle immediately after the destruction of the transformer stations.

D. Special Assignment

An airplane piloted by First Lieutenant Shiga will drop flares and scatter leaflets.

The truth of the matter was that Isao was still disturbed about the assignment to kill Kurahara. It was a task that he really wanted to reserve for himself, but something prevented him from doing so. Sawa's words had somehow struck home.

Isao felt that even now as they were talking, Sawa might take it into his head to go out and kill Kurahara on his own initiative. If he did, they would have no choice but to delay their full-scale plan until the public outcry had died down. Then again, perhaps Sawa had been merely bluffing, trying to force Isao's assent, and would actually do nothing at all.

If Isao were to kill Kurahara, disregarding all that Sawa had said, he would be fulfilling the role he had always seen for himself. Obviously Kurahara would be the man most closely guarded. Isao had used the pretext of friendship in yielding Kurahara to Izutsu, that cheerful and credulous young man of extravagant bravery. Izutsu had been over-whelmed with gratitude, but Isao, deep within him, felt that for the first time in his life he had flinched from something.

As for using the airplane, it had been Lieutenant Hori's counsel that caused the substitution of flares and leaflets for bombs. Hori, however, had guaranteed that his staunch friend Lieutenant Shiga would participate.

Weapons were a problem. Of the twenty young men, ten of them had access to a Japanese sword, but, in the assaults upon the transformer stations, a sword might perhaps prove a hindrance. If they carried concealed daggers, that would suffice. As for the various explosives to be used, their aim was to obtain some of the most recently developed kind.

"Sagara. Read us the list of the items we need."

"All right," said Sagara, and he began to read in a low voice, as if fearful of being overheard:

"1. A large piece of bleached cotton: one length of about sixteen feet to be used for a banner proclaiming our ideals, to be set up at the place where we commit suicide. The rest of the material to provide a belly band for each man.

2. Headbands, armbands, pins for armbands, and rubber-soled footwear to equip twenty men.

3. Paper: one ream of white, two or three of varicolored, a large enough supply for printing the leaflets.

4. Benzine: for incendiary use. One or two cans each to be purchased from three or four dealers by different men.

5. One mimeograph machine and accessories.

6. Writing brushes, ink, etc.

7. Bandages, styptic drugs, strong liquor to be used as a restorative.

8. Canteens.

9. Flashlights.

"That's about all. We'll buy everything individually and then assemble it in a good hiding place somewhere. Once we're back in Tokyo we'll get busy finding a place."

"Do we have enough money set aside?"

"Yes. Iinuma has saved eighty-five yen in all, and putting this with the savings of the rest of us, we have a total of three hundred and twenty-five yen. And then, just before we came up here, I received a letter to the 'Meiji History Study Club' with no return address. I brought it along so that I could open it in front of everybody. It might be money. I feel a little uneasy about it."

Sagara opened the envelope to find ten one-hundred yen bills. A shock ran through the group. Sagara read aloud the single sheet of stationery with two or three lines upon it: "I had some forest land at home sold off, and that's where this money came from. It's clean. Please use it as you like. Sawa."

"Sawa?" Isao felt his heart thump when he heard the name. Sawa was again behaving in incomprehensible fashion. Even if Isao were to believe that the money was indeed "clean," Sawa's purpose in giving it eluded him. Did he intend this gift as a substitute for his offer to assassinate Kurahara? Or did he mean this vast sum of one thousand yen as an apologetic farewell contribution before acting alone?

But Isao had to give an immediate answer. "It's from Mr. Sawa at the school," he said. "He's secretly one of us. So it's all right to take it."

"Well, what a windfall! There's no need to worry about

finances now. The Divine Assistance is with us." Sagara gleefully raised the money up to the level of his glasses as though offering thanks to the gods.

"Now we have to get down to details. First, let's settle the time of day and the date. Naturally, the time is critical to our plan. If it's too late at night, the effects of the power stoppage will be insignificant. So ten p.m. would be the limit, I think. And, within an hour after that, the attack on the bank. Now for the date . . ." As he spoke, Isao saw in his mind's eye the vague image of Tomo Otaguro in the shrine at Shingai, prostrate before the gods as he awaited their will.

The priest had offered two Ukei formulations in the midday summer heat of the sanctuary:

To bring an end to misgovernment by admonishing authority even to the forfeiture of life.

To cut down the unworthy ministers by striking in darkness with the sword.

The gods had favored neither, however. Now it was their latter wish that Isao and his comrades were presenting to the gods.

Summer and fall, Kumamoto and Kai, the Meiji era and the Showa era—such were the differences. But the swords of these young men were thirsty for blood, and they indeed wanted to strike in the darkness of night.

The story told in that small pamphlet had at some point or other burst through the dam of literary convention and poured out upon the present. Reading that story had ignited a flame in the hearts of these young men, and now they could not be content until the fire within them had set off a conflagration.

> As the white swan soars to heaven,
> Leave no traces here below.

The poem of Master Oen suddenly came to Isao's mind, as freshly and vividly as if it had been composed only the day before.

No one ventured an opinion. The boys sat in silence,

earnestly studying Isao's expression. He himself had raised his eyes to the sky above the cliff on the other side of the river. The brightness that edged the cloud fragments was now somewhat more subdued. But the streaked pattern, as though a fine-toothed comb had been at work, still held firm. Isao felt that the eyes of the gods might glance down through this.

Evening darkness had already claimed the cliff's rock face. Only the white water of the rapids below stood out in the gloom. He himself had become a character in a romance. Perhaps he and his comrades were on the verge of a glory that would long be remembered. True or not, the cold evening wind conveyed the chill of a bronze memorial tablet. The moment seemed suited to a manifestation of the gods. . . .

No revelation came. Nothing at all about a date or a time. Nothing came down out of the lofty brilliance of the cloud-streaked evening sky to seize hold of him. No immediate communication of wordless feeling. It was as though a koto's strings had snapped and not a single note could be plucked from them.

But even so, the gods had not expressed their disapproval as clearly as they had to Tomo Otaguro. They had not made their rejection obvious.

Isao struggled with the implications. Now at this moment a group of young men, all of them under twenty and vibrant with youth, had their eyes fixed upon him, their eyes sparkling with fervor, while he himself kept gazing up at the divine brightness above the towering rock wall. Matters had moved relentlessly to this point, and never would the moment be more apt. Some sort of revelation had to take place. Yet the gods had neither consented nor denied. They had abandoned the decision, like a sandal casually let slip there in the brightness of the heavens, as if imitating the uncertainty and imperfection of this world.

Isao had to answer immediately. Something in his heart closed up for a moment, just as a clam closes its shell, for a time covering over its "pure" flesh which should always be open to the cleansing waters. A tiny evil concept had scampered like a sea louse across one corner of his heart. Though the memory of closing up in defense may be vague, once done it would no doubt take on the force of custom. After two or three times, it must seem as common as eating and drinking.

Isao did not think of himself as lying. If something was not designated by the gods as either true or false, then it would be highly presumptive for a human being rashly to think of it as a lie. Isao's case was no different from that of a bird that had to give nourishment to its young. They had to be fed, and had to be fed at once.

"It's December third, ten o'clock at night. That seems to be the will of the gods. Let's make it definite. There's over a month remaining, so I think we'll have plenty of time to prepare. And now, Sagara, you're forgetting something important. Our struggle will be pure and without blemish, like a white lily. And so in order that men in years to come can speak of the 'War of the Lilies,' I want each of you, when you go into battle, to make certain that you carry in your breast pocket a petal from one of the Saigusa Festival lilies that General Kito's daughter distributed to us. The protection of the harsh god of the Sai Shrine will surely be with us. Now, as to the date being December third, a Friday, is there anyone who objects? If so, speak up. Maybe it's inconvenient for someone."

"If we're all going to die," one boy responded in a loud voice, "how could it be inconvenient?" Everyone laughed.

"All right then, let's go on to the reports on individual projects. Ohashi, Serikawa, let's hear the report on your investigation of the Mejiro station and your plan for bombing it."

At Isao's order, Ohashi and Serikawa tried to defer to each other, but finally the articulate Ohashi began the account. Whenever Serikawa spoke to Isao he squared his shoulders and was as tense as a raw recruit, but because his strong feelings choked the flow of his words, the others had difficulty understanding him. Still, his reliability in performance was peerless. Never had he failed to carry out to the letter any order. When he spoke passionately of something, his voice sounded as if he were weeping. Presenting clearly detailed reports was not his forte, and so the task fell to the clever and articulate Ohashi, with Serikawa standing beside him and nodding vigorously at every significant point.

"When we arrived at the Mejiro transformer station, there was a man dressed in overalls at the entrance. He was repairing some copper wire. Now when Serikawa and I went to other stations and told them we were night school students in an electrical school and asked to inspect the station, someone always wanted to see our identity cards or made some other objection, and we were quickly sent on our way. But this man in overalls was surprisingly friendly, and had us come up to the second floor. When we climbed the stairs, there were three clerks working in an office, and one of them told the man in overalls to show us around. So this fellow got out of his regular work, and cheerfully showed us all over the place. He seemed to take great pride in it. Whenever we asked about the equipment or anything, he gave us a full explanation. And so we found out that that station had both a water-cooled and an oil-cooled transformer.

"In general, the most critical parts of a transformer station are the transformer, the switchboard, and the water pump for cooling. Just to destroy the water pump, all you'd have to do would be to smash the pump motor switch with a hammer or something, and then toss in a hand-grenade. But that wouldn't be too effective. Of course if you destroy the water pump it'll stop the flow of water to cool the transformer, the equipment will overheat, and it'll become useless. But that would take a certain amount of time—in the first place, the other oil-cooled transformer would go on working.

"However, from the standpoint of ease of attack, since the pump is outside of the main building and there's no one guarding it, it would be the simplest. For a really crippling attack, the best thing would be to have one man kill the guard and go into the building itself. Then the other man would set the explosives by the switchboard, and once the fuse was lit, they could withdraw. But if some unforeseen obstacle should arise, all you could do would be to destroy the pump.

"Now as for those men who are going to investigate other stations, we think that the best way for you to get inside would be to see if you know somebody who is a student in an electrical school and borrow his identity card. And that's all we have to tell you."

Isao was pleased with the clarity and succinctness of their report.

"Good. Next, Takasé. Give us your report on getting a plan of the interior of the Bank of Japan."

"All right," answered Takasé, whose partner, Inoué, was absent. His voice was hoarse from his lung affliction, but his shoulders were powerful, and his reddened, feverish eyes were fixed piercingly on Isao. "To tell the truth, I puzzled over this for quite a while and couldn't come up with a good plan. Then I decided that the only way would be to get taken on as a night security guard, but before they'll hire you, the bank has you investigated thoroughly and you have to pass a very demanding physical examination. Since I had no hope of passing the physical, I approached Inoué on it. He's second degree in judo, you know. And so Inoué, ready to lay down his life at any time, set about it without the least fear or hesitation. He went to see the dean of student activities and told him that he wanted to work as a night security guard in order to help with his tuition, and the dean wrote a recommendation for him. With this and his certificate of the second degree in judo, he went to the bank and was hired with no difficulty. When he goes to work, he takes along some harmless books and pretends to be studying them. I went to see him once; the other guards seem to have a very good opinion of him. He told me that at their night supper they sometimes

treat him to a bowl of noodles. And though Inoué is the man
he is, he said he couldn't help feeling a little guilty to think
that the time was coming when he was going to burn all this
down."

The sound of youthful laughter rose in the dark.

"Until the day we go into action, Inoué will continue to
work as a security guard at the bank, keeping up an innocent
appearance. And since we'll have assistance from the inside,
Lieutenant Hori and the rest of us should work out some
kind of signal so that Inoué will know when to open the door.
As for the plan of the interior, Inoué and I will take the
responsibility of having that drawn up by two weeks before
the day itself, and we intend to show it to Lieutenant Hori.
Inoué says that, instead of letting himself seem suspicious by
investigating the layout of the bank too hastily, he makes a
point of learning all about it in a natural way while being
diligent in his work. He's certainly a grim sort of fellow. But
his eyes are narrow and he looks very amiable when he
laughs, so people take to him easily." Takasé glanced at his
watch. "Oh, it's about time for the tellers and clerks to go
home, and Inoué will be starting his shift. He was really sorry
he couldn't come up here, but the work he's doing now is absolutely vital. That's the end of my report."

While other such reports were being delivered in rather
meandering fashion, Isao, who had heard them all before, was
able to let his thoughts wander. But as he did, names that he
would prefer to avoid thinking about—his father, Sawa,
Honda, Kurahara—rose up at once in his mind to harass him
like a cluster of swirling moths. Isao took forcible hold of
the tiller and turned the vessel of his mind toward more desirable thoughts, thoughts that flashed, thoughts that provoked rapture: At the top of a cliff at sunrise, while paying
reverence to the sun . . . while looking down upon the sparkling sea, at the base of a tall, noble pine . . . to kill myself.
Yet, after the uprising, it would be difficult to get from Tokyo
to an ideal seaside cliff. If the attacks on the transformer sta-

tions were successful, all transportation would be disrupted, even escape by train might be out of the question. There seemed little hope that an adroit withdrawal from the assassination locales followed by a flight of some distance would indeed be possible.

Nevertheless, Isao would not give up his dream: somewhere a place awaited him where all the elements that belonged to an unblemished enactment of seppuku came together. The vision he clung to, of course, was the scene atop Omigataké when the six comrades of the League of the Divine Wind turned their swords against themselves. The vision of dying on a mountain peak, as the sky gradually lightens to reveal trailing clouds and white pendants fluttering in the morning breeze.

Isao had no desire to decide now upon a place for himself. To make a choice beforehand that the events following the rising might frustrate would be pointless. He would leave himself free. He would let himself be guided by the Divine Will, whose signs would ever be at hand. Surely somewhere the wind would blow through the pines at daybreak, somewhere, when he loosened his kimono, the keen winter air of the seashore would set his flesh tingling, somewhere the blood that stained his corpse and the trunk of the red pine beside which it lay would soon gleam brightly in the rising sun.

Suppose he succeeded in fleeing to the plaza before the Imperial Palace. . . . An awesome thought took form in Isao's mind. He might even swim the palace moat, shattering the film of ice that covered it, and climb the steep bank on the other side. There, hidden among the pines atop the bank, he could wait for morning to come. Perhaps he could look out beyond the vast array of ships at anchor off Tsukishima to see the dawn breaking over the bay, and then, just before the Marunouchi skyline opposite him stood out in the first rays of the sun, he could thrust his blade home!

25

Honda was not unaware of the gossip that he was somehow a changed man after his return from Tokyo. For him the once so imposing façade of present reality had fallen away. And his profession, involving as it did the minute analysis of the stuff of present reality, seemed suddenly to have lost all its savor.

Honda was frequently sunk in thought and failed to answer remarks made to him by his colleagues. When word of this reached the ears of the Chief Justice, he became concerned that the strain of overwork might have clouded his subordinate's peerless clarity of mind.

Though he dutifully considered the work spread before him on his desk in the judges' chambers, Honda, more often than not, would shudder as his thoughts returned still once more to the scene that evening in Yanagawa, the moment when Kiyoaki's dream of so many years before was realized in every detail. And he also recalled what had happened the following morning, shortly before he took the train back to Osaka, when he yielded to a strange impulse to go to Aoyama Cemetery to visit Kiyoaki's grave.

His mother seemed startled as he hurried out the door that morning earlier than necessary to catch his train. But Honda had the driver take him to Aoyama first. The car went up a road through the huge cemetery to the circular drive that lay in its very center. After getting out of the car here and telling the driver to wait, he walked quickly along the road toward the Matsugae family plot. Even if he had forgotten the way, the great torii that marked the Matsugae plot would have been visible.

Honda walked along the road for only a short distance before turning off on a path that wound among the graves, the morning light at his back. When he turned to look over his shoulder he saw the late autumn sun shining but weakly through a thin screen of pines. The rays that filtered through the dark evergreen branches and fell among the pointed stone shafts seemed to subdue rather than heighten the luster of the new marble gravestones.

Honda followed the path. In order to reach the Matsugae plot, whose torii seemed already to be looming up over him, he had to turn right on a still narrower path covered with moss and fallen leaves. The massive white marble torii of the Matsugaes towered over the small gravestones as if they were courtiers gathered in attendance. It had been modeled after the "Omiya-sama" torii on the grounds of the Matsugae estate. This example of Meiji grandeur now struck Honda's eye as somewhat tasteless.

The first thing that caught his attention after he passed beneath the torii was a memorial stone, an enormous slab of rock which seemed about fifteen feet high. The seal-style characters of the title of the epitaph had been drawn by Prince Sanjo and engraved by a famous Chinese artist, who, besides carving the details of Kiyoaki's grandfather's life, praised himself with the words:

> Gazing up at this monument,
> A myriad generations will be struck with awe.

In the shadow of the memorial stone were the graves of all the Matsugaes, each one with its own epitaph, but so overpowering was the enormous stone that one hardly noticed them. To the right of this stone, on a level reached by climbing a few steps, was a section set off by a marble fence, and here, side by side, were the graves of Kiyoaki and his grandfather. Since the place was familiar to Honda, he hardly

glanced at the memorial slab as he at once turned to his right
and climbed the stone steps.

Though the two graves were side by side, they obviously
had a different rank. His grandfather's huge gravestone rose
up in the very center of the fenced area, and four Nishinoya
stone lanterns kept solemn watch at either side of the path
approaching it. To the right stood Kiyoaki's more modest
gravestone, an evident intrusion upon the symmetry of his
grandfather's domain. Kiyoaki's seemed small beside the mass
of stonework that was his grandfather's, though it rose to the
respectable height of six feet from its foundation. But the
stone itself, the water urn, the flower vase with the family
crest—everything was in exactly the same design as his grandfather's, cut from the same kind of stone, only the scale altered. Chiseled gracefully upon the darkened marble in the
ancient square-cut characters was: KIYOAKI MATSUGAE. There
were no flowers in the vase, but there were some glossy sprigs
of Chinese anise.

Honda stood before the grave for a few moments before
offering a prayer. He could conceive of nothing less fitting
than that a young man who had given his life so wholeheartedly to emotion should now rest beneath this mound of
stone. The Kiyoaki of Honda's memories certainly had the
hint of death about him. But even that aura of death was like
a transparent flame, as if in him death itself was brilliant and
volatile. This cold stone had nothing at all to say of Kiyoaki.

Honda looked away, letting his gaze wander over the
stretch of cemetery beyond the grave of Kiyoaki's grandfather. Among the wintry trees the circular drive where his
car stood was white beneath the morning sun. And in the
midst of dark-hued evergreens there were the gravestones of
other families, facing away from him, that seemed to be
heaped up to overflowing on either side with floral offerings
of yellow and purple chrysanthemums.

Oddly enough, Honda felt a protest stirring within him.
Rather than press his palms together, he wanted to summon

Kiyoaki rudely and then take him by the shoulders and shake him. In his frustration Honda let his eyes stray to the marble fence that marked off the grave site with such precision, and there, atop a railing, he caught sight of a very small tendril of red-tinged ivy. When he walked over for a closer look, he saw how it had worked its way stealthily up the polished marble, clinging firmly to the surface so as not to slip, and had at length climbed to the top of the railing, whence it now was reaching out toward Kiyoaki's gravestone. Yellow veins were delicately sketched upon the spread-open red leaves, which were like fine candies, their tips dyed a deep scarlet. At the sight of this, Honda's heart at last became somewhat more tranquil, and he turned back once more to Kiyoaki's grave. He bowed his head deeply. He pressed his palms together. He shut his eyes. No sound came to disturb him.

All at once, an intuition struck him with unmistakable force. Honda shuddered. No one, the intuition told him, was within this grave.

 **26**

Isao had not yet shown Lieutenant Hori either the summary of the plan for the rising or the draft of the declaration to be dropped from an airplane. The Lieutenant was fully taken up with the fall maneuvers, and he had not acceded to Isao's request for a meeting. More than a month remained before the appointed day. Once into November, the Lieutenant was supposed to spend all his spare time in directing their efforts.

After he had returned home, Isao had been warmly welcomed as usual by his mother, and by Sawa and the other students. Sawa, perhaps because there was no chance to talk with Isao alone, had not once referred to the problem that he had recently discussed with such heat. And so Isao had not yet found an opportunity to thank him for the money.

The evening of his return, his father had gone out to attend some meeting, and, since the Academy students had told Isao that they would like to hear about the training camp at Yanagawa, he decided that he would eat with them in the dining hall that night. His mother took special pains to prepare a fine meal for them.

"With just you and the boys there, you'll be able to talk a lot more freely," said his mother, handing him a colorful porcelain platter of sashimi as he stood in the hallway. The house custom forbade boys in the kitchen. "So please take this in for me." Slices of halfbeak, sea bream, mackerel, flounder, and yellowtail lay beautifully arranged upon the platter, the kind of treat that hardly ever brightened a schoolboy's diet. He felt suspicious of this unlooked-for generosity. As for Miné herself, she was struck by the icy look on her son's handsome face as he reluctantly took the platter. In the darkness of the corridor his features seemed set and unresponsive.

"Why are you being so extravagant?" he asked her.

"It's just a little celebration on your coming home."

"But I was only gone a week, to the next prefecture. What would you do if I had been overseas?"

Isao could not keep his mind free of Kurahara and his money. Nothing made him so miserable in his own home as being under the constant menace of that name. The name was like a toxin that lay heavy in the atmosphere of the Academy of Patriotism, in the water, in every particle of food.

"Here I go to great lengths to give you a nice dinner, and you're not the least bit happy about it!"

Isao looked full into the eyes of his grumbling mother, whose pupils were wavering uneasily like the bubble in a spirit level. As he did so, her expression went blank, and she suddenly shifted her gaze away from him.

Perhaps, Isao thought, this treat was no more than one of his mother's whims. But his underlying anxiety was such, he realized, that his mood could be nothing but suspicious. Anything out of the ordinary in the household, whether good or bad, was enough to make him uneasy. The least alteration pained him.

"Master Kaido scolded you, didn't he?" she said, her tone jocular and even coquettish. "I heard all about it from your father." As she spoke, it seemed to Isao that droplets of her saliva sprayed over the limpid slices of halfbeak sashimi, and he felt a twinge of revulsion. The thought of his mother's saliva falling like a sudden shower upon the fresh sashimi and green seaweed garnish almost distracted him from the other uncleanliness that was troubling him.

"It was nothing of importance."

Isao's answer, given without the trace of a smile, was hardly satisfactory to her.

"Why must you be like this? You talk to me as if I'm a stranger, no matter how much I worry about you."

With a sudden movement, Miné picked up a slice of sashimi from the platter and thrust it into Isao's mouth. He was holding the platter, and could not block the rapid thrust of her hand. Probably opening his mouth to take it was an automatic reaction to the urgency of her gesture. His eyes watering from this forced feeding, he watched as she turned hastily as though to hide her tears and went back into the kitchen. Being thus treated like a son going off to war stirred his resentment.

His mother's sorrow lay in his mouth like a foreign body. He was annoyed at the way the sashimi clung to his teeth.

What was going on? Everything had been knocked from its proper course. Still, it was hard to believe that his mother's intuition had discerned in his eyes the determination to die.

When he walked into the dining hall carrying the platter of sashimi, the students greeted Isao with loud cheers. The usual faces around the table suddenly seemed quite alien to him. He was the only one there who was set upon action. But this crew went on as before, doing nothing but composing their poems about loyal devotion, about noble resolves, about Restoration, about seething passions. And Sawa's face, too, had its place among them, Sawa who was smiling like an indolent Zen monk. Sawa had taken no action even up to now, and it seemed clear that the decision not to admit him to their group had been a wise one.

Isao felt keenly that he must develop the knack of masking his feelings in dealing with others. He had now become a man quite out of the ordinary. Even if nothing in his bearing showed this, the least carelessness might let people get wind of it. They might detect that within him was the odor of a burning fuse.

"We hear that Master Kaido severely chastises his favorite students, the ones he loves the most, and that you had the experience yourself," said one of the students, making it plain to Isao that they all knew about the incident.

"What did you do with that pheasant?"

"We all ate it for dinner."

"I'll bet it tasted good. But, Isao, we had no idea you were such a good shot."

"Oh, I didn't do the shooting," Isao answered cheerfully. "Just as Master Kaido said, it was the 'harsh god' in me that shot, and so there was no question of missing."

"One of these days I hope some pretty young thing will bring out the 'mild god' in Isao."

Everyone went on eating and talking, except for Sawa. His smile persisted, and he said not a word. During the cheerful exchanges, Isao found himself unable to keep his eyes from straying in this man's direction. Then, suddenly, Sawa broke in to check the flow of chatter.

"I would like to recite a poem in celebration of Isao's having completed his training camp and become an even stronger man," he said.

As he chanted the poem, Sawa's voice reverberated loudly in the hushed dining hall. It was pitched somewhat high, his lungs straining from the force of his passion, like a horse neighing as it senses an approaching storm:

> "Purging away the evils of the West,
> Let us be faithful to our land.
> Stalwart, giving no ear to traitor's pleas,
> We shall hand down our great cause
> Without the least fear of death."

Isao immediately recognized the poem as one written by Inokichi Miura, but these last words of the young company commander involved in the Sakai Incident were not at all suited to a festive occasion.

As soon as he had acknowledged the applause, Sawa went on: "Now just one more. This is something that would rejoice the heart of Master Kaido."

After this introduction, he recited a poem of Kohei Tomobayashi:

> "We who were a people
> Of a land pure and holy
> Foolishly became Buddha's lackeys
> And preached that we were all one.
> Now we shall throw out Buddha,
> (Grieve not too much, Buddha!)
> We who were a people
> of a land pure and holy."

At the words "Foolishly became Buddha's lackeys" everyone laughed, the image of Master Kaido's face before them. And the admonition "Grieve not too much, Buddha!" also provoked laughter.

Though he laughed with the others, in his heart Isao was still responding to the emotion latent in Sawa's first poem beneath its clarity and openness, which was that of a young man's angry death. This Sawa, who had vowed to die, showed not the least sign of shame at being still alive, but seemed instead to be trying to implant in Isao the fervor of a youth who had brought his life to a furious conclusion at the dawn of the Meiji era. Isao felt the keen thrust of shame. Rather than Sawa himself suffering from a shame that was rightly his, that shame pierced Isao.

It was a shame that came from the conviction that Sawa, and Sawa alone, had seen in him both the pleasure and the arrogant pride of a young man luxuriating in the sweet feeling of having made up his mind to die. Sawa, in a sense, had purchased Isao's shame with his money.

27

ON NOVEMBER SEVENTH Lieutenant Hori sent word that Isao was to come at once to his billet. Isao went there. The Lieutenant was sitting down, still in uniform. Something was different about him. As soon as he entered the room, Isao had a premonition of trouble.

"How about having supper with me? I told them downstairs that you would." As he spoke, the Lieutenant stood up and turned on the lamp.

"I'd rather hear what you have to say."

"Don't be in such a rush."

Devoid of furnishings as it was, the austere eight-mat room had taken on the aspect of a brightly lit empty box. It was cold inside, but there was no trace of fire in the hibachi. From the hallway outside the closed door came the sound of a consciously military tread. The footsteps passed, turned back again, and then, apparently from the head of the staircase, there was a shout: "Hey, old fellow! Hurry up and bring my supper." The footsteps passed again and retreated down the corridor.

"That Lieutenant's in the room at the end of the hall on the other side. He can't hear what you say, so don't worry. The man next door is gone today. He's duty officer this week."

These words sounded somehow evasive in Isao's ears. He had not come here to say anything himself but to listen to the Lieutenant.

Lieutenant Hori lit a cigarette. A piece of tobacco clung to his lip, and as he dislodged it with the tip of one of his large fingernails, he crushed the now empty Golden Bat cigarette pack with his other hand. For the briefest of moments, the openings between the Lieutenant's fingers revealed bat wings, golden against a green background, being crushed ruthlessly within his fist. He had some time or other mentioned to Isao that his monthly salary was eighty-five yen. And now this memory, together with the cold of the room, together with the loneliness of billet life, rose up from the noise of the paper being crumpled.

"Has something happened?" asked Isao, taking the initiative.

The Lieutenant only grunted.

Finally Isao gave voice to his worst fear: "I see. It's gotten out."

"No, that's not it. Rest easy on that point. The fact is, I'm suddenly being sent off to Manchuria. An order came down from headquarters. I'm the only one going from the Third Regiment. It's very hush-hush. I haven't told anyone else, but I'm assigned to an independent Manchurian security force."

"When do you leave?"

"November fifteenth."

"But . . . that's only a week away."

"That's right."

Isao felt as if the sliding doors before his eyes were about to come falling in upon him. The Lieutenant's leadership was now lost to them. They had been by no means intending to leave everything up to him, but the expert guidance of a military man would be of inestimable help in the assault upon the Bank of Japan. Furthermore, they had been looking forward to the Lieutenant's detailed tactical and organizational instructions during this final month. Isao had the spirit but he lacked the technique.

"Is there no way for you to stay longer?" asked Isao, unable to keep the regret out of his voice.

"It's an order. You can't change a thing like that."

After this final word, both of them remained silent for some time. Image after image passed through Isao's mind as he kept trying to settle upon the role that now would best suit the Lieutenant. As he gave himself over to such wishful thinking, throwing aside common sense, he felt as though the Lieutenant were about to change himself into an ideal figure. There was the example of Harukata Kaya, who made his heroic decision just before the rising. The image that held Isao's mind was that of the Lieutenant abruptly resigning his commission and becoming just another man from the provinces, sacrificing himself to lead Isao and his comrades in the rising. Isao felt, on that summer afternoon when they practiced the kendo forms in the drill hall amid the cries of cicadas, that this was the very spirit that had flashed from the Lieutenant's eyes.

But perhaps the Lieutenant had already made this decision, and, after letting Isao be sufficiently distressed, would declare his intention.

"In that case, the Lieutenant will not be participating?"

"I didn't say that . . ."

Isao's eyes flashed as he heard the Lieutenant's prompt denial.

"You will take part then?"

"In the Army, an order is an order. But if you move the

date up before the fifteenth of November, I'll be happy to
take part."

As soon as he heard this, Isao was struck by the absurdity
of the Lieutenant's words, and realized at once that he had
no intention of taking part. The Lieutenant was well aware
that it was impossible to have the rising within a week, and
so his offer had been meaningless. Isao was even more bitterly disappointed at the Lieutenant's sophistry than at his
failure to join in the rising.

Now Isao began to suspect that the Lieutenant had had a
good reason for remaining in uniform. When he made his
announcement, he had to be clothed with unassailable dignity. Indeed, as he sat opposite Isao across the rough table,
he kept himself in a stiffly formal position, his shoulders
squared in his military tunic. His insignia glittered on the
broad shoulders that inspired such confidence, and he held
his firm and powerful chin rigid above the red infantry badge
at his collar with the golden "3" affixed to it. He was deliberately showing off his strength, to announce that he could
not lend it to their cause.

"That's out of the question," answered Isao, but with no
hint of defeat. By so answering he felt that, quite unexpectedly, he had moved into a broader and freer position.

The Lieutenant, apparently not noticing the sudden change
in him, began lecturing Isao as if he had been crushed: "If
you think it's out of the question, give it up. All right? From
the very beginning I had certain doubts—about deficiencies
in planning, the inadequate number of men involved and
therefore the absurdity of trying to bring about martial law,
the project's premature timing. . . . I believe it has become
quite hopeless. Now neither heaven nor the times seem to be
with us. Your resolve is a splendid one. I was aware of that,
and that's why I helped you, but to act now would be utterly
in vain. You see? Wait for the right time. This business here
of my sudden transfer—that's the voice of heaven speaking,
telling you 'Stop!' I won't be in Manchuria long. Wait till I

come back. And then I'll be glad to take part. So the thing to do until then is to go over your strategy and tighten up the loose ends, and do more research. Even in Manchuria, I'll be thinking of you young men and the pleasant times we had together. . . . Well, how about it? Will you take my advice and tell me straight out that you're not going through with it? Don't you think that the real man is the one who can be decisive, and check his forward rush?"

Isao was silent. He was surprised to find himself not at all surprised by the Lieutenant's words. And he was well aware that the longer his silence, the more uneasy the Lieutenant would become.

Somehow Isao had grown accustomed to the idea that when one reality crumbles, another crystallizes and a new order comes into existence. The Lieutenant had already been cast out by the new order. And so his gallant uniformed figure spun aimlessly about the edges of this impenetrable mass of pellucid crystal. Isao had made his way to a higher degree of purity, to a nobler level of tragedy.

Perhaps the Lieutenant had imagined that this young man would be thrown into a panic and would cling to his knees and plead tearfully. Isao, however, sat stiffly upright, saying nothing, his features even colder and more composed than before. When he spoke, his words were so far removed from his customary sincerity that there was danger that the Lieutenant might perceive that he was being mocked.

"But would you at least be so kind as to put us in touch with Lieutenant Shiga? I do want to beg his assistance in distributing the leaflets."

As he spoke, Isao was determined that the Lieutenant's eyes would never look upon the draft for the leaflet that lay within his briefcase. Lieutenant Hori, however, still failing to notice any change in him, gave a candid answer.

"No. That won't do. Give it up, I told you. You haven't even answered me yet. Do you think I enjoy saying this? The project just won't work, that's all, so I have to swallow my own feelings and warn you against going on. It's not the result of any spur-of-the-moment decision. And now that I've told you to give it up, I'll tell you also that I don't want you to count on any assistance whatsoever from the Army. I shouldn't have to mention that I didn't decide without consulting Lieutenant Shiga. You can understand that much, can't you?" The Lieutenant paused for a moment. "Of course if you yourselves want to carry it through on your own, that's up to you. But insofar as I was once your advisor, I warn you against it from the bottom of my heart. I can't bear to see you throw away your young lives. Don't you understand? Give it up!" the Lieutenant shouted as though issuing a command on the drill field, his eyes fixed on Isao's face.

What he might do, Isao thought, was simply to promise then and there to abandon his plans. That was it! For if the Lieutenant were left with a vague answer, he might become anxious and use the week remaining before his departure to devise a means to frustrate the project. But would not this sort of deception violate his own purity?

What the Lieutenant said next worked a sudden change in Isao's mood.

"You understand? And I don't want even the smallest scrap of notepaper remaining with either my name or Shiga's on it. I put this to you all the more strongly if you have any intentions of going against my advice to give it up. Get rid of our names as quick as you can."

"Yes, sir. We shall do that," Isao answered smoothly. "I understand all that you have said. I guarantee that no trace of your names will remain. As for abandoning the plan, it would be impossible to persuade everyone, so I will delay the date indefinitely. The effect will be the same."

"You'll do that? I've gotten across to you?" The Lieutenant's expression suddenly turned jovial.

"You have, sir."

"Good for you! There's no need for another episode of the League of the Divine Wind. We will bring about a Restoration, at whatever cost. And, without fail, there'll come a day when we'll have the chance to fight side by side. What do you say to a drink?" The Lieutenant took a bottle of whiskey from the wall cabinet as he made his offer, but Isao firmly refused and got up to leave. Because he did not want to give the impression of sulking, he had to do his best to seem cheerful.

Isao left the inn through the latticework door with the nameplate "Kitazaki" beside it. The rain was not falling as hard as it had the first afternoon that he had come there, but the pavement glistened beneath a winter shower. He was without rain gear, but, wanting to walk alone for a while to collect his thoughts, he turned in the direction of Ryudo. The high brick wall of the Third Regiment's compound rose on the left side of the street, and its smooth red surface gleamed wetly in the feeble glow cast by the street lights. No one else was out walking. Up to this moment he had been resolved to marshal firmly all of his mental power, but just then his will was betrayed by sudden tears.

He remembered an incident that had occurred when he was a fervent member of the kendo team and had been privileged to practice with the famous kendo master Fukuchi, who happened to visit the drill hall. Frustrated at every turn by the master's fluid defense, Isao had attacked with reckless force, only to be thwarted once more. Just as he was instinctively pulling back, a hoarse voice spoke quietly from behind the bars of his opponent's mask.

"Don't retreat. You need some work here, I think."

28

Isao's comrades had gathered to wait for him at their secret headquarters, the newly rented house in Yotsuya Samon. Since Lieutenant Hori had asked to see Isao alone, everyone had presumed that the Lieutenant had some rather important instructions for him.

They had named their hideaway Kamikazé, divine wind, as a symbol of their link with the League. To meet in Kamikazé, therefore, meant to meet in this two-story, four-room house reached by getting off the streetcar at Samon and walking about a hundred and twenty yards. The landlord had been happy to rent it to them even though they were students, and it was only lately that they learned the reason: a suicide had been committed there last summer and no one else was willing to take it. The entire south face of the house was covered with siding held by split-bamboo verticals, with only two small windows, and the veranda faced east, another unusual feature. When the previous tenants were moving out, an old woman of the family, her heart set against leaving, fastened a rope to the railing of the stairway and hanged herself. Sagara had heard the story at the neighborhood bakery and reported it to the others. The woman at the bakery had told him that much as she stuffed a paper bag with poppyseed-covered bean jam buns, grasped the two top corners of the bag with her fingers, nimbly twirled it once to close it, and passed it across the counter to him.

When Isao slid open the door of the entranceway and stepped in, the group on the second floor, hearing the noise, gathered at the head of the stairs, the skirts of their blue splashed-pattern kimonos rustling against one another in the dim corridor.

"What's the news?" asked Izutsu, his voice filled with a joy born of his own optimism. When Isao merely made his way past him on the stairway without answering, everyone felt the setback as if it were an electric shock. A locked cabinet at the end of the second-floor hallway was used to store their arms. Whenever Isao came here, he would have Sagara unlock it so that he himself could immediately check the number of swords. But today, forgetting even that, he went directly into the parlor. The shoulders of his jacket were soaked from the rain, and after he sat down, he felt a chill run through his body. His friends had been eating peanuts and shells were scattered over spread-out newspapers. Lying there in the lamplight, the shells seemed dull and pale, contorted with tension.

Seated cross-legged, Isao nervously picked up a peanut and cracked it as the others were gathering around him. The shell gave way, squeaking beneath the pressure of his fingertips, and split into two parts, a peanut in each.

"Lieutenant Hori has been transferred to Manchuria. Not only does he refuse to give us any further help, but he insists that we drop everything. As for our airplane, Lieutenant Shiga too has abandoned us. So we have no link with the military. I think it's time to consider what we should do."

Isao delivered all this in a single burst. The impression reflected in the faces around him was like that of brimming water abruptly receding. He sought out each one, compelled by the feeling that he had to make visual contact with them all. Now was the moment when purity was stripped naked. And no one but Isao embodied it.

Izutsu showed his lovely recklessness. He spoke out gallantly, his face flushed and glowing, as though Isao's news had been the best possible.

"I say: rework our plan, well and good. But there's no need to put off the date. Spirit is what counts—determination! These soldier boys! When it comes right down to it, all they're concerned about is their careers."

Isao strained his ears to catch any adverse reaction to this, but he heard nothing. The silence was like that of a number of small animals, each holding its breath within the shelter of its own thicket. Not unnaturally, Isao was tempted to be a little ruthless. He felt that he had no choice but to act with arbitrary force.

"It is just as Izutsu says. We strike on the day set. Aside from the problem of leadership, all that we've lost is the chance to drop our leaflets by airplane and to get our hands on some light machine guns. We'll print the declaration, at any rate, and then we can decide how to distribute it. Have we already bought a mimeograph machine?"

"We'll do it tomorrow," answered Sagara.

"Good. We have our swords. And so it has turned out that for the Showa League of the Divine Wind, too, the ultimate reliance will be upon the Japanese sword. Nothing could be more fitting. Let's reduce the scope of our attack, but double its intensity. We have all made our vows, and I know every man here will be loyal to the end."

His words were indeed greeted with loud shouts of approval, but the blaze did not leap up as high as Isao had expected. If this sort of flame falls only a trifle short of what one had hoped for, then one's heart cannot help but sense a proportionate measure of coldness.

Serikawa alone showed high excitement.

"We'll do it! We'll do it," he shouted, kicking about and scattering the shells that littered the floor. He gripped Isao's hand firmly and shook it. As usual, he was on the verge of tears. This young man affected Isao like a match girl who uses blatant emotional appeal to force a sale. It was a manifestation he had little need for at the moment.

That night all stayed until late discussing the means of cutting back on their plans. Two factions formed, one in favor of giving up the assault on the Bank of Japan, the other, of following through on it. Since no agreement was reached, another meeting was set for the following night, and they adjourned.

As everyone was leaving, three boys, Seyama, Tsujimura, and Ui, told Isao that they had something further to discuss with him. Sagara and Izutsu were going to stay too, but Isao sent them home, also dismissing Yoneda and Sakakibara, who were supposed to have been on night watch at the house.

The four returned to the room, which had no touch of fire to warm it. Though he was yet to hear their story, Isao well knew what they were going to say to him.

The high school student, Seyama, began to do all the talking. With a pair of fire tongs, he chipped at the crusted ash in the cold hibachi, and the scars of pimples showed on his cheeks, as, head down, he spoke in a numbed voice.

"As for what I've got to say, please understand that it's out of friendship. Anyway, I think we should postpone the attack for a while. I didn't bring it up in front of everybody because I thought it might give the wrong idea, as if I were throwing cold water on the discussion of the attack itself. Now as far as that goes, we made our vows too at the shrine in the presence of the gods. But a vow—a vow with the condition that there won't be any big change in the circumstances —isn't that made in the same spirit as a promise?"

"A vow and a promise are different!"

It was Tsujimura who broke in indignantly. The effect of his words was to anticipate the response expected from Isao and seem to act as his spokesman, a device that hinted of a subtle sycophancy toward Seyama. And the way Seyama took this as a cue irritated Isao still more.

"Oh, they're different? I shouldn't have confused them like that. Please disregard my slip of the tongue. But if we have any idea of bringing about martial law, the cooperation of the military is essential. What's really needed is not just dropping a declaration from an airplane but, as you said in the beginning, bombing the Diet. And wouldn't whether or not we had professional help be the big factor in coordinating local attacks? Wouldn't going ahead without it, depending only upon our spirit and our swords, be much too risky? We ought to be careful not to get carried away by spirit, I think."

"It would be a risk," said Isao, speaking for the first time, his voice low. "That's certain. The comrades of the League took a risk." So composed was his manner, so evident the fact that he had already given up trying to persuade them, that the three fell silent and exchanged glances.

A somber waterfall was falling within Isao's heart. His self-esteem was being slowly worn away. But he acted as he did because the precious thing that concerned him now was not his self-esteem. As a consequence, however, the abandoned self-esteem took its revenge upon him with a pain that could not be shunted aside. And beyond that pain lay his purity, like the clear evening sky seen through rifted clouds. As though in prayerful reverie, Isao saw the faces of those plunderers of the nation who deserved to be assassinated. The more isolated and bereft of strength he became, the more oppressive grew their fleshy, opulent reality. The stench of their evil worsened every moment. Isao and his comrades were plunged into a world of ever-growing uncertainty and anxiety, a world like the reflection of the moon adrift on a night sea. It was the plunderers' crimes that did this, their crimes that had changed his world into something so unsure, so unworthy of belief. The grotesque reality of these men who confronted Isao—there lay the source of all the world's perfidy. When he killed them, when his untarnished blade cut cleanly into that flesh swollen with fat and ravaged by high blood pressure, only then, for the first time, could the world be put to rights again. And until then . . .

"If you want to quit, I'm not going to stop you."

Isao would have had no chance to check these words, so readily did they pass his lips.

"Just a minute," protested Seyama, flustered and swallowing hard. "All we meant was, if our proposal wasn't accepted we'd have no choice but to quit."

"Your proposal isn't accepted." As he answered, Isao's voice seemed to him to be coming from a long way off.

There was a meeting every day thereafter.

On the first day, no one followed the three deserters. On the second, after a violent argument between the two factions, the four men of the smaller one withdrew. Then two men quit the day after that. Thus the number of the comrades, Isao included, was reduced to eleven. The day set for the rising was a bare three weeks ahead.

Isao came thirty minutes late to the meeting of November twelfth, the sixth meeting since Lieutenant Hori's abandonment of them on November seventh. When he climbed to the second floor, his ten comrades were already assembled. And seated there also was one uninvited guest. Isao did not see this man at first because he had settled himself in a corner, somewhat removed from the others. It was Sawa.

Sawa had obviously taken into consideration Isao's surprise and anger at his coming, and Isao realized that there would be no point in making a childish display that would give Sawa the advantage. The first thought that crossed his mind was that everything was finished now that Sawa knew their hideaway. For if one of the ten had secretly gone to Sawa for help, he could no longer trust any of them. But then he quickly ruled this out as an unworthy thought. It was much more likely that one of the deserters had gone to Sawa, hoping to soothe the pangs of conscience by asking him to take his place.

"I thought all of you would be hungry, so I brought some Osaka sushi," said Sawa, his squat figure like a wooden temple drum as he sat cross-legged upon the only pillow in the house. He was dressed, to his evident discomfort, in an old Western-style suit, and the man who was so scrupulous about the state of his underwear had fastened his bulging necktie around a sweat-stained collar.

"Thank you," said Isao, as calmly as possible.

"Surely it's all right, my coming here, isn't it? After all, what am I but a backer, so to speak? Come on, help yourself to some of this. All of them were stubborn. They held out, wouldn't take up their chopsticks until you came. They're good comrades, I tell you. And what greater joy can a man have than having comrades who'll stand fast for him?"

Since he could do little else, Isao replied with a touch of false enthusiasm: "All right. Let's go ahead." He reached out to take the first piece.

As he was eating, Isao tried to think how best to deal with Sawa, but chewing interfered with his calculations. Besides, the silence while they ate the sushi was a relief to him. Three more weeks. How many more times before he died, he wondered, would he experience this untidy pleasure of eating? He thought of the episode in *The League of the Divine Wind* of Tateo Narazaki eating and drinking heartily before he cut open his stomach. When he looked around, he saw that all the others too were eating in silence.

"Are you going to introduce me to your comrades?" asked Sawa, beaming. "I see two or three familiar faces from the Academy."

"This is Izutsu. This is Sagara. And then Serikawa, Hasegawa, Miyaké, Miyahara, Kimura, Fujita, Takasé, and Inoué," answered Isao, introducing each of them.

Now that he thought of it, Isao realized that of the unit assigned to attack the transformer stations, only three men, Hasegawa, Sagara, and Serikawa, were still with him. As for the Bank of Japan unit, Inoué remained steadfast together with Takasé, though their assignment would be different. Not a man was missing from the assassination unit. Isao's intention had been to assign the more daring of his comrades to these two latter units, and his judgment of character had proved unerring.

The cheerfully rash Izutsu, the clever little Sagara with his glasses, the boyish son of a country priest Serikawa, the taciturn but often droll Hasegawa, the sincere Miyaké with his long head, Miyahara with the hard and somber expression of a dried insect, Kimura with his love of literature and his profound reverence for the Emperor, the ever-silent but passionate Fujita, Takasé whose strong, broad shoulders belied his tuberculosis, the huge but mild-looking Inoué with his second degree in judo . . . These were his true comrades, the ones who had survived every test. These youths who were left knew what confronting death meant. Here beneath a ceiling lamp whose dim light fell upon tatami mats smelling of mold, Isao saw before him the corroboration of his own burning conviction. The petals of a drooping flower decay and fall away, leaving not a single one, but the hardy stamens stand firm together, still lustrous. And these keen-tipped stamens can pierce the blue of the sky. The more hopeless their dream became, the more stubbornly he and his comrades thrust their bodies together, leaving no opening for rational argument, forming themselves into a block of chalcedony shaped for killing.

"You're fine young men," said Sawa. "Those young people at the Academy of Patriotism should hang their heads." Then, having tried a bit of the *Kodan Club* style on them, he went at it in earnest: "Gentlemen, this is what it's come to: either this very night you number me among you or else you've got to kill me here and now. There're no two ways about it. And watch it that you don't let me walk away. For then you'd never know what I might spread about. I never took a single vow yet, remember. Well, then, gentlemen, either you trust me all the way or you don't trust me a bit. You can only do one or the other. And from the standpoint of your own advantage, I think that the clever thing to do would be to trust me. Getting rid of me would only do you harm, believe me. Well, gentlemen, what do you think?"

When Isao hesitated before answering, Sawa startled them by beginning to recite the vows in a loud voice: "Be it thus that we, emulating the purity of the League of the Divine Wind, hazard ourselves for the task of purging away all evil deities and perverse spirits. Be it thus that we, forging deep friendship among ourselves, aid one another as comrades in responding to the perils that confront the nation."

As he listened to Sawa's recitation, the words "forging deep friendship" struck Isao to the heart.

"Be it thus that we, never seeking power and giving no thought to personal advancement, go forth to certain death to become the foundation stones for the Restoration."

"How do you know our vows?" Isao asked accusingly, a touch of boyish grievance in his voice despite himself. With the keen instinct of the hunter, unexpected in a body so blunt and massive, Sawa seized upon Isao's weakness at once.

"Divine inspiration! Well, now I've made my vows. If you want me to seal them in blood, I'm ready."

Isao glanced briefly at the faces of his comrades, and then a smile formed on his lips around which there was a light trace of beard.

"There's no way of getting the best of you, Mr. Sawa. So . . . please join us."

"Thank you."

The joy evident in Sawa's face was overwhelming. He radiated the innocence that marks the absolute rejection of prudence. Isao now, for the first time, noticed that Sawa's teeth were no less white than the underwear that he washed so unremittingly.

The meeting that evening turned out to be productive. Sawa spoke earnestly and persuaded the others to abandon such exalted hopes as the proclamation of martial law and to concentrate their full force upon the assassinations.

The sword of justice need flash but once in the darkness. The light that shone from its blade would tell the world that the dawn was not far off. But men knew that a single glint from a Japanese sword was like the pale blue of daybreak along a mountain ridge.

Assassins had to be lone wolves, argued Sawa. There were twelve of them in the room, and therefore they had to make the chillingly bold decision to kill twelve. The date of December third could remain unchanged, but, having ruled out the attacks on the transformer stations, they should aim for a time just before dawn, rather than at night. Dawn was when these rich men, poor sleepers because of their years, lay awake in their beds. This was when the faint light would reveal their faces and so prevent mistakes. This was when they listened, heads on their pillows, to the twittering of the first sparrows of the morning, and calculated how best that day to spray all of Japan with the poisonous breath of their rule. This was the time to aim for. Now each man had to investigate the sleeping accommodations of his victim and then carry through his task with a burning sincerity that flamed up to the heavens.

Such was Sawa's counsel, and its adoption resulted in the assassination plan being altered as follows, in order to wipe out the principal figures of the economic world:

> Busuké Kurahara—Sawa
> Toru Shinkawa—Iinuma
> Juemon Nagasaki—Miyahara
> Nobuhisa Masuda—Kimura
> Shonosuké Yagi—Izutsu
> Hiroshi Teramoto—Fujita
> Zembei Ota—Miyaké
> Ryuichi Kamiya—Takasé
> Minoru Gota—Inoué
> Sadataro Matsubara—Sagara
> Genjiro Takai—Serikawa
> Toshikazu Kobinata—Hasegawa

This was a plan that struck at every great capitalist family in Japan. All the *zaibatsu*-controlled heavy industries, iron and steel, light metals, shipbuilding—an illustrious name from each of these sectors was on the list. That morning of mass killing would, beyond any doubt, send a severe shock through the economic structure of the nation.

Isao was amazed at the skill in persuasion shown by Sawa, who had set aside Kurahara for himself. Izutsu's boldness had been aroused by the very strength of Kurahara's guard, but Sawa easily turned him aside, saying: "The Kuraharas dismiss the police on guard at their home every night at nine and don't let them return until eight the next morning. He'll be the easiest one to attack, so leave it for an old man like me."

Sawa reached down inside his trousers and drew out the dagger in its plain wooden sheath that he had shown to Isao. "From now on, I'll come here every day, and I'll show you how to go about killing a man," he said. "It would be good to make a straw dummy. The most important thing is practice. I'll show you how it's done. . . . All right? There's your enemy. He's shaking with fear. A pitiful fellow, ordinary-looking, on the old side—a Japanese just like you. Pity is taboo! The evil of these men has taken such deep root inside them that they're not even aware of it themselves. You've got to keep your eye on that evil. Do you see it? Whether you see it or not will decide whether you succeed or fail. You've got to destroy the flesh that's blocking your way. You've got to get at the evil that's festering inside. Here, let's try this. Look!"

Sawa faced toward the wall and gathered his strength, his shoulders hunched.

As Isao watched he realized that before one could attack with one's whole being like Sawa, there were many rivers to be leaped over. And one clouded stream that never ran dry was that choked with the scum of humanism, the poison spewed out by the factory at its headwaters. There it was: its lights burning brilliantly as it worked even through the night—the factory of Western European ideals. The pollution from that factory degraded the exalted fervor to kill; it withered the green of the sakaki's leaves.

So be it then. The leaping, head-on attack! The body, bamboo stave held high, breaking through an invisible barrier all unaware and coming out on the other side. The quick and marvelous emotional abrasion gives off sparks. One's enemy, as though of his own accord, presses heavily against the point of one's sword and impales himself. Just as prickly seeds cling to the sleeves when a man makes his way through a thicket, so the assassin's kimono becomes splotched with blood without his noticing it.

Sawa pressed his right elbow against his lower side, and then, with his left hand pushing down upon his right wrist to prevent the blade from turning up, his icy blade seeming to spring directly from his fat body, he screamed: "Yaaah!" and struck the wall with full force, slashing through it.

The following day Isao began to investigate the layout of the Shinkawa house. The house stood on a knoll and was surrounded by a high wall. Isao discovered, however, one place at the top of a slope behind the house where a portion of the upper wall had been cut out to accommodate an ancient pine in the garden, a branch of which curved out over the street. Here it would be easy to get a footing, climb up into the tree, and then slip down into the garden. The trunk had, of course, been surrounded with barbed wire as a guard against burglars, but, if one disregarded a few cuts, this was nothing to be concerned about.

The Shinkawas often went away on the weekends, but would no doubt be found sleeping at home on Friday night. Since the Baron and his wife were so fond of English customs, perhaps they slept in a double bed; in any case, they surely shared the same bedroom. A mansion so large would have many bedrooms, but it seemed likely that the Shinkawas would naturally take advantage of the pleasant southern exposure. The view of the sea was from the east, however, and therefore Isao felt that their room would be in the southeast corner of the house, thus combining comfort with the beauty of the view.

Trying to sketch the plan of the house, with its many wings, was no easy matter. By chance Isao happened to come across an old issue of the magazine *Bungei Shunju* in which an affected essay by Toru Shinkawa caught his eye. Shinkawa was one who had long prided himself on his literary ability, but phrases such as "my wife this," "my wife that" were conspicuous in his style. Perhaps this was merely an unconscious affectation, but possibly he was insinuating a criticism of the Japanese custom of avoiding direct references to one's spouse.

The essay was entitled "Gibbon Through the Night," and from it Isao was able to draw this essential portion:

> By any standard Gibbon's work is a masterpiece. It goes without saying that I am far too deficient in scholarship and intellect to comprehend its wisdom, but I may safely contend that no Japanese translation can possibly convey the monumental significance of *The Decline and Fall of the Roman Empire*. The lavishly illustrated 1909 edition edited by Professor Bury, seven volumes, unabridged, is absolutely without peer. When I give myself over to the pleasure of reading Gibbon by the light afforded by my bedside lamp, the hour inevitably grows far advanced. The breathing of my sleeping wife beside me, the rustle of the pages of my Bury edition of Gibbon, and the ticking of the antique clock purchased from LeRoi's of Paris become by and by the only sounds that occupy the silence of my bedroom, forming a kind of delicate nocturnal trio. And the small lamp that illumines Gibbon's pages is, within the whole house, the last torch of the intellect to be extinguished each night.

When he read this, Isao pictured to himself how, once he had slipped into the garden under cover of darkness, he could take up a position at the southeast corner of the mansion. Then if he saw a light shining through a window curtain, and if the light kept burning after all the others had gone out, he would be able to tell the Baron's room. To accomplish this he would have to slip into the garden late in the evening and conceal himself there until the last light had disappeared. This kind of residence would no doubt have night watchmen patrolling its garden, but the shelter of the trees would certainly offer him ample place to hide.

After having considered the problem up to this point, Isao experienced doubt from another quarter. How strange it was that the Baron, whom everyone knew to be in constant peril, should deliberately write in a public journal in a fashion to expose himself to further danger. Could it be possible that this essay was meant as a trap?

29

As NOVEMBER was drawing to a close, Isao found himself fighting with the desire to say farewell to Makiko Kito in a way that would seem casual. He had neglected her recently. He had been busy, for one thing. The circumstances of his enterprise had been frequently altered, and he had been able to spare little time or feeling for anything else. And then there was something about saying farewell after making the decision to die that embarrassed him. Besides, he was afraid he might become so tense before Makiko that his powerful emotions would get the better of him.

He felt that the most beautiful thing would be to die without seeing her, but, as the world viewed it, to do so would be a breach of etiquette. Furthermore, each of the young men would go to his death carrying a petal from the sacred lilies

Makiko had given them. Makiko, then, was the *miko* who would preside over the divinely sanctioned conflict that was the War of the Lilies. How could it be otherwise, then, but that Isao, as the emissary of his comrades, go to Makiko to take an inconspicuous leave of her? This thought finally gave him courage.

Isao shuddered at the possibility that he might not find her at home if he paid a sudden visit. Given his mood, he would hardly be able to force himself to come a second time to say farewell. She had to appear at the door that night to greet him, allowing him a last glimpse of that beautiful face.

Though it was not in accordance with custom and though he realized that it violated the casualness he wanted, Isao ventured to telephone to make sure that Makiko was home. It happened that his family had received a gift of oysters that day, and he was able to say that he wanted to bring some of them over.

One of his father's old students, who lived in Hiroshima, sent oysters every year in season, and it would be only natural for his mother to have him take some of them to the Kitos, who had treated him with such kindness. The coincidence was fortunate.

Dressed in his student uniform with his feet thrust into clogs, Isao left the house carrying a little keg of oysters. Since it was already long past the dinner hour, there was no reason to hurry.

As one who was sworn to die and about to take an unspoken farewell, Isao resented the incongruity of his gift. The splashing sound that came from the keg as he walked was like low waves lapping at the base of a sheer cliff. He imagined the sea as crammed into that small dark space, its freshness giving way to pollution.

Probably it was the last time he would follow this familiar path. It would also be his farewell to the thirty-six stone steps he knew so well. As he climbed them, the steps seemed to cascade down through the darkness like a waterfall. The cold of the night was bone-chilling even though there was no wind. Suddenly he had an odd feeling that he wanted to turn and look back at the way he had come. Two or three hemp palms grew on the slope on the south side of the house. The hairy fiber that covered their trunks seemed to entangle the stars in the winter sky. There were only a few lights in the houses below, but the eaves of the stores by the Hakusanmaé streetcar stop shone brightly. He saw no streetcar, but the scraping noise of one echoed in the night like an old drawer being pulled out.

The scene was quite ordinary. There was nothing that had to do with death and the spilling of blood. Even the sight of the four or five bonsai in a neat row upon the drying frame outside a house whose shutters were already closed brought to his mind how life would go on along its ordinary course after his death. His death, he was sure, would ever be beyond the grasp of the people living in that house. The turmoil that he and his comrades stirred would not disturb their sleep.

He entered the gate of the Kito home. He pressed the bell. Makiko slid open the door at once as though she had been lying in wait in the entrance hall.

Any other time, he would have slipped off his clogs and stepped up into the house, but he was afraid that if he talked to Makiko too long, his expression would betray his emotions. And so he merely handed her the small keg and said: "My mother asked me to bring you this. It's a few of the oysters we received from Hiroshima."

"Thank you. This is certainly not an everyday present! Well then, do come in."

"Today I can't. Please excuse me."

"Why not?"

"I've got to study."

"What a fibber! When did you start grinding away so at your books?"

Makiko insisted upon Isao's staying and then disappeared into the house. He heard the General's voice telling her to invite him in.

Isao shut his eyes and gave himself over greedily to the image of Makiko before him a moment ago. Her beautiful smiling face with its fair skin—he wanted to store this image in his heart just as it was, unflawed. But if he were too eager, it would shatter like a mirror that has slipped from one's grasp.

What was best, he thought, was to leave at once. If he did so, the Kitos would, he was sure, take his abrupt departure as nothing more than a bit of boyish rudeness and would later perceive its true significance as his farewell. The dim light of the entrance hall served well to hide Isao's expression.

The whiteness of the flat stone where one removed one's shoes stood out in the chill pool of darkness that pressed against the floor platform, which seemed to Isao like a quay where a ship might berth. He himself was a ship that was about to cast off. The floor's edge, then, was the trim quay where people were finally received or denied, or bade farewell. And he was a ship loaded down with a full cargo of emotion, riding low in the dark winter sea of death.

Isao turned to leave the entrance hall, just as Makiko re-appeared. She cried out: "What's this? Why are you going? After Father said to have you come in."

"Please excuse me," answered Isao, pulling the sliding door shut behind him. His heart pounded as if he had accomplished something difficult. He felt like running, but then he reflected that to run would be unfitting and ruin everything. Departing by a different route would be enough. Instead of going back down the stone steps, he could turn toward the rear of the house, in the direction of Hakusan Shrine. He could return home by going through the shrine precincts. But as Isao was about to turn onto the path, deserted this late at night, that led through Hakusanmaé to the shrine itself, he caught a glimpse over his shoulder of Makiko's white shawl.

She was coming along behind him, not pursuing at all but keeping the same pace.

Isao went on walking. He had made the decision never to see Makiko again. He was on a path along the edge of Haku-san Park, which was at the rear of the shrine. To pass through the shrine grounds he would have to stoop and go beneath an elevated passageway just ahead, that joined the forehall with the shrine office. Light shone faintly through the close-worked lattice of the passageway.

Makiko finally called out. Isao had to stop. But he felt that if he looked back at her some ill-omened event might occur.

Instead of answering her, Isao turned away and walked to the top of a small hill opposite the park. A flagpole stood on the crest. The front of the hill was a steep drop covered with a growth of trees and shrubbery.

Finally he heard Makiko's quiet voice at his shoulder.

"Why are you angry?"

Her voice hung in the darkness, charged with anxiety. Isao had to face her.

Her silvery white shawl concealed her mouth. But the faint light coming from the distant shops revealed tears shining in her eyes. Isao felt as if he were choking.

"I'm not angry at anything."

"You came to say farewell. It's true, isn't it?"

Makiko pronounced this non sequitur with assurance, as though she were placing a white chess piece upon a new square.

Isao said nothing as he kept his eyes upon the scene below. A tall, sinewy zelkova tree, its upper roots exposed, lifted its branches to spread a delicate tracery across the face of the night and dim the stars caught within its branches. Two or three persimmon trees stood on the edge of the cliff, their scanty leaves black against the sky. Beyond the valley the land rose again, and the brightness of the shopping district misted the eaves of the houses along the hilltop. From here, a good many lights still seemed to be burning, but the effect

was not at all that of a bustling city. Rather, the bright points
were like small stones lying at the bottom of a brook.

"It's true, isn't it?" said Makiko once again.

This time her voice was very close to him, inflaming his
cheek. It was then that he felt Makiko's hands pressing upon
the back of his neck. Her cold fingers were like a sword blade
against the close-cropped nape. When the time came to receive the finishing stroke, when his neck shivered in anticipa-
tion of the falling blade, no doubt he would feel a chill like
this. Isao shuddered, but his eyes told him nothing.

And yet for Makiko to have stretched out her arms and
clasped his neck as she was doing, she had to be standing
before him. This is what Isao had not perceived. Whether
she had been incredibly quick or incredibly slow, she must
have moved in front of him. And he did not see her.

Makiko's face was no more visible than before. What he
could see was something blacker than the night, the rich
abundance of her hair just at the level of his chest. She had
buried her face there. The perfume that rose from her seemed
to screen his vision. His senses were fully taken up with that
scent. Isao's feet trembled in his clogs and the thongs creaked
faintly. His footing seemed to be giving way, and like a man
seized by a drowning person, he reached out in self-protection
and clasped Makiko in his arms.

He embraced her, but what he felt beneath her light coat
was no more than the firmness of her bulky, tight-wound obi
with its padded layers and its huge bow. This was a substance that seemed to put him at a greater distance from
Makiko than before he had embraced her. And yet what this
sensation conveyed to Isao was the reality behind all his
mental images of a woman's body. No nakedness could seem
so utterly naked.

Here began his rapture. Suddenly it was like a runaway
stallion breaking free of the yoke. A wild strength flowed into
his arms as he held the woman. He clasped her tighter, feeling their two bodies shake like the mast of a plunging ship.

The face that had been buried in his chest was lifted. Makiko had lifted her face! Her expression was just what he had dreamed night after night that it would be when he said his last farewell. Tears sparkled on that lovely white face that was without a trace of makeup. Her tight-shut eyes looked at Isao with a force stronger than that of vision. Her face was like a delicate bubble that now floated before his eyes after having risen from some unimaginable depth. In the darkness her lips trembled as she sighed again and again. Isao could not bear having her lips so close to his. To banish them, all he could do was touch his own lips to hers. As naturally as one leaf falls and comes to rest upon another, Isao came upon the first and final kiss of his life. Makiko's lips reminded him of the red leaves of the cherry trees that he had seen in Yanagawa. He was startled by the sweetness that began to flow gently through him once their mouths were joined. The world trembled at the point of contact between their lips. From this point radiated a transformation that altered his very flesh. The sensation of being steeped in something indescribably warm and smooth reached a climax when he realized that he had drunk in some of Makiko's saliva.

When they finally drew their lips apart, they clung to each other and wept.

"Tell me just one thing. When will it be? Tomorrow? The day after?"

Because he realized that, were he in possession of himself, he would never answer such a question, Isao told her at once.

"It's December third."

"Only three days from now. Will I see you again?"

"No. I'm afraid that's impossible."

They began to walk in silence. Makiko chose a roundabout route, and Isao had to follow her through a small open space in Hakusan Park and down a dark path along the outbuildings where the shrine's sacred palanquins were kept.

"I know what I'll do," said Makiko in the darkness beside him. "I can take the train to Sakurai tomorrow and go to

Omiwa Shrine. I'll pray for your good fortune in battle at the
Sai Shrine. I'll bring back a talisman for each of you, and
see that you have them by December second. How many
should I get?"

"Eleven. . . . No, there're twelve of us."

A kind of shyness kept Isao from daring to tell Makiko
that each man would undertake his mission with a petal of
her lilies hidden upon him.

The two of them entered the lighted area in front of the
shrine, but there was no sign of anyone else being there.
Since she did not want to cause any trouble at the Academy,
Makiko asked him how to get to their hideaway, and he wrote
the directions on a slip of paper and gave it to her.

Such light as there was had only one source, a small night
lantern donated by a Hakusanshito photo studio. It cast a
feeble glow over the stone guardian dogs, the gold-lettered
tablet, the embossed carving of a dragon breathing fire, and
the wooden steps leading to the shrine. Only the white pendants that hung from the sacred ropes stood out with any
clarity. Weak though the light was, it reached as far as the
white wall of the shrine office, some twenty feet away. Shadows of sakaki leaves made a lovely pattern upon it.

Each of them prayed silently. Then they passed beneath
the torii and parted at the top of the long stone stairway.

30

ON THE MORNING of December first, Isao, pretending that he was off to school, went directly to the hideaway.
Sawa had been sent on an errand by the headmaster and was

unable to attend the meeting, but the other ten were all present. The action was now only two days away, and, though it was necessary to work out some details, the main purpose of the meeting was to renew everyone's resolution to take his own life, whatever difficulty he might find himself in, immediately after the blow had been struck.

The expressions on the faces of his comrades seemed to Isao to be clear and determined. The group had sold two regular swords and bought six short swords. Thus each now had his own sharp-bladed dagger. But someone made the suggestion that, as an extra precaution, it would be well if they all had a hidden dagger too, and the others agreed. They knew that poison was the most effective way to commit a hasty suicide, but they spurned this womanish means of putting an end to life.

The practice was to lock the door of the house when the group was assembled. When a knock sounded, everyone presumed that Sawa had come after all, stealing time from the task he was sent to do.

Izutsu went downstairs and called out: "Mr. Sawa?"

"Yes," came the answer in a low voice, but when Izutsu slid the door open, a stranger entered, pushed his way past, and began running up the stairs, still in his street shoes.

"Get away!" Izutsu shouted, as a second and third man rushed in and twisted his arms behind him.

The comrades who tried to escape by jumping down into the backyard from the overhanging roof were seized by detectives who had moved in from the rear. Isao snatched up one of the daggers in front of him to thrust it into his own stomach, but a detective caught his wrist. In the struggle that followed, the officer suffered a cut finger. Inoué grappled with the detectives and threw one of them, but two or three others brought him down.

And so the eleven were handcuffed and brought to the Yotsuya police station. On the afternoon of the same day, Sawa was arrested as he was returning to the Academy.

 **31**

TWELVE ULTRANATIONALIST RADICALS ARRESTED
IN HIDEOUT

SWORDS AND SEDITIOUS LITERATURE SEIZED
SERIOUS PLOT SAY AUTHORITIES

Honda's first reaction when he saw the headlines in the morning paper was "Again, eh?" and nothing more, but his calm was abruptly shattered when his eye caught the name Isao Iinuma on the list of those arrested. He wanted to place a call to Tokyo at once and talk to Iinuma at the Academy, but worldly prudence prevented this. The headlines the following morning were even larger:

FULL DETAILS ON "SHOWA DIVINE WIND" AFFAIR
AIM TO DELIVER CRUSHING BLOW TO FINANCIAL WORLD
EACH MEMBER TO ASSASSINATE ONE MAN
RINGLEADER NINETEEN-YEAR-OLD YOUTH

A picture of Isao appeared for the first time. The reproduction was very coarse, but there was no mistaking those incredibly clear eyes whose brilliance had so affected Honda when the boy and his father had come to dinner, those eyes with their piercing gaze, which could never blend into the pattern of ordinary amenities. No doubt they had been looking forward to this day.

Belatedly Honda regretted his tendency to be capable of discernment only after a matter had been strained through the meshes of the law.

Isao was already past eighteen and would therefore not be

treated as a juvenile before the law. According to the article, the entire group, except for the middle-aged eccentric named Sawa, was made up of youths in their late teens or early twenties, and so some no doubt would be tried as juveniles. But for Isao there was no chance of this.

Honda visualized the worst possible legal situation. Something seemed missing from the vague newspaper articles. On the surface this affair was merely the rash assassination plot of some heedless boys, but the investigation might well turn up a far wider and deeper conspiracy.

As a matter of fact, the military authorities, wanting to refute wild rumors and to allay the prejudice provoked by the May Fifteenth Incident, had made a statement carried in that day's paper: "No Army officers had any connection whatsoever with this recent incident. Unfortunately, every time an incident of this sort occurs there are those ready to believe that young officers must be involved. Ever since the May Fifteenth Incident, the greatest concern has been shown for the rigid enforcement of discipline in every unit throughout the Armed Forces. The extraordinary energy that we have displayed in putting our house in order is a matter of public knowledge."

Such was the statement, but its effect, however groundless, was to excite the suspicion that some greater power was indeed at work behind the plotters.

If the scope of the affair broadened, and any intent were revealed that would come under Article 77 of the Criminal Code, "Subverting the Constitution," the situation would become critical. The newspaper accounts were not clear as to whether the unconsummated aspect or rather the element of premeditation would be uppermost when the case was brought to trial. Honda remembered *The League of the Divine Wind*, which he had read at Isao's urging. He could not help but feel a sense of ill omen at Isao and his comrades' choice in calling themselves the Showa League of the Divine Wind.

He dreamed of Kiyoaki that night. Kiyoaki seemed to be
asking for help, and also to be lamenting his premature
death. When Honda awoke, his mind was made up.

Honda's reputation at the Courthouse seemed not quite
as high as it had been. When he talked with his colleagues,
their manner since his return from Tokyo in the fall had
somehow cooled. The rumors in vogue alleged that either
family trouble or woman trouble had made Honda a changed
man. And his once highly regarded discernment was no
longer so esteemed. The Chief Justice, though he kept it to
himself, was grieved when he became aware of the situation.
For no one had been more appreciative than he of Honda's
rise to eminence.

For the vast majority of men, romantic dreams are inevitably bound up with a woman. And so when his colleagues
intuitively diagnosed the affliction lodged within him since
his fall trip to Tokyo as involvement with a woman, they
were at least correct in giving it a romantic coloring. Their
intuition was indeed remarkable in shrewdly picturing Honda
as one who had strayed from the way of reason and was now
wandering aimlessly along some overgrown path of emotion.
But what might have been expected in a twenty-year-old
youth was deemed improper in a man Honda's age, entirely
human though the failing was. And this was where most of
the disapproval was focused.

Members of a profession in which reason was of the essence, his colleagues could hardly be expected to view with
respect any man who, unknown to himself, had contracted
the disease of romanticism. And then from the viewpoint of
national righteousness, though Honda had not gone so far as
to commit any crime, he had certainly defiled himself with an
"unwholesome" attitude.

But most surprised of all at this state of affairs was Honda
himself. The eagle's nest that he had constructed at a dizzy-
ing height in the structure of legalism, which by now had

become second nature to him, was—something wholly unforeseen!—threatened with the floodwaters of dreams, with
the infiltration of poetry. More awesome yet, the dream that
assaulted him did not destroy either the transcendence of human reason, which he had always believed in, or his proud
pleasure at living with more concern for principles than for
phenomena. The effect was rather to strengthen his beliefs,
to heighten his pleasure. For he could now glimpse towering
up brightly beyond the principles of this world an unbreach-
able wall of principle. Once he saw it, so dazzling was this
glimpse of the ultimate that he was unable to go back to the
placid, everyday faith he had known before. And this was not
to retreat but to advance. It was not to look back but to look
ahead. Kiyoaki had certainly been reborn as Isao, and from
this fact, beyond one kind of law, Honda had begun to see
into the essential truth of law.

He suddenly remembered that in his youth, from the time
he had heard the sermon of the Abbess of Gesshu, the European philosophy of natural law had lost its appeal for him,
and he had been much attracted by the ancient Indian Laws
of Manu, whose provisions extended even to reincarnation.
Something had already taken root in his heart then. A law
whose nature was not to impose order upon chaos but to point
to the principles that lay within chaos and so give form to a
legal code, just as the surface of the water caught the reflected image of the moon—such a law could well have
sprung from a source more profound than the European worship of reason that undergirded natural law. Honda's instinc-
tive feeling, therefore, may have been sound, but this was not
the kind of soundness looked for in a judge, the guardian of
the operative law. He could easily imagine how unsettling it
must have been to his colleagues to have a man of this sort
working with them in the same building. To have one dust-
covered desk in a room filled with the spirit of good order.
From the viewpoint of reason, nothing so resembled the
stains on an untidy man's clothes as an obsession with

dreams. Dreams somehow turn one into a slovenly figure. A soiled collar, the back of the shirt wrinkled as though slept in, trousers baggy—something similar overtakes the garment of the spirit. Though he had done nothing, though he had said nothing, Honda had, at some time or other, come to violate the code of public morality, and so he knew that, in the eyes of his colleagues, he was like wastepaper scattered along the path of a neatly kept park.

As for his home life, his wife Rié said nothing at all. Rié was not a woman who would intrude curiously into her husband's private thoughts. She must have realized that he had changed, and that he seemed preoccupied. But Rié said nothing.

It was not any fear of ridicule or insult, then, that kept Honda from confiding in his wife, but a certain sense of shyness. This subtle kind of bashfulness gave a special character to their marriage. Perhaps this was the most beautiful aspect of their rather quiet and old-fashioned relationship. And though Honda himself may have been faintly aware that something in his recent discovery and change of outlook infringed upon it, husband and wife made use of this extremely beautiful characteristic to preserve silence and the unrevealed secret.

Rié must have wondered why her husband's work had recently become so burdensome. The dishes that she took such pains to prepare for his evening meal failed to give him the pleasure that they had before. She did not grumble. She did not wear a sad expression. Nor did she punish him by putting on a brave cheerfulness. At some point or other a childish court-doll face, the vague look she had whenever her kidneys troubled her, had become her everyday face. Though always smiling and amiable, she never showed any expectation. The force that had shaped Rié into the woman she was belonged in part to her father, in part to her husband. At least, Honda had never given his wife cause to suffer from jealousy.

Although the affair of Isao was widely covered in the newspapers, her husband said nothing about it, and so Rié too said nothing. But then one night at dinner, when further silence seemed unnatural, she spoke out casually: "That's a terrible thing about Mr. Iinuma's son. When I saw him here, I thought he was such a serious and well-behaved boy . . ."

"Well, with this kind of crime, it's the serious and well-behaved ones you're most likely to find involved," said Honda in rebuttal. But so gentle and bemused was his manner that Rié became concerned.

Honda's mind was in turmoil. Because his failure in trying to save Kiyoaki was the keenest regret of his youth, he felt that he must succeed this time. He had to rescue *him* from danger and scandal no matter what the cost.

The favor of the public would be something to count on. The extraordinary youth of the conspirators seemed to keep people from becoming too aroused against them, and, beyond that, Honda sensed that a feeling of sympathy was already in the air.

Honda made his decision the morning after he had dreamed about Kiyoaki.

When Iinuma met Honda at Tokyo Station on his arrival from Osaka, he was wearing an inverness with a seal collar and his moustache seemed to be quivering in the late December cold. The weariness of his long wait on the platform was evident in his voice and in his watery and bloodshot eyes. As soon as Honda descended, Iinuma clasped his hand, commanded a student to relieve him of his bags at once, and then began to pour an insistent stream of thanks into Honda's ear.

"How grateful I am that you chose to come! I feel that I have all conceivable power aligned with me. No boy could be luckier than that son of mine. But what a momentous resolution, Judge Honda, you have made in our behalf!"

After instructing the student to take his luggage to his mother's house, Honda accepted Iinuma's invitation and went to have dinner with him at a Ginza restaurant called the Gincharyo. The streets were gay with Christmas decorations. Honda had heard that Tokyo's population was now 5,300,000, and when he looked at the crowded streets, it seemed that hunger and the depression were like conflagrations burning in some corner of a distant land, things too far off to be visible from here.

"When my wife read your letter, she too wept tears of joy. We put it upon the altar of the gods, and we pay it reverence each morning and evening. But wasn't your judgeship a lifetime appointment? Why did you resign it?"

"Illness. No one can help that. However much they tried to keep me on, I had the doctor's certificate to defend myself."

"But what kind of illness?"

"A nervous breakdown."

"Not really?"

Iinuma said nothing further, but the frankness of the momentary misgiving that showed in his eyes gave Honda a warm feeling toward him. Honda knew that a flash of frankness from an unsavory defendant could create a measure of goodwill in a judge, no matter how much care he took to avoid emotion. He tried to get some idea of the feeling that a lawyer would have for his client. No doubt it ought to be more theatrical. The goodwill that passed through a judge's mind would naturally have some ethical motivation, but a lawyer's feelings had to be fully exploited.

"It was a matter of being relieved of duty at my own request. So I'm still a judge as far as that goes, but now my status is that of a retired judge. Tomorrow I'm going to join the Bar Association, and then my career as a lawyer will begin. It's the work that I've decided to do, and so I intend to put everything I have into it. The truth is that since I rose no higher before resigning, I'm not going to bring too much prestige to my career as a lawyer. But the whole thing was my choosing, and I have to accept the consequences. After

all, it's up to you to select your own lawyer. But as for com-
pensation, I explained to you in my letter . . ."

"Oh, Judge Honda! How can you be so benevolent toward
us? It would be despicable of me to take advantage of your
good nature, but under the circumstances . . ."

"Very well then. Let us agree that I receive nothing at all.
I'll undertake it on that condition only."

"Judge Honda . . . I am at a loss for words." Sitting in a
stiff, formal position, Iinuma bowed his head again and
again. "But after a decision of such grave consequences,
wasn't your wife taken aback? And your mother too, wasn't
she upset? It seems to me that they would be greatly opposed."

"My wife was perfectly calm about it. When I phoned my
mother to tell her, she caught her breath for a moment, but
then she simply said that I should do as I thought best."

"Really? What a fine mother! What a fine wife! Judge
Honda, your wife and your mother are remarkable women.
My wife, now, couldn't possibly match it. Sometime you must
teach me the secret of wife-training. I have to try to instill in
my wife a little of what yours has. But I suppose it's too late
for that."

For the first time, the formality between guest and host
gave way, and both of them laughed. As they did, a nostalgia
welled up in Honda's heart. He felt as though twenty years
had been rolled back and the student Honda and the tutor
Iinuma were meeting to discuss how best to come to the
rescue of the absent Kiyoaki.

The lights of the Ginza flashed beyond the frosted glass of
the window. But just as the gaudy night life could not altogether escape the reality of famine and bad times, so inside
the night had a double aspect all too evident. Even the colorful scraps of fish that they had left uneaten upon the platter
suggested a link to the cold darkness of a detention cell at
night. And the past too, its unfulfilled hopes acknowledged

with some reluctance, was linked to the present of these two men now in their prime.

Never again in his life, Honda thought, would he make a renunciation of such magnitude, and he determined to fix in his memory the bizarre passion that now seethed within him. He could recall nothing comparable to the inner fervor and exhilaration he felt after making the decision that all the world would call foolish, a decision made at a time of life when his powers of discretion should have been at their height!

It was for him to thank Isao rather than for Isao to thank him. If he had not been electrified by Kiyoaki's rebirth in Isao and by Isao's conduct, Honda might have turned into a man who would be delighted to live on an iceberg. For what he had looked upon as tranquility had been a kind of ice. His concept of perfection had been a kind of desiccation. His ability to view things in an unorthodox fashion had seemed to him merely immature, but the truth was he had had no idea of what maturity meant.

Iinuma, as though spurred on by something, had drunk one cup of saké after another, wetting the ends of his neat moustache. As Honda studied those drops of saké, he thought of them as bits of ideology innocently clinging to the moustache of this man who had earned his living by commercializing a passionately held belief. Having made faith his livelihood, ideology his means of support, Iinuma's follies and excesses had given his face a certain fatuous look of self-deception. Still sitting in a formal position and drinking heavily, with a vigor that showed no sign of concern for his son shivering in a cold cell, he played up his emotion and his very affectation of emotion as a kind of role. His driving manner seemed as stereotyped as a painted black dragon on a screen in the entrance hall of an inn. He had chosen to cultivate his beliefs as a mannerism. A long period had passed since his youth when, with his dark, deep-set eyes, he had given such an overpowering, almost physical, impression of gloom. Now it was not surprising that his worldly reverses, his agonies, and, above all, his humiliations, made him throw out his chest in pride at his son's glory.

As Honda sat musing, he saw that Iinuma had wordlessly committed something to his son. The old humiliations of the father entrusted to the purity of the son, who goes against the powerful of this world with fierce cry and drawn sword.

Honda felt that he had to hear a frank word about Isao from Iinuma.

"Would you say," he asked, "that the truth is that your son fulfills a dream that you've had ever since the days when you were Matsugae's tutor?"

"No," answered Iinuma with a touch of defiance. "He's my son. That's all he is." But then after this denial, he began to talk of Kiyoaki. "When I stop and think today, the young master dying the way he did was probably the only thing that could have happened. It must have been the will of heaven. As for Isao, well, he's pretty much like his father. He's young, and the times are different, so he's got involved in something like this. Yes, I tried to instill the samurai virtues in the young master, but maybe it was my own boorishness that pushed me to do it. I suppose the young master did die of frustration . . ." Here Iinuma's voice broke as his emotions got the better of him. As soon as he yielded in the least to his feelings, the result, it seemed, was like a dam giving way. "But still . . . he acted as his heart told him to act, and I'm sure that, if nothing else, he had that much satisfaction. At least, as time goes by, that's what I find myself wanting more and more to believe. Otherwise, I would find it unbearable, though that's my own selfish view. At any rate, the young master lived and died in a way suited to himself. As for me, an outsider, and all my anxiety, everything I tried was pointless and a waste of effort.

"Isao, though, is my own son. I raised him very strictly in accordance with my beliefs. And his response was all that I could have wanted. I was delighted at his reaching the third degree in kendo before he was out of his teens, but since then, needless to say, he's gotten out of hand. Perhaps he was too deeply influenced by my own life. But there was more to it than that. He was too anxious to be freed from his father's guidance. He put too much trust in himself, and this was the root cause of his going astray. Now in this affair, if through your great effort, Judge Honda, the sentence imposed is somehow a light one, the chastisement will do that boy a world of good. Surely there's no chance of the death penalty or life imprisonment, is there?"

"You needn't worry about that," said Honda in laconic reassurance.

"Ah, Judge Honda! Thank you for everything. Father and son, Isao and I have had no greater benefactor in our lives than you."

"You'd do well to spare your gratitude until after the trial."

Iinuma bowed his head again. Now that he had let himself indulge in sentiment, the conventional vulgarity of his expression suddenly vanished. As he became drunker, his eyes began to water in an unsettling manner, and his whole body seemed to give off the feeling, like an invisible vapor, that there was something he wanted to say.

"I know what you're thinking, Judge Honda," Iinuma finally declared. The pitch of his voice rose somewhat as he went on. "I know, I tell you. It's that I'm impure beyond words and my son is pure. That's what you're thinking."

"Not really." Somewhat irked, Honda made his reply vague.

"No, that's it. There's no doubt about it. And since I've gone so far, let me go further: my boy was arrested just two days before they were to strike. Who do you think he has to thank for that?"

"Well now . . ." Honda knew that Iinuma was on the verge of saying something better left unsaid, but there was no way to stop him.

"You're doing so much for us, Judge, I find it painful to

make this revelation after all your kindness, but I suppose a
client shouldn't keep anything from his lawyer. So I'll make
a clean breast of it. I'm the one. I secretly reported my son to
the police. At the last possible moment I saved my son's life."

"Why did you do it?"

"Why? Because if I hadn't, my son's life would have
ended."

"But, putting aside the good or evil of what had been
planned, didn't you feel in any way that perhaps you should
let your son achieve what he set out to do?"

"It was because I looked ahead. I'm always looking ahead,
Judge." Flushed from drink, Iinuma abruptly reached for his
seal-collared inverness which lay upon a clothing box in the
corner of the room. Heedless of the dust he scattered, he
shook open the coat with a flapping noise and held it up like
a mantle. "Here," he said. "This is me. This inverness is myself. There is no sleight-of-hand involved. The inverness is
the father. It's like the dark sky of a winter night. So the folds
of the inverness reach far and wide, covering whatever spot
the son might place his foot upon. The son runs about wanting to see the light, but he cannot. The huge black inverness
is spread wide over his head. As long as the night continues,
the inverness sternly makes him acknowledge the night.
When the morning comes, the inverness falls to earth and lets
the son's eyes be dazzled by the light. Such is the father. Am
I not right, Judge Honda? My son didn't want to acknowledge this inverness, and he did what he wanted to do. Therefore it's only natural that he be taken to task. For it's still
night, and the inverness knows this and wants to prevent the
son from going to his death.

"These leftist scum—the more pressure you put on them,
the stronger they get. Japan is invaded by their germs and
those who made Japan so weak as to be susceptible to them
are the politicians and the businessmen. I knew all about it
without my son telling me. And those in the advance guard
ready to leap to the defense of the Imperial Family when a

crisis threatens the nation are, as hardly needs saying, we ourselves. But there's the matter of picking the time. There's such a thing as the favorable moment. Determination alone counts for nothing. Thus I have to conclude that my son is too young. The necessary discernment is still beyond him.

"I, the father, have the determination. Indeed, I may say that my patriotism, my agony of soul, exceeds that of my son. My son tried to hide everything from me that he was intent on carrying out—wouldn't you say he was blind to his father?

"I always look ahead. Rather than take action, the best course is to achieve results without acting. Am I right or not? I heard that at the time of the May Fifteenth Incident there was a flood of petitions asking leniency. So the naïve purity of the young defendants will surely evoke public sympathy. We can count on that. And my boy, rather than losing his life, will come home covered with glory. His whole life long, he'll have no worries as to where his next meal is coming from. Because the world will forever hold him in awe as Isao Iinuma of the Showa League of the Divine Wind."

Honda was at first struck dumb, but then he wondered if Iinuma was being altogether candid.

By Iinuma's account, the primary savior of Isao was Isao's father, and Honda, in coming to the son's rescue, was merely an agent assigned to bring about the realization of Iinuma's plan. No words could more effectively negate the goodwill shown by Honda in throwing aside his career and undertaking Isao's defense without a fee. Nor could any words more defile the nobility in Honda's action.

But, oddly enough, Honda was not angered. The person he was concerned about defending was Isao, not his father. However blemished the father, his blemishes had nothing to do with his son. They had not the least effect upon the son's purity of intention.

Beyond this, Honda, who should have been offended to some degree by Iinuma's boorish display, had another reason for remaining unperturbed. For as Iinuma, having said all this, kept hastily pouring himself more to drink in this little room from which he had long since excluded the waitress, Honda was aware of a tremor in his hairy hands. And here Honda perceived a sentiment that Iinuma would never voice, something that was probably the deepest motive of his betrayal. The son, in other words, had been on the verge of achieving a bloody glory and a sublime death, and the father had been unable to restrain his jealousy.

32

His HIGHNESS Prince Harunori Toin was another to whom the affair had been a severe shock. He was not apt to remember those who came once or twice to pay their respects, but the memory of Isao's visit that night was still vivid in his mind. And, especially since Lieutenant Hori had brought the boy, he could not take a detached view of this incident. Naturally, as soon as the affair broke, the Prince made a long-distance telephone call to his steward to seal his lips about Isao's visit. But since the steward was, in effect, a minion of the Imperial Household Ministry, the Prince could put little trust in him.

For some time now, the Prince had found in the Lieutenant a like-minded companion with whom he could deplore the times. The gentlemen of the Imperial Household Ministry were not amused at this. They frequently admonished him for granting audiences indiscriminately, without regard to rank. But this very conduct grew out of resentment at the Ministry's constraints, requiring him to report even the shortest trip, and so he could hardly be expected to listen meekly to this advice.

Since his appointment as regimental commander in Yama-guchi, the Prince had shown a certain intemperance in speech and action which had not gone unnoticed by the Imperial Household Minister and the Director of the Division of Special Affairs. Waiting until Harunori came up to Tokyo, they arranged to call on him for a friendly visit, in order to admonish him gently. The Prince heard them out without a word, and made no reply even after they were finished. A long silence ensued.

The Minister and the Director had expected the Prince to charge them angrily with meddling in military affairs. If he did so, their resources were at an end.

The Prince's expression was extremely subdued, however, and the moment for him to lash out at them was already past. Finally, his slender eyes half open but radiating dignity, the Prince looked from one official to the other and then said: "This is not the first time I have had to suffer your interference. If you must interfere, I hope you will devote equal attention to the rest of the Imperial Family. How is it that I alone have long had to bear the brunt of this?"

Before the Minister could so much as protest, the Prince, struggling to keep his deep anger in check, began to deliver a tirade.

"Years ago, when Marquis Matsugae affronted me with the greatest impertinence regarding the woman who was to be my wife, the Imperial Household Ministry supported the Marquis and gave me no help whatsoever. It was a blatant case of the Imperial Family being insulted by one of its own subjects! Who is the Imperial Household Ministry meant to serve? Should it be any cause for wonder that since then I have viewed the maneuverings of you gentlemen with suspicion?"

The Imperial Household Minister and the Director of the Division of Special Affairs could offer nothing in reply, and they hastily took their leave.

Lending an ear to the violent words of Lieutenant Hori

and two or three other young officers had been a great diversion for the Prince, and he enjoyed being looked up to as the
blue sky showing through the dark clouds that hung over
Japan. A grievous wound lay deep within his heart. He was
happy that this was a kind of beacon to some men, and that
his sad, maverick spirit had become the source of hope for
many. However, he was not at all inclined to take action.

Once the affair of Isao and his companions had come to
light, nothing more was heard from Lieutenant Hori in Manchuria. The Prince had only his memory of that single audience granted Isao to draw on, but now, when he recalled
the light blazing in the young man's clear eyes on that summer night, he realized that they had been the eyes of one
sworn to die.

The copy of *The League of the Divine Wind* given to him
by Isao, which he had read only hastily at the time, was still
on the book shelf in the commandant's room. And so the
Prince, hoping to search out the true meaning of the affair,
took up the book again and read through it during his spare
moments away from his military duties. More than the force
of the story itself, what seemed to flare out from every line of
the book was the intensity of Isao's eyes that night and the
fire of his words.

The rough simplicity of a shared military life was something of a boon to the Prince, who had been altogether sheltered from the world, and he found it extremely congenial.
Yet here too, there was deference and regard for rank. Not
until he met that young civilian had he encountered such
burning purity, and at searingly close range. And so the conversation of that night had been unforgettable.

What was loyalty? Soldiers had no need to wonder about
that, the fiery young man had said. Their loyalty as soldiers
was part of their duty.

Those words, the Prince realized, had struck home. Adopting a gruff, martial manner, the Prince had fitted himself to
the obvious standard of loyalty of the soldier. Probably he

had sought refuge in it in flight from a host of threatening sorrows. He knew nothing firsthand of the kind of loyalty that burns and destroys the flesh.

Nor had he had any reason to take notice of its possible existence. The night Isao was brought to him was the first time that the Prince had had an authentic encounter with such fiery loyalty, with such raw and uncontained loyalty. The experience had thrilled him.

Prince Harunori was, of course, ready at any moment to give his life for the Emperor. Some fourteen years older than His Majesty, who was thirty-one, the Prince had a love for the Emperor like that of an affectionate older brother. But these were serene, quiet feelings, a pleasant loyalty like the shade cast by a huge tree. Then too, the Prince habitually viewed with some suspicion the loyalty of those beneath him, and kept his distance from it.

Deeply impressed by Isao, Prince Toin had dedicated himself more gladly than ever to the simplicity of the military spirit. And now it occurred to him that the reason no evidence of military involvement in this incident had come to light was that the accused had kept silent to protect Lieutenant Hori. This speculation increased his sympathy all the more.

Prince Toin recalled a passage from *The League of the Divine Wind* that Isao must have read with keen appreciation, applying it to himself: "Most of them did not take to refinement. They loved the moon shining on the banks of the Shirakawa with the love of men who believed that it was the last harvest moon they would see in this life. They prized the cherry blossoms like men for whom this spring's blossoms were the last that would ever bloom." The hot blood of such young men made the forty-five-year-old regimental commander's heart stir excitedly within his breast.

Prince Toin began to ponder earnestly whether or not he could save these boys. All his life, whenever he became weary of thinking, whenever a problem seemed to have no solution, his practice had been to listen to Western-style music.

He called his orderly and had him light a fire in the chilly parlor of this large official residence. Then he selected a record and laid it on the turntable with his own hand.

Because he wanted to listen to something pleasant, he had chosen Richard Strauss's "Till Eulenspiegel" performed by the Berlin Philharmonic under the direction of Wilhelm Furtwängler, and he dismissed his orderly so that he could enjoy it alone.

"Till Eulenspiegel" was a satiric sixteenth-century folk tale. Hauptmann's play and Strauss's tone poem based upon it were famous.

The late December wind whistled through the broad, dark garden outside the commandant's residence, and seemed to blend with the sound of the flames in the stove.

Without so much as loosening the collar of his Army tunic, Prince Toin settled himself in an armchair with a white linen slipcover that was cold to the touch. He crossed his legs in their military breeches, and the tip of one foot in its white cotton sock hung motionless in midair. The buttons at the knee of breeches like these constricted the upper calf, and so one usually unfastened them when one's boots were off, but the Prince paid no attention to the slight discomfort of this congestion. He caressed the waxed and curled tip of his moustache lightly, as if touching the tail feathers of some fierce bird.

It was a long time since he had listened to this record. He wanted something entertaining, but when he heard the first weak sounds of the horn that played Till's theme he had the immediate feeling that his choice had been wrong, that this was not the kind of music he would enjoy hearing now. For this was not a gay and mischievous Till, but a sad and lonely one, as transparent as crystal, a character fashioned by the conductor himself.

But Prince Toin kept on listening. From Till's going into a frenzy, when he seemed to make the silvery bundle of his nerves into a duster that beat its way throughout the parlor, up until the end, when he received his sentence of death and was executed, Prince Toin heard it all. When the record was done, he got to his feet abruptly and rang the bell summoning his orderly. He instructed him to put in a long-distance call to Tokyo and to get his steward on the line.

The Prince had come to a decision. On the occasion of his return to Tokyo for the approaching New Year's holidays, he would request a few minutes with His Majesty, during which he would make bold to bring to the Imperial attention the unparalleled loyalty of Isao and his companions. And when some gracious response had come forth from His Majesty, the Prince would convey this in strictest confidence to the Chief Justice of the Supreme Court. But first, before the year ended, he had to invite the lawyer in charge of Isao's defense to discuss with him all the ramifications of the case.

By telephone, then, he ordered the steward to find out the name of the lawyer and to have him come to the Toin residence on a date immediately following the Prince's arrival in Tokyo on December twenty-ninth.

Until he was able to find a suitable place of his own, Honda had established himself in a room that was part of the office of a friend of his on the fifth floor of the Marunouchi Building. The friend was also a lawyer, and a college classmate.

One day an official came from the Toin residence to convey a confidential request from His Highness. Since this was indeed something unprecedented, Honda was startled. When he saw the little man in a black suit walking stealthily across the brown linoleum floor without making a sound, Honda felt an indescribable distaste, and, after he had led him into the conference room, the sensation grew more acute. The little man had a frozen yet uneasy expression as he looked around the small conference room, which was separated from the office by a wall of rippled glass. He was anxious about being overheard.

His face was like that of a pale fish fitted with gold-rimmed glasses. It told of living in a habitat of cold, dark waters never visited by the light of the sun, of breathing only with trepidation beneath the tangled seaweed of red tape.

Honda, who still had a little of the haughtiness of a judge, started off by brusquely neglecting the civilities.

"As far as guarding secrets goes, that's our business, and so I would urge you to put your mind at rest. And, especially since your errand has to do with such an august personage, I will exercise the greatest care imaginable."

The official spoke in an extremely low voice, as if he had a lung ailment, and Honda was obliged to lean forward from the edge of his chair to hear him.

"No, no, there's no question of any sort of secrecy being involved. His Highness is pleased to take some interest in this affair, and he merely requests that you be gracious enough to visit his residence on December thirtieth. And if you would then have the goodness to tell him frankly whatever lies within the scope of your knowledge, he would be more than gratified. However . . ." Here the little man stammered spasmodically, as though trying to choke back an attack of hiccups. "However, as to . . . that is, if His Highness were to learn of what I have to say next, a grave problem would result, and I would therefore beg that you refrain from mentioning it to him."

"I understand. Please speak freely."

"Well . . . since this is an opinion that is by no means held by me alone, I would be pleased if you would be sensitive in this regard. But in the event, as it were, of your happening to catch a cold on the appointed day and being thus prevented from coming, and if you were to notify us of it, that too would be entirely agreeable. Since His Highness's desire has been duly communicated to you."

Honda stared in amazement at the expressionless face of this delegate sent by Prince Toin. His mission was to deliver an invitation, but he hinted that Honda should contrive to slip out of it. To receive such an invitation from Prince Toin, nineteen years after his indirect involvement in Kiyoaki's death, was a strange turn of fate, and Honda had become ill at ease as soon as he had heard His Highness's request. But now, confronted with so odd a message, he became determined to pay his respects at the Toin residence.

"Very well. Then, if on that day I am without the least trace of a cold and the very picture of health, I am to present myself to His Highness. Is that correct?"

For the first time the official's face showed a slight expression. A sad discomfiture lingered briefly on the cold tip of his nose. But then, as though nothing had happened, the voice like the breeze blowing through bamboo grass went on.

"Yes, of course, of course. So please be good enough to come to the Shiba Residence at ten o'clock on the morning of December thirtieth. I will have informed the guard at the main gate, and you need merely give your name."

Though Honda had been a student at Peers School, he had never had the experience of visiting the home of a member of the Imperial Family, perhaps because no personage so exalted had happened to be in the same class with him. Nor had he ever sought the opportunity.

Honda knew that the Prince had been involved in Kiyoaki's death, but no doubt the Prince was unaware that Honda had been Kiyoaki's friend. Since, in all justice, Prince Toin had been an injured party in that affair, the best course was to say nothing about it unless His Highness brought it up. A mention of Kiyoaki's name would in itself be an insult. Honda, of course, well realized this and knew how he must conduct himself.

On the basis of the official's manner the previous day, however, Honda's intuition told him that Prince Toin, for whatever reason, seemed to have a sympathetic attitude toward this most recent affair—never dreaming that Isao was none other than Kiyoaki reborn!

Whatever the official might think of it, Honda made up his mind that, just as the Prince had requested, he would tell him everything he knew, giving a true picture of the affair without saying anything that bordered upon disrespect.

Thus when he went out on the day set, his mind was tranquil. The winter rain, begun the previous day, was still falling, and the rivulets that streamed down through the gravel of the sloping path that led to the Toin residence wet Honda's shoes. The official himself greeted him at the entrance hall, but though courtesy informed his every word and action, the coldness of his manner was strikingly apparent. Indeed the white skin of this little man seemed to secrete coldness.

The visitor's parlor was a strange little room. Two of its walls formed an obtuse angle containing a door and a window which opened upon a rain-soaked balcony. A third wall was fitted with a *tokonoma*-like alcove, and the incense burning in it filled the room with a tenacious fragrance intensified by the heat coming from the glowing gas stove.

At length Prince Toin, the stately figure of a regimental commander in a dark brown suit, made his appearance, his cheerful manner calculated to put his guest at ease.

"Well, here I've brought you out in mid-morning. How kind of you to come!" said the Prince in a voice much too loud for the occasion.

Honda offered his card and bowed low.

"Please make yourself comfortable. My reason for asking you to come has to do with this affair that you are concerned with. I am told you have gone so far as to resign your judgeship in order to undertake the defense of these youths."

"That is correct, Your Highness. One of them is the only son of an acquaintance of mine."

"Iinuma, I take it?" asked Prince Toin with the straightforwardness of a soldier.

The window was clouded with drops of moisture from the heat. The winter rain seemed a mist as it fell upon the bleak trees in the broad garden and upon the pine and hemp palms outside the window, each of which was wound with straw mats to protect it from frost. A white-gloved butler served English-style tea. He filled the white china cups with a graceful amber stream issuing from the slender spout of a silver teapot. Honda withdrew his fingers from the sudden heat that his silver spoon transmitted. The too keen warmth all at once reminded him of the punishment provisions of the Imperial Code, which seemed to vibrate there in the silver.

"The fact is, someone once brought Isao Iinuma to my house," said the Prince calmly. "At that time he made a strong impression upon me. He expressed himself very passionately; he seemed absolutely sincere. And he has quite a head on his shoulders. A superior mind. No matter what tricky questions I put to him, his response was invariably to the point. A somewhat dangerous boy, but one with nothing frivolous about him. That such a worthy youth should stumble like this is indeed cause for regret. And so when I heard that you had cast aside your profession to become his lawyer, I was delighted and wished to meet you."

"The boy, Your Highness, is wholly devoted to the Emperor. On the occasion of his coming here, did he express himself in such terms to Your Highness?"

"Yes. He said that loyalty was presenting to the Emperor steaming rice balls made with his own hands. And after that, whatever the result, loyalty demanded cutting open his stomach. He gave me a book called *The League of the Divine Wind.* . . . But surely he won't kill himself, will he?"

"Both the police and the prison authorities are alert to that possibility, so there seems to be no need for concern. But, Your Highness . . ." said Honda, gradually growing bolder and turning the conversation in the direction he wanted, "Your Highness, to what degree do you countenance the conduct of these boys? How far would you go in supporting them, not only in the actions that have already come to light but in their entire plot? Or, indeed, would you deign to

countenance whatever came forth from their burning sincerity?"

"That's not an easy question," said the Prince. There was a
disconcerted expression on his face as he halted his teacup in
front of his moustache, a wavering ribbon of steam rising
from the cup. At that moment Honda felt an unaccountable
urge to inform the Prince of the circumstances of Kiyoaki's
sorrowful death.

The Prince's self-esteem must have suffered a severe
wound from the incident involving Kiyoaki, but Honda was
uncertain as to whether or not passion had been the cause of
the Prince's vulnerability. If, however, years before, the
Prince's whole being had indeed become suffused with the
splendor radiated by that bright phantom that draws all men
—high and low, rich and poor alike—to death, to hell, if he
owed his wound to that passion, altogether ignorant, altogether noble, that blinds men with its splendor . . . And
then as to Satoko, if it had been she herself and no one else
who had turned the Prince's passion to ashes . . . If that
could be made known here and now . . . no more consoling
requiem could be offered for Kiyoaki. Nothing, Honda
thought, could more comfort Kiyoaki's soul. Love and loyalty
sprang from the same source. If Prince Toin would give
some clear evidence of this, Honda would find in himself the
sincere dedication to risk everything to protect the Prince.
Thus, though Kiyoaki's name was a forbidden word, Honda,
using this present issue as a metaphor of the storm of passion
that had brought Kiyoaki to his death, now had the courage
to test the Prince by speaking of something that up to now he
had kept back for fear of showing disrespect. It might perhaps be to Isao's disadvantage in the trial, and perhaps, as a
lawyer, he should leave it unsaid. But he could not suppress
the thought that the voices of Kiyoaki and Isao were crying
out together within him.

"The truth is, Your Highness, that according to what the
investigation brought out, though this is still a matter of the

deepest secrecy, it seems that the Iinuma group had something more in mind than the assassination of certain men of the financial world."

"Something new has come out?"

"Their plot was, of course, nipped in the bud, but, as might be expected of such youths, they were moved by the earnest desire to see the governing power in the benevolent hands of His Majesty."

"That's understandable."

"Their primary objective was, I believe, the formation of a cabinet headed by a member of the Imperial Family. I find it very difficult to say this, but the police discovered leaflets secretly printed by them in which Your Highness's name has a prominent place."

"My name?" exclaimed the Prince, his expression abruptly altered.

"The leaflets had been mimeographed with the intention of distributing them speedily after the assassinations, in order to make the populace believe the falsehood that the Emperor had vested Your Highness with authority to take action. Once the Prosecutor's Office became aware of them, their attitude hardened immeasurably. And my task is now all the more difficult. Depending upon how they handle it, this could result in the charges becoming extremely grave."

"That is an offense against the Emperor! It's absurd. It's a shocking thing."

Though the Prince's voice grew louder, this did not conceal a note of fear. Honda, still intent on testing the Prince's state of mind, quietly asked another question. He looked steadily into the Prince's almond eyes.

"It is rude of me to ask this, Your Highness, but could it be that in the military too there was similar sentiment?"

"Not at all. The military was not in the least involved. It's absurd to try to link it to the military. The whole thing came out of the fevered brains of schoolboys."

Prince Toin, Honda realized, was angrily shutting the door

in his guest's face to protect the Army. Honda's most cherished hope was shattered.

"Imagine a boy that intelligent coming up with such nonsense!" said the Prince as though muttering to himself. "I am profoundly disappointed. And of all things, to use my name! To exploit my name that way after a single meeting, the name of an imperial prince! He's lost all sense of obligation—at least he doesn't know where to stop. He doesn't understand that there could be no greater disloyalty than an offense against the Emperor. Is this his concept of loyalty? Of sincerity? How distressing that young men are like that!" There was no longer any trace of the magnanimity of a leader of troops. His heart had suddenly turned cold. And Honda, as he listened, had easily perceived the instant change in His Highness's zeal. The fire that had burned in the imperial breast had been extinguished, embers and all.

Prince Toin was thinking how well it was that he had decided to meet with this lawyer. Now when he paid his respects to His Majesty at the New Year, he would make no mention of this to him, and thus he would avoid later mortification. But misgivings swarmed in his mind. It hardly seemed possible that such an offense could have been planned by schoolboys. How strange that he had heard nothing at all from Lieutenant Hori since this affair! Prince Toin had felt sorry to learn of his transfer to Manchuria, but now, as he considered the matter, he began to wonder if the Lieutenant might not have volunteered to go, fleeing before the affair broke. If that was the case, the Prince had been used, had been betrayed by this officer in whom he had placed such trust.

Since his hatred had its root in fear, it kept growing. For a long while Prince Toin's attitude toward those in the Imperial Household Ministry and toward that little group who made up the upper class had been one of distrust and revulsion. And now the odor of treachery had risen even from the one place where his mind had been at rest. That smell was all too familiar. He had only to reflect, and the memory came to him of how, ever since his childhood, it had been on all sides of him. The odor of a fox's den. No matter how he tried to banish it, this odor permeated his exalted surroundings, sinister, affronting the nostrils, an excremental stench of treachery.

Honda glanced through the window at the falling rain. The glass was becoming more and more clouded. The color of the fresh mats wrapped protectively around the hemp palms in the foreground shone dully amid the rain-soaked scene, giving the impression of khaki-uniformed men crowding about the window. Honda knew that he was about to take a dangerous gamble, one that never would have occurred to him during his years as a judge. Of course he had not arrived at the Prince's residence with such a strategy already in mind. But with the pitiful ashes of His Highness's passion before his eyes, a sudden, reckless hope sprung up within him. This approach would be entirely different, no longer a matter of the Prince's interest in saving Isao. The approach left to Honda, one that was far more cogent, would have the effect of smoothly diverting Prince Toin to an effort to save Isao without his having the least intention of doing so. At this moment there was no one but Honda to instill such a resolution in the Prince, nor would there be another opportunity like this. And so, though with much trepidation, he felt obliged to urge this skillfully upon the Prince. The incendiary literature in question was in the hands of the prosecution, still unknown to the general public.

Trying to speak as calmly as possible, Honda said: "With regard to those pamphlets in which Your Highness's name occurs, if they are allowed to remain as they are, and if this results in any awkward consequences for Your Highness, I am afraid that an extremely unfortunate situation will arise."

"Awkward consequences? From something with which I had no connection?"

For the first time the Prince turned eyes upon Honda in which anger showed clearly. He raised his voice only a little, however, revealing that he felt some fear about giving way to anger. But his anger was precious to Honda. He felt that he had to make the most of it.

"I beg your pardon, Your Highness. But it seems to me that this material is dangerous, and in spite of my concern for Your Highness's welfare, I haven't the power to see that it's suppressed. Unless you take action speedily, it will sooner or later become public knowledge, and though you are involved in no way in this affair, grounds will be given for speculation that you are involved."

"Do you mean that I have the power to suppress it?"

"Yes, Your Highness. You do have that power."

"How?"

"It is simply a matter of Your Highness so directing the Imperial Household Minister," Honda answered without hesitation.

"You're telling me to bend my knee to the Imperial Household Minister?" The Prince's voice finally became as loud as before. The fingers with which he tapped the arm of his chair trembled with anger. His impressive eyes, their pupils fixed, were wide open. He looked as stern as if shouting orders to his troops from horseback.

"Not at all, Your Highness. If you but give the order, the Minister will arrange things in an agreeable manner. For when I was a judge and an occasion rose that had some bearing upon the Imperial Family, I always treated the matter with extreme deference. The Imperial Household Minister will confer with the Minister of Justice, the Minister of Justice will give orders to the Attorney General, and the existence of those leaflets may well be totally disregarded."

"Could that be done so easily?" the Prince asked with a little sigh. Before him was the face of the Imperial Household Minister, wearing that disagreeable soft smile of his.

"Yes, Your Highness. Given Your Highness's authority . . ." Honda's tone was so earnest and decisive that Prince
Toin seemed much encouraged.

With this, Honda thought, one dangerous and ominous
shadow hanging over Isao's crime had been swept away. But
this happily accomplished, what was now to be feared was
the Public Prosecutor's subtle revenge.

33

AFTER HAVING SPENT the New Year's in a police
cell, Isao was transferred to Ichigaya Prison at the end of
January when he was indicted. Through the weave of the
basketlike headcover that prisoners wore he glimpsed the
dirty remnants of a two-day snowfall piled in shaded spots
along the streets. The many colors of the advertising banners
hanging before the market stalls were heightened by the
afternoon rays of the winter sun. The fifteen-foot iron door
of the south entrance to the prison opened with a high screech
from its hinges, admitted the car carrying Isao, and closed
again.

Ichigaya Prison had been completed in 1904, and was of
frame construction, its exterior covered with gray mortar
and its interior walls almost all of white plaster. After entering through the south gate, the prisoners awaiting trial got
out of their vehicle and walked through a covered passageway which brought them to an inspection room called "Central."

This bare room was more than sixty feet square. One wall
was lined with narrow wooden cubicles like telephone booths.

Here prisoners waited their turn. On the other side was a toilet with a glass door. The officer in charge sat on a high platform surrounded by a wooden enclosure, and just beyond, its floor covered only with a thin matting, was a place to change clothes.

The cold was severe. Isao was led with the others to the changing place, and there he was made to strip to the last stitch. He had to open his mouth and have even his back teeth examined. Guards carefully peered into the orifices of his ears and his nose. His arms were spread, and the front part of his body was scrutinized. Then he had to get down on all fours and be examined from the rear. Handled in this rude fashion, one's own body began to seem alien, and only one's thoughts remained secure. This state of mind was already a refuge from humiliation. Stripped of clothing, goose flesh over his entire body, Isao was feeling the lash of cold sparing no part of him, when a brilliant red and blue phantom appeared to him. What was it? He had happened to recall the tattoo artist, a habitual gambler, with whom he had found himself in a common detention cell. The man had been taken with Isao's skin and had repeatedly begged him to let himself be tattooed, free of charge, once they were out of prison. He told Isao that he wanted to cover the fresh skin of his back with lions and peonies. Why lions and peonies? Perhaps because that sort of red and blue pattern, like the reflection of glowing evening clouds upon the dark waters of a marsh covering a valley floor, was a sunset burst of color that rose out of the very nadir of humiliation. No doubt the tattoo artist had seen the setting sun reflected deep in some valley. And nothing but lions and peonies would suffice to capture it. . . .

However, when Isao felt a guard's hand touch the moles on his side and squeeze them momentarily, he realized once again that he could never commit suicide out of humiliation. During his sleepless nights in the detention cell he had toyed with the thought of killing himself. But the concept of suicide remained for Isao what it had always been, something extraordinarily bright and luxurious.

Prisoners awaiting trial could wear their own clothes, but since Isao had to hand over his present clothing to be steam-fumigated, he was obliged to wear blue prison garb for a day. He also had to gather together his personal belongings and, aside from what he needed for everyday use, turn these over to a guard. Then from the officer in charge, high upon his platform, he heard various instructions, on gifts sent in, interviews, letters, and the like. It was already night.

Other than the times he was led before the District Court for preliminary hearings, handcuffed and with a rope around his waist, Isao spent his days in a cell all to himself in Block 13 of Ichigaya Prison. At seven in the morning, a steam whistle blew, the signal to rise. The whistle was located above the kitchen, drawing its energy from the boilers. Though its noise was piercing, it seemed filled with the cheerful, steamy warmth of life. At seven thirty in the evening the same whistle gave the signal for retiring. One night Isao heard a cry while the whistle was blowing and shouts of abuse immediately afterwards. This was repeated the following night. On the second night, Isao realized that that cry, under cover of the whistle, was a prisoner shouting "Long live the revolution!" in unison with a comrade whose cell window was in the wall opposite him. The shouts of abuse were those of a guard who had overheard them. Isao never heard this prisoner's voice again, perhaps because he had been removed to a punishment cell. Human beings, Isao realized, could descend to communicating their feelings like dogs barking in the distance on a cold night. It was as though he could hear even the restless shuffling about of chained dogs and the scratching of nails upon a concrete floor.

Isao too, of course, missed his comrades. But even in the common detention cell where he was put after being taken by bus to await his preliminary hearings, he was unable to learn anything about them, much less look upon their faces.

The gradual lengthening of the days was the only sign of the approach of spring. The straw matting that covered the floor of his cell still seemed to be woven of frost. And the chill made his knees stiff.

Isao longed to see his comrades who had been arrested with him; and as for those who had slipped so effortlessly away right before they were to strike, when he thought of them, rather than anger, he felt something mystical. Their sudden falling away had brought with it a sense of tranquility, the lightness of a tree newly pruned. But what was at the heart of this mystery? What had brought about this reverse? The longer he pondered these questions, the more he avoided the word "betrayal."

Before he was thrown into prison, Isao was never one to dwell upon the past. If he thought about it at all, his mind would instantly turn to the League of the Divine Wind and the sixth year of the Meiji era. Now, however, everything forced upon Isao a consideration of the most recent past. The immediate cause of so swift a downfall for him and his sworn companions was Lieutenant Hori, of course, but, from the outset, his comrades had made their vows without waiting to assure themselves that the enterprise was possible. Something had abruptly given way, an avalanche within the heart, something that could not be stemmed. Isao himself had not been unaware of that interior avalanche. At that time, however, not one of the vowed group who had remained true would have been able, Isao was quite sure, to foresee their present situation. What they had thought of then was death. They were completely given over to fighting and dying. Indeed they had lacked the caution necessary to accomplish their aims. They had been confident in the thought that their rashness could bring on nothing other than death. How had they come to this humiliating and agonizing end? Isao's concept of purity had been that of a noble bird meant to perish by flying so high that the sun would sear its wings. He had never dreamed that any hand could capture that bird alive. As for Sawa, who was not with them at the time of their capture, Isao had no idea how he was faring now, but, even though he did not want to think of him, Sawa's face flashed disagreeably from somewhere deep among the emotions that clogged Isao's breast.

Article 14 of the Peace Preservation Laws put the matter bluntly: "All secret organizations are forbidden." And loyalist organizations such as that of Isao and his companions, firmly bound together in a blood brotherhood, ready to spill their hot blood so that they could rise up to the heavens, were proscribed by their very nature. But as for political organizations bent upon further enriching the bellies of vested interests, as for corporations bent on profit, there was no objection to forming any number of these. It was in the nature of authority to fear purity more than any sort of corruption. Just as savages fear medical treatment more than disease.

Isao finally came to the questions that he had up to now been avoiding: "Does a blood brotherhood in itself invite betrayal?" This was a most dreadful thought.

If men brought their hearts together beyond a certain degree, if they were intent upon making their hearts one, did not a reaction set in after that brief fantasy had passed, a reaction that was more than simply alienation? Did it not inevitably provoke a betrayal that led to complete dissolution?

Perhaps there was some unwritten law of human nature that clearly proscribed covenants among men. Had he impudently violated such a proscription? In ordinary human relationships, good and evil, trust and mistrust appear in impure form, mixed together in small portions. But when men gather together to form a group devoted to a purity not of this world, their evil may remain, purged from each member but coalesced to form a single pure crystal. Thus in the midst of a collection of pure white gems, perhaps it was inevitable that one gem black as pitch could also be found.

If one took this concept a bit further, one encountered an extremely pessimistic line of thought: the substance of evil was to be found more in blood brotherhoods by their very nature than in betrayal. Betrayal was something that was derived from this evil, but the evil was rooted in the blood brotherhood itself. The purest evil that human efforts could attain, in other words, was probably achieved by those men who made their wills the same and who made their eyes see the world in the same way, men who went against the pattern of life's diversity, men whose spirit shattered the natural wall of the individual body, making nothing of this barrier set up to guard against mutual corrosion, men whose spirit accomplished what flesh could never accomplish. *Collaboration* and *cooperation* were weak terms bound up with anthropology. But *blood brotherhood* . . . that was a matter of eagerly joining one's spirit to the spirit of another. This in itself showed a bright scorn for the futile, laborious human process in which ontogeny was eternally recapitulating phylogeny, in which man forever tried to draw a bit closer to truth only to be frustrated by death, a process that had ever to begin again in the sleep within the amniotic fluid. By betraying this human condition the blood brotherhood tried to gain its purity, and thus it was perhaps but to be expected that it, in turn, should of its very nature incur its own betrayal. Such men had never respected humanity.

Isao, of course, did not pursue the idea that far. But he had obviously reached the point where he had to make some sort of breakthrough by thinking. He felt resentment that his intellect lacked keen and ruthless canine teeth.

Seven thirty was too early for retiring, and his sleeplessness was worsened by the twenty-watt light that burned all night long, by the faint rustle of lice beginning to stir, by the stink of urine from the oval wooden pot in the corner, by the cold that brought a flush to the face. But soon the whistles of the freight trains that passed through Ichigaya Station told Isao that it was the dead of night.

"Why, why?" he thought, gritting his teeth. "Why are people not allowed to do what is most beautiful, when ugly, shoddy acts, acts for the sake of gain, are all freely allowed?

"At a time when there is no doubt that the highest morality lies concealed only in the intent to kill, the law that punishes that intent is exercised in the sacred name of His Majesty, the sun without blemish. And so the highest morality itself is punished by the very personification of the highest morality. Who could have put together such a contradiction? Could His Majesty have any knowledge of such an appalling contrivance? Is this not a blasphemous system that a skilled disloyalty spent much time and effort to create?

"I don't understand. I don't understand it at all. And then, after we did the killing, not one of us would have disregarded his vow to kill himself at once. So if we could have done as we had meant to, not a single branch, not a single leaf of the tangled thicket of the law would have brushed so much as the tip of our sleeve or the hem of our kimono. We would have slipped marvelously through the thicket and gone rushing headlong up into the bright sky of heaven. So it was with the League of the Divine Wind. Though, I know, the tangled underbrush of the law didn't grow as thick in the sixth year of Meiji. The law is an accumulation of tireless attempts to block a man's desire to change life into an instant of poetry. Certainly it would not be right to let everybody exchange his life for a line of poetry written in a splash of blood. But the mass of men, lacking valor, pass away their lives without ever feeling the least touch of such a desire. The law, therefore, of its very nature is aimed at a tiny minority of mankind. The extraordinary purity of a handful of men, the passionate devotion that knows nothing of the world's standards . . . the law is a system that tries to degrade them to 'evil,' on the same level as robbery and crimes of passion. This is the clever trap that I fell into. And because of nothing else but somebody's betrayal!"

The whistle of a freight passing through Ichigaya Station stabbed through his thoughts. It brought to his mind a man

racked with an emotion so intense that he was like one rolling
about on the ground to put out his flaming kimono. The
heartrending cry of the man tumbling in the blackness was
wrapped in a swirl of its own fiery particles and glowed red
with its own blaze.

This train whistle; however, differed from the prison
whistle with its false warmth of life. This voice, though
twisted with anguish, somehow pulsated with a limitless freedom and offered a smooth access to the future. Another part
of the country, another day—even the rust-covered phantom
of a white, sour-faced morning suddenly appearing in the
line of mirrors above the sinks on some station platform did
not suffice to dispel the powerful attraction of strangeness
the whistle conveyed.

Then the dawn came at his prison window. From the window of the easternmost cell on the right of the three rows in
Block 13, after a night without sleep, Isao watched the red
winter sun rise.

The horizon was a high wall, and the sun clung to that
line like a soft, warm rice cake before gently climbing. The
Japan that that sun shone upon had refused the help of Isao
and his comrades, and lay prey to sickness, corruption, and
disaster.

It was after this that Isao, for the first time in his life,
began to have dreams.

Of course, it was not actually the first time he had dreamed.
But his earlier dreams had been the kind that a healthy youth
forgot with the coming of morning. Never once had a dream
lingered to affect his waking hours. Now it was different. Not
only through the morning but through his entire day, last
night's dream would persist, sometimes linked with the
memory of the dream of the night before, or to be continued
in the dream of the next night. His dreams were like bright-
colored garments put out to dry and left forgotten in the rain,
hanging on the clothes pole without ever drying. The rain

continued. Perhaps a madman lived in the house. And more printed silk robes were added to the drying pole, bright splotches of color against the somber sky.

One night he dreamed of a snake.

The setting was the tropics, perhaps the garden of a large mansion somewhere, which was surrounded by jungle so thick that the walls that bordered it could not be seen.

He seemed to be in the middle of this jungle garden, standing upon a terrace of crumbling gray stone. The house to which the terrace belonged could not be seen. There was nothing but this small, square terrace which defined a gray rocky zone of stillness, the curving stone images of cobras rising up from pillars set at each of its corners, like four outspread hands pushing back the heavy tropic air. A hot square of silence cut from the heart of the jungle.

He heard the whine of mosquitoes. He heard the buzzing of flies. Yellow butterflies flew about. The cries of birds came down to him like drops of blue water ever falling. And, now and again, came still another bird cry, a frenzied cry that seemed to tear through the very midst of the intricate tangle of green vegetation. Cicadas were shrilling.

Rather than these varied sounds, however, what most affronted the ear was a roar like that of a sudden rainstorm. It was not, of course. A passing wind was shaking the jungle growth that bound the treetops together, far above the shaded terrace, but since its effect was not felt below, the only visible sign of its passing was the movement of the flecks of sunlight that dappled the cobras' heads.

Leaves high up, caught by the wind, slipped down through the foliage, and the noise they made sounded like falling rain. Not all of them were newly torn from their branches. Tree limbs were thrust against each other to undergird the nearly impenetrable mass of vines that caught up leaves as they dropped away. A fresh wind would cause these to fall a second time, working down through the branches with a sound like heavy rain. Since the leaves were broad and parched, they made an echoing din. Each one that fell upon the stone terrace, overgrown with moss white as leprosy, was large.

The tropical light was like thousands of massed spearheads of marshaled troops. Reflections fell everywhere about Isao, as patches of sunlight filtered through the branches above. To look at that light directly would be blinding, to touch it would be to scorch one's fingers. From beyond the jungle growth, it held everything in siege. Isao felt its presence crowding in even upon the terrace.

At that moment Isao noticed a little green snake put its head through the railing. What had seemed to be an outstretched vine there suddenly grew longer. The snake was quite thick, like a waxwork figure colored in light and dark shades of green. Its lustrous, artificial-looking body was not a vine, something Isao discovered too late. Its fangs had already found their mark by the time he realized that it had coiled itself to strike at his ankle.

The chill of death came to him through the tropic air. Isao shivered.

He was suddenly cut off from the torrid heat. The venom had driven all warmth from his body. Each of his pores awakened fearfully to the coldness of death. He could breathe only with difficulty, and each breath became more shallow. Soon the world had no more breath to put into his mouth. But the movement of life went on throbbing keenly within him. Against his will, his skin, like the surface of a pond struck by a shower, grew puckered. "I was not meant to die like this. I was meant to die by cutting open my stomach. I never expected to die this way, a passive, miserable death by a chance of nature, a small touch of malice." Even as he thought this, Isao seemed to feel his body freezing into a block as solid as a fish so frozen that a hammer blow could not shatter it. When he opened his eyes, he saw that he had kicked off his quilt and was lying in his cell in the glimmering dawn light of an unusually chilly early spring morning.

Another night he had this dream.

This one was so strange and disagreeable that he tried afterwards again and again to banish it from his mind. This was a dream in which Isao was transformed into a woman.

He was not at all certain, however, what sort of woman his body had been changed into. Perhaps because he seemed to be blind, he could only grope with his hands to try to find out. He felt as if the world had been turned inside out, and he was sitting languidly in a chair by a window, his body lightly covered with sweat, possibly just after awakening from an afternoon nap.

Perhaps his previous dream of the snake was impinging upon this one. What he heard were the cries of jungle birds, the buzzing of flies, the rainlike patter of falling leaves. And then there was an odor like sandalwood—he recognized it because once he had lifted the lid and sniffed inside a sandalwood tobacco box that his father prized—a melancholy, lonely odor, the sweet, bodylike odor of old wood. Suddenly he thought of something that resembled it: the odor of the blackened embers that he had seen on the path through the rice fields in Yanagawa.

Isao felt that his flesh had lost definite form, turned into flesh that was soft and swaying. He was filled with a mist of soft, languid flesh. Everything became vague. Wherever he searched, he could find no order or structure. There was no supporting pillar. The brilliant fragments of light that had once sparkled around him, ever drawing him on, had disappeared. Comfort and discomfort, joy and sorrow—all alike slid over his skin like soap. Entranced, he soaked in a warm bath of flesh.

The bath by no means imprisoned him. He could step out whenever he liked, but the languid pleasure kept him from abandoning it, so that staying there forever, not choosing to go, had become his "freedom." Thus there was nothing to define him, to keep him under strict control. What had once wound itself tightly round and round him like a rope of platinum had slipped loose.

Everything he had so firmly believed in was meaningless. Justice was like a fly that has tumbled into a box of face powder and smothered; beliefs for which he had meant to offer up his life were sprayed with perfume and melted. All glory dissolved in the mild warmth of mud.

Sparkling snow had melted away entirely. He felt the uncertain warmth of spring mud within him. Slowly something took form from that spring mud, a womb. Isao shuddered as the thought came to him that he would soon give birth. His strength had always spurred him with violent impatience toward action, had always responded to a distant voice that conjured up the image of a vast wilderness. But now, that strength had left him. The voice was silent. The outer world, which no longer called to him, now, rather, was drawing closer to him, was touching him. And he felt too sluggish to get up and move away.

A sharp-edged mechanism of steel had died. In its place, an odor like that of decaying seaweed, an entirely organic odor, had somehow or other permeated his body. Justice, zeal, patriotism, aspirations for which to hazard one's life—all had vanished. In their place came an indescribable intimacy with the things around him—clothing, utensils, pincushions, cosmetics—an intimacy in which he seemed to flow into and merge with all the minutiae of gentle, beautiful things. It was an intimacy of smiles and winks, one that was almost obscene, outside the range of Isao's previous experience. The only thing that he had been intimate with had been the sword.

Things clung to him like paste, and, at the same time, lost all their transcendental significance.

Trying to arrive at some goal was no longer a problem. Everything was arriving here from elsewhere. Thus there was no longer a horizon, no longer any islands. And with no perspective at all evident, voyages were out of the question. There was only the endless sea.

Isao had never felt that he might want to be a woman. He had never wished for anything else but to be a man, live in a manly way, die a manly death. To be thus a man was to be required to give constant proof of one's manliness—to be more a man today than yesterday, more a man tomorrow than today. To be a man was to forge ever upward toward the peak of manhood, there to die amid the white snows of that peak.

But to be a woman? It seemed to mean being a woman at the beginning and being a woman forever.

The smoke of incense came to him. There was the echo of gongs and whistles—apparently a funeral procession passing by the window. He caught the muffled sound of people sobbing. But nothing clouded the contentment of the woman dozing on a summer afternoon. Fine beads of sweat covered her skin. Her senses had stored up a vast variety of memories. Her belly, swelling slightly as she breathed in her sleep, was puffed like a sail with the marvelous fullness of her flesh. The delicate navel, which checked that sail by tugging from within, its color the fresh, rosy tinge of the bud of a wild cherry blossom, lay quietly beneath a tiny pool of sweat. The lovely tautness of the breasts of so regal an aspect seemed all the more to express the melancholy of the flesh. The skin, stretched fine, seemed to glow as though a lantern burned within. The smoothness of the skin extended as far as the tips of the breasts, where, like waves pressing in upon an atoll, the raised texture of the areolas emerged. The areolas were the color of an orchid filled with a quiet, pervasive hostility, a poisonous color meant to attract the mouth. From that deep purple, the nipple rose up piquantly, like a pert squirrel lifting its head. The effect was mischievously playful.

When he clearly saw the figure of this sleeping woman, even though her face was shrouded with sleep and its contours blurred, Isao thought that it had to be Makiko. Then a strong whiff of the perfume Makiko had worn when they parted came to him. Isao shot out his semen, and he awakened.

An indescribable sorrow remained. Though the sensation

that he had been transformed into a woman had persisted in his dream, he could not recall the point at which the course of the dream had shifted so that he seemed to be gazing at the body of a woman whom he took to be Makiko. And this confusion was the source of his disturbed feeling. Furthermore, though it was a woman, Makiko apparently, whom he had defiled, he, the defiler, strangely enough could not rid himself of the vivid sensation that he had felt before, that the whole world was turned inside out.

The fearfully dark emotion that had enveloped him in sadness—never before had he experienced such an incomprehensible emotion—lingered on and on even after his eyes were open, and hung in the air under the dim light cast down by the feeble bulb in the ceiling like a yellowish pressed flower.

Isao did not catch the sound of the guard's hemp-soled sandals coming down the corridor, and, taken by surprise, he had no time to shut his eyes before they met the guard's peering in through the observation slot.

"Go to sleep," the guard said hoarsely, and then moved on.

Spring was drawing near.

His mother came often with packages for him, but she was never allowed to see him. She told him in a letter that Honda was going to defend him at the trial, and Isao wrote a long reply. Such good fortune was more than he had hoped for, he wrote, but he would have to refuse it unless Honda agreed to defend him together with his comrades as a group. No answer to this ever came. Nor was he given the opportunity to meet with Honda, something that should have been readily granted. In the letters he received from his mother there were many words and phrases deleted with black ink—no doubt the news of his comrades that he wanted so much to hear. No matter how he scrutinized the portions blotted out with black ink, he could not make out a single letter, nor could he deduce anything from the context.

Finally Isao began a letter to the man he felt least inclined to write to. He did his best to suppress all emotion, and he chose his words with the intent of not bringing further trouble upon Sawa, whom the authorities must at least have questioned about his contribution of money. Yet he hoped that the pangs of conscience would drive Sawa to do what he could to better their situation. He waited and waited, but no answer came, and Isao's anger took a despairing turn.

Since he had heard nothing further by way of his mother, Isao wrote a long letter of appreciation to Honda himself, addressing it in care of the Academy. In it he gave fervent expression to his desire that Honda act as defense counsel for the entire group. A reply came at once. With well-chosen words, Honda expressed his sympathy for the way Isao felt. He said that, since he had gotten into this affair, he might as well go all the way, and so he would be willing to defend them as a group, except, of course, for those who would be tried as juveniles. Nothing could have strengthened Isao more in his prison cell than this letter.

Isao was moved by the way in which Honda responded to his expressed desire to take all the punishment upon himself and have his comrades absolved: "I understand your wanting to do this, but neither judges nor lawyers conduct themselves on the basis of their emotions. Since tragic feelings are certainly not of long duration, what is important now is to remain calm. I think that I can count upon you, as an expert in kendo, to understand what I mean. Leave everything to me— that is what I am for—take earnest care of your health, and bear your lot with patience. During the exercise periods, by all means give your body a vigorous workout." Honda had correctly perceived that the sense of tragic heroism in Isao's heart, like the colors of a sunset, was gradually fading.

One day, since there was still no indication that he would be allowed to see Honda, Isao put his trust in the sympathetic manner of the judge in a preliminary hearing, and asked casually: "Your Honor, when will I be allowed to see someone?"

The judge hesitated for a moment, obviously uncertain

whether or not to reply. Then he said: "Not as long as the prohibition against it is in force."

"And who has laid that down, Your Honor?"

"The Prosecutor's Office," the judge answered, his intonation conveying his own discontent with this measure.

34

His MOTHER'S LETTERS kept on coming frequently, but no other letters had so many blotted portions. Sometimes a section would be clipped out, or even a whole page removed. His mother obviously lacked the wit to write in such a way as not to run afoul of the censor. But one day there was a change. The censor's job had apparently been taken over by a new man. The blotted portions were noticeably fewer, but, since his mother wrote under the impression that everything in her previous letters had been conveyed to him, his impatience was aggravated by the difficulty of deciphering. It was as though he were receiving later letters before their predecessors. But then there was one line, reading: "The letters . . . are piled up like a mountain. They say there are at least five thousand of them, and when I think . . . my eyes fill up with tears," in which, even though two sections had been inked over, the ink had been lightly applied as though the censor had been careless. Isao realized that the man had done so deliberately, to encourage him. In one section Isao was able to read without difficulty "letters *asking for leniency*," and in the other, though it was more obscure, "when I think *of the sympathy people have*." For the first time Isao learned about the public reaction to the affair.

He was loved! He who had never in the least wanted to be loved. Perhaps a gentle, sympathetic concern had been stirred by his youth, by the immature purity that people naturally expected in the young, by considerations of his "promising" future, and this had inspired the clemency letters. It was a conjecture that caused Isao some pain. The mass of petitions sent in after the May Fifteenth Incident must have been of a different nature.

"The world does not take me seriously." Ever since his imprisonment Isao had been haunted by that single relentless thought. "If people ever suspected the fearful, blood-smeared purity I revere, they'd hardly be able to feel any love for me."

Not feared nor, much less, hated, only loved, he found himself in a situation that wounded his pride. It was spring. Most of all, he yearned for the letters from Makiko that arrived one after another at regular intervals, well aware though he was how ill such a desire became that resolve, tough as hardened glass, that he had long embraced.

In fact, I have always been peculiarly favored, thought Isao. Something murky lay in the depths of that favor.

Was it not that the nation, the laws of the nation, perhaps in just the same way as the public, refused to take him seriously?

Then too, when he was being questioned in an interrogation room on a cold day, the police would urge him to sit closer to the hibachi, and, if he was hungry, they would bring him a dish of noodles with fried bean curd. Once an assistant inspector pointed at the flowers on the table and said, "What do you think of these camellias? Aren't they pretty? There are winter camellias blooming in my garden, and this morning I cut these and brought them here. During interrogation, you see, it's most important to be at ease, and flowers make everyone feel more congenial." The odor of a vulgarized refinement bent on using nature clung to the inspector's words, much like that given off by the white shirt that he wore day after day despite its cloud pattern of grime.

Still, three pure white camellias pushed aside tough, dark green leaves with their outspread petals. Drops of water lay upon them as though upon white lard.

"This sunshine is nice, isn't it?" said the inspector, as he asked the policeman standing by to open the window. From where Isao was sitting, the winter camellias occupied half of his field of vision. The iron bars of the window let pass the warm, abstract winter sunshine, their shadows cutting through it with a precision that made it seem still more devoid of substance.

The probing ray of sunshine like a warm hand upon his shoulder—this for Isao was something quite different from the brilliant summer sun that he had seen pressing down with glittering authority upon the heads of the troops drilling upon the Azabu Regiment parade ground. This ray spoke of the kindliness of the judicial system come down to touch him upon the shoulder after many a twist and turn. It had nothing at all to do with the summer sun of the Imperial Benevolence, Isao thought.

"With patriots like you and your friends, I don't need to worry about the future of Japan. You shouldn't have violated the law, of course, but that shining sincerity of yours is something that even we can understand. And now, about you and your friends making your vows, when and where was that?"

Isao responded automatically. That evening of the summer before, in front of the shrine . . . there rose in his mind the memory of all twenty of them clasping each other's hands, one hand over another, like white fruit whose weight bent the branches that bore it. Yet to call up the memory had become painful. As Isao answered, he looked away from the inspector, who kept watching him intently, and he gazed at the sunlight and one of the white camellias by turns. Dazzled by the sun, his eyes saw the whiteness of the camellias as pitch black, the flower a small, lustrous knot of hair. And, in the same way, the dark green leaves seemed to form a collar of pure white. He had a secret need for this play of the senses to help him withstand the discordance within him. For when he spoke the "truth"—"Yes, sir. There were twenty of us. We bowed twice and clapped twice before the shrine. And then I recited the vows, one part at a time, and the others repeated it in unison"—giving an account that was totally unembellished, the words no sooner passed his lips than, here before the judicial authorities, they seemed to grow scales and become wrapped in a falsehood that made him shudder.

And then all at once Isao heard the white winter camellia groan.

Startled, he looked back at the inspector. There was no surprise in the inspector's eyes. It was only later that Isao realized that chance had not dictated the choice of this second-floor room, with its open window, for the interrogation on this particular day. The room was across a narrow alley from a drill hall, its windows shuttered even at midday, but with lights visible through the transoms.

"You're third degree in kendo, I hear. You know, if you hadn't got yourself involved in this business and stayed with your kendo, you and I might have had a pleasant match in that hall down there."

"Are they practicing kendo now?" Isao asked, feeling sure that they were not. The inspector did not answer.

Some of the sounds that carried up to the room were like kendo yells, but the groan that had seemed to come from the white camellia had nothing of kendo about it. The crash of staves on thick-padded kendo gear was different. This was the dull, somber sound of blows striking upon flesh.

Isao recalled that the white camellia, which seemed to be sweating in the heat generated by the clear winter sunshine, had somehow become sacred after the cries and groans of the tortured had filtered through it. Free of the inspector's debased refinement, the flower began to give off the scent of the law itself. His eyes could not help looking beyond the lustrous leaves of the camellia, through the transom where lights burned at midday, at the thick ropes swinging back and forth with what must have been a heavy burden of flesh.

Isao looked into the inspector's eyes once more, and the latter answered his unspoken question: "Yes. It's a Red. Stubborn ones bring this kind of thing on themselves."

Obviously the police intended to make him realize that, in contrast, he was being treated with the utmost gentleness, that the kindly law was showering benefits upon him. But it had the opposite effect. At that moment Isao felt a choking of anger and humiliation. "My ideas—what do they amount to?" he asked himself in a rage. "If real ideas have to be beaten like that, are mine supposed to be unreal?" Isao was vexed with frustration: despite the enormity of what he had plotted, there had been no adequate reaction. If they realized the core of terrible purity within him, he thought, they would surely hate him. Though officers of the Emperor, they could not help but hate him. On the other hand, however, if their ignorance persisted, his ideas would never gain the weight of flesh, never grow wet with agonized sweat. And, as a consequence, they would never give out the loud cries of beaten flesh.

Isao glared at his cross-examiner and shouted: "Torture me! Torture me right now. Why can't you do the same thing to me? Can you tell me why not?"

"Easy now. Calm down, don't be foolish. It's very simple. You don't give us any trouble."

"And that's because my ideas are rightist?"

"That's part of it. But rightist or leftist, anyone who gives us trouble is going to pay for it. Still, when all is said and done, those Reds . . ."

"Is it because the Reds won't accept our national structure?"

"That's it. In comparison to them, Iinuma, you and your friends are patriots. Your thoughts are in the right direction. It's only that you're young. The trouble is, you're too pure, so you went to extremes. Your purpose is good. It's your methods. What about making them more gradual, toning them down a bit? If you made them a little more flexible, everything would be fine."

"No," Isao retorted, his body trembling all over. "If we made them a little more flexible, it wouldn't be the same. That 'little' is the point. Purity can't be toned down a little. If you make it a bit flexible, just a bit, it becomes a totally different idea, not the kind we hold. So if our ideas can't be watered down, and if they're a threat to the nation the way they are, that means our ideas are just as dangerous as those of the Reds. So go ahead and torture me. You have no reason not to."

"You're quite a debater, aren't you? Now, don't get so excited. I'll tell you just one thing that would be good for you to know. There's not a man among those Reds that asked to be tortured, as you're doing. They take it if they have to. They're not like you, they don't respond to us even if we torture them."

35

MAKIKO'S LETTERS, though she naturally avoided straightforward expressions, were filled with assurances that her feelings toward Isao were just as before, and she always took care to include two or three poems that her father had revised for her. The censor's cherry blossom seal affixed in red to the letter was no different, but when Isao considered how easily her letters alone came through, without any significant deletions, he suspected some help from General Kito. Still, there was hardly any sign that his own replies had reached their destination.

Never questioning nor responding to questions, neither al-
luding to present circumstances nor ignoring them, neither
conveying information nor withholding it, Makiko wrote of
this and that, of beautiful or entertaining things, or things
altogether innocent, in keeping with the changing seasons.
Thus she wrote of a pheasant from the Botanical Gardens
flying into their yard, as one had the previous spring; of the
records she had bought recently; of often going for a walk in
Hakusan Park with thoughts of a particular night in mind;
of seeing there one night the soiled petals of rain-scattered
cherry blossoms clinging to the children's log swing as it
moved gently back and forth beneath the faint light of a
lamp post, as though an adult couple had been sitting on it
just before; of the deep darkness around the Shinto pavilion,
brightened once, however, by a running white cat; of the
early-blooming peach blossoms that she used in practicing her
flower arranging; of freesia; of finding some starworts on a
visit to Gokoku Temple and plucking them until her sleeves
were heavily laden. . . . Since poems accompanied all this,
Isao often felt as though he had been there to share her
mood.

Makiko had in abundance the talent that his mother lacked,
and she seemed to have easily learned a style of writing that
enabled her to slip by the stern guard of the censor. Be that as
it might, the Makiko that appeared here had all too little
resemblance to Ikiko Abé, who, together with her mother-in-
law, leapt with joy as she saw the fires of insurrection spring
up in the distance, the work of her husband and his comrades
of the League of the Divine Wind. He read Makiko's letters
again and again. She never touched upon politics. Then, while
he was striving earnestly to decipher certain passages that
seemed to him to have double meanings or to hint at passion,
he suddenly felt the need to resist the sensual attraction that
these letters had for him. He was bent on finding something
other than tender regard and goodwill. But how could Makiko
have written to him with hostility? Even if there had been

something like that hidden here, he was sure that it was not intentional.

Her smooth, vivacious style was clearly a kind of tight-rope walking. How could he blame in her the exultation that an increasingly skillful tightrope walker found in the very act of risking danger? But, to go one step further, Isao could not but think that Makiko had an almost indecent zest for tightrope walking, and, under the pretext of fear of the authorities, was indulging a passion for emotional mischief.

Nowhere in her letters was there a phrase of this sort. But there was a certain scent. A playful feeling. At times Makiko seemed to be enjoying his being in prison. Cruel separation guarded the purity of emotion. The pangs of being apart were transformed into quiet joy. Danger aroused the sensual. Uncertainty fostered dreams.

Makiko conveyed in artless phrases the pleasure she felt at knowing how his heart trembled, as if from the seductive breeze blowing in through his cell window. This relationship between the two of them, though it verged on cruelty, was for Makiko the fulfillment of a cherished dream. Once Isao thought in such terms, he could see proof everywhere in her letters. Apparently Makiko had discovered in this kind of situation a kingdom of her own.

His senses, sharpened by prison life, told him this was true, and Isao suddenly became furious. He wanted to tear the letters to shreds.

In order to turn his mind in another direction and to strengthen his will, he asked that his parents be allowed to send him *The League of the Divine Wind*, but he was, of course, refused. Prisoners could purchase some magazines, but these was limited to such as *Science for Children*, *Today*, *Eloquence*, *Kodan Club*, *King*, and *Diamond*.

Whether a prison book or not, only one book a week was allowed, and none of those made available by the authorities were the sort to set his heart afire. When, therefore, he was allowed to receive a book that he had asked for some time ago from his father, Dr. Tetsujiro Inoué's *The Philosophy of the Japanese Wang Yang-ming School*, Isao was indescribably happy. He had been looking forward to reading about Chusai Oshio in it. Heihachiro (known as Chusai) resigned his position as a police official in 1830, at the age of thirty-seven, and devoted himself to writing and lecturing. He became famous as a scholar of the Wang Yang-ming school, and he was also an expert in the use of the spear. During the great famine from 1833 to 1836, no statesman or wealthy merchant came forward to aid the starving people; moreover, when Chusai sold all of his prized books to alleviate distress, it was viewed as an act to curry public favor, and his foster son, Kakunosuké, was subjected to reprimand. Finally, on February 19, 1837, he raised an armed force and, with this body of a few hundred men, burned down the storehouses of rich merchants and distributed gold and grain to the people. More than a fourth of Osaka was ravaged by fire, but Chusai's men were at last defeated, and he himself died by blowing himself up with an explosive charge. He was forty-four years old.

Chusai Oshio realized in his own person the Wang Yang-ming concept of unity of thought and action, embodying the dictum: "To know and not to act is not to know." What appealed to Isao, however, even more than Chusai's Wang Yang-ming fusion of thought and action, spirit and reason, was his concept of life and death.

Dr. Inoué explained that: "With regard to death, Chusai's view was quite similar to the Buddhist nirvana."

The "Great Void," according to Chusai's teaching, was not a negative condition in which all the workings of the human spirit were obliterated. He taught, rather, that here the light of intuition was able to shine in all its brilliance, simply by means of the elimination of personal appetite. To become a part of the Great Void, Chusai said, to give oneself over wholly to the ever-present and ever-lasting Great Void, was to enter the sphere of eternity.

"Once the spirit is given over to the Great Void," Inoué

wrote, "even though the body perish, there remains something that does not. Thus there is no fearing the death of the body but only the death of the spirit. Knowing that the essential spirit will not die, one need fear nothing in the world. This, then, is the basis for one's resolution. And no matter what arises, it has no power to shake this resolution. Thus it might be said that this is to recognize the will of heaven."

In the course of his discussion, Dr. Inoué drew many quotations from *An Account of the Purification of the Heart.* One of these particularly struck Isao: "There is no fearing the death of the body, but only the death of the spirit." To Isao, in his present condition, these were words like hammer blows.

On May twentieth the preliminary hearing was concluded and a decision handed down, the main part of which read: "This case is to be brought to trial before the Tokyo District Court." Honda's hopes for a dismissal at the preliminary hearing were dashed.

The trial would most likely begin at the end of June. The prohibition against visitors remained in force during the period preceding this, but a present came from Makiko, which Isao opened in a state of high excitement. It was a wild lily from the Saigusa Festival.

Since it had been subjected to the guards' handling at the end of its long journey, the lily was a little withered and drooping. Still, it had a freshness and luster far greater than those that Isao and his comrades had intended to conceal on their persons on the morning of their attack. This lily still seemed to have a trace of the morning dew that fell upon the open place before the shrine of the gods.

Makiko must have made a special trip to Nara in order to give this one lily to him. And, from all the lilies that she brought back, she must have chosen this one for its superb whiteness and beauty.

Isao reflected. The previous year at about this same time, he had been filled with a sense of freedom and strength. Beneath Sanko Falls on the holy mountain of the gods, he had snuffed out the fire still smoldering from the victorious kendo combat before the shrine. And with a purified heart, he had then given himself over to his act of worship, gathering the mass of lilies that were to be offered to the gods. Sweat had covered his forehead wrapped with a white *hachimaki* as he pulled the laden cart along the road to Nara. The village of Sakurai had been bright in the summer sun. Isao's youthfulness and the green of the mountainside had been in harmony.

Lilies were like a crest marking that memory. And afterwards they had become the symbol of his resolution. Since that day, lilies had been at the center of everything—his fervor, his vows, his anxiety, his dreams, his readiness for death, his yearning for glory. The pillar that supported his dark plan, the soaring pillar of his resolution—always shining in the gloom at its top were the ornamental lilies that concealed the bolts holding it fast.

He gazed at the lily he held in his hand. He rolled the bent stem between his palms, feeling the leaves rubbing against his skin as the drooping lily revolved. Then it abruptly fell away from him, scattering a bit of dull golden dust. The sunlight at his window had become stronger. Isao felt that the lilies of last year had been reborn.

36

When the ruling of the preliminary hearing was delivered to Isao, he saw Sawa's name among the defendants, and he felt ashamed of the suspicions that he had been entertaining for so long. He had only to think of Sawa's face, of his name, for that shameful, unpleasant feeling to surge up irresistibly. Sometimes in this mood he felt that he had to have someone to play the role of informer. If not Sawa, who then? His suspicions, since they could not be dismissed, required an object. Otherwise, how could he sustain himself?

What was most frightening, however, was what came next if Sawa, by far the most likely, was no longer to be considered. Isao was fearful of transferring the suspicion he had felt toward Sawa to some other person. At the time of his capture, ten others were with him: Miyahara, Kimura, Izutsu, Fujita, Miyaké, Takasé, Inoué, Sagara, Serikawa, and Hasegawa. Of these, the absence of the names of Serikawa and Sagara from the list of defendants was but to be expected because, being under eighteen, they would be tried as juveniles. Isao thought about Sagara and Serikawa: the one always so close at hand as if he were Isao's shadow—small, alert, bespectacled Sagara; the other the boyish son of a Shinto priest in the Tohoku region—Serikawa, who had burst out in tearful protest before the shrine: "I can't go back!" Under no circumstances could Isao think of those two as betraying him. Someone on the outside then? Isao feared pursuing this further. For he felt that something lay hidden, the same sort of feeling that checked one from searching through a clump of grass in which one fears to discover white bones.

Those who had fallen away knew, of course, that December third was the date set. But the last man to desert them knew nothing more than what they had had in mind three weeks before that day. Since the plan had thereafter been drastically altered, there was no reason why the date set could not have been either postponed or moved up or simply canceled. Even if one of the deserters had informed on them, Isao still could not fathom why the police had refrained from intervening until two days before they were to strike. Should not the simplification of the plan have made it likely that they would strike at an earlier date?

Isao kept struggling not to think about these things. But even as he did, just as the moth drawn to the flame must turn its eyes back upon it, no matter how it tries to look away, his mind returned to the foreboding thoughts he wanted most to avoid.

The day of the opening of the trial, June twenty-fifth, was fair. The heat was intense.

The patrol wagon carrying the defendants passed by the moat surrounding the Imperial Palace, its waters glittering in the sunlight, and entered the confines of the red brick Courthouse through the rear gate. The Tokyo District Court was on the first floor. Isao came into the courtroom wearing a white splashed-pattern kimono and *hakama*, which had been brought to the prison for him. The amber luster of the judges' bench struck his eyes. When the guard removed his handcuffs at the door, he made Isao turn, out of kindness, so that he had a momentary look in the direction of the spectators. There sat his father and mother, whom he had not seen for half a year. When his eyes met his mother's, she covered her mouth with a handkerchief. She seemed to be choking back sobs. Makiko was nowhere to be seen.

The defendants formed a single line, their backs to the spectators. Thus arrayed with his comrades, Isao felt his courage mounting. Izutsu was right beside him. Though they could neither exchange words nor look at each other, Isao sensed that Izutsu's body was trembling. He knew this was not due to his friend's standing before the bench. The excitement of seeing Isao after so long was conveyed by every tremor of his friend's hot, sweaty body.

Right before Isao and the others was the defendants' box. Beyond it was the dazzling light mahogany of the judges' bench, the grain visible in the wood of its panels. It was majestically proportioned, and to its rear stood a doorway of the same light mahogany, a gable in the baroque manner crowning its solemnity. The three judges, the Chief Judge in the center, sat upon chairs, each of which had a corolla carved upon its back. The court stenographer sat to the right of the defendants, and over on the left was the prosecutor. The purple arabesque embroidered upon the front and spreading to the shoulders of the judges' black robes glinted dully. And there was also purple piping upon the haughty black judges' caps. Obviously this was like no other place in the world.

When he was somewhat more composed, Isao glanced to the right, where the defense counsel sat, and saw Honda staring full at him.

The Chief Judge asked his name and age. Since his arrest, Isao had become accustomed to being addressed authoritatively from above, but this was his first experience of being summoned by a voice from such an eminence, a voice that seemed to embody the rationale of the entire nation and to fall like distant lightning from a sky filled with brilliant mist.

"Isao Iinuma, Your Honor. Twenty," he answered.

37

THE SECOND SESSION of the trial was held on July nineteenth. The weather was fair, but an occasional breeze through the courtroom fluttered the legal papers, and so the attendants shut the windows halfway. Again and again Isao had to resist the temptation to scratch a bedbug bite on his side, which was aggravating his sweaty discomfort.

As soon as the session began, the Chief Judge rejected one of the witnesses that the prosecutor had requested at the first session. Delighted, Honda rolled a red pencil quietly across the papers that covered his desk. This was an idiosyncracy that he had somehow acquired around the time he became a judge in 1929, and one he had been making an effort to suppress ever since. Now, four years later, it had reasserted itself. It was a bad habit for a judge, because of its disturbing effect upon defendants, but in his present position Honda could indulge it to his heart's content.

The rejected witness was Lieutenant Hori. Here indeed was a witness that would have presented problems.

Honda noted the sudden look of disappointment that darkened the prosecutor's face, as though a gust of wind had ruffled the surface of a pond. Hori's name appeared any number of times in the minutes of the preliminary examinations and hearings, as well as in the hearings to which the deserters had been summoned to give information. Isao alone had never mentioned the name. To be sure, Hori's function in the plan was extremely vague, and his name did not appear on the final list seized by the police. This was in the form of a chart upon which each of the names of the twelve major financiers was joined by a line to the name of one of the twelve defendants. The police had found it at the hideaway in Yotsuya. Still, there was nothing in it that clearly indicated assassination.

Most of the twelve defendants said that Lieutenant Hori had been an inspiration to them, but only one of the twelve testified that he had exercised any leadership. Among the deserters, many testified that they had never met Hori nor even heard his name mentioned. Essentially, then, aside from the confused testimony of the defendants, the prosecutor had no evidence whatsoever to back up his suspicion of a large-scale plot prior to the massive defections.

As to the leaflets falsely proclaiming that imperial authority had been granted to Prince Toin, the dangerous evidence that the Prosecutor's Office had set eyes upon, darkness had swallowed them up. Once the prosecutor had seen the disproportion between the ambitious proclamation and the scanty resources of the would-be assassins, it was obvious how vital a witness the Lieutenant had become for him. Honda perceived Sawa's hand at work in this turn of events which so irritated the prosecutor. Iinuma had hinted as much.

"That Sawa's a good fellow," Iinuma had said. "He wanted to join his fate with Isao's, whatever the consequences. He was going to help Isao carry out his plan, without a word to me, and then follow him in suicide. So perhaps the one that was hurt the most by my informing was Sawa. But he's a mature man, after all, and must have made careful preparations in case of failure. Since deserters are the greatest source of danger in this kind of activity, I'm sure he sprung into action as soon as they dropped out. He must have gone around to give each one a thorough talking-to. Maybe he said: 'If this affair is nipped in the bud, you're going to be called to give testimony. It takes hardly anything to change a witness like you into an accomplice. Just in case you don't want this to happen, you'd better say that the military influenced you only in spirit. Otherwise this is going to turn into a big affair, you'll all be implicated, and you'll be sticking your neck into the noose.'

"Sawa was all for going through with the action, but, on the other hand, I'm sure he was prepared for any eventuality, and had taken prudent means to do away with evidence. This is the kind of wisdom that's hard to find in young people."

At the beginning of the session, when the Chief Judge, singularly expressionless, rejected Lieutenant Hori as a witness on the grounds that he had no direct connection with the case, Honda had immediately told himself: "Ah! This is thanks to the statement by that 'highly placed military authority' that came out in the paper."

Ever since the May Fifteenth Incident, the military had been extremely sensitive to the public reaction stirred by this sort of event. And they would be especially nervous in this case because Lieutenant Hori was an officer marked indelibly in connection with the May Fifteenth Incident. Since he had been rushed over to Manchuria for this among other reasons, it would be most distressing if he should be called back, himself under suspicion, to testify before a civilian court. If he did appear, whatever the content of his testimony, the credibility of the "highly placed military authority" who issued that statement immediately after the arrests would henceforth be open to question, and, consequently, the dignity of the military itself would be injured.

Given this state of mind, the military was without doubt keeping a sharp eye on this trial. And so as soon as the motion had been made to summon Lieutenant Hori, they had quite evidently been disgruntled with the prosecutor and were counting upon the judge to give the motion that expressionless dismissal.

In any case, the Prosecutor's Office had learned from the questioning conducted by the police that the students had met with the Lieutenant in the "Kitazaki" lodging house for mili-

tary personnel, at the rear of the compound of the Azabu
Third Regiment.

Thus Honda read beyond the irritation and impatience on
the prosecutor's features to deduce the sources of his frustration.

His conclusions were as follows: the prosecutor was not at
all happy with the simple indictment for preparation to commit murder that came out of the preliminary hearings. What
he wanted, however it could be attained, was to make the
affair bigger, to make it become, if possible, an indictment
for conspiracy to commit insurrection. Only by so doing, the
prosecutor believed, could the evil root of this affair be torn
out. This state of mind, however, seemed to have disturbed
the logic of his procedure. By taking so many pains to prove
that the defendants had curtailed an original plan that had
been large-scale, the prosecutor had been remiss in gathering
the essential elements for proving preparation to commit
murder.

"To aim for this weak spot," thought Honda, "and, with
one thrust if possible, render even the murder preparation
charge unproved—that's what I must do. And so my greatest
worry will be Isao's purity and honesty. I have to confuse
him. My witnesses will be directed both against our oppo-
nents and against our own side."

Honda felt his heart calling out to Isao's clear eyes, excep-
tionally beautiful and gallant, even among those of all his
fellow defendants. When he had heard of the affair, Honda
had thought that Isao's furiously gazing eyes were most appropriate, but now, seeing them again, he felt that they were
unsuited to these circumstances.

"Beautiful eyes!" Honda exclaimed to himself. "Clear and
shining, forever disconcerting others. Peerless young eyes radiating a censure that seems from another world, as if one
were suddenly plunged beneath the waters of Sanko Falls.
Go ahead, express what you like. Confess to anything at all.
Be deeply wounded. You're at the age when you should be

learning the means to defend yourself. By speaking out without restraint, you will at last learn that no one is willing to believe the truth, one of the most valuable lessons a man can learn about life. This is the only wisdom that I have to convey to eyes as beautiful as yours."

Then Honda began to study the face of Judge Hisamatsu, who sat in the Chief Judge's place upon the bench. The Chief Judge was somewhat past sixty, and faint splotches marked the dry, white skin of his handsome features. He wore gold-rimmed glasses. Despite the clarity of his enunciation, now and then, as he spoke, one heard inorganic sounds like the elegant click of ivory chess pieces striking together. Though this lent his speech something of the chill dignity of the glittering chrysanthemum crest above the door of the Courthouse, it was apparently merely due to his false teeth.

Judge Hisamatsu's character was in high repute, and Honda too admired his probity. But the reason why he was still a judge of the lower court at his age was that he could hardly be called brilliant. According to what lawyers had to say among themselves, though he looked as if reason reigned supreme in him, he was in fact easily moved, and his efforts to affect a cold exterior in order to combat his inner flames were given away by the sudden reddening of the old man's dry, white cheeks when he felt violent anger or deep emotion.

Honda, however, knew something about what went on inside a judge. And how intense were a judge's inner struggles! Emotion, sentiment, desire, personal concern, ambition, shame, fanaticism, and all sorts of other flotsam—the fragments of planks, the wastepaper, the oil slick, the orange peel, the fish, the seaweed filling the sea of human nature that was ever pushing against the lone seawall that kept it in check: legal justice. Such was the struggle.

Among the indirect evidence supporting the indictment was the defendants' having sold their swords in exchange for daggers, a matter to which Judge Hisamatsu seemed to attach considerable importance. As soon as he had ruled that the Lieutenant could not be summoned, he began the examination of the evidence.

JUDGE HISAMATSU: I have some questions for Isao Iinuma. You sold your swords and bought daggers in exchange preparatory to acting. Was that because you had assassination in mind?

IINUMA: Yes, Your Honor. That was the purpose.

JUDGE: What day and what month was that?

IINUMA: It was November eighteenth, as I remember it.

JUDGE: You sold two swords on that day and purchased six daggers with the money. Is that correct?

IINUMA: Yes, Your Honor.

JUDGE: Did you yourself go to do the exchanging?

IINUMA: No, Your Honor. I asked two of my comrades to do so.

JUDGE: Who were they?

IINUMA: Izutsu and Inoué.

JUDGE: Why did you give each of them a sword to exchange like that?

IINUMA: I thought that if someone saw a young man bringing in two swords to sell, it might attract attention. I picked the two men who would have the most cheerful and well-behaved appearance, and I sent them to dealers who were some distance apart. If the sword buyer asked why they were selling, I told them to say that they had been practicing swordsmanship but had given it up, so they wanted to exchange their swords for some daggers with plain wooden sheaths for themselves and their brothers. If exchanging the two swords would bring six daggers, these and the six we already had would give us enough for the twelve of us.

JUDGE: Izutsu. Tell us what happened when you brought the sword in to exchange it.

IZUTSU: Yes, Your Honor. I went to a shop called Murakoshi's Swords at Number Three Koji-machi. I tried to look as nonchalant as I could as I said I wanted to sell my sword. A little old lady holding a cat was behind the counter. And I thought to myself how uneasy that cat would be if this was a samisen shop.

JUDGE: That is not to the point.

IZUTSU: Yes, Your Honor. When I told the old lady what I wanted, she went to the back of the shop right away, and the dealer himself came out, a grumpy-looking fellow with a bad complexion. He unsheathed the blade and examined it. With a contemptuous expression on his face, he looked at it from all different angles, finally removing the hilt fasteners and examining the part of the blade that fitted inside. "Just as I thought," he said. "The maker's name was added later." Without even asking why I wanted to sell it, he set a price and gave me three wooden-sheathed daggers in exchange. I took a good look at their blades and then walked out.

JUDGE: He didn't ask your name or address?

IZUTSU: No, Your Honor. He didn't ask me anything at all.

JUDGE: What do you say, Mr. Honda? Do you wish to ask Iinuma or Izutsu any questions?

HONDA: I'd like to question Izutsu, Your Honor.

JUDGE: Very well.

HONDA: When you went to sell the sword, had Iinuma told you that swords would be awkward for an assassination and that it was therefore necessary to exchange them for daggers?

IZUTSU: Well, no, sir, he didn't say it in so many words as I remember.

HONDA: So he didn't specify anything of the sort but merely told you to go and exchange the swords, and you went without knowing the purpose?

IZUTSU: Well . . . yes, sir. But I certainly had a good idea of it. It seemed obvious.

HONDA: Then it wasn't a matter at that time of a sudden change in the nature of your resolution?

IZUTSU: No, sir. I don't think that was it.

HONDA: The sword you brought to the dealer, was it your own?

IZUTSU: No, sir, it was not. It was Iinuma's sword.

HONDA: What kind of weapon was in your own possession?

IZUTSU: I had a dagger right from the beginning.

HONDA: When did you obtain it?

IZUTSU: Well, sir . . . yes, it was last summer. It was after we had made our vows before the shrine on the campus. I felt that it would be unmanly of me not to have a dagger at least. So I went to my uncle who is a collector, and I got one from him.

HONDA: I see. And at that time, then, you had no clear and definite idea of the use to which you would put it?

IZUTSU: No, sir. I only felt that someday, somehow I would like to use it. . . .

HONDA: Very well. Now when was it that you came to a clear realization of the definite use to which it could be put?

IZUTSU: I think it was when I was given the mission of assassinating Mr. Shonosuké Yagi.

HONDA: What I'm asking is when the realization first came to you that, in order to commit an assassination, a dagger was indispensable.

IZUTSU: Well, sir . . . as for that, I don't remember too well.

HONDA: Your Honor, I would like to ask Iinuma a few questions.

JUDGE: Very well.

HONDA: What kind of sword did you have?

IINUMA: The sword that I gave Izutsu to sell was signed by Tadayoshi of Bizen. When I reached the third rank in kendo the year before last, my father gave it to me as a present.

HONDA: Did you not exchange that valuable sword for daggers in order to use one of them to commit suicide?

IINUMA: Pardon, sir?

HONDA: You testified as to your fondness for the book *The*

League of the Divine Wind and said how the suicides of
the men of the League had aroused your admiration. And
you further testified that you wished to die in that manner, and that you had praised such a death to your comrades. On the battlefield the men of the League fought
with their swords, but, when it came to suicide, they used
daggers. And so judging from this . . .

IINUMA: Yes, sir. Now I remember. At the meeting on the
day of the arrest, someone said: "In case of emergency,
each one should carry a second dagger hidden on his person." Everyone agreed. This emergency dagger would be
definitely for committing suicide, but we were arrested
before we could buy more.

HONDA: In that case, up to that time you had not considered
buying weapons for such emergency use?

IINUMA: No, sir.

HONDA: But before that you had been firmly resolved upon
suicide?

IINUMA: Yes, sir.

HONDA: In that case, this exchanging swords for daggers,
might one say that you had killing yourselves in mind as
much as killing others—that is to say, a double purpose?

IINUMA: Yes, sir, you could say that.

HONDA: Your action, therefore, in exchanging your ordinary
weapons for daggers had a twofold purpose: assassination and suicide. And at the time in question these deadly
weapons were not exclusively bound up with the idea of
assassination. Is that right?

IINUMA: Ah . . . yes, sir.

PROSECUTOR: Your Honor, I object. The defense's line of
questioning is obviously tendentious.

JUDGE: That should be enough questions from the defense.
The matter of exchanging the swords has now been sufficiently covered. The prosecution may therefore call its
witnesses.

. . .

Honda, as he sat behind his desk, was fairly content. By his questions he had somewhat confused the logic of linking the obtaining of the daggers to the intent to murder. Honda was concerned, however, about Judge Hisamatsu's apparent lack of interest in the ideological aspects of the case. Right from the opening of the trial, the judge, by virtue of his authority, could have elicited from Isao any number of statements about his political beliefs, but he had made no attempt to do so.

The spectators looked over to the entrance of the courtroom, toward the uncertain tapping sound of a cane. An old man appeared. He was very tall but bent, shielding himself by clutching the front of his linen summer kimono, as though he were striving desperately to catch hold of something. The sunken eyes alone, beneath the white head of hair, were directed upwards. He made his way to the witness box, where he stood supporting himself on his cane.

The judge rose and read the written oath. The witness signed this with a trembling hand and put his seal upon it. A chair was provided for him before his testimony began.

In a voice so low the spectators could hardly hear him, the old man answered the judge's questions: "My name is Reikichi Kitazaki. I am seventy-eight years old."

JUDGE: The witness has been the proprietor of the place in question for some time, I understand.

KITAZAKI: Yes, Your Honor, I have. I opened my rooming house for military personnel at the time of the war with Russia, and I have continued to operate it up to the present time. Among my officer guests were many who went on to fame, becoming major generals and lieutenant generals. My establishment has a reputation for being a fortunate lodging house. It's a rather shabby, dilapidated place, but I have been honored with the favor of military gentlemen, especially the officers of the Azabu Third

Regiment. I have no wife, and, though it be frugal, I make my living without being a burden upon anyone.

JUDGE: Does the prosecution have any questions to ask?

PROSECUTOR: Yes, Your Honor. How long has First Lieutenant of Infantry Hori been a guest at your house?

KITAZAKI: Well, sir . . . let me see now. Three years . . . no, two years. . . . My memory is not what it used to be. Oh my . . . yes, it's been about two years, I think. . . .

PROSECUTOR: Lieutenant Hori was promoted to first lieutenant three years ago. In March of 1930, that is. When he became a guest at your house, then, he was already a first lieutenant. Is that correct?

KITAZAKI: Yes, sir, of that I'm sure. The gentleman wore two stars from the very beginning. And I have no memory of there being a promotion celebration.

PROSECUTOR: In that case, it's a matter of less than three years and more than one?

KITAZAKI: Yes, sir. That is correct.

PROSECUTOR: Did Lieutenant Hori have many visitors?

KITAZAKI: Yes, sir, very often indeed. Not once was there a woman guest, but young men, students, were forever coming and going. They liked to hear him talk. And the Lieutenant, for his part, was fond of them. If dinner time came, he would send out to the neighborhood shops for food. He treated them well and would empty out his pockets for them.

PROSECUTOR: How long has he shown such a predilection?

KITAZAKI: That, sir, was from the very beginning. Yes.

PROSECUTOR: Did the Lieutenant have much to say to you concerning his visitors?

KITAZAKI: Oh, no. In that regard he was not at all like Lieutenant Miura. He was not affable with me and hardly had a word to say. So there was no likelihood at all of his confiding in me about his guests. . . .

PROSECUTOR: One moment please. What about this Lieutenant Miura?

KITAZAKI: A gentleman who has been a long-time guest. His room is on the second floor—at the opposite end of the corridor from Lieutenant Hori. He has a rough manner, but he is good-natured.

PROSECUTOR: Please tell us whether or not there is anything special that you remember about Lieutenant Hori's visitors.

KITAZAKI: Well, sir, I will. On this particular night, I was bringing Lieutenant Miura his dinner, and when I was passing Lieutenant Hori's room, the door was closed, and, all of a sudden, from the inside I heard the Lieutenant shouting as though he were giving an order on the drill field. It rattled me considerably.

PROSECUTOR: What did Lieutenant Hori say?

KITAZAKI: That I remember clearly. "Don't you understand? Give it up!" he shouted angrily.

PROSECUTOR: Do you have any idea what he meant by "Give it up"?

KITAZAKI: Well, no, sir. After all, it was something shouted as I was just going by, and I was hard put to keep from dropping my tray. And since, as you see, I'm not good on my feet anyway, it was all I could do to hurry on to Lieutenant Miura's room. You see, Lieutenant Miura was really famished that night. Earlier he had called down to me: "Hey, old fellow! Hurry up and bring my supper." And now if I dropped his tray, I thought, I'd have Lieutenant Miura shouting at me. When I put the tray down in front of Lieutenant Miura, he grinned and said: "He's going at it, isn't he?" And that was all. He didn't say another word about it. I think that's one of the good things about military men.

PROSECUTOR: How many visitors were in Lieutenant Hori's room on the night in question?

KITAZAKI: Well, I believe there was one. Yes . . . that was it, one.

PROSECUTOR: And when was this night that Lieutenant Hori said, "Give it up"? This is an extremely critical point, so please try to remember exactly. What year, what month, what day? Do you keep a diary?

KITAZAKI: No, sir. No chance of that.

PROSECUTOR: Perhaps you didn't understand my question?

KITAZAKI: Pardon?

PROSECUTOR: Do you keep a diary?

KITAZAKI: Oh, a diary? No, sir, I do not keep one.

PROSECUTOR: Well, then, what year, what month, what day was it?

KITAZAKI: Well, I'm fairly sure it was last year. Yes, it was. And because I didn't think it was at all strange that the sliding door should be closed, I know it wasn't summer—maybe not even early summer or early fall. The weather must have been cold, but it wasn't too cold out, so it could have been last spring as late as April, or else from October on. The time of day was dinner time, at night, but as for the day itself . . . well, sir, on that, I'm not quite sure.

PROSECUTOR: So it was April or October, or perhaps March or November. Can't you be more specific?

KITAZAKI: No, sir. But I'm trying hard to remember. Let's see. . . . Yes, it was October or November.

PROSECUTOR: But which was it: October or November?

KITAZAKI: On that point, I'm not sure.

PROSECUTOR: Could one say that it was either the end of October or the beginning of November?

KITAZAKI: Yes, sir. That's fine with me. Forgive me for being so useless.

PROSECUTOR: Who was the visitor that night?

KITAZAKI: I don't know his name. Lieutenant Hori would

only tell me how many young visitors he was expecting,
and when they were supposed to come.

PROSECUTOR: His visitor that night was also young?

KITAZAKI: Yes, sir. It was a student, I believe.

PROSECUTOR: Would you be able to recognize him again?

KITAZAKI: Well, sir . . . perhaps.

PROSECUTOR: Please turn around, Mr. Kitazaki. Is the one
who visited the Lieutenant that night there among the
defendants? You may if you like get up and examine each
of their faces.

Isao let the tall, bent old man come over to him and
stare full into his face. The sunken eyes were clouded like an
oyster. A web of dark red veins encroached upon the whites,
and the pupils were so beset by their surroundings that they
seemed shrunk to lusterless black moles.

Isao was forbidden to speak, but his eyes challenged the
old man: "It was me that time, wasn't it?" Even with Isao's
face right before him, however, Kitazaki's gaze seemed somehow to be hindered, as though some shadowy, undefined
presence were hovering between the two of them and he were
being drawn into it.

The cane scraped lightly against the floor. The old man
was now studying Izutsu's face. Since he had spent much
more time in front of Isao than anyone else, Isao was sure
that Kitazaki had recognized him.

The old man returned to the witness stand. His elbow resting upon his cane, his hand pressed to his forehead, he stared
blankly, as though worn out by the effort to chase down the
memory, as elusive as mist, that fled before him.

The prosecutor took up the questioning again, a note of
irritation evident in his tone.

"Well now, did you recognize him there?"

Kitazaki did not look at the prosecutor as he answered in
a barely audible voice but seemed to be addressing his own
image faintly reflected in the paneling of the judges' bench.

"I can't be sure, sir. But that first defendant . . ."

"Iinuma, you mean?"

"I do not know his name. But the face of that young man on the far left . . . I am certain that he came to my house at some time. It may have had nothing to do with Lieutenant Hori, though."

"In that case, maybe he was a guest of Lieutenant Miura?"

"No, sir. It was not that. Quite some time ago, there was a young man who came to stay with a woman in the rear parlor. I think he is the one. . . ."

"Iinuma brought a woman to your house?"

"I cannot be certain. But it was someone like him."

"And when was this?"

"Well, as I look back now, I think it was, yes, some twenty years ago."

"Twenty years? Iinuma brought a woman to your house twenty years ago?"

So taken aback was the prosecutor that the spectators burst into laughter. But this reaction did not unsettle the old man in the least. He doggedly repeated his answer.

"Yes, sir. That is correct. I think it was some twenty years ago."

The incompetence of the witness was now clear to everyone. People were laughing at Kitazaki's senility. Initially, Honda too had the same reaction, but then when the old man earnestly repeated "some twenty years," his amusement suddenly gave way to a shiver.

Honda had once heard from Kiyoaki the details of his tryst with Satoko in the back room of Kitazaki's lodging house. Other than their being the same ages there were no outward similarities between Kiyoaki and Isao. But still this Kitazaki, so close to death himself, had confused in his mind the memories of the two. Only the intensities of hue of all the things that had happened in his old house were blended together, transcending time. Passionate love of years past, passionate dedication in the present—these two had merged vaguely to-

gether in exceeding normal bounds, in becoming early fail-
ures. From the marsh of memories of a lifetime rose two superb lotuses, red and white, and these must have been seen as
a single flower. But through this misapprehension, Honda was
sure, in Kitazaki's senile old mind a stagnant, gray marsh had
suddenly been lit up by strange, clear beams of light. The old
man, eager to seize this extraordinary brilliance, had stubbornly repeated what he had said, undismayed by either the
ridicule of the spectators or the anger of the prosecutor.

Having grasped this, Honda then had the feeling that the
dazzlingly polished brown judges' bench and the robes of
solemn black were suddenly fading before the intense brilliance of the summer sun pouring down outside the windows.
As though struck by those powerful rays, the awesome, finely
tuned mechanism of the legal order seemed to be melting
swiftly away before him like an ice castle. Honda knew that
Kitazaki had glimpsed that great bond of light, invisible to
ordinary eyes. The summer brightness, which gave a sparkle
to each needle of the pines outside the windows, surely had as
its source a rope of light more forbidding, more magnificent
than the legal order on display within this room.

"Does the defense wish to examine the witness?"

When he heard the judge's question, Honda, still dazed,
could only reply: "No, Your Honor."

"Very well. Thank you, Mr. Kitazaki. The witness is dismissed," said the judge.

". . . At this time I would like permission to call as a
witness someone present who has not been formally summoned," said Honda. "Her name is Makiko Kito. For the sake
of the defendant Iinuma and the other defendants too, I would
like to have her questioned with regard to Iinuma's change of
mind three days before the day set for their action. And since
I will present as evidence the diary entries made by the witness at this time, I hope that the questioning can be based
upon these."

There was no provision for the calling of witnesses in this manner in criminal proceedings, but, depending upon the nature of the testimony to be given, a judge would usually grant permission after conferring with the prosecutor and the assistant judges, and Honda intended to take advantage of this custom.

The judge asked the prosecutor's opinion, and he acquiesced coldly, as though he considered it unworthy of his concern. After turning first to the judge on his right, consulting in a whisper, and then doing the same with the judge on his left, Judge Hisamatsu replied to Honda.

"Very well. You may do so."

Accordingly, Makiko appeared at the entrance to the courtroom. She wore a dark blue, waterfall stripe Akashi kimono bound with a Hakata obi. In the midst of summer, Makiko's naturally white complexion, cool as ice, gave a tranquil, distant look to her face, framed in a border of the jet-black hair hiding her ears and the blue neck of the kimono. Below her lively, moist eyes, her skin was faintly touched, like the coming on of twilight, with the signs of aging. Affixed to the slightly slanted cord that held her obi in place was the figure of a trout done in dark jade. Its hard green luster seemed to impose a crisp firmness upon the easy flowing lines of Makiko's attire. There was a subtle tension beneath her unruffled exterior. But no one could tell whether the cold expression on her face concealed sorrow or contempt.

Makiko made her way to the witness stand without so much as glancing in Isao's direction. All that he saw of her then was the cool seam that ran down the back of her kimono and the huge bow in which her obi was fastened.

"I hereby swear that, in accordance with my conscience, I will speak the truth, neither concealing nor adding anything thereto."

The judge read the oath as before, and Makiko signed the book, which was brought to the witness stand, with a hand that showed no sign of trembling. Then she drew from her sleeve the small case containing her seal, and, taking the slender ivory seal, she pressed it firmly to the paper so that her lovely fingers bent back. Watching from the side, Honda caught a glimpse of red ink between her fingers like a splash of blood.

On Honda's desk was the diary that Makiko had been willing to make public. Just as he had requested, Honda had offered this as evidence. Just as he had requested, he had called Makiko as a witness. But Honda could only guess at what the intent of the judge was in allowing this.

JUDGE: What are the circumstances of your being acquainted with the defendant?

MAKIKO: My father, Your Honor, is a friend of Mr. Iinuma's father. And furthermore, since my father enjoys the company of young men, Mr. Iinuma was a frequent guest at our house. And the relationship was much closer than that with relatives.

JUDGE: When was the last time you saw the defendant, and where was it?

MAKIKO: The evening of last November twenty-ninth. He came to the house.

JUDGE: The content of your diary that is being offered as evidence is altogether accurate?

MAKIKO: Yes, Your Honor, it is.

JUDGE: The defense may now question the witness.

HONDA: Yes, Your Honor. Miss Kito, this is your diary of last year, isn't it?

MAKIKO: Yes, sir.

HONDA: This diary is the sort in which the pages are not marked with dates, allowing you to write as much as you like, and you've kept such diaries faithfully for years. Is that correct?

MAKIKO: Yes, sir, that is correct. And so I can at times put in *waka* and the like.

HONDA: Your method from long past has been to leave a blank line between entries and not begin a new page each day?

MAKIKO: Yes, sir. In the last two or three years I've been writing so much that if I started a new page each day, even in
a diary without printed dates, I would run out of pages
by fall. So it doesn't look neat, but that is how I make
entries every day.

HONDA: Very well, then. Last year, 1932, that is, as to the
entry of November twenty-ninth, this was not something
that you wrote later, but you can testify that it was written that very night?

MAKIKO: Yes, sir. I've never let a day go by without writing
in my diary. That day too I made an entry before going
to bed.

HONDA: Now, in that entry of November twenty-ninth, 1932,
I shall read aloud just the portion that pertains to the defendant Iinuma:

> . . . Tonight at around eight o'clock, Isao paid an
> unexpected visit. Though I had not seen him in quite
> some time, I was thinking of him tonight, why I don't
> know, and perhaps it was my odd faculty for premonition
> that impelled me toward the entrance hall before the bell
> rang. As usual, he was wearing his student uniform and
> had clogs on his feet, but when I looked at his face I
> sensed that something had happened. He seemed stiff
> and formal. He suddenly thrust toward me a small keg
> he was carrying and said: "My mother asked me to
> bring you this. It's a few of the oysters we received from
> Hiroshima." In the darkness of the entrance hall, the
> water inside the barrel made a sound like a clucking
> tongue.
>
> Fidgeting about, he made the excuse that he had
> studying to do and so had to go, but the lie was written
> all over his face. I never would have expected such a
> thing from the Isao I knew. Pressing him to stay, I ac-
> cepted the keg and went to tell Father, who cordially
> said: "Have him come in."
>
> I rushed back to the entrance hall. Isao was already
> slipping out the door. I hurried out after him. I wanted
> at all costs to find out what was troubling him.

I am sure he knew that I was following him, but he neither turned around nor altered his pace. When we had reached the front of Hakusan Park, I called out to him: "What are you angry about?" and he finally stopped. He turned around to face me, and he smiled in a grim, embarrassed manner. We then sat down upon a bench in the park, and we talked there, in the cold night wind.

I asked him how he and his group were getting on. For some time he and his comrades have been gathering at the house and talking about how intolerable are the present circumstances of Japan, and I too have been a part of this, often treating them all to a supper of sukiyaki and the like. And I had been thinking that it was the activity of this group that had been keeping Isao away from the house in recent days.

Isao answered me with a woeful expression: "What I really meant to do in coming to your house was to talk to you about the group. But when I saw your face, since I had said such brave things before, I was embarrassed and couldn't say anything. And so I stole away." The words were spoken slowly and painfully.

The story that came out from my questions was as follows: Without my having been aware of it, the direction of his group's activities had gotten altogether out of hand, and the truth of the matter was that each of those involved, to hide his own fears and to measure the courage of the group, had grown ever more violently vocal, and as the numbers increased of those who fell away because this bravado unnerved them, the handful who remained bluffed all the harder. And while their actual resolution grew ever weaker, their words and their plans kept mounting toward a fantastic bloody retribution. They no longer knew what to do with each other. Since none of them could show a trace of weakness in his words, an outsider would no doubt have been appalled by what went on at their meetings, but in fact no one any longer really wanted to take action. With the situation as it was, however, not one of them had the courage to insist on giving up their plan, for fear that he would be branded a coward. Furthermore, if things went on this way, the danger would grow more acute. All unwillingly, they would rush ahead on a collision course with the deed that they had no intention of performing. Isao himself, their leader, no longer wanted to go through with it. Was there no way of drawing back? And the real purpose in his coming to the house tonight had been to ask advice. Those were the circumstances.

I used every argument I could think of to urge him to give it up. The manly thing to do was to put an end to things. And so, even if his comrades turned their backs on him now, the time would certainly come when they would understand. There were many other ways to serve one's country. And, if he didn't mind, I would be willing to try to persuade his comrades from a woman's standpoint. But when he replied that that would only embarrass him, I thought he was right and I acquiesced.

When we parted before Hakusan Shrine, Isao turned to me after we had prayed together and said: "Thanks to you, I feel good again. I have no intention of going through with it. As soon as I find the chance, I'll tell everyone that it's off." He laughed cheerfully when he said this, and so I was somewhat relieved. But still, in my breast there was a lingering uneasiness.

As I write this my head is clear and alert, and I shall not be able to sleep tonight. If some misfortune should overtake that fine young man in whom my father, too, has placed such hope, I think I can say that Japan herself will suffer a great loss. My heart is heavy tonight. I am in no mood to write poems.

That is the entry. Can you assure us that you are the one who wrote it?

MAKIKO: Yes, sir. I wrote it.

HONDA: And afterwards, you neither changed anything nor added anything?

MAKIKO: No, sir, It was just as you see it.

JUDGE: If that's the case then, according to your observation, the defendant Iinuma, on the night in question, gave up all intention of committing a crime?

MAKIKO: Yes, Your Honor, that is correct.

JUDGE: Did Iinuma say anything to you about the day chosen or anything similar?

MAKIKO: No, Your Honor. He did not.

JUDGE: Do you think perhaps that he might have wished to conceal that from you?

MAKIKO: He had already told me, Your Honor, that he had given up his project, so he would consider it pointless, I think, to talk about such things as the day he had once set for it. He was always so honest that I feel sure I would have known if he had been lying.

JUDGE: Your relationship with the defendant seems to be a rather close one.

MAKIKO: I suppose I thought of him as a younger brother.

JUDGE: Well, if you two were so close then, didn't you, considering the lingering uneasiness that you mentioned in your diary, feel any urge to work secretly to make sure that they turned back?

MAKIKO: I felt that a woman's meddling would only make matters worse, so I just kept praying. And while I was doing this, I learned of the arrests. It was a shock to me.

JUDGE: Did you speak of the events of that night to your father or to anyone else?

MAKIKO: No, Your Honor.

JUDGE: Wouldn't it have been natural to tell your father— considering that the matter was so grave, and considering, moreover, how the circumstances had changed?

MAKIKO: When I returned that night, my father asked me no questions. In the first place, my father has a military man's point of view, and he had always held the sincere fervor of youth in high regard. So I had no desire to speak to my father of Isao's change of heart. I felt that he might take it amiss because of his affection for Isao. And, even without my saying anything, I felt that it would come to his knowledge. So I kept the matter sealed in my heart.

JUDGE: Does the prosecutor wish to question the witness?

PROSECUTOR: No, Your Honor.

JUDGE: The witness is hereby dismissed. Thank you, Miss
Kito.

Makiko bowed, and, after turning her back with the huge
bow in which her white Hakata obi was tied, she walked out
of the courtroom without a glance in the direction of the defendants.

Isao clenched his fists. Sweat simmered inside them.

Makiko had committed perjury! The most brazen kind of
perjury! She had given testimony that Isao knew to be an outright lie, risking the danger that, if discovered, she would be
liable not only to the charge of perjury but also, according to
circumstances, to that of criminal complicity.

As for Honda, undoubtedly he must have summoned Makiko without knowing that she was lying. Honda would surely
not go so far as to jeopardize his whole career by conspiring
with Makiko. Honda, therefore, believed the story Makiko
told in her diary!

Isao felt at a loss. If Makiko was not to be indicted for
perjury, he had no other course open to him but one that involved the sacrifice of that purity he so valued.

And then, too, if Makiko had actually made such an entry
that night (and it would seem that here, at least, she was telling the truth), how could she, immediately after that tragically beautiful farewell, have changed their encounter into a
scene so surpassingly ugly? Was that cunning trick prompted
by hostility? By an unaccountable desire to defile herself?
No, it could be nothing of the sort. Wise Makiko, perceiving
the advent of a day like today, had come home from parting
with him to prepare her defenses against the moment when
she would be called as a witness. And why? For no other reason but to save him.

There was no longer any question about Makiko having
been their betrayer, Isao thought. Then it occurred to him
that the court was not likely to allow an informer to be called
as a witness to support indirect evidence for the defense. Had

Makiko been the informer who had brought them to trial, the contradiction between the information she had given them and her testimony today would have been apparent. Amid the unpleasant scenes that his imagination flashed before him as his heart beat fast, he could at least discard the image of Makiko as informer. And this brought him momentary relief.

Makiko's only conceivable motive was love, a love that dared to face danger in full view of the public. Such a love! For this love Makiko did not hesitate to besmirch that which was most precious to him. Moreover, what was bitterest of all, he had to make a response to her love. He could not designate Makiko as a perjurer. On the other hand, no one but he knew the circumstances of that night, and so there was no one in the world but Isao who could call her testimony a lie. And Makiko was well aware of this. She testified as she did precisely because she was aware of it. The trap that she had set for him was that he had no choice but to save himself if he was to save her, however repugnant the means. Furthermore, he was sure, Makiko knew that Isao would do nothing else. . . . Isao struggled to shake off somehow the bonds that were constricting him.

He considered a further aspect. How did Makiko's false testimony strike the ears of his comrades beside him? Isao was confident that they trusted him. Still, they could hardly dismiss testimony so openly given as a tissue of lies!

The silence of his comrades while Makiko was testifying was like that of beasts tied up in their pens at night, their secret snarlings and their stealthy scratching at palings sharply intensifying an atmosphere of inexpressible discontent and the smothering stink of urine. Isao knew that his comrades were reacting with every fiber of their bodies. Even the noise of one of them scraping his heel against the back of the chair Isao heard as a reprimand directed at him. The anxiety about betrayal that had oppressed him in prison—that formless anxiety one feels in groping for a needle lost in the darkness—now its circumstances were reversed. Isao sensed a black poison spreading rapidly through the heart of each of his comrades. He could hear a network of cracks beginning to cover the entire surface of the white porcelain vase of his purity.

Let them be disgusted with him. Let them contemn him. That he could bear. What he could not bear was what they would naturally infer from Makiko's testimony: that so sudden arrest—might it not have resulted from Isao's betraying them to the authorities?

There was but one means to clear away this intolerable suspicion. There was but one person to clear it away. Isao himself, in other words, had to take the stand and expose Makiko's perjury.

Meanwhile, Honda himself was far from satisfied of the truth of Makiko's diary entry. He did not believe that the judges would accept the evidence of the diary at face value. He knew, however, that Isao would never do anything to cause Makiko to be charged with perjury. Isao, too, Honda was sure, clearly realized that Makiko's sole concern was to save him.

He hoped to bring about a struggle between his client and his witness. Isao's secret chamber—his clear purity of dedication—would be aglow with a woman's burning passion, as with the scarlet rays of the setting sun. Each of them, armed with the sword of ultimate truth, would have to destroy the power of the other's world—there was no other way. This was a kind of struggle that Isao in his twenty years of life had never imagined, had never dreamed of. It was, furthermore, a battle one had to learn to fight, a certain necessity of life.

Isao had an inordinate belief in his own world. Honda had to smash this for him. Why? Because this was the most dangerous of faiths. A thing that was endangering Isao's life.

If Isao had executed his plan as he wished, suicide following upon assassination, he would perhaps have brought his life to a conclusion without ever having encountered "another person." The "big shots" he killed would never have been other persons whom he had to confront. He would have viewed these men as nothing more than ugly dummies to be destroyed by the pure zeal of youth. Indeed, when Isao's sword blade cut into such ugly old flesh, Isao would probably have felt a fondness for his victim, more so than if he were a blood relative, since this man would have been like an icon that embodied the concept that Isao had cherished for so long. For in his written testimony also, he had stated that he "would never kill out of hatred." His crime would have been one of pure abstraction. To say, however, that Isao knew nothing of hatred would be to say that he had never loved anyone at all.

Just now, perhaps, he was knowing hatred. The shadow of something alien had for the first time entered his world of purity. No matter how keen his blade, how quick his footwork, how swift his blows, this was something alien and powerful from the outer world, something he could neither control nor suppress. He was, in short, learning that the "outside" existed in the very substance of the flawless sphere in which he lived.

As he watched the retreating figure of the witness, the Chief Judge slipped off his reading glasses. The bright summer sunlight that spilled into the courtroom lit his face with its bad complexion and paperlike skin.

"He is thinking something. What is he thinking?" Honda asked himself with a quiver of interest as he watched the judge.

It was not plausible that a venerable judge would allow himself, in public, to be captivated by the crisp loveliness of a rear view of Makiko. Judge Hisamatsu on his high bench seemed, rather, to be keeping a lonely watch from the high tower of age and legal justice. With his farsighted old eyes he could command a wide, distant view, a gift that his superiors esteemed in him. Consequently, Honda was certain that, beyond Makiko's flawless conduct and attitude under questioning and during the reading of the diary entry, the judge's intention was to weigh more heavily the composure with which she walked away. To look beyond a desolate, barren plain of feeling, to where a view of a summer obi was growing distant. . . . Now, surely, he has inferred something. Though Judge Hisamatsu had no reputation for brilliance, it was not strange that he was thoroughly versed in human nature.

The judge turned to Isao: "Is the testimony that Miss Kito just gave correct?" he asked. With a firm thrust of his forefinger Honda held fast the red pencil which he was about to roll down his desk, and pricked up his ears.

Isao stood up. Honda felt a little apprehensive as he noted that Isao's fists were tightly clenched, and even trembling slightly. At the neck of his somewhat loosely wrapped summer kimono, drops of sweat glistened upon the white skin of his chest.

"Yes, Your Honor," Isao answered. "It is correct."

JUDGE: You visited the home of Makiko Kito the evening of November twenty-ninth, and you told her of your own volition that you had changed your mind about your resolution?

IINUMA: Yes, Your Honor.

JUDGE: And the conversation took place just as she described it?

IINUMA: Yes, Your Honor. . . . However . . .

JUDGE: However? What do you mean "however"?

IINUMA: I did not tell her what I really felt.

JUDGE: And what do you mean by that?

IINUMA: What I really felt. . . . The truth is, Your Honor . . . that both Miss Kito and General Kito have been very kind to me for a long time. And so I wanted to make a brief farewell before I carried out my resolution. And since, for some time now, I had been letting her know something of my thoughts, I wanted to prevent her from becoming involved in any way whatsoever in the aftermath of our action. Therefore I deliberately acted as though my nerve had failed, and, in order to make her believe that, I told her nothing but lies. I wanted to see her gravely disappointed in me . . . and, by that means, break off my—attachment. Everything I said to her that night was a lie. She was completely taken in.

JUDGE: I see. Well, then, do you mean to say that on the night in question your resolution was as firm as ever?

IINUMA: Yes, Your Honor.

JUDGE: Aren't you just saying this in a hasty attempt to redress matters in front of your companions, who just heard from the mouth of Miss Kito testimony that portrayed you as weak and irresolute?

IINUMA: No, Your Honor. That's not it at all.

JUDGE: It seems to me that the witness, Miss Kito, is not the sort of person who is easily deceived. On the night in question, while Miss Kito heard you out, didn't you have the impression that she was merely pretending to be deceived?

IINUMA: Not at all, Your Honor. I was being very serious about it.

As Honda was listening to this exchange, he secretly applauded the desperate means that Isao had unexpectedly seized upon to extricate himself. Hemmed in as he was, Isao had at last learned the sophistication of adults. He had now discovered on his own the one device by which he could save Makiko and yet save himself. For the moment at least, Isao was not a young and heedless beast that knows nothing but how to hurl itself forward.

Honda calculated. When the charge was preparation to murder, the prosecution could not merely show intention but had to demonstrate that some concrete preparatory action had been taken. Since, therefore, Makiko's testimony pertained only to intention and had nothing to do with acts, in the broader context of the trial, it was neither a plus nor a minus. But when one considered the judges' own state of mind with regard to the defendants, that was a different matter. For article 201, which dealt with preparation to murder, had a provision specifying that punishment could be remitted, depending upon the circumstances.

How each judge assessed the circumstances would vary according to his character. Honda could find nothing in previous decisions of Judge Hisamatsu that would enable him to be confident of understanding his character. The wise course, accordingly, was to offer for the formation of the judge's assessment two kinds of mutually opposed data.

If the judge was psychologically inclined, he would base his opinion on Isao's renunciation of criminal intent, which Makiko's testimony alleged. If the judge was one who favored commitment to a belief, an ideal, then perhaps the unswerving purity of resolution, which Isao's own testimony insisted upon, would move him. The essential thing was to be prepared to offer adequate material of both kinds, whichever view the judge might take.

"Say what you like. Insist as much as you like," said Honda again in the depths of his heart to Isao. "Pour out your sincerity. Let the thoughts you describe reek of blood, but don't by any means let yourself go beyond the realm of concepts. That's the one way that you can save yourself."

JUDGE: Well now, Iinuma . . . you have talked of "the action" and of your "belief." You had much to say on this in the written testimony. But what do you think about the connection between thought and deed?

IINUMA: Pardon, Your Honor?

JUDGE: Put it like this: why isn't belief enough? Can't patriotism simply remain a belief? Why must one go beyond that toward illegal acts, such as you had in mind? I would like to hear your opinion on this.

IINUMA: Yes, Your Honor. In the philosophy of Wang Yang-ming there is something that is called congruity of thought and action: "To know and not to act is not yet to know." And it was this philosophy that I strove to put into practice. If one knows of the decadence of Japan today, the dark clouds that envelop her future, the impoverished state of the farmers and the despair of the poor, if one knows all this is due to political corruption and to the unpatriotic nature of the *zaibatsu*, who thrive on this corruption, and knows that here is the source of the evil which shuts out the light of our most revered Emperor's benevolence—with such knowledge, I think, the meaning of "to know and to act" becomes self-evident.

JUDGE: That's extremely abstract, I'd say. Take as much time as you need, but explain the development of your feelings, your indignation, your resolution.

IINUMA: Very well, Your Honor. I gave myself over to the practice of kendo from boyhood, but when I realized that around the time of the Meiji Restoration youths had swords with which they fought actual combats, struck down injustice, and fulfilled the great task of the Restoration, I felt an indescribable dissatisfaction with the bamboo sword and the kendo of the drill halls. But as yet I had formed no definite idea of the sort of action that was right for me.

In 1930 there was the London Naval Conference, and even in school I was told what humiliating conditions had been forced upon us and how national security was imperiled. Just as my eyes were being opened to the dangers threatening the nation, there occurred the incident of Sagoya shooting Premier Hamaguchi. I then realized that the dark cloud that covered Japan was not something to be lightly shrugged off, and from that time on, I listened to what the teachers and older students had to say about current events, and, on my own, I began to read all sorts of things.

Gradually, I became acquainted with the problems of society. I was shocked at the inaction of the government in the face of the chronic depression that had been dragging on since the worldwide panic.

A mass of jobless wage-earners that reached two million, men who had formerly worked away from home and sent money back, now returned to their farming villages to aggravate the poverty already reigning there. I learned that there were great crowds at Yugyo Temple in Fujisawa where the monks dished out rice gruel to the unemployed who were walking home to the country, lacking the money for train fare. And yet the government, despite the gravity of the situation, responded only with nonchalant indifference, Minister of the Interior Antachi declaring: "Relief measures for the unemployed would make people frivolous and lazy, so I will do all I can to avoid such a harmful policy."

Then in 1931, bad harvests struck Tohoku and Hokkaido. Whatever could be sold was sold, land and homes were lost, and the situation was such that whole families lived in stables, and people held starvation at bay by eating acorns and roots. Even in front of the township hall one saw notices such as: "Anyone wishing to sell his daughters, inquire within." It was not at all rare for a soldier on his way off to war to bid a tearful farewell to his younger sister being sold to a brothel.

Beyond the hardship of the bad harvests, the stringent economic policy of the government after the lifting of the embargo on the export of gold laid ever heavier burdens on the farmers, and the panic in agriculture mounted to new heights. The Land of Abundant Rice, which was ancient Japan, was transformed into a wasteland populated by people sobbing from the pangs of hunger. And then the importing of rice, when there was more than enough rice within Japan, caused the price of rice to plunge disastrously. Meanwhile tenant farming grew by leaps and bounds, and more than half the crop a tenant produced had to go as rent, with not a single grain of rice going into the mouth of the farmer himself. The farmers had not one yen of currency. Trade was carried out by bartering. A pack of Shikishima cigarettes went for two quarts of rice, a haircut was four quarts, a pack of Golden Bat cigarettes was a hundred bunches of turnips, and twenty-six pounds of cocoons would bring in ten yen. That was the situation.

As you know, Your Honor, the farmers are breaking out in protest everywhere. There is danger that the farming villages will go Red. Even in the breasts of the young men who are being called to the imperial colors as loyal subjects one cannot find unalloyed patriotism, and that evil is beginning to infect the armed forces.

Giving no thought to these crises, the government plods along in the path of corruption. The *zaibatsu* has amassed vast sums through dollar buying and other policies ruinous to the nation, and no one pays any heed to the wretched misery of the masses. As a result of my varied reading and other research, I came to feel strongly that what had debased Japan to this extent was not just the sins of politicians. Much of the responsibility lay with the *zaibatsu*, who manipulated these politicians to satisfy their greedy craving for profit.

I never thought, however, of going over to the leftists. For the ideology of the leftists bore hostility toward the most revered person of His Sacred Majesty.

Japan from ancient days has been a land whose character was to reverence His Sacred Majesty, a harmonious land where the Emperor was held to be the head of the vast family that was the Japanese people. Here, I need hardly say, is the true image of the Emperor's Land, a national character as everlasting as heaven and earth.

But what of this decadent Japan filled with people suffering from hunger? Why has this become such a degenerate age despite the revered person of the Emperor? Isn't it the unparalleled virtue of the Emperor's Land that the exalted ministers who serve at his side and the starving farmers in the remote villages of Tohoku are alike his children without difference or distinction? At first I firmly believed that the day would certainly come when the poor would be saved by the benevolence of His Sacred Majesty. Japan and the Japanese had for the time being gone somewhat astray. With the passage of time, the Yamato Spirit would reawaken in the hearts of her loyal subjects, and the whole nation working together would make the Emperor's Land what it had been before. Such were the hopes that I once held. I had faith that the dark clouds would one day be blown away and that a bright and clear future lay ahead for Japan.

Wait as I might, however, that day did not come. The longer I waited, the darker the clouds became. Then I happened to read a book that struck me with the force of a revelation. This was the book of Tsunanori Yamao: *The League of the Divine Wind*. After I finished it, I was a different person. I realized that to go on merely sitting and waiting was hardly the behavior proper to a loyal man. Till that moment I had known nothing of desperate loyalty. Nor had I known that, once the flame of loyalty blazed up within one, it was necessary to die.

Over there the sun is shining. We cannot see it from here, but even the turgid gray light around us surely has the sun as its source, and so in one corner of the sky the sun must be shining. This sun is the true image of His Sacred Majesty. If the people could only bathe themselves in its rays, they would shout with joy. The desolate plain would then become fertile at once, and Japan, beyond any shadow of a doubt, would become once more the Land of Abundant Rice.

But the low-lying cloud of darkness covers the land and shuts off the light of the sun. Heaven and earth are cruelly kept apart, heaven and earth, which have but to meet to embrace smilingly, cannot even view each other's sad faces. The sorrowful cries of the people cover the land but cannot reach the ears of heaven. To scream out is in vain, to weep, in vain, to protest, in vain. But if their voices could reach the ears of heaven, the power of heaven, as easily as you move your little finger, could clear away those dark clouds, could transform a marshy wasteland to a shining countryside.

Who was to carry word to heaven? Who, mounting to heaven through death, was to take upon himself the vital function of messenger? I perceived that this was what the valiant men of the League of the Divine Wind intended by their faith in the Ukei.

If we look on idly, heaven and earth will never be joined. To join heaven and earth, some decisive deed of purity is necessary. To accomplish so resolute an action, you have to stake your life, giving no thought to personal gain or loss. You have to turn into a dragon and stir up a whirlwind, tear the dark, brooding clouds asunder and soar up into the azure-blue sky.

Of course I thought of gathering a vast number of arms and men and sweeping the sky clear of darkness before mounting to heaven. But I gradually came to realize that that was unnecessary. The valiant men of the League, wielding their Japanese swords, fought their way into a camp of infantry armed with modern weapons. All I had to do was to direct myself at that spot where the clouds were darkest, that point where their soiled texture was thickest and most filthy. All I had to do was to tear open a hole there, with all my might, and soar to heaven alone.

I never thought in terms of killing people, only of destroying the deadly spirit that was poisoning Japan. And to do so I had to tear away the robe of flesh with which this spirit was garbed. By this action the souls of those whom we cut down would also become pure, and the bright, wholesome Yamato Spirit would come alive in their hearts again. And they, with my comrades and me, would rise to heaven. For we in turn, after destroying their flesh, had to commit seppuku immediately. Why? Because if we did not cast aside our own flesh as soon as possible, we could not fulfill our duty as bearers of an urgent message for heaven.

Even speculating on the Imperial Mind is disloyal. Loyalty, I think, is nothing else but to throw down one's life in reverence for the Imperial Will. It is to tear asunder the dark clouds, climb to heaven, and plunge into the sun, plunge into the midst of the Imperial Mind.

This, then, is what my comrades and I pledged within our hearts.

Honda watched the face of the Chief Judge with unblinking gaze. As Isao had gone on with his explanation, the white, splotched skin covering the judge's old cheeks, Honda observed, had gradually taken on the red glow of youth. When Isao had finished and took his seat, Judge Hisamatsu began to shuffle busily the papers before him, but obviously this was a device to hide his emotion. After a time the judge spoke.

JUDGE: So that's it then? Does the prosecution have anything to say?

PROSECUTOR: Yes, Your Honor. To take things in proper order, I would like to say something with regard to the witness Miss Kito. I am sure that, when she was summoned, this court was exercising due consideration. Nevertheless, in my own view, I must not only say that her testimony was entirely irrelevant but, without going so far as to declare it perjury, contend that the credibility of the diary seems extremely questionable. As for the value of the diary as written evidence, then, I would register a forceful doubt. Now, with regard to the witness's testimony that she was as fond of the defendant as if he were "a younger brother," one would expect emotional involvement, in view of the long and cordial relationship between the Iinuma and Kito families. The defendant Iinuma himself spoke of an "attachment," and so one might well imagine that a tacit understanding existed between these two. Consequently, I regret to say that, in both Miss Kito's testimony and the defendant Iinuma's account of that night, one can detect a kind of unnatural exaggeration. In short, I believe that the summoning of this witness was not a proper step.

Now to consider the long account that the defendant Iinuma has just given us: elements of fantasy and abstraction predominate in it. At first it would seem that he was fervently pouring out all that he had intended, but one has the impression that he deliberately obscured some significant aspects. For example, how did he come to abandon the plan to gather a large number of arms and men and sweep away the dark clouds altogether, thinking it would be sufficient to tear open the clouds at one spot only? That is a gap in his account that cannot be ignored. I believe that the defendant deliberately omitted the particulars of the matter at this point.

On the other hand, though the witness Mr. Kitazaki's memory was not clear with regard to the time, he testified that Lieutenant Hori had shouted angrily, "Don't you understand? Give it up!" either toward the end of October or the beginning of November of last year. I submit that this testimony contributes vitally relevant evidence. For it clearly has a bearing upon the defendant Iinuma's account of the weapon exchange which he describes as having taken place on November eighteenth. If this weapon exchange had taken place earlier, if the night on which the Lieutenant shouted "Give it up" had been after it, the affair would be different. It is otherwise, however, and so the various parts fit together.

The judge, after conferring with the prosecutor and the defense counsel about the date and time of the next session, announced that the second session was at an end.

38

THE VERDICT was handed down on December 26, 1933, just before the year-end holiday. Though it was not the "not guilty" decision Honda had hoped for, it read: "The punishment to which the defendants are liable is hereby dismissed." It was a decision that utilized a provision in Article 201 of the Criminal Code, pertaining to preparation for murder: "Dependent upon the circumstances, however, punishment may be remitted."

The verdict acknowledged that preparation to commit murder had indeed taken place, but the defendants, with the exception of Sawa, were extremely young, their motives were pure, and they had obviously been carried away by excessive patriotism. Furthermore, there was inadequate evidence that, after plotting, they had not indeed turned aside from their criminal intent. The logic behind the remission of punishment for all the defendants was thus set forth in detail.

Then as to the older Sawa, had he been an initiator of the conspiracy, he would not have escaped, but since he had joined when it was already underway and seemed to have taken no particular leadership role, he benefited from the same remission of sentence.

Had there been a "not guilty" decision, the probability would have been strong that the prosecutor would have appealed, but as matters stood, Honda was hopeful that he would not do so. In any case, they would know within a week.

All the defendants were released, and they returned home to their parents.

On the evening of the twenty-sixth, there was a private dinner at the Academy of Patriotism to celebrate Isao's return. Honda was the guest of honor, and Iinuma and his wife, Isao, Sawa, and the student body took part in the conviviality. Makiko was invited but did not come.

Up until the time the banquet began, Isao sat listening to the radio as though in a stupor. He heard the six o'clock Fairytale Theater, Hanako Muraoka's Children's Newspaper at six twenty, a talk by the chief surgeon of the Konoe Division on "Means to Be Taken by the Citizenry in the Event of Poison Gas Attack" at six twenty-five, and while he was listening to Harold Palmer's six fifty-five Current Topics, he was compelled to get up and hurry to the dining room. Since returning home, he had merely smiled and said nothing.

His mother had met him at the door, weeping without restraint, and then, after putting on a shiny, freshly laundered apron, she retired into the kitchen and threw herself into the task of chopping vegetables. The kitchen was crowded with rejoicing housewives who had come to help her. As his mother gave orders, her busy fingertips seemed to send forth unseen rays directed at the platters everywhere, and these were instantly filled with multicolored sashimi and broiled fish and meats. Women's laughter from the kitchen echoed in Isao's ears like sounds from another world.

Iinuma and the Academy students had met Isao and Sawa, and, on the way home, all had stopped to offer reverence before the Imperial Palace and at Meiji Shrine, and as soon as they had returned to the Academy, they went to worship as one family in the shrine located in one wing. Only after this was Isao able to enjoy the leisure of a hot bath. All the gods had been thanked, and now at this banquet it remained to thank the one who, in the world of humans, deserved the most thanks: Honda. Iinuma, in his formal kimono with family crest, rose from his seat, moved down to a humble place with his son and Sawa on either side of him, and, turning to Honda, bowed low.

Isao did as he was told. Even his smile appeared to be one

demanded of him. Sounds were ringing in his ears. Things
were stirring and bustling. Things were glittering and dancing before his eyes. Things he had long dreamed of were being conveyed to his mouth. His senses were surely operative
yet they diffused reality. The food seemed as insubstantial as
delicacies tasted in dreams. The twelve-mat room in which he
sat seemed to become permeated with a painful brilliance and
suddenly transformed into a vast hall of a hundred or two
hundred mats, where, far in the distance, a throng had gathered for a festive banquet. They were people with whom he
had nothing to do.

It was Honda who quickly noticed that Isao had lost that
piercing stare of his.

Iinuma smiled at Honda's concern. "Naturally he's still
somewhat numb," he said in a low voice. "I had a similar experience. Of course in my case it wasn't so long, but even at
that, I was in a state of collapse for a week or so afterwards.
I couldn't really feel free. . . . There's nothing to worry
about, Mr. Honda. But here now, do you know why I'm having this party for the boy? It's just to make this the day to
celebrate his becoming an adult. He won't be twenty-one for a
while yet, but there's no doubt that this day will be one of the
most memorable of his life, the day of his rebirth. From now
on tonight I'll be giving him rather rough treatment, but I
intend to really open Isao's eyes and treat him as a full-fledged
adult. And I know, sir, that you understand how I feel as a
father and won't try to stop me."

Isao, in the meantime, sat drinking with Sawa, both of
them surrounded by students. Sawa was entertaining everyone by recounting prison experiences in a loud voice while
Isao merely smiled and remained silent.

The youngest student, Tsumura, who idolized Isao, grew
irritated as one funny story followed another, wanting to
hear the icy severity of Isao's words. His attention never wa-
vered from him, but, since Isao offered nothing at all, Tsumura finally took the initiative and whispered to him: "Isao,

did you hear the disgusting thing Kurahara did?"

The name Kurahara struck Isao's ears like a peal of thunder. As soon as he heard that name, the realm of reality which had seemed so distant suddenly impinged itself upon his senses like sweat-drenched underwear clinging to one's skin.

"Kurahara? What about him?"

"Something I saw in yesterday's paper. The *Imperial Way* gave its whole front page to it," Tsumura answered, citing the name of a right-wing newspaper. "It was really disgusting." He pulled a folded-up tabloid newspaper from his jacket pocket and showed it to Isao. Then he peered intently over Isao's shoulder as he read the article, his breath hot, his angry eyes seeming to burn holes through the paper. "It was really disgusting," he repeated.

The newspaper was crudely printed, with broken type evident here and there. The story it carried did not appear in major newspapers but was an article reprinted by permission of a Shinto publication connected with the Grand Shrine of Isé.

According to the article, Kurahara had, on December fifteenth, attended a session of the Kansai Bankers Association, and on his return had stopped at Isé, where he had stuffed himself with a dinner of Matsuzaka beef, which he especially favored. And on the following morning, he went together with the Prefectural Governor to offer worship at the Inner Shrine of Isé.

With them were their secretaries and a number of other underlings, but Kurahara and the Governor were accorded special treatment by having two folding chairs set up for them on the gravel pathway. At the sacred branch ceremonial too, two previously prepared sakaki sprigs were handed over to them. Both stood and, holding their sprigs aloft, listened to the ritual prayers. Then suddenly Kurahara, apparently feeling an itch on his back, transferred the sprig to his left hand and tried to scratch the spot, but could not reach it. He took the sprig in his right hand once more and this time reached behind him with his left. Again he failed to reach it.

The ritual prayers continued, still without any hint of coming to an end. Kurahara hesitated a moment, then, hindered as he was by the sakaki branch, decided to lay it down on the chair. Then he put both hands behind his back and scratched. At that moment the prayers finally ended, and two assistant priests indicated that the two men were to offer their sprigs.

Kurahara, forgetting that he had put aside his sprig, joined issue with the Governor in a contest of mutual deferring. Finally the Governor yielded, and stepped forward to make his offering. At this moment the priests were shocked to see that the sakaki sprig was gone from Kurahara's hand, but it was too late. For Kurahara, relieved that the Governor had preceded him, had sat down for the time being, crushing beneath his buttocks the sprig that lay on his chair. In the midst of the Shinto music accompanying the ritual, this faux pas was quickly passed off without attracting too much attention. Before many people had noticed, Kurahara, furnished with a fresh sprig, was stepping forward to offer worship. But, among the young priests who witnessed this, there was one who could not restrain his indignation. It was he who wrote about it in the Shrine journal, an article that came to the attention of the *Imperial Way*.

Kurahara could not have committed a greater sacrilege. Tsumura's indignation was reasonable enough. Even though it was a simple blunder on Kurahara's part, the night before he was to offer worship he had filled his belly with the flesh of beasts, and, furthermore, rather than begging forgiveness for the breach that he had committed before the gods, he had dared to advance with his second sakaki sprig into the very presence of divinity, and, as men looked on, had committed the still greater sin of glossing over his previous transgressions with a solemnly enacted sacrilege. Still, Isao concluded, this was not reason enough to kill him. But then, turning to look at young Tsumura, he noticed the boyish anger in those clear eyes. Somehow Isao felt ashamed.

This momentary misgiving seemed to rob the hand that held the newspaper of its strength. Sawa reached out the next instant and snatched the paper away.

"Forget it. Forget it. Don't bother your head about it," said Sawa. Isao could not be sure how drunk the man really was as he wrapped a fat, too white arm around his shoulder and urged saké upon him. For the first time Isao noticed how somberly pale Sawa's skin had become.

The saké bottle made its rounds, everyone sang and clapped, some stood up to entertain, and, at length, the headmaster declared that the party was over. Then Iinuma suggested that Honda, Isao, and Sawa join him around the *kotatsu* table in his own room to resume drinking while his wife served them.

This was the first time Honda had set foot in this room. It was ten mats in size, and in its center he was startled to find, spread in bright splendor, a Yuzen silk *kotatsu* quilt of sensuous beauty with the palace oxcart pattern. Perceptive as he was, Honda immediately guessed that this was a product of the taste for aristocratic indulgence that Miné still clung to. At the banquet too, Honda had been taken aback to see how the wooden rice tubs were covered with quilted blue cotton.

When he observed the interchanges between husband and wife, Honda's intuition told him that Iinuma, somewhere in his heart, had never forgiven his wife's past. Whether it was the distant past, which involved Marquis Matsugae, or some event in the more recent past, he did not know. For Iinuma's unrelenting attitude was somehow evident in his manner, and, correspondingly, Miné had a certain obsequiousness that seemed to keep on begging her husband's forgiveness. Nonetheless, it was odd that Iinuma should tolerate all over his house, reminders of the source of his wife's youthful lewdness, that gaudy style of beauty, so contrary to his own tastes, that could be seen in this sort of *kotatsu* quilt. Perhaps,

Honda thought, Iinuma himself, in the depths of his heart, concealed a nostalgia for this kind of taste appropriate to a maid in the service of a noble household.

Honda was invited to sit in front of the *tokonoma*. Miné kept her gaze fastened to the large bottle of saké resting in the copper kettle on the hibachi, from time to time touching it quickly with the tips of her long, skillful fingers as though it were an easily aroused animal. No matter how extreme her politeness, Honda felt, she had something of the mischievous young girl about her. The four men, warming themselves in the *kotatsu*, began to drink saké, taking some dried mullet roe with it.

"Tonight, Isao, drink as much as you want." As Iinuma offered the bottle to his son, he darted a stealthy glance at Honda. Apparently this was the start of the "rough treatment" that he had given notice of earlier. "Tonight, in front of Mr. Honda here, I am going to say something that will probably set you back on your heels. I'm doing it because from today on, you're an adult in mind and body, and, as your father, I'm going to treat you as a full-fledged man so that you'll know all the ins and outs of life, and can become a worthy successor to me. I'll put it to you bluntly: it's obvious that the police got you a year ago because somebody had informed. Who do you think that somebody was? If you have any idea, tell me."

"I have no idea."

"Don't hold back. If you think you know, tell me. It's all right."

"I don't know."

"I'll tell you. It was your father here. Well, are you surprised?"

"Yes. . . ."

Honda noticed with a sense of foreboding that at that moment Isao's expression bore not a trace of real surprise. That same instant Iinuma turned his eyes away from Isao and hurried on with what he was saying.

"Well? What do you think? Do you think there could be a father so cold-hearted as to hand over his own beloved son to the police? A father who, with a laugh, could turn his son over to the police? Eh? Well, I dared to do just that. But . . . I did it weeping. It's the truth. Isn't it, Miné?"

"Yes, it's the truth. Your father was weeping as he did it," said Miné, chiming in from across the hibachi. Coolly, but with no sign of disrespect, Isao put a question to his father.

"I see now that it was you who reported us to the police, Father. But who reported what we were planning to you?"

Iinuma's neat moustache trembled slightly. Startled, he put a hand to it as though pressing down a butterfly that was trying to fly away.

"I started keeping a close watch on it long ago. It was your mistake to think your father's eyes were like two knotholes."

"Is that right?"

"Of course that's right. But why in the world did I hurry out and get you arrested? That's what I really want you to understand.

"To tell the truth, I was greatly impressed by what you intended to do. I thought it was magnificent. I even envied you. I wanted to let you go through with it, if only I could. But that meant sitting and watching you rush to your death. If I'd left you alone, you'd have gone through with it. You'd have died.

"But you've got to understand that I'm not like other fathers, not wanting to lose their boys, who would even frustrate their sons' greatest hopes just to save their lives. Get this point straight. I wanted to save your life, and I wanted to see your plan go through. But what should I do? I thought about it all night long, and finally I arrived at a solution. Saving you like this means, in the long run, taking everything into consideration, the fulfillment of your plan in an even greater way.

"Do you understand, Isao? Just to die isn't everything. Just holding your life cheap isn't loyalty. In the eyes of The Most

Revered Son of Heaven, the life of each of the Emperor's treasures is a precious thing.

It's been obvious since the May Fifteenth Incident, people are fed up with political corruption. They have admired and applauded incidents like this. Then, too, you and your companions were young. You were pure. You had everything needed for sympathy and appreciation. Furthermore, if you were apprehended one step away from your goal, people would have a sense of relief, all the more reason to applaud you. Not by committing the act, but by being caught on the verge of it, you could become greater heroes. And because of this, to strike in the future will be easier. When a truly large-scale Restoration takes place, you will be a force to be reckoned with, and then you can fight magnificently. I was right. The number of letters that came in asking for a reduction of sentence after your arrest, the tenor of the newspaper accounts —everything showed how much people were on your side. I did what was best, Isao.

"What I did, in other words, was in imitation of the lion who heaves the cub he loves so much down into a deep ravine in order to toughen him up. Now you've made your way from the bottom of the ravine in splendid fashion. You've proved yourself a man. Isn't that right, Miné?"

"Yes, it's just as your father says, Isao. You've come through in splendid fashion. It's all due to your father's love, like the love of the lion for its cub. You must thank him for what he did. It was all done out of love for you."

Just as, when one digs a hole in the sand by the water's edge, however hard one tries, the sides give way before the water that wells up, so the elaborate speech that Iinuma had begun to deliver so triumphantly, Honda thought, was giving way before the uncomfortable silence of the listener at his side. Indeed as soon as the words had passed Iinuma's lips, the sands of silence were already trickling down upon the watery surface gleaming in the sun. Honda looked at Isao. He looked at Sawa. Shoulders squared, Isao was letting his head hang forward. Sawa was taking a surreptitious drink from his saké cup.

Honda had no idea whether or not Iinuma had intended from the beginning to say what he said next, but, whatever the case, Iinuma feared silence.

"Now listen. Up to now, I've been talking about something that you could understand well. But, Isao, here is something more you need to know to become an adult. You've got to swallow the bitter wisdom that women and children never taste. There's a gate that every man has to go through. With your experience this past year, you've gone through it in body. Now your soul has to go through it too.

"Up to now I have said nothing about this, but . . . the Academy of Patriotism—who do you suppose is the man responsible for its present prosperity? Whom do we have to thank, do you suppose?"

"I don't know."

"If I say it, the name is going to set you back on your heels. But it is nobody else but Baron Shinkawa. Don't either you or Sawa ever mention a word of this to the students. This is the Academy's greatest secret. This building—the truth is that it's due to an anonymous contribution of Baron Shinkawa. And I in my turn, of course, have had to hustle in various ways on his behalf. The Baron, on his part, has not thrown money away in vain. Otherwise, how do you think he could have pulled through the recent storm of abuse over dollar buying?"

Honda looked at Isao's face once again. This time the coldness and utter lack of surprise made Honda shudder. Iinuma was still talking.

"So that was the relationship with Baron Shinkawa, and shortly before the May Fifteenth Incident I got a summons from the Baron. Since the money was passed to me every month secretly through his secretary, it was something extraordinary that made him want to meet with me face to face.

"I won't mention the amount, but he handed over to me a

huge stack of bills and said: 'This money has nothing to do
with my safety. I'll tell you frankly: it's to protect Busuké
Kurahara. Because he's the sort of person he is, you see, he'd
never pay out money for his safety. I have received many
favors from Mr. Kurahara which I should repay. And so,
without telling him, I'm giving you this on my own. So please,
then, let this money act as a safeguard for Kurahara. If it's
not enough, just let me know, and I'll give you more.' And
so, then, I——"

"So you took it, Father?"

"I did. I took it. Because I was so moved by Baron Shinkawa's feeling for his old friend. From then on, things went
very well indeed with the Academy, as you and Sawa know."

"That's why you reported us to the police then, to protect
Kurahara?"

"So you'd think, I imagine. That's the way a child would
see it. No matter how much money they gave me, whom do
you think I'd put first: a big shot of the world of finance who
is no relative of mine, or my own boy?"

"I see. You took the best possible course, one that insured
saving your son's life as well as saving Kurahara's and honoring your obligation to Baron Shinkawa."

Honda was finally heartened to see for the first time in Isao's
eyes the fire that had once been there.

"No. That shows how naïvely you look at things. Do you
understand me? You've got to learn that in this world of ours
everything is tangled and twisted together. You'll never get
free of all that until you go up to heaven. The harder you try
to shake it off, the tighter it will cling to you. But as long as
you keep your faith, the tangle is nothing to worry about. It
doesn't worry me a bit, Isao.

"As far as I was concerned, no matter how much money I
took, you could have cut down Shinkawa and Kurahara, and
it wouldn't have bothered me. Afterwards I'd make amends
by cutting open my own belly. I was prepared for something
like that from the moment I took the money. If a merchant

doesn't hand over the goods when he receives payment, that's
fraud. But it's different with a patriot. Money is money, fidelity is fidelity. Two different things. Money is used in
money matters, and fidelity can be kept by seppuku. That's all.

"You see, I want you to be prepared for these situations.
That's why I'm telling you all this. To defile yourself, yet
not really be defiled—that's true purity. If you're fastidious
about defilement, you're not going to do anything. You'll
never become a real man, Isao.

"Having said this much, I think you must understand my
intentions. I didn't turn you in to save Kurahara's life. Nor
was it to save your own life either. If I had thought that that
was the way to eternal glory for you, to throw away your life
in that action, I would have rejoiced and let you go to your
death. I didn't do that simply because I didn't think it was.
Do you understand me? I said it before, so I won't repeat myself. I prized your goal, I cherished you as my son—and precisely because of this I took the step of denouncing you. I took
the step, drinking tears of blood. Didn't I, Miné?"

"Isao, you'll suffer for it, if you don't show gratitude for
your father's affection."

His head hanging, Isao said nothing. The saké he had
drunk had brought a rosy flush to his cheeks. His hands on
the *kotatsu* quilt trembled slightly.

Honda, looking at Isao, suddenly realized what it was that
he had been wanting so earnestly to tell him. Throughout
Iinuma's long, self-seeking admonition, Honda had been
bursting to say something. Once he said it, Isao's world would
crumble, and his eyes might be opened, so that he could race
across the wide fields in the bright light of the sun, afraid of
nothing. And yet, if he said it to console Isao, who sat there
with drooping head, there was the danger that what he told
him might instead turn Isao's supreme moment of suffering,
never to be lived again, into something altogether meaningless. What Honda wanted to communicate was the secret of
Kiyoaki's rebirth in Isao. But when Isao raised his head and

there were tears running down his cheeks, Honda completely lost the urge to free the secret he had guarded until now and let it beat its wings like a released bird.

Isao spoke out, like a dog yelping with eager restlessness: "I've lived for the sake of an illusion. I've patterned my life upon an illusion. And this punishment has come on me because of this illusion. . . . How I wish I had something that's not an illusion."

"If you become an adult, you'll get it."

"An adult? I'd rather . . . Yes! Maybe I ought to be reborn a woman. If I were a woman, I could live without chasing after illusions. Couldn't I, Mother?"

Isao laughed suddenly, as if something had cracked.

"What are you saying?" Miné answered, rather angrily. "Reborn a woman! How silly of you! You're drunk, aren't you—to come out with something like that."

Soon, after more saké, Isao fell asleep with his cheek upon the quilt that covered the *kotatsu*. Sawa took charge of him and led him to his room. The concerned Honda, deciding to make this the occasion for his own going, got up and followed them.

Showing a tender solicitude, Sawa, without a word, put Isao to bed for the night. When he had done so, Iinuma called him from the other end of the corridor, and Honda found himself alone with the sleeping Isao.

Isao's sleeping face, his skin flushed from drink, showed signs of distress, and his breathing was harsh. But even as he slept, his brows were contracted in manly fashion. Suddenly, as he tossed about on his *futon*, Isao shouted out in his sleep, loudly but too indistinct for Honda to hear clearly: "Far to the south. Very hot . . . in the rose sunshine of a southern land . . ."

At that point Sawa returned for Honda. And so, even though this confused message cried out from a drunken sleep lingered in his mind, Honda begged Sawa to look after Isao, and turned his steps toward the entrance hall. He had risked everything in coming to Isao's rescue, and today he had at last won his gamble. Honda wondered, therefore, why he felt such a sense of futility.

 39

THE FOLLOWING DAY was fair.

In the morning there was a visitor, Detective Tsuboi from the neighborhood police station. This middle-aged man, who had risen to second degree in kendo, relayed to Isao the message that the police chief hoped once again that Isao would be kind enough to come to the drill hall on Sundays to instruct the neighborhood boys in kendo.

"Yes, indeed," he said, "though his position prevents him coming out to praise you publicly, the Chief tells us in private that he's struck with admiration for you. And the parents of the boys too are anxious for somebody like you to instruct their sons in kendo, so that the true Japanese spirit will be instilled in them. If there's no appeal, we would like you to come as soon as the new year is underway. Of course I don't think there's much chance of an appeal."

Isao studied the trousers of the plainclothesman, in which a crease was only dimly visible, and, as he did, he thought of himself as he might look teaching children kendo, with age overtaking him. His white hair in a purple headband would shine wherever it was not covered by the towel bound in Kansai manner behind his mask.

After the detective had gone, Sawa asked Isao to come to

his room, and said: "It certainly feels good to flop down on a tatami again, with a cushion under my head, and skim through a whole year's stack of *Kodan Club*. By the way, even if you're supposed to be on your good behavior, a young fellow like you can't stay around the house like this. You're allowed to go out as long as I accompany you. So what do you say to us going to see a movie or something tonight?"

"Well, maybe," said Isao vaguely. Then he added, to be more polite, "I could go to visit my friend, though."

"Oh, no, not that! The best thing is for you not to see each other for the time being. You might say something that's better left unsaid."

"I suppose so." Isao had not mentioned the name of the person he wanted very much to see.

"Is there anything you'd like to ask me?" Sawa said after a somewhat uncomfortable silence.

"Yes. There's one thing I still don't understand in what my father said. Who told my father what we were up to? It must have been just before we were arrested."

Sawa's hitherto carefree manner vanished. The sudden, withdrawn silence made Isao uneasy. It was a silence that seemed to poison the atmosphere. Isao found it hard to bear, and he stared intently at the faded brown binding of the tatami where the bright sunshine that poured through the clear glass of the window seemed to dig its claws into the fabric.

"Do you really want to know? If I tell you, you'll have no regrets?"

"No, I want to know the whole truth."

"All right. I'll tell you what I know. I'm saying this because the master himself went as far with you as he did. What happened was that the night before the arrest, on the night of November thirtieth of last year, that is, a call came for the master from Miss Makiko. I answered the phone. The master came to the phone, and what they talked about, I don't know. But afterwards, the master got ready to go out, and he left without taking anybody with him. And that's all I know."

As he continued, Sawa's kindliness took on the steadfast warmth of a blanket draped over the shoulders of a shivering man.

"I realize that you're fond of Miss Makiko. And that Miss Makiko is fond of you. Maybe on her side the fervor is a good deal stronger. But it's because she feels the way she does that we have this terrible result. I sized up her true nature when she stepped into the witness box during the trial. A frightful woman, I thought to myself. That was my honest feeling, I tell you. She was gambling all she had on saving your life, but, at the same time, the truth is that she was happy to see you in a prison cell. Do you follow me?

"What I mean is, that marriage of hers—you've got to understand why it ended so tragically in divorce. Her husband loved Makiko, but at the same time he was quite a playboy. The ordinary wife would have put up with it, but this one was proud, and she wouldn't have it. She loved him, and that made it even harder to bear. So, not caring what people might say, she went home to her family's house.

"Because she's that kind of person, then, when she falls in love with another man, it's no ordinary matter. The more she loves, the more anxious she becomes about the future when she might lose her lover. Because she's had an unhappy experience, she'll never believe in a man again. And so naturally, when a man she loves does come along, she wants to make sure that he stays hers and hers alone, even if he is put out of her reach, even if she has to bear the infinite suffering of not being able to be with this man. And as for a place where a man has no chance at all to play around, a place where, as far as a woman's concerned, there's the least cause for worry—where would that be, do you think? Jail, where else? She fell in love with you, so you landed in jail. What

more could a man want, come to think of it? I wish I were in
your shoes."

Not looking at Isao, Sawa chattered on heedlessly as he
rubbed the pale skin of his swollen cheek.

"Keep clear of a dangerous woman like that from now
on. I'll see that you meet lots of lovely women. The master
said something to me about this, and he's given me plenty of
spending money. Sure, it must have come from Kurahara,
indirectly, but it's just as the master said: Money is money;
fidelity is fidelity. You've never been with a woman, I bet.

"Will you come along to a movie tonight? At the Shiba-
zono there's a foreign film. Or there's the Hikawa Theater,
near the college, where we could see a movie starring Chiezo.
Then we could have a drink at Hyakkendana and head for
Maruyama. We've got to perform the 'coming of age ceremony,' just as the master said. If there's an appeal, the game
will be up. So now's the time to get it over with."

"Let's talk about this once the appeal is dropped."

"But look, if there is one, what then?"

"We'll worry about that when the time comes," Isao
answered stubbornly.

40

ON DECEMBER TWENTY-EIGHTH too the sun was
shining. Isao held back. The next day, December twenty-
ninth, was the day on which the ceremonies attending the
naming of the Crown Prince would take place, and rather
than darken the morning papers with an ominous headline
on such a festive day, it would be more excusable to act later

on the festive day itself, as long as the ceremonies were completed and the celebration at an end. Because of the possibility of an appeal, it was dangerous to wait any longer.

December twenty-ninth was still another clear day.

He asked Sawa to participate with him in a lantern procession to the Imperial Palace, and when the two left the house, Isao was wearing his overcoat over his school uniform, and they both were carrying lanterns decorated with the characters for "celebration." While they were eating an early dinner in a Ginza restaurant, they watched a streetcar float decorated with chrysanthemums making its way through the crowds in the street outside, the sign "CONGRATULATIONS" glowing in lights, and its motorman standing with his chest thrust out proudly beneath his blue uniform and brass buttons.

The human wave of lantern-bearers surged forward from Sukiyabashi toward the Imperial Palace. The lanterns with the sun emblem that each one held above his head were reflected in the waters of the moat, and lit up the pines standing in the winter twilight. The many lanterns massed in the plaza before the palace put to flight the shadows lingering beneath the trees and filled the whole area with a shifting brightness at variance with the time of day. The shouts of Banzai went on, never abating. The flames in the uplifted lanterns of the marchers highlighted the shadows of their mouths and throats. Now the faces were steeped in shadow; now they were suddenly lit with shimmering brilliance.

Before long, Sawa was torn away from Isao. After searching hopelessly in the vast throng for some four hours, Sawa returned to the Academy to report what happened.

Isao went back to the Ginza, and at a shop there he bought a dagger and a knife, both with plain wooden sheaths. The knife he put into the inside pocket of his jacket, and the dagger he concealed in his overcoat pocket.

In a hurry, he hailed a cab to Shimbashi Station, where he boarded a train for Atami. It was empty. He had a four-passenger compartment all to himself as he pulled a clipping from his pocket and read it once again. It was a page taken from the New Year's issue of *Kodan Club* borrowed from Sawa, and on it was a boxed item entitled "How the Big Shots in Politics and Finance Greet the New Year."

"Busuké Kurahara customarily sees the old year out in very simple fashion," read the portion that Isao was concerned with. "Having no liking even for golf, at the end of every year, as soon as offices are closed, he slips away to his villa at Inamura in Izusan. His greatest pleasure is looking after the tangerine orchards there in which he takes such pride. The orchards in the neighborhood are usually harvested before the year is out, but Kurahara likes to leave the tangerines hanging in bunches so that he may admire them up until the New Year's holidays are well underway. Then, except for giving some to his friends, he donates the entire harvest to welfare hospitals and orphanages. This amply bespeaks the unassuming personality and the admirable warmth of this man, who could be called the Pope of the world of finance."

Isao took a bus from Atami Station and got off at Inamura. It was already past ten o'clock. The night was still, and he could hear the sound of the sea. The village was beside the road, but wooden shutters were closed everywhere, and no light shone through. Isao turned up his overcoat collar against the chill wind from the ocean. Halfway down the slope, which fell away toward the sea, stood a large stone gate. A light burned outside it, and Isao could easily make out KURAHARA on the nameplate. On the other side, beyond a huge front garden, was a house wrapped in stillness, which, here and there, showed lights burning. There was a walled embankment topped with a hedge all the way around.

On the other side of the road was a mulberry field. At the edge of it, fastened to a mulberry bush, was a tin sign: TAN-GERINES FOR SALE. The tin rattled in the wind. Isao hid behind the sign. He had heard footsteps coming up the twisting path from the ocean.

A policeman was climbing the slope. He made his way up slowly, stopped in front of the gate for a moment, and then, the noise of his saber trailing behind him, disappeared along the narrow path that followed the wall.

Isao came out from behind the sign, and, exercising great caution, crossed the road. As he did so, he caught a glimpse of the sea, black beneath a moonless sky.

Scaling the wall presented no problem, but the hedge at the top concealed barbed wire which tore at his overcoat.

Besides plum trees, hemp palms, and pines, the garden of the villa held many tangerine trees planted right up to the house itself, presumably so that the master could appreciate them. The darkness was filled with the fragrance of their ripe fruit. The dried leaves of one giant palm, blown by the wind from the ocean, startled Isao with its sound like wooden clappers.

The ground beneath his feet yielded at every step, as if nourished by an abundance of fertilizer. Bit by bit, he drew closer to a corner of the house from which bright light was coming. The tiled roof was of Japanese design, but the window and siding indicated that the room within was Western style. The window was hung with lace curtains. Isao leaned against the wall, raised himself on tiptoe, and was able to see part of the room.

There was a chimney opening on one side of the room, indicating a Western-style fireplace. A woman was standing with her back to the window, revealing the bow of her obi. When she moved away, there appeared the somewhat plump but stern-looking face of an old man of small stature, dressed in kimono and a greenish brown sleeveless jacket. Isao knew that it had to be Kurahara.

There was some exchange with the woman. When she left, Isao saw the flash of a tray. She had brought Kurahara his tea, it seemed. With the woman gone, Kurahara was alone in the room.

Kurahara apparently sat down in a deep armchair facing the fire. All that could be seen from the window now was his bald forehead that seemed to shimmer from the flames burning in the grate. Perhaps he was reading something while he sipped the tea left at his side, or perhaps he was deep in thought.

Isao looked around for an entrance. A stairway of two or three stone steps led up from the garden to a doorway. He saw a faint light coming from the crevices of the door. The door was secured with only a metal latch. Isao took his dagger out from his overcoat and then threw off the coat, letting it fall to the soft ground in the darkness. At the foot of the stone steps he drew the dagger and discarded its sheath. The naked blade, as though giving off light of its own, shone pale.

He climbed the steps stealthily and slid the tip of his dagger between the door and its frame, slipping it underneath the latch. The latch was extremely heavy. When it finally snapped upward, the noise it made echoed like the tick of a grandfather's clock. There was no way of knowing if anything had changed within the room, but the noise must have attracted Kurahara's attention. Isao twisted the doorknob and rushed inside.

Kurahara stood up with his back to the fireplace. He did not cry out, however. A thin film of ice seemed to have spread across his features.

"Who are you? What are you doing here?" demanded the hoarse, weak voice.

"Take the punishment you deserve for profaning the Grand Shrine of Isé," said Isao. The clarity and modulation of his voice assured him of his self-possession.

"What?" An expression of altogether unfeigned incomprehension came to Kurahara's face. For a moment he was obviously groping for a memory, but without success. And at the same time he was looking at Isao with eyes that revealed the terror of being confronted in dreadful isolation with a mad-

man. Avoiding the fire behind him, Kurahara shrank back
against the wall beside the fireplace. This decided Isao's next
movement.

As Sawa had once taught him, Isao bent his back like a
cat, pressed his right elbow firmly into his side, and, gripping
his right wrist with his left hand so that the blade would not
go upward, plunged the blade into Kurahara with all his
strength.

Rather than the feel of the dagger piercing the other's body,
the main sensation was the shock of the butt of the hilt
striking his own stomach with reflexive force. Then, determined to make sure of his man, Isao gripped his shoulder
and pressed down, wanting to stab more deeply, but he was
taken aback to discover how much lower that shoulder was
than he had thought. And then the flesh that he was pressing
down had none of the softness that goes with plumpness but
was as rigid as a board.

As he looked down at him, the face of his victim seemed relaxed, rather than in pain. The eyes were open, the mouth
gaped carelessly. The upper set of false teeth had come loose
and was jutting out.

Tugging at the dagger, Isao became furious in his frustration. His victim's whole weight now lay upon the blade.
Kurahara collapsed, growing heavier still, the blade at his
center of gravity. Finally, gripping the other's shoulder with
his left hand, Isao raised his right knee, and, pushing against
Kurahara's thigh, he pulled the dagger free. The blood that
spurted out splashed Isao's knee. Kurahara, as though in pursuit of his own blood, toppled forward.

Turning swiftly, Isao was about to run from the room
when a door leading to the hallway opened, and he was face to
face with the woman whom he had seen a little while before.
The woman screamed. Isao darted aside and raced out into
the garden through the door that he had entered by. He could
still see the afterimage of the terrified woman's eyes, with
their prominent whites.

He ran at full speed down through the garden toward the
sea. Behind him the household was in turmoil, as one cry
after the other was raised. He felt the sounds and lights were
fixing themselves upon him and rushing in pursuit.

As he ran, he reached inside his jacket to make sure that
his knife was there. The dagger in his hand, however, gave
him greater assurance, and he gripped it tightly while he
rushed headlong. His breath was labored, and he had twisted
his knee. He was made well aware of how his legs had weak-
ened during his year in prison.

Tangerine orchards by the ocean were usually cultivated in
terraced fields. Each of Kurahara's tangerine trees, as though
on a platformed stage, was set upon a level of its own. The
innumerable, varied levels, bound by the stone walls, each
received its share of sunlight at its subtly varied angle, and,
though each level slightly differed from the others, all of
them fell away down to the shoreline. The average height
of the tangerine trees was eight or nine feet. The roots
were heavily mulched with straw, and the branches reached
upward in all directions from a point quite near the
ground.

Isao ran from one level to another. The fruit-laden
branches blocked his way at every turn in the darkness. As
though in a maze, he struggled not to lose his way. The sea
could not be far off, but he was unable to reach it.

He burst out of the trees at last, however, and his field of
vision suddenly widened. Before him were the sky and the
sea. A flight of stone steps descended clinging to the sheer
face of the cliff, and a gate at the edge of the orchard gave
access to it.

Isao tore off a tangerine. It was then that he realized that
he no longer held his dagger. He must have dropped it when
he was running through the trees, and clutching and dodging
branches.

The orchard gate opened easily. At the bottom of the steps,
he saw the white spray leaping high as the waves worried the

rocks. For the first time he became conscious of the echo of the sea.

Whether the land beyond the orchard was Kurahara's or not, Isao did not know. It was a cliff covered with an old growth of trees, and a path threaded its way through the grove. Isao was weary from fleeing, but, once more, he rushed headlong down the path, as the tree branches lashed his face and the undergrowth clutched at his running feet.

Finally he came to a place where the cliff was gouged out to form something like a cavern. A greenish, twisted mass of rock had been partly eroded away, and from its top the branches of a great evergreen tree hung low over this ledge. A slender stream of water, sheltered by ferns, meandered over the rock surface, flowed through the grass, and apparently fell off into the sea below.

Here Isao hid himself. He quieted his throbbing pulse. There was nothing to be heard but the sea and the wind. Since his throat was painfully dry, he tore the skin off his tangerine and roughly thrust the fruit into his mouth all at once. He smelled blood. It had splotched the tangerine skin and half-dried there. But the odor did not much alter the sweetness of the juice that was running down his throat. Beyond the dry weeds, beyond the tall pampas grass, beyond the low-hanging evergreen branches, with their clustered needles and entangled vines, lay the night sea. Though there was no moon, the sea reflected the faint glow of the sky, and the waters gleamed black.

Isao sat upright upon the damp earth, his legs folded beneath him. He removed his uniform jacket. From the inside pocket, he took out the knife. His whole being experienced such relief at finding it safe there that he almost lost his balance. Though he still wore his wool shirt and undershirt, the wind from the sea chilled his body as soon as his jacket was off.

"The sun will not rise for some time," Isao said to himself, "and I can't afford to wait. There is no shining disk climbing upward. There is no noble pine to shelter me. Nor is there a sparkling sea."

He stripped off the remainder of his upper garments, but, as his body tensed, the cold seemed to vanish. He unfastened his trousers, exposing his stomach. As he drew his knife out of its sheath, he heard cries and the sound of running footsteps from the direction of the orchard above.

"The ocean. He must have got away in a boat," one pursuer called out shrilly.

Isao drew in a deep breath and shut his eyes as he ran his left hand caressingly over his stomach. Grasping the knife with his right hand, he pressed its point against his body, and guided it to the correct place with the fingertips of his left hand. Then, with a powerful thrust of his arm, he plunged the knife into his stomach. The instant that the blade tore open his flesh, the bright disk of the sun soared up and exploded behind his eyelids.

ABOUT THE AUTHOR

ON NOVEMBER 25, 1970, Yukio Mishima committed seppuku (ritual suicide). Forty-five years old and at the peak of a brilliant literary career, he had that morning written the last word of the final novel of his tetralogy, *The Sea of Fertility*. "The tetralogy is his masterpiece, as he knew," Donald Keene has said.

Mishima had written much about suicide and early death, and often told his friends he wished to die young. After he conceived the idea of *The Sea of Fertility* in 1964, he frequently said he would die when it was completed. In fact the second of the four novels, *Runaway Horses*, is a remarkable literary rehearsal of his seppuku. Just before his suicide, he wrote his closest friends that he felt empty, having put into the tetralogy everything he thought and felt about life and this world. "The title, *The Sea of Fertility*," he told Keene, "is intended to suggest the arid sea of the moon that belies its name. Or I might say that it superimposes the image of cosmic nihilism on that of the fertile sea."

Mishima's works have been compared to the works of Proust, Gide, and Sartre, and his obsession with courage and the manly virtues has been likened to Hemingway's. Arthur Miller said, "I felt Mishima had an admirable style. He was surrealistic. He was very erotic. He had an economy of means to create enormous myths—his novels are compressed visions." A British magazine called him "one of the outstanding modern writers of fiction, possessing a complex, subtle and frightening imaginative power."

He was often wrongly called a rightist because of his private "army" of a hundred unarmed young men, but it was not on the blacklist of the careful Japanese police because it had never been involved in violence and differed from conventional rightist organizations. It was a theatrical fantasy conceived by a poet, as was his death, about which Selig Harrison of the Washington *Post* wrote, "He forced the Japanese to consider where they are going more dramatically than anyone else since World War II, and he has done so with a distinctively Japanese symbolism."

Mishima was born into a samurai family and imbued with the code that apotheosized complete control over mind and body, and loyalty to the Emperor—the same code that produced the austerity and self-sacrifice of Zen. Much of the tetralogy shows that he viewed the self-seeking arrogance and corruption of the militarists of the thirties (and their contemporary successors) as inimical to the samurai code.

His first novel was published in his school magazine when he was thirteen. A perceptive teacher encouraged him and persuaded a magazine to publish a story, *The Forest in Full Bloom*, in 1941, when Mishima (a pen name the teacher suggested) was sixteen. Three years later, when he entered Tokyo Imperial University, his first collection of stories was published under the same title and pen name. The first printing sold out in a week. In 1946 he brought two essays in manuscript to Kawabata, later the Nobel Prize winner, whose protégé he became. Altogether, 257 books by him, including 15 novels, have been published in Japan, and 77 translations here and in Europe.

Mishima reverenced and mastered the martial arts of Japan, creating a beautiful body he hoped age would never make ugly. He began to practice body-building in 1955, and kendo (dueling with bamboo staves) in 1959. In 1966 he took up karate as well. By 1968 he had become a kendo master of the fifth rank.

He traveled widely and often, and two travel books and many collections of articles are among his works. He also wrote countless short stories and thirty-three plays, in some of which he acted. Some ten films have been made from his novels; *The Sound of Waves* (1954, American edition 1956) was filmed twice, and one of the director Ichikawa's masterpieces, *Enjo*, was based on *The Temple of the Golden Pavilion* (1956, American edition 1959). Also available in English are *Five Modern Nō Plays* (1957) and the novels *After the Banquet* (1960, American edition 1963), *The Sailor Who Fell from Grace with the Sea* (1963, American edition 1965), *Forbidden Colors* (1951, American edition 1968), *Thirst for Love* (1950, American edition 1969), and *Spring Snow* (1972), volume one of *The Sea of Fertility*.

A NOTE ON THE TYPE

THIS BOOK was set in Monticello, a Linotype revival of the original Roman No. 1 cut by Archibald Binny and cast in 1796 by the Philadelphia type foundry Binny & Ronaldson. The face was named Monticello in honor of its use in the monumental fifty-volume *Papers of Thomas Jefferson*, published by Princeton University Press. Monticello is a transitional type design, embodying certain features of Bulmer and Baskerville, but it is a distinguished face in its own right.

Typography and binding design by Kenneth A. Miyamoto.

The book was composed, printed, and bound by Kingsport Press, Inc., Kingsport, Tennessee.